R.C. PRENTICE

The Masque

A Zoe Dill Mystery

The Masque
Published by HugelMar
Denver, CO

ISBN: 978-1-7353011-0-5
FICTION / Mystery & Detective / Private Investigators

Cover design by Natasha Brown Designs
Interior design by Victoria Wolf, wolfdesignandmarketing.com

HugelMar

Prologue

GREGG NEAL WAS NOT FEELING GOOD. He had just re-bandaged his hand with a two-inch square pad that he had had to secure with freezer tape. He was unable to find the roll of adhesive tape he had used earlier. Or rather, he could not seem to put his hands, moving sluggishly through the bathroom drawer, around it. The freezer tape was on the counter in the kitchen; a day earlier he had put away two quarts of stewed spring onions from his neighbor's yard down the street. Good for chili rellenos. Good for tamales.

He trudged with difficulty back into the front room, flopped gratefully into the recliner. *Whew! Those whiskey sours were stronger than I'd thought. How many did I have?*

His palm throbbed, although the bleeding seemed to be slowing. But now he felt like he was getting the flu; his body felt sensitive all over but numb at the same time. He recalled that his legs did not seem to be working right. Now, sitting in his well-broken in, overstuffed, fake-leather recliner, he fully regretted getting so blotto with Stan. Wine to start, then beers with dinner at the Coyote Café followed by brandies followed by the one or two or three (?) whiskey sours when they'd come back to the gallery. *Had Stan put something in my drink? No! That was absurd!*

Stan had wobbled out on his own power after they had gotten away with more than half of the fifth and after they'd had their stumble-tumble resulting in the broken spear. Stan had stood up to go, proclaiming that he would toddle off to a room he'd reserved at the De Vargas Hotel. *Why had he done that?* On previous visits he had always stayed with Gregg. *Oh, well.* Gregg had stood up to see him out and as he came up beside Stan, Stan had taken a step, lurched, bumped into Gregg, and Gregg had started to go down. He did go down. He tried to grab the table but succeeded instead only in grabbing hold of the business end of one of the spears, and the sharp point had gone straight into his hand. The spear had broken against the table's edge that, in the end, he had not been able to grab. Stan helped him up, then deposited him in the recliner chair.

He didn't know what he was going to do with those spears anyway. It was the pottery that he appreciated. *Why had Stan insisted on stumbling back to his room at the De Vargas?*

Greggory Neal, Stanley Joiner, Woodard Glenn and the other partners—those that were still around—got together every six months in what was now a ritual: a raucous meal at the Coyote Café where the two local hosts, Gregg and Woody, would divide the other partners up amongst themselves; Gregg always took Stan and one more. Woody had more room—lots more room: five whole houses he could put them up in. Gregg only had the single guest bedroom in his one-room eyrie; Stan always took the fold-out sofa bed in the parlor. The next day was all business: selecting the inventory, temporarily stored in Woody's capacious quarters, that one of the visitors always brought, to be divided among the five, after a current re-evaluation, and in Gregg's case, his share to be repacked and stored in the cellar, to be doled out to discerning customers.

But last week Stan had called Gregg, excited about a cache that he had secured from Peru: ancient textiles, contemporary pottery, historic artifacts.

He had arranged to have them shipped in a circuitous route, first to a port on the Amazon River— *"Icky-something,"* Gregg recalled— and then loaded onto a small plane that had made the short trip into Colombia, where it landed in an equally obscure jungle village. Paying a modest gratuity to customs officials, Stan had then gotten the items—crates of pots and a clutch of spears—loaded onto a much larger cargo plane, this time repacked so that the textiles seemed to be merely part of the packing materials for the pots, that landed in Miami and passed through customs with minimal inspection, with payment of a fee based on an evaluation provided by a well-known dealer in Native and contemporary arts, who regularly made the rounds between Bogotá, Mexico City, and Miami Beach.

Ready to get up from the recliner and toddle off to bed, Gregg found that he could not move. In fact, he had difficulty turning his head to see where the Teacher's had gotten to for one last drink and equally to turn it the other direction to espy the ormolu clock on the buffet. The numb feeling was not unpleasant and maybe just another little drink would do him good and what was wrong with dozing for a little while in the recliner anyway? But now he seemed to have trouble breathing and he really should get up and pee and what time was it anyway? And then it occurred to him: a paralysis was setting in. He'd had a stroke. *Nine-one-one. Where's the phone?* But he knew, even if he found it, he couldn't operate it anyway. He realized: he was dying, and there was nothing he could do about it…

1

WEDNESDAY, APRIL 16, 7:36 AM

WESTERN CONNECTICUT COLLEGE,
WESTON, CONNECTICUT

DAMIA ZOELLER DILL REACHED DOWN and pulled her jeans up
onto the bed, then dropped them back onto the floor, once she had extracted
her phone. Zoe—for that was what she called herself and preferred others to
call her—texted her friend Tess: *Hi rnnglate tell rosy ta zo*. She was not really
running late, but she wanted options. Zoe and Tess Gormley, her soul-mate
and also a senior, like Zoe, had met in first year Discoveries class and had
tried to take classes together ever since they both realized they were doing
the same thing: Five-year MA degrees with BAs "on the way." But once they
had embarked on their different programs—Tess in religious studies and
Zoe in art and art history—they had seen less of each other, meeting up
regularly only in Kung Fu class, which they had agreed to take together on
Tuesday evenings. Tess had stuck with the class religiously; Zoe had tried to
do so, but now in her last year, she had decided she would allow herself Kung
Fu only if she had accomplished sufficient progress on her thesis on what

she had designated as her "writing Tuesday." Now, in their last semesters, however, they were both jammed into their last mutual requirement: an "Intro to Anthropology" class with first-years. Tess would tell their affable, slightly-more-than-middle-aged professor, Ignacio "Rosy" Rosales to not mark Zoe absent (just late), if she decided not to sprint out of bed and begin her day just yet. She turned the phone off, slid it back into her jeans' back pocket, dropped the jeans, and slithered back down under the bedcovers to consider her options.

There were options. She could slide her left hand down along her left thigh and over to Nick, snuffling in his sleep beside her, over his right thigh and into fondling territory. Nick always tumbled straight into slumber-land, following the spasms and squalls of rumpy-pumpy, on his side like a normal person, either front to back or back to front with her. But in the morning, when she rolled over, there he always was on his back. *What normal person sleeps on their back!* she thought. But Nick was not a normal person. He was brilliant. He was funny. He was entertaining. He was hard working. And he was an enigma, on purpose.

He did not have a driving license. "We need to support public transport," he insisted. The college provided a Beavercard pass free of charge. "A bicycle can be had for less than a hundred dollars," he would point out. But he did not own one, using the city's minimal-charge rent-a-bike system with a six-months-for-sixty-dollars swipe card, or the Beavercard; otherwise, Nick paid cash for everything, even if he had to stuff wads of twenties into his pockets, which he never had any trouble retrieving with his ATM card, the closest thing to a credit card, as far as Zoe knew, that Nick had.

Zoe had long wondered where all that money came from. Inheritance? Nick was vague about his parents, although he occasionally mentioned one of them at odd points in conversations: they always seemed to be handily credentialed with former jobs or degrees when he needed them. Legitimate earnings? Well, true, he had a full fellowship from NYU and an adjunct teaching post as what amounted to a teaching assistant here; those two bits of personal data were the only ones which he shared, conspiratorially, with Zoe: "I've got to be careful to make sure NYU doesn't get wind of this; I'm meant to not work so I can devote full time to the dissertation." Which he sometimes did, putting in, he promised Zoe, twelve- and fifteen-hour days when he did not teach and when Zoe was off in Croton working at Cannings' Antiques during the day and serving what the Cat and Custard's menu listed as "libations" and "provisionings" in the evenings.

When in Croton, Zoe camped out on a futon in the living room of Ellie Bortz, an old family friend, who had basically raised her. Sunday afternoons—or sometimes evenings if they were really slammed—she left the shop, driving back to Western Connecticut State College, a forty-minute commute in good weather and light traffic; an hour and a half at worst.

Where Nick periodically disappeared to was a question that was always at the back or her mind. He would often return long after she was a-slumber, late Sunday night or in the wee hours of Monday morning and sometimes even cancelled class or arranged for a guest discussion leader—she was delighted when he asked that it be her—while he went off somewhere. He would never say where to, even when Zoe got hot under the collar, teary-eyed, and belligerent about what she had settled into calling "your *secret wife*, Nick." He always smiled and said merely, "Hey—I'm consulting!" But he never revealed where or with whom, and did not tell her where he was going until almost the last minute, no matter how much she fumed, which she surely was justified in doing when she was his substitute lecturer. She occasionally found ticket stubs for the Metroliner lying around or caught him checking schedules for Amtrak's Northeast Regional on his phone.

But now she knew. She had discovered his secret, or at least part of it. He was an "authenticator." He authenticated pieces of art. Still, she did not know exactly what corners of the art world, where provenances were dubious and caveats invariably accompanied authentications, he was finding on those trips. But now she was quite sure: those ATM twenties came from those corners, where he did indeed produce those authentications of paintings.

She had been surprised to discover, early on in their relationships, that he was so much older than she. She had known he was probably older than his students and professors thought he was; no driving license meant there was no way to check. But then, when they took their great, fantastic, life-changing (for her) grand trip, she got a good look at his passport: it turned out he was seven years older than she. With a fine head of black hair, a nice, tight butt, and not a wrinkle on his sharply-featured face, he remained perpetually attractive. But it was all very fine for him to prolong the art history joy ride until he'd run out of coasting power. He would probably find something else to do; or maybe he had already found it. And Zoe did not like the idea that he might one day stuff his pockets with twenties, pack his rucksack, and tell her, "Well, Zoe, this is it: I've got an opportunity in (pick a city) to (do consulting, enter yet another PhD program, take a new teaching post) and so it's been nice knowing you…"

There was a lot that was alluring but also alarming about Nicholas Zachary Taylor (yes, he had told her, when she had first encountered him, that really was his name and he was, indeed, a descendant of the American president of the same name). But now that she was about to graduate in a few weeks, her ticket on the joy ride was about to expire; she knew from talking with one of her fellow waitress friends at "the Cat" that being an expired undergraduate student clinging to a jaded non-quite-PhD-ed grad-uate student fermented frustration, feelings of irrelevance, and a sense of dead-endedness. Zoe found Nick's insistence that once she had her master's degree she should come along with him and be his assistant on his consulting to be a just barely tasteful way of saying, "come along and be my concubine." *Just what would that be, Nick Taylor's "assistant"?* Well … he would tell her all about it once she had her degree and they were out of this two-bit town and he knew he had a commitment from her. *Give her commitment to an enigma? Hah! Hardly!*

At first, the idea had been intriguing. Nick had hinted at how less-than-stellar her other options were: working full time at a pub? Or in the dusty, dim terrain of antiques and collectibles? Commuting upwards of an hour each way, every day, and pretending that throwing her sleeping bag on a futon on Ellie's floor was a good deal? Well, the proprietors of the antiques shop, Cait and Robb Murray, had mentioned more than once that after she graduated, they would increase her hours to nearly full time, at least during what they said was their busiest times. She had done her internship there, arranged by Dr. Sloan, and then stayed on part-time when the Murrays declared they wanted to hire her outright. Christmas and football and basketball seasons brought steady mobs of pub-life and beer-and-grub-seekers that would let her take up the slack at Cannings' with more hours at the Cat. "Oh, come on, Zoe, you're better than that!" had been Nick's response.

And I am *better than that*, she thought. Unknown to him, she had accepted the University of Washington's offer of a three-year fellowship in their PhD program. *Won't that set me on my way to seeing who I really am and what* I *can really do at the end of these five years of college and three years-and-a-half of Nick? Who's to say that* I *can't also "consult"? About the origins and whims and styles, the movements and crafters and outfitters of nineteenth century American accessories, for example?*

It was now nearly eight o'clock. She could just make it to Intro if she could stand foregoing a shower and sprinted. She contemplated Nick, snoring softly beside her. She started to put her hand under the covers to find him, then thought, *no, I can do without an encore of last night's shag-and-shiitake evening. No, I'll not try Rosy's patience. I'll caper through classes, get to Croton before dark tonight, break the news first to Cait and Robb and then to Gary at the Cat about going off to Washington. I'll not be having a career as a waitress and I'll not be having a career in the antiques and collectibles field, registering inventory, making nice with browsers, or even going out on buying trips.*

Formerly the Friday classes had kept her out of the "Intro" course for the last three years, because she really had to—and liked to work—on Fridays; now that the schedules had been completely redone—the M-W-F one-hour classes replaced with M-W and T-Th blocks—she would not take advantage of Rosy's kind nature. *Yes, I'll throw on my clothes, grab my satchel, whisper "bye-bye" to Nick, sprint to class, and hopefully slip in during the shuffle and babble of sorting places and assembling order.* And announcing her decision to accept the fellowship to her employers across the state line would be the beginning of a "bye-bye" that she would extend until Nick got the message: the first step in a new act on a new stage with a new story that would be hers, not his.

But as she rolled out of Nick's bed, her breath caught on an almost-sob.

2

BANNERS EMBLAZONED, "Darwin" and "Cosmic Connections" banged in an April post-squall wind, as Jen and Thad Pritchard stood outside the American Museum of Natural History, contemplating the huge bronze statue of Teddy Roosevelt, mounted, with bronze Indians striding —or trudging—along at either side. It was very warm for mid-April; an overnight rain had cleansed the air and spring—in the form of leafing trees and tweeting birds—announced itself. Bits of blue peeked out from a dun-gray sky; Starbucks containers rattled along the sidewalk, propelled by gusts of wind. Holding her shoulder-length brown hair in a left-handed grip, head down, Jen shouted at Thad, "We should have worn raincoats."

"No," said Thad, "the rain's over." He glanced ever so quickly up at the thick gray clouds hanging heavy. "Besides," he hissed, "the whole effect is lost underneath stupid raincoats. We'd look like trenchy FBI agents, or like fly-blown, down-on-our-luck riff-raff." They were, in fact, dressed in their best: an Armani suit with Hermes tie for him; a Roberto Cavalli business suit with Vince Camuto Fido boots for her: all from eBay, used, half-priced.

Jen raised an eyebrow and opened her mouth to say something, but thought better of it. Jen and Thad mounted the column-flanked steps, entered the museum, and bought their entry tickets. They found themselves in a loud, public place. Now that they were irrevocably committed to putting the plan into operation, she could admit to some qualms. "It's good for us but I don't understand why he didn't want to come to the shop."

"I know you don't understand, but it doesn't matter: the instructions were to meet him here. Our good fortune," said Thad.

With entry receipts and pamphlets in hand, they studied the floor plan. "Fifteen dollars a pop just to probably get stood up or be offered some fake 'Aztec idol," said Jen. "But okay: it looks like we go around here through the Roosevelt Rotunda and turn right at the birds. Then sit."

"We go 'round the Benin Bronzes exhibit in the Hall of African Peoples, find the diorama, whatever that is, and the bench nearest it, *then* sit," stated Thad, studying the diagram in the pamphlet, putting that aggravating exactitude of his into his voice. They navigated Tyrannosaurus rex (or whatever it was), the stuffed elephants in the Asian Peoples Hall, and found the Africa Hall. They skirted the Benin Bronzes exhibit featuring a warrior head flanked by two enormous carved ivory tusks. They found the diorama and the bench, and sat, hands in laps, facing the diorama.

Eight minutes later, Jen turned to Thad. She moved her Valentino purse, slung over her left shoulder, so she could reach her hand in. She hauled out her phone, glanced at it, then dropped it back into the purse. "We've been here exactly seven-and-a-half minutes. Didn't he say he'd meet us here at ten fifteen?"

"Yes. But the voice on the phone was not exactly a 'he.'"

"What do you mean *not exactly*?" queried Jen. "The voice on the speaker phone in the shop was definitely a he."

"Well, this voice on the Cannings' mobile sounded like someone disguising their voice to sound—what's the word—androgynous? Anyway, the voice said *someone* would meet us here at ten fifteen. Maybe…" Thad's exasperation level was mounting. The whole situation was tense enough and they did not need to moodle around. But he had not misunderstood the voice coming out of the speaker phone on Saturday: *A unique and valuable piece. Don't open shop day after tomorrow.* (That's today, Monday. Odd the shop should be usually open on a Monday.) *Come with partner. Be sitting on bench in Africa Hall, American Museum of Natural History, facing diorama with man hunting, woman carrying child. Benin Bronzes exhibit will be on your left. At ten fifteen.*

"Maybe," Thad resumed, "he got caught in a grease fire under the East River."

"You think someone who has a whatever—what is it?—a 'unique and valuable piece, not seen in the light of day since the 1890s?'—is going to stumble onto the IRT with it?" objected Jen.

"The Interborough-Rapid-Transit? What century are you living in? There is no IRT anymore. Everything's MTA, Metropolitan-Transit-Authority now, anyway." Thad registered Jen's "harrumph," even if it was not articulated.

Jen reflected on just how stuck she—and she supposed Thad, as well—had got in a lacuna, a crevice in time and space, that relegated them to the seedy and very unglamorous margins of the vintage art-and-antiques trade. *All because in our reckless youth! Now we seek cover from exposure that at the time could be provided only by fences, pot-hunters, and petty clever thieves who knew how to disguise, obfuscate, hide, repackage the things we peddled and ourselves as well*, she thought. Emerging back into semi-respectability in the heady days of recovery from the Black Monday recession of the early 1990s, they had ridden the crest of the wave of nostalgia for "things past" (and cheap gentrification) that sent young techies fleeing mid-century modern and pushed them into the urban-renewing warehouse districts of inner cities and the farmsteads left abandoned and derelict by the discouraged and defeated residuals of the "back-to-the-land" enthusiasm of the 1970s, pulling these back-to-the-land retros into rediscovery of appropriate accessorizing via Lalique, Rosewood, Van Briggle, Tiffany. The hard Bonnie-and-Clyde artlessness that had plunged her seventeen-year-old self into complicity with adventurers, whose mystique of cleverness and sophistication still seemed to fuel her and Thad, had thinned to a scrim that might still vail their languor and enervation from clients and cohorts, but now seemed so threadbare and blemished that her thirty-nine-year-old—no, make that forty-year-old self— desperately wanted to cast it aside. *But what would be revealed*, she pondered, *if I did pull back the scrim? A one-semester dropout from the Boston Art Institute who had diddled and fiddled away twenty years cloaked in a phony identity and now—if I dared leave behind Jon—Thad—and his effective but perilously glued-together bravado that persuaded the clients and cohorts to buy, sell or move the goods, what would I do?*

Two young-looking women herded a gaggle of excited school kids that rolled in, beached itself in front of the Benin Bronzes bas-relief, and took her mind off her fruitless ruminating. The kids seemed to know the drill. About half of them sat and immediately lifted faces up, staring at the warriors. The reddish-brown warriors, in helmets with what would have been rows of coral beads around their necks in real life, stared back. The other half of the troop stood in back. One of the two young women, the one with dreadlocks—*Or were they more properly styled as braids?*—began a recitation. The gabbling dropped to whispers and murmurs. Jen found herself listening intently but had trouble hearing because the young woman largely faced the bas-relief, turning to the gaggle only occasionally. "... fourteenth century ... alloy ... neighboring kingdom of Dahomey ... *cire perdue*—now what does that mean?"

"Lost wax!" chanted several children in response.

Jen pointed to her watch. "It's ten twenty six."

"Shhhh!" said Thad. "We're meant to be quiet"

"Nobody else is."

The gaggle with herders moved on, around the corner of a large free-standing case and out of sight. The room might have been empty. The museum must have cranked up the air conditioning in honor of spring. It was freezing cold. An elderly overweight woman (*she borders on the obese,* thought Jen), walking with difficulty with two metal canes, limp-shuffled in front of them, halted, glanced briefly at the bas-relief fragment, and then went the way of the gaggle.

Jen craned her head. Thad did the same. The senior citizen had stopped at a mask exhibit on the wall to their left. A man in a dark suit, bowler hat, and highly polished black brogues, also viewed the mask exhibit, a slick, black, expensive-looking saddlebag over his shoulder. They caught the merest glimpse of him as he moved away to his left, skirting the free-standing case. Grandma-with-the-canes did the same, although much more slowly, both of them disappearing toward a portal to the next room.

Thad wondered: *Are these two together? Not likely. The man looks deliberately vintage— someone from the 1940s, but with no gray hair and therefore likely younger than he was trying to look—also younger than the quite clearly elderly woman.* A Noel Coward image popped into Thad's mind. *Or was it David Niven? Could one of them be the client? And could they have a Benin Bronze head on offer? But they would not have gotten into the museum with a Benin Bronze head in tow.* Thad leaned into Jen. "What do you want to bet that sort of David-Niven-looking character is our dude, checking us out?"

"David Niven?"

"The old-timey actor. *Casino Royale, The Pink Panther, Eighty Days Around the World...*"

"Well," responded Jen, "I'll bet it's not Grandma-with-the-canes."

Now another gaggle of kids—presumably more school kids—entered but they were quiet as books. Older, also herded by two young women, they walked in front of Thad and Jen, stopped in front of the bas-relief, stared reflectively, then moved on toward the masks. Thad bent forward a little, craned his neck, and noted a security guard with lips caressing a walky-talky—*no, of course it was not a walky-talky,* he thought, *it's a mobile phone*—just in back of the school group at the mask exhibit.

Jen followed his lead and also craned her neck, then turned, glanced down, dug the phone out of her purse again, and held it up to Thad's face. "It's 10:42. I think we've been stood up, or worse, *set* up."

Thad issued an audible "quit-making-life-difficult" sigh and turned back to stare at the Benin.

"What are we being set up *for*? You think that doofus couple had dodgy goods stored in their basement? Give it another fifteen. We'll give it up at eleven."

"Good. You do that. You sit here. I don't know why we both have to sit here. I could be punching the button and making the snake rattle."

"Okay. You go wander around and commune with your poison snake, if you can find it, ha-ha. They took that exhibit out years ago. I'll call you from Oswego."

"Or from Sing-Sing…"

A gray-bearded, but fit-looking man wearing an outback hat, very rumpled shirt, and safari pants overflowing with pocket flaps stopped in front of the Benin, pivoted, flashing a huge grin full of tea-colored teeth, then turned back toward the Benin, then clomped away toward the masks. His footwear—brown boots that seemed over-sized—squeaked on the floor. All the school children were gone. So were David Niven and Grandma-with-the-canes. Thad lowered his head slightly and *sotto-voce*'d, "What do you want to bet that's our man?"

Thad's thigh vibrated and his pants pocket burped. He flipped the phone open. "Canning here."

A woman's voice responded. "Please come to the cafeteria. Not the fourth floor café, but rather, the cafeteria." Click.

Jen's full, sensuous lips formed an *O* and her eyebrows almost met her slick brown bangs.

"We're to go to the cafeteria."

"No."

"What do you mean, 'no'?"

"I mean no. Didn't you say the voice on the speaker phone in the shop was a man's voice?"

Thad answered with a giant shrug. "Yeah."

"Then we're being set up. If the guy on the phone was a guy and this is a woman, isn't that fishy?"

Thad replied with a thigh-slap. "Who knows? Let's get going. We'll soon find out." Thad rose and started walking briskly.

Following, Jen whispered loudly, "What do we do when we get there? Are we meant to sit somewhere special? What do we do if no one shows again? How far around the world do we follow this vocal apparition?"

They moved through the museum and found the cafeteria on the lower floor. Lattes substituted for their favorite coffee, Kenya-Kagumoini. "Now what do we do? Just wait to be discovered? How is he-she going to discover us in this obscure corner?"

Thad gave her his giant shrug and thigh slap.

"I don't want to have lunch here," said Jen. "It's costly and the servers are dishing out bird portions."

"I don't think we need worry about that." Thad was looking past her. He had a bemused, whimsical look on his face. Jen turned. Several feet away, their presumed contact stood, taking them in.

"Good morning." Jen turned. It was Grandma-with-the-canes. She sat down across from them, putting her canes on the adjacent chair with a clatter. "Good of you to come," she said. promptly. "I'm Dahlia." She proffered no other name, and no card—which was fine with Thad, since they were relieved of giving her one. *We have to remember we're the Cannings*, he thought. They frittered away a couple of lattes and ten minutes, chit-chatting about the museum, the weather, the Benin exhibit.

Eventually, Thad decided to get to the point. "So, forgive me if we get to business, but—what is it exactly that you have? And why did you specially choose our shop? And why not bring what you have directly there?"

Dahlia sat back in her chair and was silent a moment, then shook her head. "I can't tell you, exactly, what we have."

"Well … well…" Thad started cartwheeling his hands.

"I have a number of items. But mainly I have a proposition for you. I don't want to discuss it here. In fact, I had thought here would be a good place to do so but now it turns out … well, let's just say there seem to be big ears in the vicinity. We'll have to arrange another rendezvous."

Jen and Thad looked at each other, then looked around for the big ears. Jen reflected: *The sooner and the farther away we are from Cannings' in Croton Corners, the better.* "Well, actually…" (Thad) "You see, we have a much larger place upstate, a kind of *entrepôt*, if you will" (Jen), "where most of our material is temporarily stored…" (Thad). "Yes," Jen broke in. "It just isn't worth our time in the down months. So, we only open on Fridays, Saturdays, and Sundays January through March." *Good lies!* She thought. *Would Dahlia bother to check up? But it would take legwork. Probably she wouldn't. And there's something to be said for not having a website!* "And sometimes not even then if the weather's bad. We can ship something out from our *entrepôt* up there or come down to Croton if someone contacts us. Really, the place upstairs from the shop is just a bedsit…"

"So, we would like to invite you to our *entrepôt*," continued Thad, "which is also our home, our real home, in what is one of the major antiques hubs on the East Coast"—*Wonder if she bought that?* Jen thought—"where we can spend a leisurely weekend examining the objects in question, and spend some time developing plans." Thad sat back, in finishing mode.

"And hear your proposition," added Jen.

Would Dahlia take that as a good enough explanation for why, if they had a nice convenient bedsit in Croton Corners, less than an hour from Grand Central, they would prefer to meet her—or them—in a drafty old quasi-mansion in a "seen-better-days" small city still smarting from the collapse of the Haymarket in the 1890s?

Jen decided to improvise further: "And we don't have room for everything in Croton Corners. Not that we've got a lot now, but sometimes we get in shipments from Europe or Mexico or India—huge ones with huge things, like doors and tables and sleighs and…"

Dahlia was frowning, Jen thought skeptically. But then Dahlia nodded and said, "Understood. But I don't do weekends. We will arrive this coming Wednesday, day after tomorrow, in the afternoon, for tea. And we will bring, not all the goods we have, but rather, a sample. Now give us directions."

3

"OH, ELLIE," MOANED CAITLYN. "God almighty, it was horrible." She took a sip of the hot chocolate. "Thanks for this. I'm just glad it wasn't you they tied up. Or that it wasn't Zoe. It could have been either of you."

"It's the least I can do," replied Ellie. "And it wouldn't have been either of us. I was meant to be here to help out *this morning*, wasn't it? *Not yesterday*. So, you two could have your day, today, in the city. And Zoe doesn't come in until Thursday."

Of a certain age, and with a personal history that she deliberately kept obscure, Ellie, for her part, cultivated a vaguely international lilt to her speech. She did not seem to mind losing a few sales when she flipped the "Closed" sign on her door to wander down the street and sit in a collectible chair in Cannings' to chat, or to entertain a particularly interesting visitor to her chocolate shop. Ellie had pried the Murrays' life stories out of them within the first week of their assuming the Cannings' mantle.

Ellie—her business cards said Eleanor Eisely Bortz, but who could get their tongues around that?—regarded—and treated—chocolate the way the

Aztecs had done: as a sacred gift from the gods, enjoyable and stimulating but also comforting and healing. It provided strength and fortitude for battle. And her friends Caitlyn and Robb Murray had certainly done battle. Two doors down, her shop offered packaged chocolates but also hot chocolate and hot chocolate lattes, coffee added if customers insisted and were willing to pay extra. "I'm surprised you're even open today."

"We're not," said Robb curtly.

"Well, God Almighty," stated Caitlyn stentorially. "We might as well be open. After all, we've been told that nothing really happened to us, haven't we? There was no break-in, there was no robbery, there wasn't even a kidnapping. Just us squirming around on the floor, tied and trussed like stuffed chickens."

Cait and Ellie sat in lushly upholstered, pale yellow chairs, quoting the Louis XVI style (in fact, they were accurate, sturdy reproductions) amidst glass-fronted cases of dark, rich mahogany, delicate filigreed, straight-backed chairs, an art-deco mirror with an ad carved into its face, credenzas, a heavy, ponderous dining table, end tables and coffee tables, a Duncan Phyfe mahogany cabinet filled with books and bric-a-brac, Toby mugs and Hummel figurines, but also some very fine Hopi and Santa Clara pots. A deep, open bookcase held mostly obsolete, hand-operated kitchen gadgets and stacks of no-nonsense blue-rimmed flatware alongside green-ribbed depression glass. From the ceiling, a few feet behind them, positioned so that those who entered could see it easily without craning their necks, hung a large green-and-red-on-white hand-painted sign, rusting just enough to be rustic: "Cannings' Antiques."

On one end table stood a shoebox stacked with postcards, some well-thumbed; on another end table a glass-fronted post office box, "113," presented obviously serious "collecteana": two rows of glassine-sleeved letter-cards. Scattered around on various display areas sat items only describable as folk art: a peach crate slat box, a monkey-on-a-pole toy, a mauve-colored terracotta apatosaurus, a set of nested Russian dolls, Mexican clay figures, copper foot and bed warmers, a set of hinged cubes that could display Santa

Claus, the Wise Men at Epiphany, the Easter Bunny, or girls dancing around the May Pole, depending on how they were flopped. Several pictures hung on the walls: three on the south wall were forest-and-stream scenes, quoting the Hudson River style, all by the same minor artist that no one had ever heard of; two more paintings, watercolors and pen-and-ink, hung on the opposite wall behind the long counter where the cash register sat along with two locked cases of jewelry. Altogether, the shop wanted to offer itself as a prowler's paradise, brimming with collectibles, high-end replicas, genuine antiques, quirky accessories, folksy hand-mades, and pleasantly rustic junk.

Ellie lifted the pair of glasses hanging around her neck up to her face and peered through them, then let them drop. "But surely tying someone up is illegal?"

"Oh, Golly!" chimed in Robb in his deep-throated oratory voice. He was sitting at a large walnut desk at the rear of the shop, grateful to be able to feel the desk's solidity, its assurance of security at this time. "It *is* illegal. But it's only 'unlawful restraint,' not even with bodily injury, since thrashing around on the floor with numbed and chafed wrists and ankles doesn't count."

"What about my phone?" complained Caitlyn. "God Almighty! That guy took my phone!"

"Misdemeanor," said Robb. "He might as well have taken the coffee pot. It's like pick pocketing —six months with five months off for good behavior in the county jail."

"So, just exactly what happened?" asked Ellie. "And what do you think they were doing here?"

Robb rose to join Ellie and Caitlyn. He was a big man—six foot-three and well over 200 pounds—he always waffled when asked his exact weight (of course most often by Cait)—but he navigated deftly around the Duncan Phyfe mahogany cabinet, a double drop-leaf table, a marble-topped server and a tall, free-standing case, glassed on three sides, housing a complete Southern Plains women's fancy dance regalia. The latter was labeled with a small hand-lettered index card noting it had been collected in a Kiowa community in Oklahoma in 1923. He beckoned them to the rear of the store. "Come on back. We'll give you the guided tour. You can see where they dumped us and how they smashed through the back door, then dragged one of our antique chairs back here and out the door and propped it under the doorknob on the outside so we couldn't budge it from in here!"

Ellie and Caitlyn got up and followed him through a beaded-curtained doorway into a small room that would have been dark except for the glow from a Larissa Tiffany lamp sitting atop a very large, flat-top desk, not nearly as neat as the one the public saw out front, the nineteenth-century English cylinder at which Robb had been seated. Magazines, catalogues, and sticky notes littered the top, but it sported the latest model Acer PC and a coffee maker in addition to the lamp. "Aren't you afraid of leaving things unattended?" said Ellie.

"No customer is going to undo that yellow police tape."

"Well, I did," inserted Ellie.

Robb barreled on. "We'd just come back here to wrap up the day..."

"Actually, it was Robb who was going to do that," interrupted Cait. "I'd just gotten the coffee pot and was about to head back here and wash it out in the bathroom. I always wish we had a separate sink back here when I do that but then I think of the mess to bring the plumbing out from the bathroom. Anyway, I was still up front when those two came in."

"But you were still open," stated Ellie firmly.

"Yes, yes. Robb passed me on the way back to the vault with the receipts from the till. I was planning to drop the pot back on the coffee maker, then lock and bolt the door. It was just after seven o'clock."

"Heh, heh, heh," said Robb mockingly. "But they did that for us."

"So, I'd pulled down the shade but had the coffee pot in my hand," continued Cait, "and for some reason I didn't lock the door. I had the coffee maker in one hand, so there I was just standing in front of the door, and there they were, in crash helmets and those red-and-white-and-black Lycra outfits cyclists wear and, of course, face masks. We couldn't even tell if they were men or women. They said nothing, not a word—just tore the door open. The one gave me a shove, grabbed me, got me down, slapped duct tape all over my face, trussed me up. I managed one little scream; then all I could do was choke."

"Yeah. The other one shut the door and threw the bolt, turned out the front lights, then came for me," said Robb, "before I knew what was happening. Knocked me down, then sat on me. The one that had Cait—we think it was a very athletic woman—yanked Cait over to where I was…"

"By my *hair*!" Cait clenched her fist.

Robb continued: "It was the surprise factor. That guy wouldn't have gotten me otherwise—but he came charging and tripped me. When I went down, I knocked my head pretty good on the corner of the desk"—he touched the bandage on his head. "Then they turned us over, stuffed scarves over our faces, and wound duct tape all around our heads. They yanked our hands behind our backs and tied them with plastic rope. It really hurt—chafed our wrists. All I got out was a 'Hey…!'"

"Oh, it sounds *dreadful*!" said Ellie.

"I heard him, the other intruder," said Cait breathlessly, remembering. "And I hoped, oh, Robb'll get him. He'll knock him flat unless he has a gun or knife."

"But I don't think they had either," Robb continued; "The guy grabbed one of my legs and kind of whipped me around, then cinched my legs. The other one came back, dragging Cait. They slapped more duct tape on both our faces. They really did truss us—you know, hog-tied us, hands behind back, tied to feet. Oh, Golly! It was hopeless!"

"Robb—stop saying 'trussed, trussed, trussed'! They *tied us up!* But it was weird," said Cait. "They tied our wrists, but you know, after a while we figured out we could squirm around so I could work the tape off Robb's face and he could do the same for me, and we got the gag-scarfs off, too."

"And this is the really weird thing: they took down our pants, including underwear, all the way down to our ankles."

"It was so … it was so *humiliating*!" wailed Cait.

"We thought pantsing us was to intimidate us and immobilize us all that much more," said Robb. "Then they went into the front of the shop. We could hear them rummaging around. They came back with guess what—"

Cait picked up the narrative: "Two of those ceramic chamber pots! And two of those small brown pottery jugs filled with water! We could just get our fingers around them and more or less feed each other with water."

"And get this." Now Robb almost chortled. "Then they opened our mini-fridge, took out a hunk of cheese, cut big hunks off with a Swiss army knife, put it on a plate, and then left through the alley door! But—now get *this*! Before they finally left, one of them went back into the shop and came back with one of our nice antique chairs. We couldn't figure it out until we started banging on the back door. I figured it might give after a while and we finally did get it just a half-inch ajar but, you know, it opens out and then we tumbled to it."

"And like we showed you, they'd rammed the chair under the doorknob outside," explained Cait, bobbing her head up and down. "So, we couldn't shove the back door open."

"Yeah. Our nice antique chair got waterlogged in that rain. But you know, by golly, it was like they didn't want to kill us or even harm us," said Robb. "And another funny thing: the receipts were all over the floor—mostly credit card receipts but some cash and a few checks. They didn't take any of it."

"And how long did all this take?" asked Ellie.

"Golly, not long. Fifteen minutes, maybe. Twenty at most," responded Robb.

"And all this time they didn't say a word—not a word!" said Cait. "I mean, God almighty, it was weird!" Cait shook her head. "They left us water, food and potty—and made it so we could use it by taking down our pants! And believe me I did—I was shaking—now I really know what 'shook up' means."

"So, you're sure they didn't take anything?" Ellie questioned querulously.

Robb heaved a big sigh. "Not a thing. After we scooted up to the front window and started banging on it, now and then, in between bangings, we did a mental inventory. We've checked and checked."

"Well, hold on now! They took my phone!" said Cait adamantly.

"Too true, too true. At least it was only the Cannings' phone—the shop phone. We keep our personal phones upstairs." Robb thrust a finger into the air at the ceiling.

"And how did they manage to go strolling around town in balaclavas without anybody noticing?"

"Well, it was probably actually closer to seven thirty when we began closing up and it was raining lightly. So—darkening and dusky. They must have been somewhere close, watching—watching for when our last customer exited so they could rush in and overwhelm us," said Robb matter-of-factly.

"Anyway, we managed to push up the shade with our heads. But we went back and forth about how we could get our pants back up or how to attract some attention." Cait looked at Ellie and blinked her eyes smarmily.

"Finally, the bakery guy across the street—what's his name? Fernand? He had to park on this side because, he told us, he was expecting a dough delivery in the back and you have to park on this side on Mondays. He didn't see us but he heard us banging and he stopped and hesitated and then came over. Boy was he surprised!" chuckled Robb. He sat back, seemingly exhausted with the ordeal of recall, but relieved at the same time. "It must have been about three o'clock in the morning by then."

"And it took forever for the police to get here," complained Cait. "Of course, they had to break in."

"But you weren't otherwise hurt?" queried Ellie.

"No, no. We weren't hurt. Just our dignity. Lying here with our pants down. And this cut." Robb touched his bandaged forehead again.

"I'm just glad it wasn't *you* they tied up, Ellie," said Cait.

"Well as I said, I wasn't to be here to help out until this morning, was I? So you two could have your day in the city."

"Yes—and we would have really appreciated that. Closing on Mondays would make sense because almost everything else in Croton Corners is closed, but Gary's is open on Mondays and so is the Antique Emporium just out of town. They're open seven days a week, 52 a year!"

"No, they close at Thanksgiving and the day after Christmas until after New Year's," interrupted Cait.

"Anyway. So why not us too? And Zoe can't come in except on Thursdays and Fridays and of course the weekend, so it's usually Friday if it's any day at all that we get our 'day in the city' or a quick trip to Bucks County because Zoe can take over. And in a pinch, you come in on Mondays, and we really appreciate that. We wouldn't have chosen today except our mystery antique peddlers phoned yesterday morning and insisted it had to be today that we met them in the city."

"What was it exactly that you were meant to do?" They had moved back into the shop proper, and were now seated on three of a set of four early twentieth century reproduction Bergère chairs at the back. "You were to do a transaction at the Natural History Museum, right?" affirmed Ellie.

"Well, who knows how serious that was!" said Robb. "Caitlyn took this call on Friday, about how somebody had something we'd really be interested in but they couldn't come to the shop—something about how it was hard for them to get around but they lived on Central Park West near the museum, so couldn't we meet them there. Well, we knew today would be really slow, after Easter weekend, so we figured why not?"

"Yes, it's slow for me too," said Ellie. "After Easter business plummets. Until school's out, then kids get chocolate! It's their reward! For getting dragged into antique shops, what I mean. Oh—no offense intended!" She looked quickly from Robb to Caitlyn and back.

"Oh, Golly! None taken! Anyway, it seems it may have had nothing to do with the museum and now I wonder if there's not some connection between what we were supposed to encounter there and what happened to us here," said Robb. "Like, maybe, there's some kind of competition going on between a couple of different purveyors? And party number two didn't want us to meet up with party number one, so they made sure we'd be literally tied up so that even if we got free by morning, we'd be in no shape to charge off to New York?"

"And now I'm sort of glad we never got there. We'd be meeting them just about now," said Cait. "I'm pretty sure our would-be purveyors are a gang of thieves with contraband to sell and our intruders here were just another gang."

"Yeah," said Robb. "Or maybe part of the same gang? It now does seem part of the whole setup. But it doesn't make sense. Caitlyn listened to the call more carefully than I did..."

"I'd put it on speaker phone so I could hear better; I was just wrapping up piece of Grueby for a customer when the call came in. The guy on the phone nattered on about how somebody had something we'd really be interested in but they couldn't come to the shop."

"But getting back to your ordeal. Didn't anybody see them?" queried Ellie skeptically. "Surely someone saw them barging in!"

"Yeah, sure," said Robb. "But what's to see? A couple of cyclists getting a last ride in before the storm rolled in. There must have been dozens of cyclists around here yesterday. And they slipped in so quickly..."

"Anyway, if we hadn't been put out of commission, we really would have been meeting our mysterious contacts and then making a day of it in the city," said Caitlyn. "I didn't expect anything to come of this hugger-mugger rendezvous with the kooks with the what-not in the Hall of African Peoples. So, after meeting up with them, we were going to hunt up lunch, browse our competition in SoHo and then, dinner. All business expenses of course!"

"Do you have any idea what it was they wanted to show—or I suppose— sell you?"

"Probably strings of amber beads they got in Morocco," said Robb. "'See?' They'd say in front of some African exhibit. 'Just like real Africans wear.'"

"But why would things African interest Cannings'?"

"Well, that's what we were wondering," agreed Cait. "But really, rendez-vousing in the Africa Hall was probably just a ruse. I don't think they were going to offer us anything African. I think it was going to be a truckload of

European patrimony looted from an east side apartment or two, or maybe even from one of those townhouses-turned-villas in Beacon Hill."

"But that's curious, isn't it?" puzzled Ellie.

"What is?" queried Robb.

"They called you on the landline. Why didn't they call you on the mobile, the one you use for business?"

"Yeah. That's my phone. The one they took. They probably did! Try it, I mean. We hardly ever answer it," said Jen dismissively. "Let it go to voicemail. We mainly use if for calling out."

"We let it go to voicemail then go through the messages upstairs between closing and supper," said Robb. "We delete the junk messages and then respond to the real ones either then or next morning."

"Yeah—and besides that, half the time it's lying around on the desk in back, or sometimes we just forget it and leave it upstairs," added Cait. "Or it's burping in your pocket, Robb, unattended."

"And remember?" reflected Robb. "I was saying just the other day that business should be picking up because it seemed like we were getting more calls for the last week or two."

"Which we never answered," said Cait.

"Yeah," added Robb. "They'd give it three, four rings, then ring off before it went to voicemail, and of course there was never any message left. That was probably them."

"Leaving a message would have given you their number, right?" observed Ellie brightly.

"Well, no," objected Robb, shaking his head. "People call anonymously all the time. 'Caller ID blocked.'"

"I'm pretty sure I remember 'private caller' on the display," said Cait ruefully. "It's really easy to block your number when you call, especially if you get one of those so-called 'burners.'"

"Yeah," Robb said. "So, I guess they finally decided to try the landline."

Caitlyn and Robert Murray, a just-short-of and just-a-little-more-than middle-aged couple had bought "Cannings' Antiques and Collectibles" four years previously. Cait had been introduced to art on a regular basis by parents seeking a cosmopolitan alternative to the quirky hand-made and hand-me-down local "collectibles" that abounded in the weekly summer and fall fêtes to be found all over their semi-rural home territory. They had done a constant rotation of the Philadelphia, the Barnes, the Michener, the Woodmere art museums. But oddly, Cait had consistently gravitated to the Deco exhibits at the Philadelphia and as she entered her teenage years, arranged with a few friends to tour the summer flea markets, rather than take in the latest "great art" in the museums.

Caitlyn, née Kernberger, had a mini-presentation prepared for customers who were receptive to chatting: she was proud of being ("at least" she would always say) sixth generation Pennsylvania Dutch—born and raised in the heart of antique country. "And of course," she would add, "we're not really Dutch. We're Deutsch-German, or at least originally German-speakers. My ancestors were Hutterites—persecuted followers of the religious reformer, Jan Hus. They were pacifists, anti-war. We originally fled to Russia, invited by Peter the Great. Then the Russians got weird and we had to leave again. Amish, Mennonites, Hutterites, Doukhobors— we're all cut from the same cloth. But I guess my family's kind of renegades squared, because we're dissidents from the dissidents! My great-grandfather got really hacked off when the Germans sank that ship? The Lusitania? He signed up with the army and got sent to France at the end of World War One, met my great-grandmother, and *voilà*! We've been all mixed up ever since!" It was a speech that she had honed to a cutting edge; she could insert it quickly into a casual conversation and then withdraw just in time to assure credentialization as a genuine, generations-old "Dutch Country" antiques aficionado but not pitch the tempted browser into boredom and "flee-the-shop" mode.

If pressed, she and Robb might ramble through a few more byways of their personal histories for a particularly intensely focused, deep-pocketed buyer who wanted to chat while their delivery details were getting written up or their dozens of purchases were being wrapped. Cait and Robb had learned early on that the antiques and collectibles business was spiked with fly-by-nighter opportunists amongst the mostly staid and stodgy dedicated browsers who tracked the fairs and shows and kept an eye on what was moving in and out of shops. But these opportunists were an important clientele because they often bought and sold in cash only, paying sales tax but never charging it, or were scouting for wealthy customers, who trusted these "scouts" to give them tips on how to kit out their newly acquired mansions.

The Murrays had encountered Cannings' through a young couple who had visited their stall in Bucks County, looking for items with which to restock their shop, which turned out to be Cannings'. Only the couple's interest in not being from where they were from, that is, from New York City, had brought them in contact with the Murrays. Scouting for antiques at the Bucks and Lancaster county fêtes and flea markets, the couple had traded personal histories and stories with the Murrays over jars of apple butter and hand-made weather vanes. It turned out the couple actually wanted out of the shop-owning business. They found that living in an upscale backwater, iced-in for nearly six months of the year, had made them stir-crazy. Still in their thirties, they wanted more action. Having owned it for only a year, they were purchasing it on a kind of payment plan and they were looking to get out of their contract with the previous owner, who had himself had it for only a short time, eighteen months.

The young Cannings' owners had encountered Robb and Cait in much the same way Robb and Cait had encountered each other. Cait had met Robb in their native Bucks County. Wandering the stalls of the long-standing weekend famers-and-flea market antiques fair and swap meet, she had recognized Robb from her childhood. He recognized her from his teenage years at his father's "antique farm machinery" stall as the little girl who liked gizmos and gadgets that spun and cranked. Robb had gone from farm-family-skidding-into-bankruptcy to dealer-in-seed-and-farm-chemicals to dealer-in-tillers-tractors-and-combines, but had finally returned to the flea market as dealer-in-antique-and-in-need-of-repair-farm-machinery when his parents had moved into senior care, and the agricultural sector had cleaved into the un-mechanized Amish and the industrial mega-farms, contracted to a handful of international corporations. He had then settled in as purveyor-of-any-junk-you-want to the tourists and accessorizers.

Cait had been trying as she put it, "to get my life together" after a number of adventures with a succession of lovers, and one husband, from New Mexico to Maine. She had returned to her roots and re-invented herself with spectacular success, starting a honey-and-bee-product business ("Bea's Bee Needs": spiced honeys, lip balm, nutmeg-and-curry spiced salves; wrinkle crème), marketing to local shops but also on MySpace and then You-Tube. She had retrofitted her parents' old barn for processing and hired a professional bee-keeper, keeping the bees on an old estate that two couples were bringing back into productivity as a compost-fed, organic, vegan oasis growing designer vegetables and dealing folk art out of their house. Soon Robb had installed Bea's Needs alongside his corn huskers and butter churns, and had gracefully persuaded Cait ("Bea") to move from her parents' place to his seedy farm shack. Taking over a little shop tucked away on the Hudson River was the farthest thing from their minds.

For their part, while searching for collectibles in Bucks County, the young Cannings' owners found that trips to the stalls and flea markets of Bucks and Lancaster counties—recommended by the previous owner, from whom they were in the process of purchasing Cannings'—had proved stimulating and engaging. ("You'll pick up the odd inventory here and there but mostly you'll want to chat up the folks who are making the rounds like you are—buying stuff," the previous owner had told them. "Sometimes they're shop owners themselves but a lot of times they're small-time dealers working out of their basements or real collectors themselves and they'll check out your place—this place—and maybe take you on as one of their feeders.") But this scenario turned out to be optimistic at best and bogus at worst. The young couple enjoyed their almost weekly Saturday-to-Monday jaunts out to Amish country in the light and bright months of the farmers' market season and the shop's persona gradually shifted from antiques to folk art. But a year out, they were suffering boredom and something of a cash flow dilemma. Custom was seldom during the winter months. They did not fit the mold of "artisan shop keeper" that seemed to permeate the ethos of commerce in Croton Corners. If it had not been for the occasional visit from the chocolate shop lady, with her Miss Marple-ish commentaries on world affairs and her stories of life in the surprisingly torrid schemes and contrivances of students and faculty at Smith College, mid-century, they would have slid into months-long moodiness.

So, when the young couple encountered an odd stall full of antique farm and kitchen equipment, folk-art-like violins made out of match sticks and jewelry boxes made of peach crates, and little jars of bee pollen honey products, they chatted up the proprietors of "Robb's and Cait's Emporium," and were intrigued to find that the older couple were as equally "in transition" as they, themselves. Cait explained that the bee products were hers; everything else was Robb's. He had recently sold all of his family's farm except for a barn after the death of his father from a heart attack and his mother's placement in the Alzheimer's unit of an assisted living facility. She, Cait, had returned to her Pennsylvania roots, moving in with her parents, after her various adventures, and now had a half-interest in the bee product business.

But for Robb, they explained to the couple, business in the winter months was worse than it was for Cannings'. It was non-existent. And falling into the flea-market-and-local product world of Friday-to-Sunday stall-erection-and-take-down was, for both of them, a kind of resignation to strenuous hum-drumness that somehow smacked of taking a fall-back position, and also a kind of failure.

Once they had learned from the young couple that Cannings' was something they wanted "out of," Cait and Robb decided that Cannings' was just what they wanted to "get into," along with marriage and an exit from Bucks County, rust-and-missing part machinery dealing, and bees. Cait found another successful woman entrepreneur who had a similar line of products and was only too happy to acquire a new line and a legation of loyal customers. Cait became the junior silent partner in bee products and the senior and very vocal partner in Cannings' Antiques. She and Robb, now married, financed the taking over of the purchase agreement from the young couple along with the payment plan, to which the previous owner agreed, largely from the proceeds from Bea's Needs. In turn, the young couple were relieved of their burden.

Cannings' Antiques had a closet-sized toilet; a sink, a mini-fridge, a two-ring hob, and a microwave oven in an equally closet-sized kitchen and a tiny office downstairs, at the back, and a full bath, bedroom and sitting room upstairs. The owner previous to the young couple had had the good taste not to rename the business (if he had done so, it would have been "Sugg's") and Robb and Cait had renewed the painted "Cannings'" sign on the front window and hanging shingle. Suggs had begun to move into Native American "crafts," and had slowly been building inventory through a wholesale firm in New York, when the recession threw a wet blanket on fine antiques and art and brought in a warming breeze for the appeal of low-priced folk art and collectibles. The Murrays kept Suggs' inventory, including the Native American material, as well as the considerable collection of folk art that the young couple had laid in. But with the bank bailouts relieving the wealthy and semi-wealthy from the anxiety of a possible end to trickle-down economics, accessorizing in afford-able collectibles once again was becoming a reasonable obsession. And Robb and Cait moved the shop aggressively back into high-end American items, which was what Cannings' had been known for, for more than thirty years, although they also still kept ties with the crafts persons, auctioneers, and retail-ers whose attention and loyalty they had cultivated over the three years that they had had their Bucks County stall, and bought from them occasionally.

The only Native American items in which the Murrays built up inventory were items that fit the definition of antique—eighty years old or more. They refused anything dubious that might have been looted from graves or from public lands. They refused any items that might be ceremonial. They found their real love was the American, Anglo-American and Franco-American furniture, mirrors, and southern pottery jugs; only very occasionally did they acquire a clumsy American portrait paining or landscape, notable only for its connection to a long-reigning but now fallen New Orleans or Atlanta dynasty or a blue-blood Brahmin Boston clan. But they also honored their largely bygone interest in folk art by stocking the occasional weathervane, sampler, or the toys and whimsies produced off and on for a couple of centuries in Bucks and Lancaster counties, Pennsylvania. Here and there in the shop was a birdhouse carved from a peach crate; a barbed wire board; a huge, heavy sculpture made from telephone insulator; a 1930s-era set of coasters, napkin rings, place settings and trivets made from bottle caps. They found that these folk art items appealed especially to families with small children; they moved well.

Ellie had seemed to take the saga of Cait's and Robb's misadventure in stride, but of course, it had not happened to her. She rose with only slight difficulty and made her way to the door. "Well! The excitement's over. No dead bodies. I'll just be going." She winked and nodded exaggeratedly. "Are you going to open tomorrow?"

"Might as well. I'll get things cleaned and patched and we'll be ready to go. I've got a man coming tomorrow afternoon to fix the damn door."

"Are you going to ask Damia to come in?"

"Zoe. No, no we can handle it."

"Are you even going to tell her?"

"I don't see why," responded Robb. "What's to tell? The doors will be fixed by Thursday."

"I think you'd better do so," advised Ellie. "You surely don't think she'd not want to work for you if she knew about it?"

"No, no, of course not."

"Well, she might have a perspective on it."

Ellie departed through the offending door. Robb arose from his chair. "I wonder what she meant by that? Anyway, I'll rummage in the back and find some cardboard and tape for the window. I guess we'll do the thieves' trick and put a chair under the doorknob and go out the back. You know, it was really foolish of us not to install that alarm system and CCTV that that guy wanted to sell us."

"Yes, yes," sighed Cait. "And an alarm system would have done us so much good, wouldn't it? God almighty, they came in before we would have set the alarm. And what would the cops do with CCTV footage of two people in ski masks and us bare-assed?"

"Good point."

The phone rang. "Landline, Robb."

"Okay, I'll get it." Robb switched directions, heading for the counter. "Hello. I'm sorry, we're closed... Oh—yes—ah—sorry, Don... Yes? Yes...? But I thought everything was copacetic—I mean, you took pictures and all this morning ... oh ... oh... Well, okay... When? Well, I guess... Okay." He replaced the phone in its slot.

Cait was standing beside him now, her face a question mark. "That was Don Barker, insurance. He's sending over an investigator."

"But I thought it was all settled. An open-and-shut case, he'd said. Damage to the shop and bodily harm to us while doing business. As soon as he gets the police report he'll send over a check? Or bring it? Right?"

"Yes, yes. That's all fine. But apparently, they're to call *their* insurers whenever there's an incident that they have to pay out on. They called them this morning just after he was here and— well, he said it was a long story. This investigator fellow thinks there's more to it. Nothing to do with us, but he just wants to check our story. Said he'd explain it all when he gets here. He thought he might even be on his way over now, or maybe he'd turn up first thing tomorrow."

"What's his name?" asked Cait.

"Ferguson. Brian Ferguson."

4

MONDAY, 3:49 PM

CROTON CORNERS, NEW YORK

IT WAS GETTING ON TOWARD FOUR O'CLOCK; Robb had placed a chair under the front door knob to secure it. But now there was a knock. "Oh, hell. *We're closed!*" he shouted.

The knock came again, louder.

"I wonder if that might be the investigator," suggested Cait.

"Oh, yeah—all right; I'll go see." Robb rose and lumbered toward the door.

Brian Ferguson always presented himself as an "insurance investigator" but actually he was a "theft and fraud investigator," who, as it turned out, usually did work on contract for this or that insurance company, or more frequently, for its underwriters, Assurance Associates, and sometimes for individuals. The consortium did an increasingly widening business with retailers, wholesalers, and collectors of art, broadly defined. Sometimes a would-be client contacted him through a representative, often an attorney, who usually did not reveal either who had recommended him or for whom he was doing the work, who needed authentication services. The client who invariably "wished to remain anonymous," was thinking of buying, or had already bought a piece of art or jewelry or an archaeological artifact that needed verification of its legality or of claims that this or that person— sometimes famous, sometimes not—had indeed worn, owned, discovered, excavated, or produced said item. If the client was to insure it, how much could it be insured for? Ferguson would give his standard reply: what he could not and would not do was provide authentication of a piece's genuineness, himself; he was not an art expert. Insurance companies would not pay for "up front" authentication. But he could provide the client with a list of "authenticators" and then recommend insurance for a certain amount on the assumption that the piece was indeed authentic.

Clients who had been robbed, or who were victims of natural disasters, were also willing to pay for his services, through their insurer, in hopes of securing replacement funds. If a client submitted a claim to an insurance company for an item that had only a bill of sale and no paper trail of where it had been and how it had got there, the process of tracking down its history could take months. In the absence of tangibility, only relying on a photograph was like trying to resurrect a raft of extinct species: no matter how sincerely a client tried to insist that the items had been in his or her possession, the task of verifying a claim of their very existence was a challenge. But usually there *was* a photograph, a bill of sale, and an authentication certificate. If the authentication certificate proved authentic, Ferguson would, keeping a straight face, tell the client he could easily recommend payment, once the expert opinion had been received and itself had been expertized.

Art thefts in the past fifty years had been on the rise, from private collections, from galleries, from museums. The thefts made art forgery easier; if a piece popped up, it might or might not be the "real thing." The most famous recent thefts were of one version of Edvard Munch's *The Scream*, found two years later, and the heist of twelve works of art from the Isabelle Gardner Museum in Boston, never recovered. No insurance investigator was called in on that one; the Gardner was uninsured. For decades the FBI had had only one full-time art theft and fraud inspector; the situation was particularly frustrating for countries such as Italy, Greece, and Turkey, that had stiff punishments—huge fines in the case of Italy—for art theft. The Investigator suspected that Italy's over-the-top, years-long dogging of a curator from a high-profile American art museum over dozens of Roman, Etruscan, and Greek vases and sculpture, ostensibly known to have been stolen and spirited out of the country, was aimed at pushing US law enforcement into greater diligence. It had not worked.

The tip from one of his colleagues about this seemingly minor case was sufficiently bizarre to merit Brian Ferguson's attention. The business had a "personal injury" clause that provided compensation at a flat rate to anyone on the premises who suffered bodily or psychological trauma, whether the victims were patrons, employees, or even owners, in exchange for signing away their right to sue. Because the two owners, according to the local agent's phone call to his insurers in New York, on the basis of a phone conversation with the owners and a preliminary police report, had been subjected to physical and psychological trauma, they each were due the one-time payment that the policy provided. But their story included some ancillary details that had triggered headquarters' policy of calling Ferguson when certain suspicious circumstances obtained. This case qualified, prima facie: not only was nothing stolen, but also the "victims," the owners of a little backwater antiques shop up the Hudson, after being subdued, had been supplied with food, drink, and rudimentary toilet facilities. The perps were, then, "nice guys." It smacked too much of the Gardner; in that heist, the crooks had apologized to the guard for having deceived him and then having to tie him up. Ferguson had persuaded his colleague at the insurance company to immediately cut a check that he could pick up and deliver to the aggrieved owners, thereby giving him an opportunity to check things out in person. He had the check in an envelope in his jacket pocket; delivery of it would offer strong persuasion to the Murrays—the shop's owners—to cooperate with him in a quid pro quo that he would propose to them.

The other suspicious aspect of this case was that, as a result of the proprietors being tied up and therefore immobilized, they had complained they had missed an appointment with someone at the American Museum of Natural History—not a museum employee—who wanted to sell them something, or make some kind of a marketing arrangement. Now that was puzzling, intriguing, and exciting. *What was the "something" that this unidentified person had to offer?* Ferguson wondered. There were enough fishy-scented "clews" to merit the investigator persuading the insurance consortium for which he worked on contract to authorize, with a cap, an expense account, per diem fee, and timeline for following up a suspicion. This suspicion shaped itself around the residue of a case that he thought of as the "Mimbres Pots Insurance Scam" from years earlier.

When he had investigated the disappearance of that over-insured shipment of well-provenanced prehistoric pottery from the Mimbres culture excavated from several private ranches in New Mexico, that had disappeared between points of origin and destination, the Investigator had gotten as far as uncovering the probable workings of a gang well known as art thieves and forger-peddlers headed by a very clever woman. He suspected they may have been involved in the Gardner heist. That woman was named Cricencia Morgenhouse. But he could never pin anything down. Presumably, the pottery had been stored somewhere, awaiting an upturn in the economy and an appreciation of potential asking prices. *Was this what was going to be on offer at the museum?*

He speculated that what Morgenhouse—if it was Morgenhouse—had to sell could have been the Mimbres pots. But equally, the missed appointment could have been with Morgenhouse peddling ritual paraphernalia that he was quite sure she had acquired at an auction in Paris a year earlier. But now, it looked as if someone else had usurped the place of the intended buyers. *Who had gone to such lengths? And why had they done so? Was it a case of another bunch of shadowy characters wanting in on the action? Or perhaps disgruntled members of the gang who had been done out of their agreed share?*

And here was yet another peculiar thing: shortly before the web site offering the pots was taken down, the dealer identified in the website as offering the Mimbres pots, Gregg Neal, had suddenly died. No suspicion of foul play, but surely more than a coincidence.

There was just a slim chance that the quirky little scenario swirling around this mom-and-pop shop in this low-profile excursion destination, which he was about to enter, was one spore on a trail leading to the re-emergence of, for want of a better handle, "the Mimbres gang," either peddling the remainder of the cache of pots or switching their interests to a different kind of black-market trade in tangible heritage objects "collected" from the First Peoples of the Americas.

If he confirmed, and hopefully added to the outline he already had, he would launch a full-scale investigation; and for that he would have to enlist the assistance of the dealers who had some apparent interest in Native American art and, therefore, who had some motivation for providing that assistance: that would be the Murrays, the intended buyers for either the remaining prehistoric pots from the cache or the ritual objects, newly acquired by Morgenhouse.

The investigator had taken a fast train up the Hudson to Croton Corners; now he scooted beneath the yellow crime scene tape and noted that the door was easy to open because the latch was broken. He peered inside. A slightly paunchy, middle-aged man with a shock of brownish hair, shot with gray, rose from a desk in the middle of the shop, turned his head, and said loudly to someone apparently in the back, "I'll handle it."

The man rose and clomped off in the direction of the still darkened front. He was joined by a woman. "We're closed," they said almost in unison.

"So ye are," replied the unknown visitor.

Cait turned her head toward the front of the shop, where she could hear some strange foreign-sounding voice. Robb was standing with the visitor—a bewhiskered man, with thin mustache and goatee, wearing a Homburg hat, in a trench coat flapping open to reveal red suspenders holding up stone-washed jeans. With his head cocked and in his trench coat, Cait thought, he looked like a cross between Humphrey Bogart's portrayal of Dashiell Hammett's Sam Spade and a photo of Henry Miller inscribed to Anaïs Nin, "from gangster-author Henry Miller," from one of her diary volumes.

He entered the shop. "But Ah'm happy to be the bearer of good cheer, good money, and also a request. Ah wonder eff Ah cood have a word with ye." Cait noted a voice that burred and clattered over words that she only understood as English after a fraction of time delay.

"Ah b'lieve Ah cood shad some laight on your recent experience!" Now the visitor hastily added something like "Ah lake these daylahtful paces uv fook aht—who'da thought o' pleece sattings oot o' Nehi b'a'll caps? Eet's nowt gray tart, boot eet's mor foon."

"Gray tart?"

"Aye, as in bad art and great art."

"Ah! Great art. No, great art was never what we intended," responded Robb.

"And Ah ha'e something for ye." He plunged his hand into his pocket, retrieved an envelope, and waved it in their faces, then placed it into Robb's outstretched hand.

"Oh, yes, right—Don phoned us. Come on in. That was quick. By the way, I'm Robb Murray and this is my wife, Cait."

"Brian Ferguson." He entered the shop as Robb and Cait gave way to let him pass and shook both their hands. "Ah was hopin' ye were; I shood'a enquired afore handing over the check!"

Ferguson then produced seven pieces of identification: a UK passport, two private investigator licenses from the City of London and the State of New York, an international driving license, a Town of Newcastle driving license, an identification card from Europol, and lastly, a picture ID from Assurance Associates. "Ah'm Brian Ferguson," he said, "but ye ken call me just Ferguson. And hare's why Ah kem chargin' op hare so quick. Ah had the bare bones o' your story related to me by the insurance adjuster at the head office. And yes, before ye ask," he continued quickly, "I am indeed British, from Northumberland. Now that ye know who I am, I am most anxious to hear the story of your ordeal."

"I'll make coffee—or tea?" offered Cait. "And maybe you can explain to us just exactly why you're so interested. The police were hardly impressed. They told us something like, 'Oh, it's just assault; nothing was taken'; no fingerprints were left, 'so there's nothing to go on and nothing to do.' The case would end with the report they made, which I guess they've made and filed. So why is the insurance company so interested?" Robb looked at the check again, as if making sure, then folded it and placed it in his shirt pocket.

Robb placed a chair back under the front door. Ferguson peeled off his trench coat. "Ehhh ... mah Macintosh..."

"Oh, I'll take that," offered Robb. He hung it on a vintage hall tree that stood just inside the door. Ferguson followed Robb over to the hall tree, removed his Homburg, and hung it on a hook.

Cait was amused to see that the suspenders were offset by a blue corduroy sports jacket with leather patches. *God almighty!* she thought. *Now he looks like a cross between Fireman Frank and Mr. Chips!*

They took seats, more or less in the same configuration that they had taken with Ellie, with Robb seated at his massive desk. Once they got used to his strange lingo, they found that Ferguson spoke with a narrative clarity, patience, a revealing diction, and a simplicity of sentence construction that rivaled Hemingway's. His heavy accent tumbled more and more toward a combination of Sean Connery's James Bond and a fairly standard Bostonian-Oxbridgian English.

"The insurance company is not interested. At least, not this insurance company and not in this case per se, but the consortium I work for on contract, Assurance Associates, may be interested. This case may be tied to another. I ... uh ... persuaded them that the most generous and prompt settlement they could possibly make would, in turn, ensure your cooperation in what I am about to tell you. But first I want to hear from you."

Robb and Cait went through the whole series of events once again, just as they had done with Ellie, but in a quieter tone and absent the hand-wringing and what Cait now recognized as her commentary verging on histrionics. They gave him a guided tour of the scene of the crime.

When they had finished, the investigator was silent for nearly half a minute. Ferguson wanted to assure himself that there were indeed enough "clews" to justify an expense account, the per diem fee, and the timeline for following up his suspicion that what had happened to the Murrays was the work of Morgenhouse. "The events and the circumstances are, indeed, sufficiently bizarre to create suspicion. No, no, no," he assured Robb and Cait, "You yourselves are not under any hint of suspicion. And I will start by saying I'm happy to encounter you once again," he addressed Robb and Cait, chuckling. "When I first made your acquaintance this morning it was in the American Museum of Natural History, where I made it a point to deliberately encounter you!"

"Huh? What?" they exclaimed. Robb started to protest, "But we weren't there…!"

"Aye! That you weren't! That's what makes this case so suspicious and intriguing, because at the time, I *thought* it was you there!" responded Ferguson, chuckling again. "I was tailing somebody. You know what tailing entails?"

Robb and Cait nodded, nonplussed.

"The individual I was tailing is temporarily living out on Long Island. I tailed her from there. She has been known to me for some time. A year ago, I got wind she had popped up again in Paris, at an auction. She's been renting a place on Long Island for the last year, living with a young man, but we also know that what we think she has, she does not have there. I've had a man keeping an eye on her on and off. She's mostly kept a very low profile, until about a week ago. What tipped me off that she was up to something was that the other day my man tailed her to the American Museum of Natural History—to the Africa room She was evidently planning something.

46

"This morning my man reported she once again took the train into the city. So, I hopped into my vehicle, raced in, and parked near Penn Station. I spied her just as she was alighting from a Long Island train. I followed her. But then I lost her for a while in the Port Authority Bus Terminal. When I found her again, I barely recognized her. She was in disguise, walking with two support canes! I knew something was up. I tailed her to the American Museum of Natural History. She headed straight for the Africa Hall, stopped dead when she came to an exhibit case of case bronze sculptures. At first, I thought she had some interest in them—she was peering intently at them. But then I realized she was actually looking through the case at a couple sitting on a bench a few yards distant. Then she retreated back into the rotunda and sat down. Well, I had to keep nonchalantly well hidden. So, all I could do was hide behind the t-rex and lie low. She looked at her wristwatch; seemed to be waiting for something. I thought, she's so slow I might sprint back to Africa and just take a look at what—or who—she was peering at, the couple sitting on the bench. Clearly, she had some interest in them but did not know them. If it was all on the up-and-up, why not just walk up to them and say, 'Here I am'? It was as if she wanted to make sure."

"Of what?" asked Cait.

"Ah—that's where it gets interesting. And you see, I'm going to have to have some allies in this—some folks who would see it as worth their while to cooperate with me—and you'll see why once I lay it all out."

"So, you know this person—her—pretty well?"

Ferguson shook his head. "I don't know her personally at all. But I know her doings all too well. I'll get to that in a minute. Anyway, I was in a dilemma: I didn't know what was going on, and now it looked like I might have two tails to do: her and you. So, I circled back and hung around between the bronzes and some masks in another case where I could turn around every now and then—and a few minutes later the fellow took out his phone. I got very close and heard him answer 'Cannings', loud and clear."

"That's us!" exclaimed Robb.

"But it wasn't!" Cait almost shouted. "God almighty! They were, they were…"

Ferguson nodded. "That's right. They were impersonating you! Now I can confirm that because I followed them to the cafeteria and managed to get myself a sweet and secure a table where I would not be unduly noticed. Now, if the couple saw me, I don't think they would make much of it—after all you do bump into people again in a museum, don't you? I was a little uncomfortable about her, but she doesn't know me from Adam so why would she suspect anything? But, on the way to the cafeteria, I managed to activate my little recording device, take off my coat, and set both down so the coat obscured the little device but did not block its receptivity. I was taking a chance that there in the museum there would be an absence of miscreants who might light-finger my coat away; well, it's a dirty old thing anyway and totally out of style.

"Anyway, then I made off as if to go to the gents. I stayed away a good long time. I figured she had done what she had to do: made some sort of contact. And I could just head back to Long Island and do a stakeout and wait for her to come back, or initiate some other kind of activity. What I really wanted was to figure out where you two came into it."

"But it wasn't us! We were here all morning, recovering from our… our 'adventure,'" protested Cait.

"Precisely. But I didn't know they weren't you, did I? Well, I gave them twenty minutes to begin their business transaction; if they were still at it, I'd just sit down behind a newspaper that I'd gone out and gotten. But when I came back, I discovered they'd cleared out. I listened to my little recorder and ascertained that you—they—were proprietors of Cannings' Antiques in Croton Corners. And that Cricencia Morgenhouse, Chris Morgen, Jane Faulks—three of the names that we know she's gone by—introduced herself as 'Dahlia' and told them she had, or has, something to peddle. But she would na' say what it was. She was suspicious that she was being, as she put it, 'surveilled.' She was right, of course. Well, I will make my way back out to

Long Island later and confer with my man and resume my 'surveilling.' But now, thanks to Metro North, here I am! So, I am gathering that this couple not only was not you but also were not sent by you, do not represent you, are in fact totally unknown to you?"

"Golly, yeah," affirmed Robb.

"That woman, the woman who rendezvoused with your impersonators is one half of a couple originally known to me as Dan Rosenstock and Jane Faulks. They were involved, some years earlier in an insurance fraud and they may have been intended as the primary brokers for a collection of antiquities that Lloyd's had agreed to insure, on behalf of a number of owners, including gallerists in Santa Fe and Arizona. The antiquities consisted of 122 boxes of prehistoric pottery from a long-vanished civilization called the Mimbres. The pottery was loaded up at a rancher's home in southern New Mexico, destined for a gallery in Santa Fe. The pottery was 'owned' by several ranchers and was being sold to several galleries and dealers in Santa Fe. When the lorry reached its destination and the boxes were opened after the 300-mile journey, they turned out to be filled with rocks, not pottery. The lorry driver claimed he had only stopped twice: once in Socorro for coffee and in Belen for a burger. The lorry was locked. The boxes had been examined and "certified" by the rancher and by a local insurance representative on behalf of Lloyd's. But clearly, there had been a switch.

"Police couldna' confirm an actual robbery because they couldna' determine that the boxes had ever contained anything but rocks, or that there were 122 cartons containing the pottery that had been actually robbed. The pottery had simply vanished. The lorry driver was questioned and released. The ranchers and dealers threw temper tantrums and denounced each other and also some possibly unknown thieves, but Lloyd's strongly suspected collusion. Extensive searches of the ranches and efforts to track down someone who had seen anything incriminating were frustratingly fruitless. After nearly a year, Lloyd's had to finally cough up $10 million. The items were undoubtedly over-insured, but we had no choice," said Ferguson.

"Insurers regularly issue policies for shipments 'in transit,'" he explained. "Such items can be insured for a gallery or a collector with a policy in which the gallery or the owners supplied descriptions and value estimates. Or a shipment can be specially covered for a fee under the shipper's policy. An attorney had turned up at Lloyd's in New York with a persuasive argument: the destination gallery in Santa Fe would neither take possession of the pots nor display them. It was simply the point of distribution for galleries and dealers who would take possession upon the pots' arrival and unpacking. The items would go out of ownership of the ranchers once they were loaded into the van, because the ranchers would not get paid until the galleries and dealers had made their selection of items and had made offers on particular pieces. So, therefore it was a special status—'items in transit'—that had to be insured."

"We know Mimbres pottery, but we don't deal in it," commented Robb. "We respect the Native American Graves Protection and Repatriation Act."

Ferguson nodded. "Yes, that's right. NAGPRA requires consultation with likely descendants if items of cultural patrimony are discovered and return of the items from graves that are found on federal property. But, in this case, NAGPRA did not ostensibly apply."

"Why do you say ostensibly?"

"Because, you see, this particular Mimbres pottery did not occur on federal land. The Archaeological Preserve had just bought the ranch from which the pottery was dug up, as well as a contiguous one, and obviously the former owner was trying to make a profit on selling the pottery before the Preserve took over. The Archaeological Preserve has a strict policy of preservation: if there is excavation, everything is duly recorded, then covered back up. Or it is left completely unexcavated. There is no way to know how many of the insured items might have come from the Preserve's ranch just prior to their acquiring it, or from other ranches, or perhaps even the bits of public land where Mimbres might be found. In fact, I think that's why the stuff disappeared: it's becoming increasingly difficult to prove it didn't come from some place that it shouldn't have. As you know, the legit dealers won't touch anything without good provenance, and if you have to go to the black market, you often have to give deep discounts."

"But I don't get why Lloyd's went for such a high value. How many pieces were there?"

"A huge cache—600, more or less. But I'm assuming you know the hallmarks of these wonderful pieces of art. Nearly every one that has ever been found has had the bottom punched out. But 72 of these did *not* have their bottoms punched out! Now, just exactly why—in fact, just exactly why most do have their bottoms punched is unknown. The standard explanation is 'to let the spirit out,' under the assumption that the spirit of the living person is embodied in the pot, and when the person dies, the pot must die too. But 72 of these did not have their bottoms punched out!"

"What about the descendants? Don't they know?" asked Cait.

"Aye, there's another rub—if and when NAGPRA might apply! Nobody is certain exactly who the descendants are. Are they the contemporary Hopi and Puebloans of the Southwest? Might they be the Pima or the Papago, who claim descent from the nearby Hohokam civilization? Or are the descendants somewhere in Mexico?" Ferguson looked from Cait to Robb, then back to Cait. "They should not have been dug up in the first place. But they were—are—highly desirable by unscrupulous dealer and collectors. These items were triple-certified: they were certified as genuine, each one with its own certificate, by an expert in the field; they were certified by the three ranchers as coming from their private holdings; and they were certified by an off-duty US marshal who affirmed that none of the pieces was covered by NAGPRA, or the Archaeological Resources Protection Act, which makes it crime to remove antiquities from federal lands. We know that the six galleries and dealers and the three ranchers agreed to divide the insurance winnings evenly. But it gets more complicated: there were actually ten interested parties, one of them listed only as 'brokers,' and therefore anonymous. We—I—suspect that was a pair of Dan Rosenstock and Jane Faulks, longtime dealers in art, antiquities, and collectibles on the black and gray markets. The gray market being any number of venues where items of dubious provenance but that are not demonstrably contraband can be sold. Rosenstock and Faulks dinna' want their names listed because they knew were already known to Lloyd's as insurance fraudsters. I will na' waste your time with the details."

"So that's what—a little over a million dollars apiece for the 'interested parties.' That's a hunk of change for each one, but it's not a lot. So, what's the connection with our imposters?" inquired Cait.

Ferguson shook his head. "I dunna' know. That puzzles me. They could be in cahoots, but if so, I dunna' know exactly how. The whole arrangement at the museum and their assuming your identities could ha'e been a ruse to throw us off the track, since Faulks specifically mentioned being surveilled.

"At any rate, we know Mr. Rosenstock and Ms. Faulks disappeared shortly after the Mimbres heist; we know that Dan Rosenstock is living in Mexico, quite comfortably, operating a gallery in San Miguel de Allende. A million grand goes pretty far down there, enough to grubstake a gallery. But Jane Faulks literally did disappear, at least from public view, until just a year ago."

"And is Mr. Rosenstock dealing in Mimbres pottery down there?"

"Och, no! He's smarter than that! But we think he and Jane Faulks—Chris Morgen—just might still be in touch with one another, and still brokering the pots for nice hefty fees collected from the principals—either the ranchers or the dealers or both."

"But I don't get it," said Robb. "Wouldn't smashing us around and trampling all over our shop just draw attention to all three of them and the situation in the museum? And you've been tailing Jane Faulks, but what do you hope to get out of doing that?"

"Ah! First, drawing attention to the situation in the museum. Aye. It would seem so. *But* the crime here creates a red herring: the focus is on the crime *here*, not the scheme unfolding *there*." Now Ferguson launched into another long monologue. "More than a year after Lloyd's had closed the investigation, a Lloyd's vice-president in London had gotten curious about the case because he collected Native American antiquities. He got especially curious when he saw, in a Sotheby's auction, three Mimbres pots on offer, originally purchased on the internet from an undisclosed seller. The frustrating thing was that, although Lloyd's had a full set of photographs of the missing pots, these did not match any of the other photos.

"That's when he called me," said Ferguson. Ferguson had poured over the photographs. "And guess what!" he said triumphantly. "The photographs had been doctored! Each one had been digitally altered: a broken rim line made continuous, a continuous line made broken, a lizard with a pattern of six diamonds made to have only five, et cetera. So, it's impossible to positively identify these as items from the 600! In fact, if they are indeed fakes, then that means at least one of the original fraud conspirators has indeed been through his share of the cache."

"And so...?" Said Cait, puzzled.

"So, I'm taking it from the other direction. If Faulks' take from the insurance scam was a million, as much as it sounds, $1,000,000 would not last Jane Faulks very long. At some point she would have to start turning that into some kind of business venture in the antiquities trade. Well, an auction was announced in Paris a year ago: an auction of an incomparably unique collection: 71 Puebloan Katsina masks. Now, Katsina masks are sacred items; American museums have returned plenty of them in recent years. How they got into museums in the first place involves many long stories. And yes, it is possible that now and then a private collector may have happened upon one, sold surreptitiously by a member of the tribe, desperate for money."

"You know a lot about this."

"Not so much. But I did a lot of reading; it seemed suspicious to me that suddenly these items—seventy-odd—were all for sale at the same time, in the same place."

"You think they were stolen?" said Cait.

"Aye. I think they were stolen, or perhaps sold, hugger-mugger, by one or more museums, just before NAGPRA went into effect, in 1991, and before they had to publish inventories of all the sacred items they had that might be repatriated to the tribes. And I think they were brought into this country by circumventing US customs."

"So, you think this Jane person was meeting 'us,'" Robb made quotation marks in the air, "to sell us one of these masks?"

"Yes. Probably more than one. And also, possibly Mimbres pots, which at this point may be fake, or may be genuine. She may have been waiting all these years to start dealing her share of the cache when she knew the other partners in the fraud had begun to run through theirs. Less competition for her, higher prices to be gotten."

"So, you know what she looks like?" said Robb.

"I tracked down photos: old ones, and not very good. They were shadowy, indistinct. But I blew them up and thought I could probably recognize her. You know, there's often more identity in how a person stands, turns, shakes hands than there is in a face. Faces can change; bodies may gain or lose weight but they tend to be wielded by their owners in an overall consistent way, throughout the lifetime. But yes, it was clearly her at the auction and also in the museum."

A clock chimed five somewhere in the store. Now, at the end of their sagas (and also the end of the day) Robb said, "Look. This is all a lot to absorb. And I don't get why we have to know all this and what our involvement is." They announced they were "beat" and were going upstairs.

Ferguson's stood up to go. "I'm satisfied that what happened, happened just as ye related it to me. But let me say that you now know there is more to this than meets the eye. I realize you are excessively tired. I'd like to propose that I look into a few things and return on say—Thursday or Friday and share as much as I can about why your experience smacks of more than what it might first seem to be."

They left it at that. Mr. Ferguson departed. Robb secured the door as best he could, they retreated to the back, trudged upstairs, and put on a pot of canned minestrone fortified with quinoa-rice and Canadian bacon that Cait cut into little squares. But before turning in, Cait needed to phone Zoe.

5

TUESDAY, 5:30 PM

WESTERN CONNECTICUT COLLEGE,
WESTON, CONNECTICUT

IT HAD BEEN A PRODUCTIVE DAY. Nick had had to go into NYU and was due back some time that night. Zoe had worked three solid hours on her paper for Dr. Sloan. It was as good as done. She'd cleared it with Dr. Sloan: yes, it was perfectly acceptable to make a twenty-five-or thirty-page paper do double duty: fulfill the assignment and also slide into her thesis as one of its chapters. "That's what we assign papers for," she had said. "We hope that it will spark students—graduate students, that is—who haven't started writing their thesis yet to do so and those that have started to make just that much more progress."

Stripped comfortably down to her panties and one of Nick's shirts, Zoe opened the night table drawer and took out a tiny gold lighter and some rolling paper. She bounced off the bed, trotted over to the door of the flat where, just to its right, sat a distressed antique washstand missing most of its parts, including one of the two double doors, the metal bowl meant to fit into the hole in its top, as well as the mirror the back frame had once held. She wrenched the washstand a half-foot away from the wall, squatted, reached behind the washstand, and yanked on a knob. With a click, a little door in the wall popped open. She drew out a can of Prince Albert smoking tobacco. Except it did not contain smoking tobacco.

A corresponding door in the hall, outside the flat, made the arrangement a pass-through; but the outside door was shut tight with a series of nail screws and the knob had been sawed off.

The building had been built probably in the 1920s. When they had asked the building owner, Mr. Bloom, who ran a dress shop on the ground floor about the little door, he had frowned, shrugged, and said, "Who knows?"

But Nick speculated it was a milk door. "Milkman trots up the stairs, opens the little door outside in the hall, slides the milk bottles in, mom comes along, opens the little door on the inside, takes out the milk."

"Maybe mail too?" Zoe had added. The flat was one large single room with a miniscule toilet-shower-sink combo in one corner and their oversized bed in the other. Before being cut up into one- and two-room flats, the apartment had probably been a good-sized family unit; this had probably been the dining room. Three other doors cut into the hallway accessed the other units.

Zoe rolled a fine, fat joint, replaced the canister's lid, slid it back into the cubby space, closed the door with a click, and shoved the washstand back into place. She plopped back on the bed, opened the lighter, flicked the wheel, sucked the joint, closed the lighter, held her breath, then exhaled. It was not very good grass. Well, maybe it had been when they had harvested it from that low valley field, clandestinely planted on a tobacco farm a year and a half ago. There had been five of them, and even divided among them, the bounty had allowed each of them to come away with a huge supply. But it had proved not very potent; it had to be well enhanced with copious amounts of Romanian red wine (palatable when well chilled), which Zoe had drawn out of the mini-fridge on which sat the two-ring electric burner. She poured a generous amount into a sturdy juice glass, took another toke, and set the bottle back onto the nightstand. She leaned back against the pillows. She reflected on how glad she was that she liked grass and wine. She hated crystal meth, drug of choice for a number of her fellow students: great high but followed by a crashing, deep downer. Coke? Too messy; cokers were always sniveling. And E? No way! She knew people who'd mixed Molly with just beer, let alone wine, and ended up in the hospital. She liked weed and wine because it was participatory; *you have to do something. You don't just pop a pill and let it take you over. And the marijuana dry throat needs wine. That's good.*

She contemplated, for, it seemed, the hundredth time, the conversation that she and Nick always seemed to be having at the tag-end of a "timeout" day ending a ragged week, at least once a month, for the last half-year. It always came on a day capped with pre- and post-dinner smokes and red wine, bookending pasta with heaps of mushrooms, or poached shad roe, or braised liver with a mound of quinoa and peas. Zoe had been delightfully surprised that Nick was just about the only person she knew who had a taste for liver. Zoe took another toke, another sip of wine; she would once again re-hash the typical conversation, which seemed to pop into her head like an unanswered memorandum. But this time she resolved to rationalize the inevitable conclusion to which it led.

The conversation went something like this:

Zoe: Nick, I don't want to be just your little thing on the side for the rest of my life, and until you tell me straight just what it is you do for a living—why you go off periodically, where you go, what you do—we can't be real partners. You talk mysteriously about being partners together, doing things together, a good life of travel and interesting work, but you never say just what that work is or is going to be.

Nick: I've told you. I can't spill it all until I know that you're really committed to me. And no, I don't mean be my marrying maiden.

Zoe: And why does commitment to you mean I can't do what you're doing—enroll in a real graduate program and get a PhD?

Nick: Because then you're tied up here, or rather there; wherever you're doing your PhD.

Zoe: But you're in a PhD program and you're not tied up at all.

Nick: Actually, I am. You think it's easy to go charging off, getting back dead exhausted, spending all day at least once a week pounding out the dissertation, grading papers, thinking up class exercises. I'll be glad when I'm done with it. Then I can take many more jobs—real ones, big ones—all over the world and not have to work around this doodly-squat TA work in butt-fuck nowhere.

Zoe: But it's the doodly-squat TA work that brought us together! If you really don't like teaching, then why can't you just get the dissertation done, get the PhD, and then come along with me wherever I get admitted to one—a PhD program. I mean, like, it might even be Columbia. I wouldn't mind commuting. We could stick right here. Or even if it's not, you can travel from wherever I am to wherever you need to periodically be.

Nick: That's true, that's true. But it would be too much like it is now—you wouldn't be able to get away and help me out. You'd be too busy taking classes.

Zoe: Well, you've never said just what it is I'm to help you with, so…

Nick: I want to branch out a little. I want to get into some other things. But I also still need to keep doing what I'm doing—to build a reputation.

Zoe: As…?

Nick: It's … it's a whole package. It … it just doesn't quite go along with being in academia.

Zoe: But you *are* in academia.

Nick: Yes, yes. It's an academic pursuit … but. But … the academics is only a stepping stone…

Blah, blah, blah; yammer, yammer, yammer; on and on and on, thought Zoe. But the conversation had moved on, at least as far as she was concerned. She had been accepted into two PhD programs in art history and connoisseurship. And University of Washington had offered her a three-year fellowship. She would be foolish not to take it. And she now knew what Nick did for a living. And yes, it would be like living inside a conundrum for her to do her PhD while at the same time being his assistant.

Nick was an authenticator. It hardly seemed possible. He did not have a PhD. He was what was colloquially known as an "ABD"—"All-But-Dissertation." It was not a real degree. Yet he put it on his curriculum vitae as if it were. And that, she presumed, credentialed him sufficiently, along with his admittedly considerable knowledge and on-going PhD work, to persuade the gullible, or simply the needing-and-wanting-to-believe owners of un-provenanced or dubious works—or outright known forgeries—that they had a possible Rembrandt, Titian, Vermeer, or a real Leger, Modigliani, Van Gogh or Manet.

Yes, unbelievably—at least to her—it seemed that Nick authenticated everything: old masters, pre-Raphaelites, cubists, fauvists, impressionists, all on the basis of his supposed—or perhaps genuine—expertise in brush strokes. His dissertation topic was exactly that: brushstrokes. And he had indeed spent hours at the Met, the MOMA, the Nelson, the Getty, the de Young, the Amon Carter, taking notes, looking from different angles, sometimes with 3-D glasses and a set of horse-blinders, entering brushstroke attributes into an excel grid on his iPad. His NEA grant had funded expeditions to the Louvre, the Picasso, the Matisse, the Tate, the Tate Modern, the National, the National Portrait, the Victoria and Albert, the Thyssen-Bornemisza the Prado and Munich's Alte Pinakothek.

During that incomparably marvelous summer, as a second-year student in the "two in five" BA-MA program, just climbing out of gen-ed and major-and-minor required courses into the specialized courses in art history and connoisseurship, she had accompanied him as his "assistant." And she *had* learned a lot, even though really, she had done little more than serve as gofer and dogs-body and of course bedmate and dinner companion, ravaging *moules-en-champagne*, stewed oysters, pâtés, mousses and bries, confits and cassoulets, half-carafes of Tavel, Sancerre, St. Émilion, Tempranillo, as gluttonously as she ravaged him. Only in London had they scrimped; it was just too expensive. They'd restricted themselves to Chinese.

They had lamented foregoing Rome, Milan, and Florence; but limited time and shrinking funds required regretted triages. But as Nick talked more and more about what he was doing and how he was doing it, on the long train rides and over the long evening dinners on café terraces and in restaurant courtyards, she began to appreciate what he was getting at and to apprehend his methodology: if you were dealing solely with painting, in oils or tempera, or even acrylic, you could indeed transcend the centuries and even cultural traditions and tease out a limited number of ways that brush and pigment on canvas or wood, gesso or linen could be applied. Sometimes they would spend a day or two not in museums, but in churches, artists' homes such as Monet's in Giverney or Zadkine's studio, or in private collections such as the Wallace. Often, in these less frequented venues, Zoe would actually be able to note down what Nick called some "basic brushstroke badges and biblios" that were signatures of this or that artist or school. Of course, she had taken art courses and had done a few paintings—water colors—that she was not embarrassed to claim, but she had realized early on, in high school, that it represented neither her forte nor her interest: she really liked learning the stories of patrons and commissions, about starving innovators and successful iconoclasts, experimental avant-gardists and workshop factories, and yes—fakes and forgers.

That was what her thesis was about: a comparison of the lives, times, economies, and products of two famous artistic workshops: Rembrandt's and Tintoretto's, with an eye to figuring out how to distinguish amongst "school of" from "by the master" and outright forgeries on the basis of historical context and events. Now, her doctoral fellowship would enable her to continue with her ideas, expand her scope, and take her to many of North America's premier museums, and maybe, just maybe, to the Rijksmuseum in the Netherlands and back to museums in London. She would then move on to the other end of the art production industry: those who bought, resold, collected, and showcased the works of not only the two masters, but also the not the so-very-famous mavens and masters of the schools and workshops, the minor, less-well-known students and understudies. And she would study the patterns that would (she hoped!) emerge when she tracked the twists and turns that their works, and the works of their students, took in wending their way into collections and museums, and how many of them had been mis-attributed to them, or not to them, and how many curators, experts, or collectors had been fooled and why. Did they always know they were acquiring a "school-of," an "attributed-to," or a "student-of"? She would, of course, have to limit her study to a small sample; but setting off on the journey would reveal its own mile markers, a journey through what she knew would be a labyrinth of false attributions, rescinded authentications, un-provenanced discoveries, and, yes, she hoped, forgeries and fakes. She mused: the Met alone had taken several hundred items off display over the years and relegated them to its "unresolved" room in the basement. The work would be tedious and time-consuming but also exciting and revealing. What she had learned in her unofficial apprenticeship with Nick would indeed be useful; and a curator and professor in Seattle with whom she was already corresponding had given her a good reason to try to get some supplemental funding to repeat those good times she had had with Nick: there was, he had written, an actual museum of fakes and forgeries in London!

Yes, it would be a parting of the ways with Nick. She couldn't help a small and short-lived cascade of tears down her cheeks; but surely, she could, she *should* move on. There were plenty of nice, honest, uncomplicated guys out there. Nick would refer to his out-of-town sojourns as "have-to-see-a-man-about-a-horse" weekends. But now she knew what it was he did. It wasn't a horse he was seeing a man about.

He had arrived back from one of his jaunts well after midnight on a Sunday, slipping into bed beside her and almost immediately falling into a deep sleep. She had sprung out of bed as usual the following morning just in time to get to her eight o'clock class only to discover her phone was out of juice. In class, she used a combination of hand-writing notes and self-texting through to her app on her laptop to assemble what would later become a journal entry on her iPad. She had reasoned that Nick would just be climbing out of bed when she returned to the flat shortly after noon. So why not take his phone? Well. She reached into the jacket pocket of his Prada suit, slung over one of the two kitchen chairs. The phone had sprung immediately to life: apparently, he had neglected to put it into password-protected lock mode. And there it was: an open file with copious notes and photos documenting his authentication of a Van Gogh! She scrolled along through the entire file that ended with the template of an authentication certificate. Would he send the authentication certificate along with the photo of the painting so the client could print it out and frame it? Or attach it to the back of the painting? And that was when Zoe knew that her work for her PhD—even for her master's—was incompatible with Nick's work. It might really have been a genuine Van Gogh. But it might not have been one.

Tintorettos, Titians, Rembrandts, Rubens, Braques, Gris, Legers, Corots—what-have-you; Zoe knew they popped up in the international art market with tedious regularity. Sotheby's, Christie's, Bonham's were constantly auctioning off "attributed-to-s," and "in-the-manner-ofs," with authentications by this or that expert, always with a caveat escape clause, only to withdraw them from the catalogue upon suffering their denunciation as fakes by yet another expert roaming the auction floor. And what happened to these works? Usually, they were quietly sold off to a dealer who then marketed them to an eager collector who was satisfied with a new authentication from, well—could be by Nick Taylor, Art Historian ABD!

There was nothing illegal about it: you can copy all the Picassos you want. You can even fake a Picasso signature on them. You can even display your fake Picassos as the real thing. The only thing you cannot do is sell them as such. And an authenticator can give an opinion this way or that, as long as the authenticator is not profiting from doing the authenticating other than collecting a fee. Some forgeries were beautiful pieces, done by talented imitators who had, perhaps, not even sold them as authentic pieces, perhaps claiming to have found them in grandma's attic, attribution and provenience unknown.

It was the dealer, then, who perhaps knowingly or not, maybe convinced and delighted at having discovered a "find," passed it on to a naïve collector as the real thing. And voilà: another newly discovered priceless gem. The old masters' students' pieces, floating around for centuries, obviously complicated the field; *but that just makes it all that more interesting for me!* thought Zoe.

One last toke. The joint was about to burn her lips. She stuck the thumb and forefinger of her left hand into her mouth and, moistened with a glob of saliva, they snapped deftly around the joint's ember. She twisted and pinched, and placed the butt-end onto the night table. She took the wine glass, maneuvered carefully off the bed, padded over to the fridge, poured a half glass, slid back onto the bed, taking a largish sip before placing the glass on the night table. *When would Nick get in? Probably as usual after midnight.* She would rise at seven and get to Rosy Rosales' Intro class just a few minutes after eight, as always. Tomorrow after class she would tell Nick: it's University of Washington and it's my PhD and it's not me assisting you and it's bye-bye. You may not make it into my dissertation by name but I know what you're all about and you'll recognize yourself. You were good for me for a while. Worldly, sophisticated, knowledgeable, fun, good in bed. You were a balm and a relief to me from the succession of palookas that took me out on dates to steak houses and bars and har-harred along with the other palookas sitting with their dates at the next table. You were, yes, I admit it—a stepping stone. Maybe I was one for you, too. You were a great dallying point, and I was your cute little thing, envy of many other girls who wanted to go out with the tall, dark, slim, slightly mysterious teaching assistant, who took the dull out of "Art Appreciation 101" once a week, turned topics inside out, stretched artist profiles into elongated sagas of hard work, pain, suffering, and beggary, took them on a fifty-minute bungee jump up and down the stack of desires, dreams, fantasies that lure the artist into hunger, disease, separation, loss, torture, addiction, disintegration, ridicule, abandonment, and sometimes— just sometimes—kudos and conquests, wild hedonic fulfillment, adulation and awe, ecstatic public triumph.

After replacing Nick's phone in his jacket pocket on that Monday just a couple weeks ago, Zoe knew that his travels, the occasional mysterious phone call, always sufficient "discretionary funds" as Nick called them for dinners out of scallops or rockfish or salmon at Jury's, for reservations in Cape Cod for Memorial Day weekend made months in advance, for dinners of pasta with fresh mushrooms almost all year round at $11.00 a pound from a grower whose basement was a supermarket of shitakes, portabellas, oysters, lion's mains, for the not-every-day costumes, came from his "seeing-a-man-about-a-horse" trips. It all added up to what Zoe had discovered on Nick's phone: a budding career that was a *cas typique* that she might in future use for her dissertation! How ironic!! Could she use it? Well, yes, as a general "for example," but no, not as a real case. She could quietly disdain Nick, neatly part from him, appreciate their time and adventures together, even credit his contribution to her understanding of art, without confronting him, exposing him, challenging him. That was not her mandate. She was a scholar and because of her interests, something of a lie detector.

She heard a noise; a kind of grunting. It repeated itself two more times before she realized it was her phone grunting in vibrate mode. Nick? But where was it? Ah, yes—still in the pocket of her jeans, draped over the desk chair. She dropped to the floor, bounded over, extracted the phone, bounded back to the bed. "Hi, Cait… Good… What?! No…! You're not. Well, that's good… Nothing stolen? Weird… Hey … why don't I come over Wednesday afternoon…? No trouble… Yeah, yeah, I'll be there by two. Sounds like a good story, at least… See you then." She pressed *End*, put the phone on the counter. *What a development! Hungry. Time for pasta. Won't wait up for Nick.*

6

SOMEONE WAS KNOCKING ON THE DOOR. "I'll get it," said Cait. It was Zoe.

Zoe came through. "Hey—Happy Earth Day! I came right after my second class was over—you're okay? No—you got hurt, Robb."

Zoe was trying for the no-longer-student look: eye liner, well-fitting Hudsons, a huge floppy man's shirt over an Eddy Bauer top, anticipating her soon-to-be-granted dual degree, a BA and MA in art history with a minor in anthropology. When Zoe had jumped at the chance to work part-time, following her internship that had been arranged by Dr. Sloan—who had been charmed with the eclectic, quaint comeliness of Cannings' when she had encountered it on a day trip along the Hudson River—Cait and Robb could not have been more pleased. Zoe had proved interested, quick, engaged, trustworthy, flexible, enthusiastic, and a workaholic, often staying after hours. "I love inventorying," she had told Cait. She had emphasized that her art-and-museum training had taught her not just how to set traps for dermestids, but also how to critically evaluate stuff; and that her anthropology had taught her how to evaluate sellers and buyers. She liked putting in full nine-to-five days when Cait and Robb were out of town, managing the store entirely with Ellie supposedly helping out but mainly providing company and chatter.

Now she and Cait sat in the Louis XVI chairs. Robb once again sat behind the desk. For the third time, Robb and Cait had gone through the whole scenario, embellishing here and there in their recounting of the events of Sunday night and the wee hours of Monday morning.

"Okay," said Zoe, placing her hands carefully in her lap. "Let's think about this. If they didn't want *stuff*, what else would they have wanted?"

Robb and Cait gave massive, exaggerated shrugs. "Well," said Robb, "The insurance people sent an investigator. He thought it was suspicious."

Zoe squinted, concentrating. "So, then this was not your standard average run-of-the-mill, ho-hum holdup."

Caitlyn straightened in her chair. "God almighty, no! It was *not!* We were tied up, rolled around on the floor…"

"But that *is* standard for a holdup! What's not is that, number one, they didn't take anything and, number two, they put you into a semi-comfort zone."

"*What!?*" wailed Cait. "How can you say…"

"Yeah, gee, thanks…" mumbled Robb.

Zoe was shaking her head vigorously, her carefully coiffed, long brown ringlets rotating and bouncing around her head. "They tie you up. They bring rope." Zoe plowed on. "They came *intending* to tie you up. But they give you two bottles of water! They go into your fridge, give you food—nice sliced smelly cheese! They put it on a plate! They give you a potty! And they even undo your pants so you can get your asses onto the potty pot if you need to…" Zoe leaned way over, clasped her hands together, and continued. "I mean, the way you explained it, they secured your ankles by taking down your pants and undoing your belt, in your case, Robb. But why strip down your undies?"

"Well, to expose us, humiliate us, intimidate us. How do you think we felt when we'd finally inched our way to that big plate glass window and gotten up underneath the shade, with our butts hanging out?"

"It wasn't your butt," said Cait, starting to giggle uncontrollably. "It was your … it was your…" Cait was now laughing uncontrollably, almost hysterically, gasping and gulping for air. "…*Right up against the window*! And you banging your head and yelling like mad!"

"Damn it, Cait, I was trying to get somebody's attention! I had to attract attention, didn't I?"

"Well," gasped Cait, "God almighty! You certainly did that, didn't you? You're lucky it was the baker from across the street who saw you and busted in the door and pulled your pants up—it could have been that cute little girl he has who comes in and sells the bread for him … or maybe…? "

Robb banged his fist on the desk. "Now stop it! It's not funny!"

Trying to recover, but also wallowing in the release, Cait gasped between guffaws, "Well, well! You certainly did that, attract attention!" She turned to Zoe. "You should have seen it! It was really…"

"Now stop!" shouted Robb.

Amidst mutual mirth-fulfilling giggles, Zoe leaned back in her chair and closed her eyes. All of them were silent for a moment. Then Zoe opened her eyes, blinked several times, and took several deep breaths. "Okay, let's see. Let's figure this out. Concentrate on that day, Sunday—and everything leading up to your—uh—encounter with the merry pranksters."

"Oh, oh, oh…" Caitlyn put a hand to her chest. "Okay. I'm concentrating," she sighed, then burst into giggles again.

Zoe tried to assume the persona of one of her professors: Professor George, who had taught her historiographical methods. "So, here's the point," said Zoe, straightening up in her chair. "So, so—like—they were being kind to you. They wanted you to be sort of comfy. You could maybe eat and pee."

"Well, come on—who cares about snacking on gourmet cheese when you're all trussed up? How do you think we felt when we'd finally inched our way to that big plate glass window and gotten up underneath the shade, with our butts hanging out?"

"They make it easy for you to scoot around. They make it so you could maybe get somebody's attention. They didn't want to hurt you. They didn't even want to rob you. They were as nice as could be to you."

"Oh, yeah, yeah, sure!" Robb's voice oozed sarcasm. Robb suddenly bloomed red and started rising from his seat.

"No, no, no, no, no. *Listen to me!*" said Zoe, waving and shaking both her hands in front of her. "They were not your normal robbers or muggers. They didn't want anything in the shop. They didn't want to put you out of commission for a long time. I'll bet you're wrong about their not taking anything. Did you check your records, your papers, your laptop? I'll be they were after information. And to do something with that information they had to immobilize you, for a time, but not forever. Just long enough for them to act on the information."

"Laptop. It would have still been on…" mused Cait. "Oh, but did we tell you? They took the shop's mobile phone—my phone."

"Okay. So, they knew there was something, some information that was on that phone that they wanted. So, it was somebody that knew you, or knew something about you that they wanted. So, who's come into the shop lately who might be a scammer like that?"

"Nobody," said Cait. "I mean, we had little old dears, moms and dads with kids and babies, looky-loos who'd just stuffed their faces at Ellie's, a couple doing redecorating… Who would guess? You mean one of those? None of them looked like your typical scammer."

"There's no such thing as the typical scammer," said Zoe. "It could have been anybody. But in class we did learn about some of the folks who have been caught. In your case, they could well be fellow antiquers. People who knew *about* you from the antiques dealers network that you wouldn't have recognized. When did that phone call come in? The one that made the appointment with you for the museum on Monday?"

"Oh … uh … let's see … Golly. I think it was Friday," said Robb.

"But *I* was here on Friday," objected Zoe. "I don't remember any phone calls…"

"That's because you *weren't* here," responded Cait. "It was really slow, remember?"

"Slower than slow," interjected Robb. "Golly, we were just sitting around."

"That's right!" Zoe nodded. "You sent me over to Gary, to the Cat and Custard, because there was nothing for me to do here. It was really slow over there too—I filled salt and pepper shakers."

"But then suddenly we were swamped," said Cait. "About four thirty people started coming in—maybe a tour bus heading for the Catskills making a rest stop…"

"So, who all was in here?" Zoe seemed intent on accounting for all the visitors that were in the shop when the phone call came in.

"There was the lady with the little boy and probably the boy's grandmother; the Park Slope couple—they swished and sashayed through here as if they were making notes for a catalogue," said Cait. "Never let up talking. They must have been in here 45 minutes. Then they went to Ellie's for chocolate and came back and were here another 45 minutes."

"Yeah. All they left with was a ceramic goose." Robb shook his head.

"Then there was that bore who was chatting you up," she nodded at Robb, "about the Van Briggle pottery works in Colorado Springs, a young couple wandering slowly through the shop but probably not going to buy anything, two loud ladies fingering the tea towels over there on the bookcase, the lady at the counter that I was helping…"

"Cait was at the counter while I was heading for the sweeties," said Robb.

"Don't call them 'sweeties'!" said Cait. "That's really rude. It's insulting."

"All right, all right. The … the … Park Slope couple."

Then, as if a light bulb had gone off, Cait stuck her finger in the air. "Wait a minute! Wait. A. Minute! Yes! Yes! *The phone!* Not my mobile—the landline! I didn't pay much attention. But that's when the phone call came in, the one that we were going to respond to yesterday morning —the guy who wanted to show us something African and we had to go to the American Museum of Natural History and sit in a certain place in the Africa room and then they would show us … something."

"Okay, all right, continue," urged Zoe.

"Well, like I said, I was wrapping and taping… No, no—they had already come in, *just* come in. I was wrapping up the Grueby vase. I heard the door jangle and this couple walked in. I looked up and registered they were there but then went back to my wrapping. The lady I was wrapping for kind of blocked my view."

"What did they look like?"

"One of them was tall. They were both slim. Our bicycle thugs were slim. The taller of them wasn't quite six feet, I'd say, and the other was more like five-five."

Zoe leaned over, put her elbow on her knee, and put her chin on her fist. "And this couple came in while you were on the phone, on *speaker* phone, blasting the whole conversation all over the shop, rendezvous details and all? And what else do you remember about them?"

"They left almost as soon as they got here," said Robb. "Looky-loos. But yes. They were here long enough to hear the details of that phone call—blasting through the shop on speaker phone."

"Aha! There you have it!" stated Zoe, in her best-in-class-smug-answer-to-the-professor's-question-affirming voice. Zoe raised her hands, palms out. "So, we're re-creating the scene here. These two people come in and you're distracted and don't pay much attention. But they were here long enough to hear the details of that phone call—blasting through the shop on speaker phone. Where to meet the contact. When. That they had something for sale, probably, and also probably something illicit," said Zoe.

"God almighty!" Cait literally slapped her head. "Somebody heard that whole conversation. That couple—those people who'd just come in …that must have been them—the impersonators in the museum! We had decided to plan a day in the city. Mondays are slow. We asked Ellie to mind the store for us; we didn't tell *you* we were going to do that because, for one thing, we weren't sure yet and, for another, we didn't want to make you feel bad about not taking over for us—we know your classes are important. And then we get this call from this kook who wants to show us some … some African beads, or something—we were to meet them in the American Museum of Natural History, in the Africa room. And so, we made the appointment. And afterwards we were going to make a day of it."

"And you made the appointment on speaker phone," continued Zoe, "And this anonymous couple were close enough to hear when the call came in."

"And apparently somebody did turn up for that appointment, impersonating *us*," interjected Robb.

"Yup. So, this couple comes back on Sunday evening just as you're closing, to immobilize you for Monday morning. Bingo. They're the ones. They're the imposters. Do you remember anything else about what they looked like?"

"Uhhh … Average height, slim, maybe forties. She had shortish hair…"

"Well, they're your imposters. Obviously, they took your phone and immobilized you because they wanted to be you! The caller on the other end would know you wouldn't be at the shop so if they were going to call, they were going to call Cannings' alternate number—the mobile. The imposters wanted to end-run you and get their hands on whatever it was they thought whoever had to peddle. That's why they tied you up but didn't take anything. That's why they didn't want to hurt you. They wanted to trump you and disable you for a while, but not for good. They knew what they were doing. They didn't break in. They didn't assault you. All they did was 'detain' you. The only way to end-run you was to put you temporarily out of commission, which they could do because you'd never met—the caller arranged everything by phone!"

"Oh, oh, oh!" said Cait emphatically but softly, "God almighty!"

"This fellow Ferguson—the fellah the insurance people sent over," interjected Robb "thought the big, big question was who we were going to meet, and whatever they had to sell, what scheme or scam they were going to propose, and also what connection there might be to some insurance scam he investigated a few years ago."

"Oh?" Zoe's curiosity was piqued. "He thinks this is an insurance scam?"

"No, not, not exactly," said Robb.

"But that's what he does," interjected Cait. "He investigates insurance stuff. And he brought us a check because we had some sort of 'bodily harm' clause in our policy for the shop."

"Yeah—he's some kind of big deal. Golly, he showed us all kinds of ID— New York state PI permit, Europol PI license…"

"And he's from England! He showed us a driver's license from some city there."

Zoe nodded. "Hmmm." *Seems like overkill for an incident that the local police are not even interested in!* she thought. "I'd like to meet this Ferguson." *Like sending in James Bond to track down mislaid cutlery!* "But right now, like, I have to get back. I've got class tomorrow morning." She rose and strode toward the door, where she turned around and announced, "But I'll be back tomorrow evening, so I can work Friday morning." She leaned over and blew a kiss onto Cait's cheek, then went over to Robb and gave the same to him. "We can talk about this some more."

"Yeah—let's do talk more about this whole thing on Friday morning," said Robb. "This Ferguson fellah might be here too. If you're up by, say, eight or eight thirty, knock on our door. We'll fix ham and eggs on the hob in the back."

"Sure!" Zoe shouted a "'bye!" as she darted out the door.

7

WEDNESDAY, 2:30 PM
OSWEGO, NEW YORK

IT WAS ONE OF THOSE MADDENINGLY open-and-shut days when the sky spits showers of fine, blowy snow, then clears, then spits again. In a large, no-longer magnificent mansion in upstate New York, on the south shore of Lake Ontario, Jen—in her latest incarnation as would-be co-proprietor of Cannings' Antiques, as well as a retailer-wholesaler in upstate New York—checked the full-length mirror. *Pretty good* she thought. She had chosen a light lemon-yellow Ann Taylor top with a quilted vest that was not meant to button and an oat-colored Eileen Fisher scarf she'd found online that matched the vest, a burgundy skirt, and her silver pumps from FootSmart. Nice. It showed off her slimness. Pretty good because she had not really been able to rightly renew her wardrobe recently. She would not think about that. She dipped her body one last time to check her subtle gray-green eye shadow, plucked and styled (but not overly so) eyebrows, the green contacts, lip color but not so you'd notice. *No, I do not look pushing-forty-years-old*, she thought. *And I'm doing this for one dowdy little old lady with a "companion"—probably an old duffer with a flat ass and paunch, chewing a cigar and scouting whiskey sours?—for a pig-in-a-poke? The old dear kept saying "we" so it can be assumed she'd turn up with a partner. Or a younger version of herself maybe? Or perhaps the "we" was the "royal we" of ancientness and hubris.*

Now, with a magnum more of pressure to keep up the ruse, Jen heard gravel crunch; she looked out the window. It was not only spitting snow now; there were little bits of accumulation around the shrubbery. A dark silver stretch limousine had drawn up. *So now here they are,* reflected Jen, *with Dahlia's announced "companion."* A man—quite a young man, at least thirty (forty?) years younger than Dahlia, anything but a dowdy, dumpy duffer—exited from the driver's seat, then opened the two back doors. *So, is this the partner?* wondered Jen, *or merely the chauffeur?* But he was not wearing a uniform. *A nephew, perhaps? General dogs-body? Maybe an apprentice—a young man learning the business and all that. Would Dahlia make it easily up the stairs? Well,* thought Jen, *I'll know that and also who this young man is soon enough.*

She stepped back from the window, clipped the netsuke-replica case and strap with her mobile inside and strapped it to her waist. *A nice touch,* she thought, *professional.* She then took out the phone and punched in the caterers' number. Thad was already downstairs. "Java Julia" and her crew were waiting around the corner in their catering truck with the food prepared, kept hot over warmers: spreads and salads, slices of corn-quinoa bread (gluten-free), Israeli couscous pasta, various little filled and wrapped thises and thats. "Surprise us," Dahlia had said. "And don't stint." Dahlia had said "tea," and Jen was savvy enough to know that meant basically lunch or supper, depending on the hour. It was going on three o'clock; this would be a substitute lunch, pre-supper. Jen was starved, but she knew chit-chat and appetizers would have to precede the main spread. She told the caterers to immediately serve chilled wine and nibblies.

Here, in frosty nowhere, there were not a lot of caterers, most of them shutting down or barely eking out a living outside of the resort-and-wedding season. They had lucked out with Java Julia. And, reflected Jen, we've lucked out with this drafty old mansion! Just the ambience for hosting the authors of what would hopefully be a profitable little adventure. *After all, "Louie-the-Landlord-Loan Shark" Delassandro does pick up the astronomical heating costs because he's afraid we'll scrimp and the pipes'll freeze (doesn't it occur to him that we would freeze too?) and burst and ruin the stuff he stored in their basement.* His *stuff in the basement.* ("I take it off my taxes," he said. "It's a business expense.") Good. Now, if need be, they could give Dahlia a tour and show off the stuff to bolster their claim of squatting in an antique hub.

Louie had been the most recent occupier of the house just before Jen and Thad had moved in. Following a messy divorce, Louie had moved into the house and decided to go into the antiques business full time; thereby the sign outside: "Suwannee Antiques." But when Jen and Thad had answered his ad ("Looking for a house? Lease from Louie!"), and Louie had learned they were in the antiques business too, he had said, "Hey! I've got just the place for you! I'm livin' in it now but hey! I rattle around in it like a fart in a lantern! It's too big for me! But it's perfect for you two—store your inventory there, use it, sell it right out of your living room!" With two fireplaces, and sitting on three lots—full of snow until just a couple of weeks ago—this and other drafty gilded-age piles rented for next to nothing; zoning restrictions prevented tearing them down and putting up condos because, as the city insisted, the old mansions were a large part of its appeal to nostalgia and thus its attraction as a resort destination.

Good old Louie; he really was a friend. Well, if Dahlia insisted on a tour, they would indeed point out the "stored inventory" that they could show off as demonstrating how potential buyers might arrange it in their own homes. Just in case she did, they made the place look as much like an upscale by-appointment-only *entrepôt* as possible. They had moved the junk out of the piano room and off the queen-sized bed in the guest room, just in case they did insist on a guided tour, assuming, quite rightly, that items for sale were also items in use. *Why would anybody want condos on the city's outskirts,* mused Jen; *well, obviously: no yard, pay a fee, everything's taken care of. But surely*, she thought, *she won't want a grand tour on those wobbly legs.*

As she descended the stairs, the doorbell rang. It was not so much a ring as a ratchet-clang: one of those old dial-your-arrival mechanisms you had to mechanically operate. Jen and Thad had had it installed—actually the whole door—to replace the plastic-laminate mid-century Home Depot bulwark that had probably replaced something like the old, solid chestnut *porte-d'entrée* that could still be seen on some house fronts. Louie had found it for them … at a stiff price. He had added the cost to their rent that month.

Dahlia stood in the doorway flanked on her right by, indeed, a late twenty-ish-early-thirty-ish man with thick blond hair, dressed in tan chinos, dress shirt, no tie, dark blue gabardine sport coat. *He looks and probably is very Ralph Lauren, and in looks, a cross between the Christopher Plumber and Omar Sharif of her childhood. Gigolo?* wondered Jen. He was balancing a portmanteau at one side. And Dahlia herself—whoa! Gone were the canes. They had been a ruse. Gone were the outsized, arthritically swaying hips. Thad invited them in. Dahlia shrugged out of a London Fog hooded trench coat, snagged by the dogs-body, who draped it over his arm. Jen saw that she was dressed in what might be a silk Nicole Farhi ecru sweater draped with a black-and-white square scarf and flared black pants that, she thought, were probably the lower half of a suit. Dahlia had shed twenty pounds. She was agile and not grandmotherly. Her hair was a multi-dimensioned black and brown and platinum, curled and styled, held in place with two silver barrettes inlaid with turquoise and coral. Dyed, undoubtedly. She carried a Hartmann overnight valise, which she handed to her companion. The whole image took fifteen years off her. But the face was the same.

"Sorry we're late," she said, "but we're here."

Jen wagged her head back and forth.

Thad shook his head up and down and declaimed fiercely with gobble-nods. "Welcome, welcome. You didn't get lost…?"

"Oh, no—your directions were just fine." But Dahlia was not happy with the Amtrak Empire State Express. "The damn train was late. Should have known. We'll just keep the limo and drive directly back. *Plus*," she emphasized, "we had to secure a separate fare for our friend here." She indicated the portmanteau with a wave of her right hand. "This is Adrian." She waved again as "Adrian" hefted the portmanteau into the entry hall. "Bring it all the way in," instructed Dahlia.

It had been arranged that Thad would greet and seat and he did so, arranging them at the oval table in the parlor, so the first round of food could be instantly brought in and served. No, Dahlia was neither fragile nor doddering.

One of the caterers brought in two standing ice buckets, one with two bottles of Clod du Bois chardonnay and the other with a magnum of Moet Brut. "Would you care for a class of chardonnay? And then, maybe when we've concluded, we could celebrate with the Champagne," offered Thad.

"Actually, I'd prefer a martini, olives, no onions, no ice," stated Dahlia firmly. She segued seamlessly: "So we're stuck with the American market." Her head sagged from Jen to Thad, her gaze resting just long enough on Jen to communicate: *get that martini, and not just one.*

Jen popped up and tried not to fairly stomp into the kitchen. *What nerve,* she thought. *What a perfect old biddy-bitch. Where does she get off ordering a martini? What does she think we are—Delmonico's?* "Anybody know how to make a martini?" she said, *sotto voce*, to the catering staff. The two caterers looked up, then around; one of them gestured and opened his mouth. Silver trays were loaded with bacon-wrapped shrimp, pigs-in-a-blanket, wontons, satay sauce, open-faced cracked crab and tapenade sandwiches. Two more bottles of chardonnay were on the sideboard. "All right—clearly you don't do martinis," said Jen emphatically. She stood on her tiptoes and reached for the Doubleday cookbook, which lived on a shelf just above the everyday-use, nobody-cares-if-what's-in-it-gets-stolen wooden file cabinet. She opened it to the index and found "Drinks, mixed." Armed with the Doubleday, Jen trotted over to rear door through which the caterers had entered. A long addition that, curiously seemed to date from the same period as the rest of the house but did not support the second story, had a door to either side. One door led to the miniscule bathroom that, she had decided, probably was meant to serve for the daily help who had come in through the back door. The other led to the pantry, an original feature, but which had been mostly converted to an office with a desk littered with old editions of *Kovel's Antiques & Collectibles* and a vintage computer that still took floppy disks, where if there were thieves—or snoopy spies or auditors—they would find a few dollars and some costume jewelry in the desk and floppies that had a wealth of very misleading information: addresses, inventories, references to events and transactions that were completely spurious and bogus.

But the pantry was, in fact, still to some extent a pantry, and retreating into it, behind cans of Goya black beans and bottles of Spanish olives, she found vermouth and gin and a beaker. She cleared a space on the desk, set everything on it, opened the Doubleday to "Drinks, mixed," poured, and mixed. Now what to use for glasses. Aha! Hand-blown, knobby blue glasses exuding "handcrafted" also sitting on a shelf. *All of this must have been sitting here,* she thought, *when we took over the house.* She and Thad did not do mixed drinks; Thad had his Glenlivet, but they were pleased with how they had cultivated their connoisseurship of wines. She re-entered the kitchen, borrowed a tray from the caterers, quickly rinsed and dried the glasses, added ice to the mixture, and put glasses and the martini-brimming beaker on the tray. After counting a minute in the interest of self-composure, she walked carefully back toward the parlor, carrying the tray. One of the caterers held the door for her.

Dahlia was sitting on the Astoria Grand Belmond sofa; Adrian had leaned the portmanteau against the sofa's arm, set down Dahlia's valise purse beside it, and taken his seat next to Dahlia. Thad had taken one of the two Bugatti wingbacks. Jen returned and sat in the other one. A Turnham coffee table separated them; Jen and Thad had hefted twin Magnussen Galloway tables up from the cellar and placed them either side of the sofa. Plenty of room for the yummies the caterers would bring in momentarily. Dahlia took her martini; Adrian did not do so. He had accepted a glass of char from Thad. Dahlia sipped without comment. Dahlia was holding forth, like a very confident Helen Mirren: trains in Europe versus trains in America; mansions over condos; the valuing of old things.

"Now, just to let you know," she said without segue, "as I told you in our very productive museum chat, our goods are perfectly legal. But! But we cannot, cannot put them ever again to auction or on the open market." She heaved a sigh, shook her head, and continued: "There is an officious, obnoxious, self-righteous little nincompoop man out in Arizona or Montana or one of those places, calling himself an anthropologist—teaches at some university or other—who has accused the pieces of being stolen." Jen thought this new persona, replacing Grandma-with-the-canes was equally well done. What an actress! Jen thought her current persona was alternating between Helen Mirren, emanating strong character and determination, and Vivian Leigh: troubled, hesitant, reluctant.

"Are they?" asked Thad, adding self-righteously, "Stolen, I mean. If so, then..."

"No, no, no. As I said, the items are perfectly legal. But the problem is that he said this on the BBC."

"Wha ... wha ... the..." Jen thought she and Thad were beginning to sound like Jimmy Stewart imitators.

"Yes. The British Broadcasting Corporation's World Service Newshour! Heard by hundreds of thousands of people around the world. So, even though there's no substantiation for the accusation, the damage has been done. We have no idea how many self-important bloggers, twits, self-styled journalists, even well-meaning collectors and antiquarians may carry on in that vein about these marvelous pieces."

"So, you have to go underground." Thad swiveled in his chair and crossed his legs. Jen could see that there was just the slightest smugness to his body language, and that he had shaken his cowlick loose.

"No. Not underground. But we have to be purposeful. We have to target truly interested people. That's where you come in."

Shit! Jen thought. *Does she know who we really are?* She was mentally shaking her head but made sure her face was a mask. *Why us? Or why the Murrays? Of all people? How did she—they—whoever they are find them—us?*

Then she realized Thad was actually saying it: "Why us?"

She's holding forth like she's used to having the upper hand, thought Jen.

"You obviously know the field. You have the contacts. Or even if you don't, your making the contacts will not raise any eyebrows. You specialize in this sort of thing and you're, well, you're nearby. And we have to do this quickly. Very quickly."

God! thought Jen. *We must seem tiny fools. Specialize in what? Oh, of course—illegal goods. Just our specialty. Is she FBI? Is this going to be entrapment?* But she kept her cool, hoping her stomach wasn't gurgling. "And *your* doing so would? I mean, making the contacts would raise eyebrows?" Jen chimed in, cocking her head.

Vivian Leigh was back. "We scouted around. Oh, yes, there are those high-end antiques places in the city. But we chose your outfit because you seem to have a certain subtlety. When we were in your shop, we noted your several cases of Indian goods—the full regalia on the manikin with the exquisite beaded choker."

"So ... so..." Thad stammered. This topic was clearly outside of their expertise. "So, this is Plains material you...?"

Dahlia topped him. "No. This is Puebloan material. We also noted your highly unusual display of Puebloan pottery—rather tucked away, I must say—but several nice Nampeyos and I think some Rose Gonzalezes along with the obligatory Maria. Or maybe it's an Adam and Santana but fine at any rate."

Now Jen decided to express her genuine puzzlement. "Yes, of course—but when were you in the shop? We didn't notice..." They were clearly out of their element here. Perhaps there was a gracious way to exit.

Dahlia topped her. Helen Mirren reappeared. "You didn't see us because you weren't there. A very nice young lady was holding forth, she said—or I guess it was that odd American expression 'holding down the fort'—while you were away, in Pennsylvania, I think. There was also a quite elderly lady who roamed around, came in and out, seemed to have some proprietary role."

"Oh, yes, of course…" *Quick save from Thad*, thought Jen and smiled just a little. "But why not just bring the items directly to the shop?" Now it was Thad who was being bold.

Dahlia seemed to ignore him. "You know about the auction, of course."

Thad opened his mouth wide and Jen pursed a silent "oh."

Dahlia continued: "In Paris. Big to-do. All sorts of interferers, interlopers, busy-bodies, do-gooders…"

"Not the…" ventured Thad.

"Yes, *that* auction. The most unique and rare, possibly the potentially most valuable, collection of Native American material culture to ever go on the block." Dahlia started shaking her head. "Not your Navajo weavings, not your silver baubles, not your Plains war bonnets…"

"Oh, *that* auction…" Jen bobbed her head and closed her eyes, hoping to look wise and knowledgeable.

"Seventy-one truly authentic, unique ceremonial masks out of several of the most reclusive and mysterious civilizations in North America: Puebloan: one-of-a-kind and actually used in rituals—some of them old and all of them, considering they have genuinely seen action—in condition ranging from acceptable to very fine." She paused.

"Ah," said Jen, then mentally kicked herself. *Cool it*, she said to herself. *Don't imply you know more than you're meant to know.*

Adrian had accepted a second glass of char from Thad. Dahlia was on her second martini. She sipped without comment. "Well, at any rate, just to be on *en garde*, I had adopted a previous persona, one from my down-in-the-dumps period—I hope you appreciate how forthright I'm being with you, and that

that means something—and Adrian was nearby bidding by telephone, but no cigar for him. So, I was glad I was there in person. We got lucky."

"We found some interested parties almost immediately—sold six of the items to Bulgarians. We did indeed make a quick trip to Prague. You can buy and sell anything in Prague," she added dismissively. "We had good success with Bulgarians there, who were intending to re-sell to Russians."

"To, to ... Bulgarians?" stammered Thad. *God! He sounds dumb,* thought Jen. *But that's good.*

Dahlia waved her hand in the air in dismissal. "Oh, yes, of course. But that market is depressed, let alone being tricky, and we were lucky to get them into the hands of collectors—and yes, they were Bulgarians and Russians; we did the negotiations in Prague, within days of the sale, because the Bulgarians and Russians were waiting for them. And we got there first."

"Well, obviously you have a market, so why not..."

Dahlia topped him. "Because." She leaned her well-manicured head toward the table and nailed Thad with her eyes. "We've exhausted that market. They would only take so many now, and we really cannot hang onto them. So, we got them here, at great cost—several small planes, landings in the Canaries, the Azores, and the Caymans, smelly little ships and more small planes to tiny islands off the Carolinas. At great expense and too much time. We've spent nearly a year getting the goods safely here."

Jen decided to finally say something that would establish her as something more than a mere consumer of spectator sport. "Here? Why here? Why not just wait it out in Europe? Surely if you brought the rest back to Prague now, the Bulgarians or the Russians ... and why couldn't you just bring them in as legitimate good for resale? Or as a personal collection?"

Dahlia and Adrian shared a look. They held each other's gaze for a couple seconds, then Adrian smiled faintly. Dahlia returned her attention to Jen and Thad and shook her head. "It's just ... it's complicated. It's just too risky. I told you. Persons in the European Parliament sniffing around. Meddling. Several years ago," continued Dahlia, "some no-account hot-shot lawyers with time on their hands brought a land claim case from some Native American tribe to the attention of the European Parliament. With the help of some self-righteous UNO nobody—she's from Greece and we all now know what those dead-beats are all about—those lawyers actually got the European Parliament to pass a resolution in support! Imagine! What business on earth does Strasbourg have mucking about in Native American land claims? At any rate, with all those aficionados in Denmark and Germany and Hungary and wherever always running off into the woods playing Indian, it put things Indian onto the Euro radar and here we are: some of those do-gooder know-nothings in Strasbourg have gotten wind of this. They're all a-twitter—literally—and it was one of their lawyers that actually tried to stop the auction." Dahlia sighed.

"And here the Geronimos and their minions would have been waiting. All the items have well-authenticated provenances, but you see there is this law—you probably know about it—that allows the Natives to make claims against pieces of art that they can argue, prima facie, might have once been housed in an American museum and made out to be"—she made quotation marks in the air—"'sacred.' We got wind of the probability that the New York attorney general notified customs to be on the lookout and that they would sequester the art while the would-be claimants and their lawyers tangled the goods up in legal mumbo-jumbo that would take years to untangle. And besides, we did not need the public spotlight that that would bring along. And you must have noted my—uh—somewhat altered appearance from our encounter in the museum."

"Well … yes…" Stammered Jen. "A … a disguise…"

"We were under surveillance there. I've narrowed our spy down to one of two characters that sauntered through; Adrian was roaming around, keeping me apprised by mobile. And I must inform you that I am sure we are under surveillance as we speak. So, you see what we're up against! That's why it's so imperative that you represent us to our potential interested parties in the Southwest."

The caterers came out with round one: caponata bruschettas, hot small portabella mushrooms stuffed (Jen knew) with Campbell's condensed mushroom soup laced with grated asiago; crusty, baked mini-weenies, shrimp-stuffed bacon rounds, veggie- and beef-filled wantons. Dahlia let the caterer fill her plate before saying, "Thank you dear." The rest of them also let the caterers fill their plates; Jen reached for the chardonnay bottle.

Dahlia helped herself again to the martini beaker and sipped without comment. They gave themselves over to serious eating. Jen and Thad were starved; this "tea" was lunch and dinner. The caterers brought in round two. A server scooped tabouli heavy with parsley from one bowl while the other offered what he announced as pea-and-caper humus. A plate of white goat cheese hunks appeared from the kitchen, along with a bowl of sizzling hot strips of what the caterer offered as pressed duck. Dahlia took heaps of both, as did Jen and Thad. Adrian still munched bruschettas but took some goat cheese. They frittered away a good forty minutes chit-chatting about everything from the ban on bigger-than-sixteen-ounce sodas to the growing market for antique barrel organs to the dearth of "those wonderful freighters from the Orient" that no longer puffed and tooted their way to the west side docks and to Wolfgang Beltracchi's highly successful art forgeries. This last topic clearly made Thad uncomfortable but Jen covered by continuing to engage Dahlia in chatting amiably about nothing in particular: the house, a retread of the Amtrak versus Deutsche Bahn and French TGV discussion, Paris cafés ("You can hardly find those down-the-stairs little bistros anymore, where they serve you just what they have but it's always superb, and you get carafe after carafe of hearty red wine," said Dahlia). Dahlia again refreshed her martini.

Finally, the caterers cleared all away, including the martini beaker, the chardonnay and the bubbly, and brought out two bottles of pinot noir and one of Muscadet as well as plates of chocolate truffles. Thad got to the point: "So, forgive me if we get to business, but—how many of these do you have and what exactly are they?"

"How many we have. We'll get to that. We are looking to move them fairly quickly, as I said. You know all the publicity might have been something of a good thing in a way, up to a point. It has really established a market, I think, for goods that have been undervalued—or not valued at all, or outright neglected because of unsubstantiated temerity and an unwillingness to face the truth, ha-ha!—among those of us who are in the know and not about to suffer intimidation."

Dahlia was getting up steam again. "All this stuff about sacred this and cultural that,"—*Her voice is going a little harsh and flat now; she's losing that verbal panache, carefully constructed*, thought Jen, *from Helen Mirren*—"is just a lot of horse pucky."

Jen stifled a guffaw. A glance at Thad revealed him holding his breath.

Dahlia rapped out her rationale. "If they were so sacred, why were they sold in the first place?"

Thad had a big swallow of nothing, then ventured, "So, so, you have provenance? Bills of sale? Authentications?"

Dahlia scoffed. "Provenience we have. Immediate provenance, certainly. Auction sale records, of course, from a venerable auction house with an impeccable address—you don't get an address like that without considerable respectability; a beautifully illustrated catalogue, with verifications from a publication of no less than the Smithsonian Institution, and references to any number of other scholarly documentary sources. If these aren't authentications, I don't know what would be."

She continued, "But, even though the items were perfectly legally acquired, we can't risk trundling them about and trying to peddle them, even semi-openly. And we can't waste time and allow our surveilers to get the jump on us while we go through contacting a baker's dozen of dealers who *might* or *might not* be interested. We know there are collectors and dealers here who will either pay what they are really worth or broker them for that. But with ARPA and NAGPRA and all of that, if they are seen here on this continent their sale could be enjoined or the items even confiscated while the tribes in question turn themselves inside out, tying themselves in knots to argue that these things that have been disused, abandoned for generations, relics of archaic rituals that no one ever does anymore, let alone even understands, still have some sort of religious significance! Masks are sacred only when used in the dance. They are not sacred afterward because the religious context is gone. If they were to be returned to the tribes, who knows where they would go? They would just get resold again. That's where many of the more recently made ones came from in the first place! From the tribes themselves! From people who could see they no longer had relevance except as *objets d'art*! And if we are to say 'hands off religious art,' well, we question the entire notion of art. Give all those paintings and statuary back to the Vatican? It's absurd!" Dahlia sat back in her chair.

Thad and Jen must have sported the epitome of blank looks, encouraging Dahlia to punt with more verbal unpacking, wading into the breach with more word flow, roping Jen and Thad into the position of fellow travelers, certain now that in lieu of her first choice for that status, she could bend these two into co-conspirators. "And NAGPRA…"

"The Native American Graves Protection and Repatriation Act," announced Thad. "But that act applies also only to stuff dug up on public lands or to items in museums proved to be religious…"

He's done his homework, thought Jen. *He's been reading up.*

Dahlia wagged a finger. "*Prima facie* identifiable as such. Unfortunately, we think some of the goods—the older material—might well have come from one or two particular museums: sequestered away just after passage of NAGPRA, but before the museums had to, by law, publish inventories of their holdings that might possibly have to be returned to tribes because they were ceremonial or religious. At some point those sequestered items were sold, and therefore did not show up on the inventories. We have to be cognizant of the possibility that we may have some of those items. And who knows? Once they've surfaced in this country, a museum or two might even claim they were stolen from them. Then where would we be?"

Dahlia leaned forward and resumed preaching mode. Had she been a schoolmarm? Jen wondered. "Let me tell you!" Her head wagged from Jen to Thad and back. "Don't let it happen to you! In this business you can be high-rolling one day and one or two little bumps appear in the road and you're suddenly in the ditch. You roll along and suddenly your basketful is all over the road and your goodie bag has been absconded with. There you are knocked all widdershins, the lock-safe's been picked, and you've got so much negative cash flow and dirty laundry flying about you might as well declare yourself a third-world country."

Whew! Talk about mixing metaphors! But okay!, thought Jen, *we're okay. Dahlia doesn't know who we are. She really does think we're that doofus couple up in Croton Corners. And if not exactly the most above-board person, well, she's Mary Poppins compared to some of the insects that have creeped all over us.*

"That's the reason this is so important to me." Dahlia sat back; she seemed deflated. *Vivian Leigh is back.* "It's my last hurrah."

"I see, I see." Thad nodded sympathetically. "But ... our cash flow isn't exactly Morgan Stanley rated. I mean, we also operate within tiny margins… If you want us to buy something from you…"

"Of course not! I envision you as brokers, not buyers. Your shop is known. Cannings' Antiques—did you inherit it?—Oh, it doesn't matter. It's been around for nearly forty years. You have panache, reputation, credibility. You have youth and energy. You can travel; you have someone to mind the shop. You haven't made mistakes."

Hah! Thought Jen. *If she only knew!*

"Well, we need to know just what you have. I mean we can guess…" Thad threw a meaningful 'of-course-we-know' look at Jen, who nodded. "But we really need to see…"

"Of course." Dahlia was again the incarnation of reasonable rationality. "That's why we're bringing you a sample. That is, if you're interested. I have to have your solemn word that you are interested, and that you will accept our terms, which we will make clear."

"Well, yes, I think if you leave us your 'sample' we can take the weekend to mull it over and…"

Dahlia was frowning. But then Dahlia nodded. "Understood," she said. "But we can't wait for the weekend. We have to have your commitment now. And we have to get things in motion by—well, certainly *by* the weekend."

She wiped a smudge of truffle off her mouth with the mini-napkins supplied, swallowed, and said: "Alright. Let's show you the goods—our sample. Here is what we're proposing: You supply us with a bond, a bond-of-trust: say, $10,000. We leave you our friend here. Then you trundle it off—at your earliest convenience—and the earlier the better—to a certain person at a certain address in a certain place in the Southwest. Adrian, open it please."

Adrian arose. Taking a key chain out of his pocket, he opened two small locks at the top and bottom of the portmanteau, then undid three clasps, and swung it open.

Jen and Thad rose from their chairs, positioned themselves in front of the portmanteau, bent down, and peered inside it.

"And you take our friend here out west, to someone who must under no circumstances know who we are, but who must be led to believe that you, yourselves, possess not only this item, but another thirteen that are even more superb. You can show him the catalogue, if you want to do so." Dahlia reached down to the valise next to her chair, took out a multi-colored brochure, and handed it to Thad.

Thad continued to scrutinize the portmanteau's interior. He handed the brochure to Jen. It was a catalogue. She sat down again and leafed through it. Each item was pictured, with smaller pictures at the bottom of the pages, apparently provenience references. Thad continued to stare at the contents of the portmanteau. Inside was a face, but not a human face. Tri-colored, the bottom half was black; the upper half was evenly divided with a horizontal line, with its right side being turquoise colored and left side, white. The face was mounted on a tan-colored leather helmet. A long, tapered beak protruded from its mouth; a feather hung from the beak's tip. A headdress of about a dozen large feathers framed the face.

"It's a mask," said Dahlia, "a Kachina mask. Ones like it are used in dances. We're not saying this one necessarily was, or necessarily wasn't. But even if it has been used, once it's used, it's retired. There are Kachina ceremonies several times a year, but any particular mask is only used once. If a similar mask is needed some years later, a new one is made. The old ones are retired and usually destroyed. For some reason, this one and several dozen other ones escaped destruction, or maybe it was arranged that a discerning collector or museum would purchase it after the ceremony."

"So, you got this … in Paris?" exclaimed Thad incredulously.

"Yes," answered Dahlia impatiently.

"And, and—exactly what, what does this, this Katrina do?" asked Thad.

"Kachina," corrected Dahlia. "It's intended to bring rain. Men make the masks and don them in a sort of dance so that that the rains will come."

"So, they put on these masks and do a rain dance. And what tribe does this?" asked Jen.

"Puebloan. The proveniences are all there, in the catalogue." She gestured to the brochure in Jen's hands.

For some reason, Jen felt disconcerted. She turned to the large bay window. Suddenly there were white-out conditions outside. But she knew it wasn't a blizzard. Not in April. The flurries would leave a half-inch on the ground and the rest of the day would just gloom.

"And so," said Thad, turning away from the portmanteau, "You want us to take this … this 'sample' out…"

"To Woodard Glenn," said Dahlia, "in Santa Fe, New Mexico."

"And he's to either buy them all outright or commission them to his friends."

"That's the idea."

"And how much do you expect somebody would pay for one of these?" asked Thad.

"Well as you can see from the catalogue, these items have high value. I should think each one would fetch ate least $35,000 a piece, some more."

"And ... and what would be the arrangement for us?"

"Well, the usual broker's fee is 15 percent. So, I should think, divided three ways..."

"Five per cent for us, five for you, and five for this Glenn Wood?"

"Woodard Glenn. Yes."

"And you have altogether fourteen of them, including this one."

"Yes." Dahlia nodded.

"So, let's say, conservatively, $25,000 for each?" calculated Jen, off the top of her head. "That's more or less, at minimum, a total of ... more than $400,000..."

"At a minimum. Probably more. I expect that once their availability is known through Woodard Glenn, there will be another mini-auction, so to speak, with people more or less bidding against one another for the choicer items."

"And you're confident that..."

Dahlia leaned back in her chair, brought her arms up in a salute worthy of British soccer and fairly shouted, "Of course I'm confident! I'm sure he was one of the telephone bidders at that auction. Woodard Glenn will jump at the chance to broker these, and his clientele will be suitably impressed. It's just the kind of thing he couldn't pass up. I'll bet he was cursing like a Trojan when he didn't get any of them! But it cost us a bundle and now we've got to get it back."

"How do you know he didn't get any of them?" queried Jen. "And if he was so anxious for them, why wasn't he there in person?"

Dahlia turned and addressed her very specifically. "As I told you. None of the telephone bids was successful. And Glenn rarely travels. He was shot down in one of those Hueys during the Vietnam War and flying gives him the heebie-jeebies. He also has a lot of pins and braces on his limbs and that complicates traveling."

"You know him well."

"No. Not well. But I've encountered him. I wish I could just go barreling out there myself. But I'm a pariah. If I come anywhere near him, he's going to react very strangely, if not downright rudely. I've gone into enough detail on that. These are just the sorts of things that he cannot resist; he needs them. When I was in contact with him years ago, he was very busy ramping up 'service' as he called it for people who buy up land in the Southwest, at a premium, that is guaranteed to have a Pueblo ruin on it. Then you call in an archaeologist, excavate it in accordance with all the right rules and procedures, and voilà: you get to keep everything that's dug up. He did this on his own property years ago. Well—a nice Kachina mask is just what you need to go with your arrangement of pots and such from your excavation. Or better yet, your ruin is a kind of pied-à-terre for upscale parties or the honored guest, decorated appropriately. That's what he's got there in Waldo. But he and his friends have moved on to some properties down around Yellowjacket, in southern Colorado. Most of those impoverished bean farmers were glad to sell. So, now those properties are being developed and they'll sell even better if the prospective owner is promised the chance to obtain something that very few are privileged to have: not just a collection of pots, but a genuine ceremonial mask to mount on the wall."

"Okay," said Thad. "So where do we find this Woodford, in Yellowjacket or in Waldo?"

"Woodard. Woodard Glenn. And you find him in neither place, initially. Contact him at his gallery in Santa Fe. Even if he's not there, once he hears what you have, he'll turn up. But with luck, he'll invite you out to Waldo to experience his 'Indian pueblo.' It really is special. He has re-created, faithfully re-created, several rooms of what is a truly in situ, carefully excavated, accurately restored Indian pueblo dating from 1150. He's partially reburied it and it's in a sort of hollow anyway so it's like a folly—you don't know it's there even if you're wandering around on his property, and it's not visible at all from the road. It has a coal-fired fireplace-cooking hearth, mud floor, elk robes separating the four little rooms, genuine ceramic material throughout—Mesa Verde effigy jars, polychrome canteens, and of course," she chuckled as if at an insider joke, "the odd Mimbres bowl. He's got his own line of

Kokopelli-decorated martini glasses and brandy snifters, and if you really are treated as honored guests, you'll sleep in comfy beds made up on adobe sleeping platforms, piled with sheepskins and lovely blankets. Those are not quite period pieces; they're contemporary Navajo weavings, but even so. And again, if he takes a liking to you, he'll feed you mutton roasted in an outdoor oven and corn pudding baked overnight in coals buried underground."

"It sounds … exotic," said Jen, somewhat doubtfully.

"But when you see it, you'll know why his clients want to imitate him. They want all of that but most of them also want electrical outlets and base-board heating systems. So, the right décor—carvings, pots, blankets—is even more important for them, so you don't notice the anachronisms."

"So, you want us to pay you $10,000 to do your work for you?" said Thad.

"No, no! As soon as you negotiate some sort of agreement with Glenn and his cohorts to deliver a set number of these masks, at a certain amount per mask, you get your bond back, plus your commission. You have to understand: we don't want you just running off with this and disposing of it in some fashion, either to Glenn or to somebody else, all on your own. If Glenn bites, or finds somebody who does, you'll get more than twice the bond you put up. All for a little trip and a week or so as guests under very pleasant circumstances. We'll leave this catalogue with you. But you are under no circumstances to reveal where you got this, nor anything about me. I have shared more with you than I intended; but you must appreciate that the utmost discretion is called for. Once you have the contract, you contact us on this." She retrieved a flip phone from her valise purse as well as a checkbook. She tore out a deposit slip from the back. "Here's everything you need. Routing number, account number. Ten thousand dollars by wire transfer by, say, tomorrow, five p.m.?" She handed the phone to Robb. "Our number is programmed in. We'll take it from there. If you'll be so kind as to show us to the door."

A few minutes later, outside, in the limousine's driving seat, Adrian was fiddling with his phone. "Let's go!" urged Dahlia. "Let's get out of here!"

"You know something funny?" Adrian turned to Dahlia, in the passenger seat. "Those people aren't the Cannings. They're Robb and Cait Murray, proprietors of Cannings' Antiques."

"It doesn't matter. To us they're Mr. and Mrs. Canning."

"And you know something else funny? Suwannee Antiques doesn't have a website."

"What does it matter? Neither do I! Besides," added Dahlia, "Suwannee Antiques doesn't need one if Cannings' has one and a shop to boot. And we don't care who they really are—Cannings, Murrays, Mr. and Mrs. Crusader Rabbit! We've got them! They're hooked! They're going to do just what we need them to do."

.

8

WEDNESDAY, 9:16 PM

OSWEGO

JEN SNUGGLED DOWN INTO the oversized sleigh bed, engulfing herself in the down comforter. Thad plopped down beside her on "his side," but on top of the coverlet, leaning against the headboard. Now with her fourth (or was it fifth?) glass of chardonnay and Thad with his Glenlivet, they assessed the situation. He opened his iPad. The portmanteau leaned against the dresser on the other side of the room.

Dahlia and Adrian had departed just short of seven o'clock, Dahlia declaring their intention to keep the hired limousine until they reached Poughkeepsie, arranging by phone to turn in the limo there and take the Harlem and Hudson line back to Grand Central. "That Amtrak is for hokey-pokeys," declared Dahlia. "Nothing like the good old New York Central. I should have known."

Somewhat dazed by their new calling, not to mention the necessity of raising the bond and arranging a bank transfer—they had exactly sixty hours—Jen and Thad had poured more wine and nibbled at the last of the snacks, while discussing the pros and cons, mostly the cons. But the end result of the somewhat disjointed dialogue was that they were trapped in this new identity, with their destinies determined, not only as Robb and Cait Murray, but also as the "shadow" employers of an unknown young lady who, Dahlia had instructed them, was perfectly capable of running the shop in their absence, assisted by "that old busybody who brings hot chocolate to everybody." Thad had listened as Dahlia had given them a snapshot description of the inventory of the shop that she and Adrian had visited several weeks back, on a slow Monday morning, while a girl with frizzy dark hair fading to blond at the tips, in white ruffled blouse and black skirt cut on the bias, busied herself while an Edith Piaf CD played softly. They had been left on their own; the girl was more interested in a large illustrated book than she was in them. "Let me know if you need anything," she had called out, in the detached manner of the standard bored employee. So obviously, Dahlia had said, they could get the girl to earn her keep for a few weeks while they went on a "buying trip," which would really be a "selling trip," a "show-and-tell," a "dog-and-pony show" meant to convince this Woody Glenn person to line up clients who would pledge to purchase the dozen-plus ritual masks. Mystified, Jen and Thad nodded, they hoped knowingly. *Who was this young woman,* wondered Jen, *and did they have to account for her? And if so, how?*

Dahlia and Adrian would let their presence in the vicinity be known only long enough to verify the bank transfer, Dahlia had said; then they would be gone. But Dahlia would be keeping an eye on Jen and Thad—"from the shadows, if you will; you can bet on that"—once they arrived in Santa Fe. Just how, she would not say. Jen and Thad were meant to depart for Santa Fe on Saturday, or Sunday at the latest.

"So here we are suddenly unremittingly committed to a road trip in our good old oil-guzzling, over-mileaged chariot to persuade a high-rolling antiquities dealer to arrange under-the-table sales of dubiously provenanced sacred ceremonial goods to high-rolling jet-setting collectors? So, are we totally crazy? What do you want to bet that they didn't go back to the city at all; they're still right here," said Thad.

"You mean, to keep an eye on us."

"Well, yeah. If that 'friend' is worth as much as they say it is, they're not going to leave it and us unwatched; or at least, they're going to be close by so they can snag us if we try to trundle off with it before they get their bond."

"So, you think they're out there? Lurking in the hedgerow?"

"Nah—but I'll be they've got some two-bit thug or PI lurking in the hedgerow."

"So, then, where are we going to get this $10,000 from?" wailed Jen.

"We'll have to contact loan shark Louie."

"And tell him what? We've gotten roped into this crazy scheme and can you just hand over $10,000?"

"Yes, basically. It's just the kind of scheme he likes. We'll show him the catalogue. We'll put up $10,000 worth of our goods as collateral."

"Okay—then why don't you call Louie before he gets too blitzed or too cozy with whoever he's out with to answer his phone. Set up a brunch appointment with him tomorrow. Our treat."

Jen hauled her iPad up from the floor. In her haste and char-befuddle-ment, she googled "Woodford Glenn," but it worked. Thad punched his phone. "Louie? Yeah, yeah. Yeah, I hear. Having a good time. That's great! Something's come up—kind of an emergency but an opportunity... Eh? Yeah, for you. Well, for us, but for you too. Dollars... Hey—how 'bout brunch tomorrow. On us. The all-you-can-eat buffet at Sparky's. Yeah. Their new daily brunch. Beignets and oysters-on-the-half-shell; bottomless mimosas and bloody marys... Say, ten thirty? Okay... Good." Thad rang off. "He said 10:45 at Sparky's. He wasn't happy with the early hour."

"What if he balks?"

"Look—we'll offer him the contents of the whole house as collateral. He could unload the ground floor alone for more than ten thousand. Or I'll offer him that coin collection we picked up —quick liquidity if we default. There's a St. Gaudens double eagle and all those Revolutionary War pennies, that set of Civil War two-cent pieces."

"Okay—anyway I found Woodard Glenn. He's real. Gallery, Canyon Road, Santa Fe. Classic Western and Native American art. Frederick Remington, Charles Russell, Carl Bodmer, Howard Smith, Joe Bieler, Dan Namingha, Howard Gorman, RC Gorman. Native American weavings, sculpture, pottery. So, we're not *totally* crazy for doing this!"

~⌇

THURSDAY, 10:50 AM

Louie Delassandro was not really a loan shark; he was a real estate speculator who had bought up some of the sagging mansions whose owners' financial crises, following the Haymarket collapse in the 1890s, had resulted in their being divided into flats, two per floor, or in many cases, boarding houses for families of workers in the iron, lead, and gypsum mines to the southeast. In the 1970s, when the mines closed, one by one, many of the properties went on the auction block for back taxes and sewer assessments. The stock market crash of 1989 made that scenario even much more likely. Young Louie, with a talent for hand-crafting wood and a modest stake inherited from an auntie, started buying them up. Young and affable, he began by renovating them himself, occasionally trading decorative wainscoting or inglenook inserts, or heirloom furniture missing a nob, a handle, a leg, for plumbing and heating installations. As tourism slowly took hold, the first couple became bed-and-breakfasts; most he eventually sold. Twenty years later, Louie had his fingers in lots of pies, mostly the result of being able to underwrite loans as an under-the-table silent mortgage partner. Jen and Thad lucked into their cavernous mansion by persuading Louie that they would gradually fix it up, and by noting that the mortgage crisis of 2008-2009 made buyers unlikely. They negotiated a long-term lease.

Now, scruffy in a dark green hoodie and bagging allagash cargo pants bunched at his ankles, he slumped at one of the sturdy but well-used tables at Sparky's. A plate of six oysters with cocktail sauce, a plate piled with six beignets, and a cup and pot of coffee almost obscured his drooping face. Thad had no trouble spotting him.

"Thad! Hey, what's going on?" said Louie, the crack in his voice betraying a long and well spiced evening that had probably ended fewer than eight hours previously.

Thad outlined the general schema, leaving out the bizarre encounter in the museum, implying vaguely that the "opportunity" had been dumped into their laps as a result of their far-flung antiques and collectibles network. Louie slurped the last of the oysters and gestured to the beignets. "Have one."

"No, thanks," replied Thad.

"Well," said Louie, chuckling. "Let's walk over to the office. You know where it's at. It's not far." Actually, it was a back room in Louie's ramshackle warehouse. "I'll fill out a standard loan agreement, then we'll walk over to the bank, have it notarized, do the transfer. It'll cost you another seventy; I'll have to do an overdraft on both accounts—business and personal—and you know the collateral is gonna be the entire contents of the house?"

"The entire contents??" squeaked Thad. But actually, he and Jen had discussed that possibility.

"Well, yeah—unless you want to waste time going over everything in the house, doing descriptions and estimate until we get to ten thousand?"

"No, no—I see what you mean. That's fine."

"But you gotta give me 'til tomorrow. I can't come up with ten thousand just like that." He snapped his fingers.

Thad shrugged. "I guess we have no choice."

9

CAIT WAS BEHIND THE COUNTER; Zoe and Robb were each with a customer. Ferguson entered the shop unobtrusively. He waited for the customer to wander off to look at the collection of kitchen gadgets. Robb approached him.

"I do have some more information, and I have a proposal for you, as I mentioned. I wonder if you'd like to hear it."

"Well, sure, I guess. But ... can we do it elsewhere?" suggested Robb. "I'd like to *not advertise* our recent misfortune as much as possible."

Cait came out from behind the counter. "Robb—why don't you and Ferguson go to the Cat and Custard. Take Zoe with you. She can smooth the way if you want something to eat and I think it would be worthwhile for Ferguson to hear her theory about what went on."

"Great!" said Robb. "We've had a steady stream in here all day and my cheese-and-liverwurst is still sitting out back half-eaten."

"No, it's not," corrected Cait. "I ate yours, too, after you just left it sitting there."

Robb shrugged. "Okay, Mr. Ferguson, why don't you and Zoe and I walk up to the Cat and Custard, get some early lunch." He called Zoe over and introduced her and Ferguson to each other.

"I don't need lunch," said Ferguson, "but I'll treat you both."

"Whatever…" said Robb.

"Good," said Cait. "Now, why don't you three run along and I'll hold down the fort here."

They walked up to the Cat and Custard. On the way, Robb filled in Ferguson about Zoe: her upcoming degree in art history, her work for them, her plans for University of Washington. "And she has a theory about all this."

There actually seemed to be two entrances to the Cat and Custard, one to a restaurant, and the other to a bar. The bar had a sign on it, "closed"; they entered the restaurant. Zoe led them to the rear, where she drew back a heavy curtain, exposing the bar. "Hi, Gary," yelled Zoe. "I'm here as a customer for the time being."

"Hi, Jo," yelled a man behind the bar as they entered.

"You can get a drink any time but the bar doesn't officially open until four," Zoe explained. They found themselves in a large room that ran the length of both the restaurant and the bar. They sat at one of the round, dark tables, purposely distressed to go with the dark overhead beams and the dark, scuffed floor.

Ferguson took off his trench coat and hat. He draped the coat over an adjacent chair. Robb noted that his beard was gone. And he was not sporting suspenders. He wore a wore a brown leather belt; his open corduroy jacket revealed a blue paisley shirt.

"Did he call you 'Joe'?" asked Ferguson, fixing Robb with a penetrating eye. "I was meant to think your name was Robert."

"*I'm* 'Jo," said Zoe. "I'm really Zo, or 'Zo-ee,' but for days after I started working here nobody could get the 'Z.' So, they kept calling me 'Joey.' So, I told everybody, like, 'Call me "Zo,"' and then they all though I must be 'Jo' for Josephine, or something. So, I just left it at that." She shrugged.

"She's not really Zoe, either," said Robb. "She's Damia, but she has objections to that wonderful classical name, so she came up with 'Zoe.'"

"I didn't 'come up with it.' It's a shortening of my middle name—a family name, Zoeller. Can you imagine going through life with the name 'Damia Dill'?"

"I rather like it," protested Robb. "It's not only classical; it's alliterative."

"Hah!" said Zoe. "'Damia Dill'? Too easily coupled with endearments like 'Dizzy' or 'Darling' or 'Doofus,' too." She rose and walked quickly to the bar where she picked up two menus. She returned and handed the menus to Robb and Ferguson.

"Okay, you can get all the regular stuff like hamburgers and cheeseburgers and you can get a 'Ploughman's Lunch'—that's just hunks of really strong cheese, dark bread, and a pickle. Comes with a Guinness. Because, as you can probably tell, this place is supposed to be an ersatz English-Scottish-Irish pub. Like, the food's supposed to be what you'd expect in an English pub, or maybe an Irish one. They specialize in pies. Like, I don't know how authentic they are but they're really good. They're all made here on the premises fresh. No Swanson's frozen TV dinners here. There's a different pie special each day: Steak pie (without the kidneys), chicken pot, liver and onions, Shepherd's, French—that's got pork in it, Brumby's—that's Australian and has ostrich, lamb. There's also a haggis pie." She looked at Ferguson. "You know what that is!" Ferguson sniggered. "Today's special is the French pie. It's really good. They offer the veg pie daily but the specific veggies differ—today it's leek and broccoli; a couple times a week it's mashed potato and fried onion alternating with shredded carrot and sweet potato, and usually on Fridays, Saturdays, and Sundays it's portabella mushroom and fried onion or a mashed pea and cremini mushroom and every now and then a fresh caper, fried bell pepper, and white bean pie. That one's wild! The capers get only partially cooked and they're *hot*.

"To get the haggis pie you have to call a day in advance. The ingredients are frozen. Hardly anybody orders it," explained Zoe. Ferguson smiled wryly. "I don't know why. What do Americans have against spleen and lung and kidneys mixed into good old oatmeal? I don't recommend the chip butty unless you're looking for an excuse to dump a gallon of vinegar on a hamburger bun stuffed with fries. But the bacon butty is another story—it's stuffed with crisp, greasy bacon, and if you get the double it's like a Dagwood with fried egg. The horseshoe gammon is a better bet if you don't want a pie. It's ham—smoked pork leg—rolled, tied into a horseshoe shape, glazed with honey and star anise seed and baked with pineapple and roasted red peppers. It comes with chips—that is, fries—and two eggs. Takes a long time to make. They only have so much of it on any day and they usually run out before lunch time is over."

Robb guffawed. "All right, so, Zoe, can you get this started for us? I'll have the pie and a Porter Stout."

"I'll have the same," said Ferguson. And of course, this is on me."

Thought this guy Ferguson didn't need lunch. "Hey, Gary," yelled Zoe, "three French pies, two Porter darks, and a sarsaparilla for me."

Robb shifted in his seat, put his elbows on the table. "All right, Mr. Ferguson, maybe you can tell Zoe just what your interest is in all this and what you've discovered. And Zoe has an idea for you."

Ferguson sat back. "I'm an investigator and although I'm not, strictly speaking an insurance investigator, I often work for insurance companies." Ferguson went through the same litany of explanation he had given Robb and Cait earlier in the week: the shipment of a well-provenanced, over-insured cache of prehistoric pottery excavated from several private ranches in New Mexico, its disappearance, the insurance settlement with the gallery owners and ranchers, the recent sudden appearance of probably faked items resembling those that were in the original cache.

"This shipment of prehistoric Mimbres pottery, well insured, was loaded onto a lorry, a remover's van—in southern New Mexico, bound for Santa Fe, where it was to be unloaded into a gallery storage space, then distributed to a number of other galleries in Santa Fe, Taos, and Arizona. The insurance covered only the event of loss or damage in transit," added

Ferguson. "Our man inventoried each single item as it was packed into the crates, and each crate—numbered—as it was loaded onto the lorry. The packing took all day, so the journey was made at night. When the lorry arrived in Santa Fe—and again, our man was on the scene to witness the unloading, as a security measure, of course—and the receivers started to unpack the crates, there was nothing in them but rocks and stones, all packed in shredded paper and sisal. Obviously, the crates were switched at some point, but when? My guess is that there were two lorries—identical in make and year—and at some point, the two lorries rendezvoused, plates and drivers were switched, and, well, Bob's your uncle."

Zoe piped up: "So why didn't 'your man,' as you call him, follow the truck on its way to Santa Fe?"

"Yes. That was a mistake. But who was to know? After sitting at a makeshift station entering data into a computer hour after hour, he said he was fried. He got a good night's sleep in Las Cruces and set out for Santa Fe the next morning. I can't blame him. And I don't think he was in on it. But I'm not so sure the receiving galleries and the originating rancher pot-hunters weren't. They finally got the insurance settlement—after two months of intensive investigation, I couldn't come up with a thing—and my guess is that at some point the galleries got their goods. They got the insurance settlement *and* the mislaid pottery."

"So where does this gang come into their situation, to what happened to Cait and Robb?" asked Zoe.

"Ah'm wonderin': could the missed appointment have been with the notorious gang—or a part of them—seeking to market the remainder of the cache of vanished artifacts?"

"Okay," said Zoe. "I get it. Like, how much was the stuff insured for?"

"It was insured for $10 million."

"Whew! And this gang got some of that?"

"Presumably," replied Ferguson. "And also, presumably, a share of the pottery."

"So, it's this couple that tied us up that's the gang? And … Golly, I just don't get it. Wouldn't they want to sell us the pottery rather than tie us up and smash us around?" said Robb, wagging his head back and forth.

"Wild!" said Zoe.

"Quite a tale," said Robb.

"Drinks, Jo," came a shout from the bar. Zoe sprang up and returned quickly with a round tray of beers and her sarsaparilla.

"Yes, but there's yet another wrinkle," said Ferguson. "Here's the other, not-as-cold case that Ah'm working on." Ferguson, the Northumberlander, was coming through a bit stronger after the pint. "There was a wee auction in Paris nearly exactly a year ago of 'Native American art.' Except that it was not 'art' at all. The Native American 'art' consisted, in fact, of masks used in ceremonies, pieces that are religious items, the possession of which over here could have set the FBI off onto a major sting. Plus, although some items had been in the possession of this or that person, they were largely 'unprovenanced'; therefore, they might well have been stolen from the tribes while their caretakers thought they were safely tucked away, awaiting their participation in the next appropriate ceremonies, or deaccessioned from museums before a law, called the Native American Graves Protection and Repatriation Act kicked in. The sellers were anonymous; many of the buyers were anonymous also, acting through telephone bids or representatives. Who, then, were the targeted buyers? And how many of those buyers were actually wholesalers, looking for resales in the black market?

"I know that one of those buyers was this woman going by the name of Jane Faulks. She undoubtedly submitted successful bids and may be in possession of up to a dozen masks. Her former partner, Dan Rosenstock, is currently living in San Miguel de Allende, Mexico, without Jane Faulks. He may have been the driver of the substitute lorry, the one that drove off with the real crates of pottery. That would mean he and Jane Faulks pulled a fast one on the other partners. So, it stands to reason they'd both go to ground. And what has Jane Faulks been doing for the last several years? Well, I know now that she is living out on Long Island.

"My idea is that the gang that orchestrated the Mimbres switch was a partnership: Jane Faulks and Dan Rosenstock. But here we are nearly seven years after the Mimbres heist and Jane Faulks has a cash flow dilemma because her slice of the insurance settlement is gone. So, she now sees her chance to sell off the remainder of her share of the stolen cache. Ah thought at first it was the pots she would be offerin' ye, Robb and Cait, there in the museum. But now, after a wee bit o' investigatin' Ah been doing, Ah think it's the masks she's peddlin'. And Ah canna' get a grip on how these two imposters—who I now know are headquartered upstate—got in on the act, or why. They seem to ha'e been tipped off that ye were going to be offered something valuable and illicit. And if Ah'm right about her being in possession of however many of the masks she has, then she's had to get out a loan to finance the Paris auction caper.

"Now my guess is the loan is due. So, putting it all together, given the elaborately planned but neatly and tidily executed nature of the Mimbres caper—it was far too clever a scheme for a couple of amateurs in the design of hoaxing and hoodwinking—this masquerading of you at the museum has Madame Faulks' signature all over it. That signature is putting the blame, the responsibility, for the misdeeds onto someone else; in the Mimbres case, the gallery owners and the ranchers, in this case, a couple of shady antiques dealers.

"And I also got a glimpse of the person the impersonators met at the museum. I'm sure it was Jane Faulks, the woman I've been following, cleverly disguised. Did I mention that that is not her actual name? But no matter. I couldn't stick around; I don't think they have yet tumbled to the fact they're being tracked. But Ms. Faulks may have done. Anyway, if she is who I think she is, then the putative Mimbres gang has resurfaced, and may be peddling the religious items from the Paris auction as 'Native American art' as well as the residue of the mislaid pottery."

"So, you've been following her—can you tell us anything about what she's been doing?" queried Zoe.

"I've had a man watching her out on Long Island. I got word from him that she was heading for the nearest Long Island Railroad station. I was lucky. I raced over to the Pennsylvania Station and waited. Sure enough, she emerged from one of the trains with a young man. He was carting along a very large portfolio. Ah dunna know where he got on. They took the shuttle to Grand Central; they boarded the Empire State Express. I rented a car and barreled up the Hudson—followed the train route as best I could. She did not get out at Albany or Utica or Rome but she did get out at Oswego, rented a limousine, drove into one of the old, once posh neighborhoods, parked. Her dogs-body or gigolo or whatever he is hauled the portfolio out of the back seat. They rang the bell and were admitted to the house. I could not swear to it but the fellah who answered the door could well have been the 'you'—he nodded at Robb—"who was sitting on the bench in the museum and had the conversation with Jane in the cafeteria."

"How do you manage to follow all these people around without getting caught out?" asked Zoe.

"First of all, I have a number of what you might call disguises," said Ferguson.

"Pies, Jo," came the voice from the kitchen.

"Hah!" shouted Zoe, then rose and marched off. She returned with the three pies on the tray and her forearm laden with a large oval platter piled with fries. She bent over and slid everything deftly onto the table, assembling the dishes around the cruet of salt, pepper, vinegar and hot sauce. "It comes with chips," she said, then took her seat.

Ferguson, obviously enjoying hearing himself talk, resumed his monologue. "For one of them, I don glasses, stick-on beard, with my trench coat here, adopt a shuffling gate. Not to mention the odd lingo; of course, nobody in the British Isles really talks like this." He winked. "But it works.

"Now, as to your couple sitting on the bench in the African Hall. I think they are being sought as go-betweens, facilitators for buyers."

"So, this seems to be a case of a couple crooks getting wind of a couple *other* crooks having something illicit to sell—whether pots or sacred masks—and setting themselves up to hoodwink the other crooks!" said Zoe. "Wild!"

"Aye! And Jane Faulks was obviously mistaken about Cannings' interest in Native American art, if she is peddling the residue of the Mimbres pots and the dance masks bought at auction. And now that I know that Jane Faulks is a principal in *this* affair, then I truly do not want this to be another bollixed cock-up. I'd like to be able to demonstrate that the masks were acquired outside the law, or at least, with intent to get around the law, and maybe even that they were outright stolen at some point. I'd like to see my sly smuggler get caught in receipt of stolen goods, or at least in violation of custom regulations. I'm hoping that catching her out in that way might persuade her to rat out her partners in the Mimbres scam. I want this to be a sting that gets Jane Faulks in illegal possession of items that violate NAGPRA and threaten her with violation of the Antiquities Act of 1906 and Archaeological Resources Protection Act of 1979 *and* leverages her exposure of the entire Mimbres scam. We threaten her and finger the other principals and perhaps retrieve at least part of the insurance payout.

"Now—the problem is that my disguises won't work for long with Jane Faulks. Not because she would recognize me as who I am; I'm quite sure she was at an auction last year in Paris. She was also 'in disguise,' so to speak, there, as well as here. Here, she was a dumpy little old lady with a vaguely old-world way of speaking, laboring along with a couple of canes. In Paris, attendance was only by invitation. I didn't have an invitation. So, I only glimpsed her as I was hanging around outside and she was going in. There, she was—from afar—a sprightly, youngish-looking woman nattily dressed, sporting a turban. If, indeed, she is the same person. And if, indeed, she is the same person that fits the description I have from nearly twenty years ago. And I can't be sure that she or one of her minions didn't spot me lurking around on St. Germain-des-Prés. But it's not that she would actually recognize me per se; she has the same kind of sniffer that I do for ferreting out the odd anomaly."

Zoe asked, "Don't you have a picture? Of this … this Jane person?"

"I took a picture, necessarily from afar, of Jane Faulks in Paris; and I'm afraid that's all I have connecting her to the dance masks. Interpol has one of Jane F. on file but it's old and grainy. It's actually a photograph of her on the only occasion that we know of, of her arrest; she was only eighteen or nineteen. And of course identification by name can't be relied on; passports, until very recently, were incredibly easy to forge, and driving licenses—well, they're a joke in terms of ID."

"And she decided to contact us, I mean our imposters, because…" Robb let Ferguson finish his sentence, presumably for Zoe's benefit.

"Because in fact, she—or one of her minions—was probably in your shop sometime in the last few months and noticed that, in fact, you deal in high-quality Native American art."

"But of course, we really don't," observed Robb. "Golly, that stuff is almost all left over from a previous owner, Suggs, who thought he wanted to special-ize in it."

"Jane doesn't know that," said Ferguson matter-of-factly, wagging his head. "All she sees is what you have on display."

"But wouldn't she be better off going directly to the Southwest and contacting those gallery owners you were talking about? Isn't that where the real market is for stuff like that?"

"Yes and no. I suspect that there was, so to speak, a falling out among thieves. She knows the interest is there, among the same gallery owners that she did the Mimbres heist for. But for some reason she disna' want to contact them directly. So, she gets you—or your imposters, rather—as the go-betweens."

Zoe nodded her head vigorously. "So, you think they had these religious items in the—what did you call it, the portmanteau? And if that turns out to be the case, you offer a kind of plea bargain thing?"

"Aye. It's a long shot. But if she spills the beans, then we call in the FBI, get a court order to attach assets, and go for another plea bargain with the other principals on the Mimbres scam. We let them off the hook or let them plead to some kind of misdemeanor, we sell off their assets, or as many as we have to. Lloyd's gets back its ten million—or part of it, at least, and finally wipes the egg off its face. Off *my* face. I'd like to convince my overseers that this case is worth running to ground for the sake of precedent and saving reputation, if nothing else."

"And the tribes get their sacred items back," said Zoe.

"Aye, right," replied Ferguson.

"Well, we'll help if we can," offered Robb, "but I don't see exactly what we can do."

"Hey..." Zoe, who had asked a few questions but otherwise had remained mostly silent up until then, but becoming increasingly more fidgety, broke in. "So, can I run out the whole scenario?" She addressed Ferguson. "Listen to this," said Zoe. "It was the information that this couple got, when they came into the shop on Friday, a week ago, that kicked off the whole thing. The dudes who tied up the Murrays were after information. It was the details of when and where to meet someone who, indeed, had something to sell, and where to meet them in order to find out what it was that they had to sell, that they got. The couple that you found in the Museum on Monday are the ones who got that information and then came back and tied up Robb here and Cait on Sunday evening, so *they couldn't* turn up to the arranged rendezvous.

"This is how it was done," continued Zoe. "Cait's busy at the counter. She puts the phone on speaker. It turns out it's the call Robb and Cait were meant to respond to on Monday. The guy—or gal—has something they want to show that they hope they'll be interested in. They don't want to risk coming to the shop. If they were on the up-and-up, if they had something that was just, like, an ordinary antique, or even a non-ordinary antique, they would have just trotted it by the shop, right?

"So, the ski mask dudes just happen to be here. I mean, there, in the shop, without their ski masks. The woman is right there at the desk. The call comes in. And they get that information because the landline is on speaker when they just happened to come into the shop. They were there long enough to hear the details of that phone call—blasting through the shop on speaker phone. Where to meet the contact. When. That they had something of interest for sale. So, these two smell an opportunity. Like, it's big. It's something that isn't just from grandma's attic." Zoe nodded her head sagely.

She addressed Robb: "You don't recognize them when they come back just before closing on Sunday because you weren't paying that much attention when they first came in and now they're duded up like robbers. These guys come in, tie you up, take nothing, leave. You'd never seen them before, but you *had*! And they weren't, like, even after information because they already had it. And they take Cait's phone so that after they make contact with Jane Faulks, they can stay in touch by phone. If the contact is made by phone, they can answer, and they could call the contact back and make details of the arrangements. They tell the contact they're 'at home' so don't call the shop. Call the shop's mobile. When the contact—this maybe-Jane-Faulks person—does so, the contact's caller ID says it's Cannings'. So, if they had to follow up with a call to the contact while they were at the museum, the caller ID would show them to be Cannings'. They wanted to get their hands on whatever it was they thought whoever had to peddle." She looked meaningfully at Ferguson, her eyes almost popping. "So now they've, like, made contact with the contact. And now we know who they are—or at least where their digs are, because Ferguson followed them—and we know who the contact is."

"That's it!" enthused Ferguson. "You've done it, Miss Zoe! You've slotted the last piece of the puzzle into place!" He turned to Robb. "The imposters are crooks themselves and are maybe nosing around your shop, Mr. Murray, to suss out how they might rope you into some sort of scam. And *zut*—the opportunity comes blasting through the speaker phone and rings their well-attuned, duplicitous crook-chimes!" He turned again to Zoe. "Crooks hoodwinking crooks! Ah lak that!"

He turned back to Robb. "So, let me make a few suggestions—or some observations, rather. First, it seems it would be in your best interests to find out who these imposters, these interlopers, are and put a stop to them. Second, you're the best people to do it because you've encountered them: you know the sounds of their voices, how they move, their body builds. It's really too bad you don't have security cameras here so we could a good look at them, but that can't be helped. But you are the last people they will expect to confront them, to expose them; you provide shock value. Just what we need to get them to reveal their mischief and to point the finger to Ms. Faulks. And third, Jane Faulks has no idea that the imposters are imposters; if you met up on the street, she'd have no idea who *you* were. You've got the shock value of exposing them, as well."

"So, we'd be the catalyst for this Faulks person agreeing to the plea bargain?" said Robb around a mouthful of meat-and-veg-pie. "We barge in, tell them, 'The gig's up, blackguards, come clean and take us to your leader, and we'll let you off the hook'?"

"Something like that," agreed Ferguson. "So, then, what I'd like to suggest is a little road trip. Out west to some of the dealers who were to be the recipients of the missing Mimbres pieces on the assumption that they are also the likely middlemen who would shift the Paris auction items to interested customers. Specifically, to one of them, named Woodard Glenn. In fact, I would bet that, at some point, that portmanteau currently residing in a run-down mansion in Oswego is going to accompany those two on a road trip out west, and you are going to follow them."

"Why can't *you* do that?"

"Ah canna' be in two places at once. I need to keep Ms. Slippery Faulks in the crosshairs. She's showed up at the imposters' headquarters. She's left something with them. We can bet that there's a deal on and things are going to go into high gear. The imposters are going to negotiate some sort of deal with someone. At some point Jane F. will appear and cinch it, or the imposters will cinch it for her. That means I have to be ready to jump. But I'd like for you also to be ready to jump, so to speak. I'd like to you to be ready to confront your would-be usurpers when Ms. Slippery Faulks surfaces again to get everything sorted and tied up. And that means we're all in the same place as they, when they do so."

"By golly, but we can't just pull up and move out and suddenly become amateur detectives!" objected Robb. "We've got a business to run! Would you pay us for all this? For closing the business for who knows how long?"

"Well, you wouldn't both have to become sleuths. One could stay here and mind the store. Zoe, maybe you could fill in—isn't term almost over?"

"Maybe," said Zoe.

"Pardon me for being crass, but would you pay us?" asked Robb.

"Aye. Funds are limited. But I could provide mileage and per diem. Per diem is $200 a day, and a fee. Say, $1,000? Or, if we are able to recover the full amount of the insurance settlement, or even a part of it, a percentage of that—say, point-oh-one percent? That's $10,000. I'll wager Lloyd's would agree to that as a modest reward, if this is successful."

Robb wagged his head back and forth. "No deal. It's chancy; it's risky; it might be dangerous—especially when it comes out that these bozos aren't who they're pretending to be. And we could miss some really good deals if there's only one of us buying and selling and running the store. Why can't your man out on Long Island do the tailing and the spying?"

"He's strictly local. Affairs on the side, fodder for divorce court sort of thing. He only kept me apprised of Jane Faulks' doings as he pursued his dirtier, more lucrative miscreants. And to hire a full-time PI is just not in the cards; they charge twice my rate, plus per diem and a travel allowance. Lloyd's have already lost millions and the statute of limitations on prosecuting this sort of crime is about to run out."

Zoe pushed her empty wooden pie paddle to the side, leaned forward, placed her elbows on the table and fixed Ferguson with her gaze. "Hey. I have a proposition for you. Hire me."

"Hire?" said Ferguson.

Zoe held up her right hand, traffic cop style. "Okay, look. Like, as soon as the, the—whatever, the signal, is given, whoever it is has to hop, right?"

"Aye," agreed Ferguson.

"By the end of the week, I'll have only two weeks of school left. Two classes require only final papers and I can submit those by email, as attachments. And the other is a take-home, open-note exam. I've got one paper just about done and the other's a no-brainer. I'm going out to U Wash anyway. I'll just do what you need me to do, then continue on. Get an early start."

"Hmmm," said Ferguson.

"I've done courses in *Peoples and Cultures of the Southwest; Southwest Prehistory; Native North America; Native Art of the Americas; Museum and Heritage Studies; Frauds, Forgers, Fakers and Filchers*—you name it in art, and I know it, not to mention antiques." Zoe took in the room with a sweep of her arm, as if it were Cannings'.

"That's right!" chuckled Robb. "She's more of an expert than we are! And surely on Native North America and its arts."

"And you know something?" said Zoe confidently. "I'm pretty sure I saw your Jane Faulks and her paramour. They came in a couple weeks ago on a Friday or Saturday when Robb and Cait were in Pennsylvania."

Ferguson had his mouth almost around a chunk of his half-eaten meat pie. He set it down. "Well…" he demurred.

"And best of all, those two bozo imposters *haven't* seen *me*. If you don't mind if I collect the per diem whether I sleep in my car or throw my sleeping bag in a camping shelter instead of staying at the Days Inn, hey—like, this is an adventure!" *And it will solve the Nick problem* she thought. *I can make a clean break. I can be as mysterious as him. I landed temporary work for the summer, I'll tell him. I'll be vague. Pursuing something for Cait and Robb. Outta here. Pack everything in boxes and ship it out to Seattle by Greyhound Bus.* "I'm smart, very knowledgeable, clever, attractive, engaging, and up-beat. Who could resist charm, blue eyes, frizzy-styled hair, and my dusky, Zorah-like, cameo face, straight out of a Matisse sketch? Not to speak of the well-filled-out-but nicely sculpted rest-of-me! So, who would ever suspect me? Couldn't I be a charming young lady acting on behalf of an anonymous buyer interested in things antique and Native American? Especially with my credentials.

"I've got what you and Robb both don't have," she continued, "flexibility. I mean, like, Robb turning up, hovering around, could blow the whole thing or, like, at least take it in an unanticipated direction. The imposters could get real grumpy or even violent when Robb turns up out in the open. I come across as just a post-teenage, post-college gal well on my way to an advanced degree and looking for a career, not like an antiques store proprietor. And you don't know where or when the imposters—the Lycra-and-ski-mask-imposter-brokers—might scoop up the rest of the masks. They may be in storage in the middle of nowhere."

Ferguson took a deep breath, scrunched his butt into the back of his chair, folded his arms and placed them on the table in front of his barely touched pie, let his breath out, and said, "Miss Zoe, your points are well taken, but that's precisely why your proposal will not work. You are indeed a quite vivacious and therefore noticeable person. The imposters may not know who you are, but Ms. Faulks might well recognize you. And what I'm going to rely on is the shock value: Cait and Robb—or maybe just Robb—turns up wherever: to the gallery, to the secret warehouse, to the back room in the dealer's home, with myself lurking nearby, and confront frauds, felons, and fellow travelers all at the same time. One or more of them capitulates and agrees to reveal the cache or caches, each more anxious than the other to turn state's evidence for a lenient sentence."

"But just the opposite could happen," said Zoe calmly, taking an overly long sip of her sarsaparilla. "Robb could come barreling in, or sauntering in, or whatever. He points his finger, says, 'Blackguards! The gig's up! Surrender the goods!' And everybody clams up, dummies down, and goes to—what did you say—goes to ground? And you come in hard on his heels and everybody just shrugs. You're back where you started, or worse, like, with violent reprisals."

Ferguson nodded. "That could happen. But remember, I'm not really after the imposters; I'm after this gang of thieves, or what's left of them, and their booty. I need Robb because he turns up, tells them the gig is up, and the imposters pee their pants, capitulate, start gabbling. Tell us where we can find Jane Faulks and how. And then we're in negotiation mode."

"Couldn't I do the same thing? I can drop all kinds of hints, like, I know who the imposters are and what they did, if you want me to do that. Or I can just scope things out. You're not the only one with disguise potential. I can dye my hair; straighten it. Just to be on the safe side, I can use a different name."

"Um…" said Ferguson.

"How dangerous do you think this would be?" asked Robb.

"I think the danger is minimal," assured Ferguson. "The imposters are most probably your fellow antiquers, Mr. Murray. They are crooked, but with a certain amount of survival quotient. 'Tis yet to be revealed, but they may well ha'e no investment in Jane Faulks' scheme, yet, whatever 'tis, and no knowledge of it. My guess is they are going to be Ms. Faulks' fall guys."

"Then why not take Zoe up on her proposal?" said Robb. "There's no way they're going to cotton on to her. All she does is check in with you about their whereabouts, right?"

"Well…"

"I'm here all weekend," said Zoe. "I can stick around until Sunday night. Think about it."

"All right. I'm going to drive back up to Oswego directly, as soon as I leave here. I will call you at some point, after I give it a good think and see what those two are up to at this point. Give me your phone number; I'll call you on my burner and tell you my decision, one way or another."

10

ZOE EXCITEDLY FILLED ELLIE IN on her conversation with Robb and Ferguson at the Cat and Custard. Ellie listened, punctuating her narrative with *ohs* and *ahas* and *oh mys*, especially when she revealed her plans to do Ferguson's spying for him. When she came to the part in her story where she shared Nick's on-going proposition for her future and her decision to break off with him, Ellie nodded sagely, commenting, "I think that's a wise decision. You don't want to be forever in his shadow."

Then Ellie rose, saying, "Well this has all been quite a surprise, but a good one. An adventure. I had my adventures years ago, you know. And now I have a surprise for *you*. You stay right there." She retreated into her bedroom, returning with a small card, which she handed to Zoe. "I was going to do this in June, on your actual birthday, but you won't be here. So, I'll do it now. I am giving you my automobile. It's not even two years old. I hardly use it. You'll need it even more, now that you're doing this work, and it will be good for you to have it out west."

"Oh, Ellie—I couldn't possibly!"

"Oh yes you can. I insist. Otherwise, it will just sit here. I have no use for it."

It was a Honda Civic, definitely an old lady's car, but it was spacious and indeed, she could sleep in it in a pinch. She could also cram a lot of her belongings into the trunk; maybe she'd need to ship only a couple of boxes. *It's a lot more car than my rattletrap VW*, she thought. "Well, thank you, thank you, thank you so much!" She rose and gave Ellie a hug and kiss.

"I'll print out the proper forms and have them signed and on the table there when you come back tonight."

The first few bars of Aretha Franklin's "Respect" sounded. Zoe reached into her back pocket and drew out her phone. It was Ferguson. "I will take you up on your proposal, for all the reasons your employers gave for no to do it and all the reasons you gave for yes to do it. But we have to act immediately. The imposters are making plans to flee. Can you be ready to go tomorrow, Saturday?"

"Holy moly!" Zoe's mind raced. Yes, she could explain to Cait and Robb. She could race back early, early tomorrow morning, pack up her things, get Tess to take the boxes to the Greyhound station. Maybe she could even stuff most of them into the Civic's ample trunk. She'd have to break the news to Gary at the Cat this evening. She'd need to text Tess right now. She did so. Then she called Ferguson. "Where are you?"

He answered, "I'm on the Thruway. And I need to give you a crash course in how to tail tomorrow morning—also some additional information."

"Why don't you do that now? You can come straight here to where I am." She looked at Ellie and raised her eyebrows. Ellie shrugged and nodded.

FRIDAY, 8:30 PM

Zoe had called Gary at the C & C and begged off working this evening; not happy, he nonetheless had said "okay" and rung off. Well, tomorrow she'd have to call him with her final news: she would not be coming back to work.

Ferguson had arrived at 7:45 p.m. After introductions, Ellie had retreated to her bedroom; Zoe and Ferguson were seated at the kitchen table. Ferguson opened his briefcase and withdrew an oversize envelope. "You'd best read this first," he told Zoe. "I'll just put in a call to the Holiday Inn, make sure I've got a room for the night."

"Would you, would you like a glass of … something? Wine? Beer?"

"Aye! A glass of wine would be superb. If there's some about I'll not trouble ye—just help myself."

"There is. In the fridge. Glasses in the cupboard."

Ferguson helped himself, then retreated to the living room. She could hear him on the phone. She opened the envelope, drew out a manila folder thick with several items.

The first item was a newspaper clipping:

Albuquerque Journal North, March 30, 2015

Greggory Tabor Neal passed away from natural causes on March 25 in his home in Santa Fe. Mr. Neal, 62, was a pioneer of the gallery scene in Santa Fe. "You could always count on Gregg to offer nothing but the highest quality in Indian arts," said longtime fellow gallery owner Woodard ("Woody") Glenn. "He will be sorely missed."

Mr. Neal was found dead in his home the afternoon of March 28 by his business partner and housemate, Sebastian Plumm, who had just returned from a buying trip to the Hopi villages. "I found him slumped in his favorite recliner chair," said Plumm. "At least he died surrounded by the things he loved."

According to Plumm, Mr. Neal had complained of fatigue and pains in his legs, as well as some stomach trouble off and on during the previous couple of months. "I thought he just had a stomach bug and maybe the aches and pains were—you know—arthritis beginning to set in. He was a few years older than I so I thought, 'Well, this is normal.'"

Santa Fe coroner Robert Garcia declined to order an autopsy, noting there was no reason to think that Mr. Neal's death was anything but heart failure. "He had apparently cut his hand on some glass or perhaps on a sliver of a wooden spear that was on the floor, broken in several pieces." It looked like Neal had entertained a visitor the night he died, said Mr. Garcia. Two glasses had been found on end tables in the living room where Mr. Neal died. "He most likely succumbed shortly after his visitor left. But there was no sign of a struggle, no indication of foul play," said the coroner.

Neither Mr. Garcia nor Mr. Plumm could speculate on who the visitor might have been. "Probably just a friend—another gallery owner. He had a lot of friends," said Mr. Plumm.

Coroner Garcia remarked that "a primitive spear was found on the floor, in several pieces. Several other spears were propped up, leaning against a large table; it looked like maybe somebody—probably Mr. Neal himself, when he was experiencing the attack—might have knocked against one of the spears, breaking it and knocking it on the floor. But there were no marks or bruises on Mr. Neal's body, except for a small cut on one of his hands. So, it's not like anybody bopped him on the head or something."

Given the state of the body, it is surmised that Mr. Neal had been dead perhaps as long as two days when Mr. Plumm found him. A memorial service will be held at the Scottish Rite Temple next Saturday.

Ferguson had returned to the kitchen and taken a chair across from Zoe. The next item was a catalogue from a Paris auction held by Sotheby's: April 12, 2013. Zoe turned the pages. The items seemed to be mostly ceremonial masks as well as some statuary and other items, all seeming to be of a ritual nature. "So, these are what Jane Faulks bid on?"

Ferguson nodded. "Aye. Some of them. Actually, she bid on most of them, and probably got up to a dozen or more."

Next was an insurance document: a set of photographs, fifty-odd pages. Here, then, was the target of Ferguson's initial investigation: an inventory, with photographs, of 606 prehistoric Mimbres pots from three ranches in Arizona. She started turning pages, but then stopped. "Is it unusual for things like this to be insured?"

"Not at all. A limited time policy with a per diem premium is almost always taken out on a shipment of valuable items when they are shipped from museum to museum or from collector to museum against breakage, unforeseen delays and yes, always theft. But Lloyd's could find no case, as precedent, of a shipment consisting solely of New World ceramic items. The closest they could come was a loan from the National Museum of Mexico to the Denver Museum of Natural History in early the 1990s, and that was mixed collection; only some of it was pottery. The lawyer for the ranchers and gallery owners argued that the equivalent case to theirs was a shipment of Meissen, Dresden, and Sevres porcelain conveyed from various collection points in Austria and West Germany to the Louvre shortly after the end of World War II. They made the argument that, in 2008 dollars, the cache would have been insured for the equivalent of $8,000 per piece. They also claimed that some of their pots would go for twice that amount."

"So … a little less than $5 million?"

"Aye. But the ranchers and gallery owners insisted on doubling that figure because of the unique aspects: all hand-made, impossible to replicate, with effigies decorating many of the pots and the fact that some did not have the bottoms smashed, as is usually the case with Mimbres."

"Right," said Zoe. "Nobody really *knows*, but they supposedly smashed the bottom to let the pot's spirit out. When it was buried along with a dead person, it is speculated that smashing the pot also released the spirit of the dead person."

Ferguson nodded "Aye. Ye do indeed know your art and collectibles, Native and otherwise. But I do know that when Lloyd's balked, the group's attorney pointed out that it was Lloyd's itself that had insured the porcelain, and that there was an 'effigy' statue only a few hundred years older—Greek or Roman, I forget which—that had recently sold at Sotheby's for $50 million. The pots, not quite as old but also many decorated with motifs from the natural world built into their structure, should be similarly valued. At any rate, there would have been several exemplars of the 'unique' pieces. So that made the whole batch worth more."

"So, about $10 million!" affirmed Zoe.

"Aye. That was surely enough. Enough to ensure that they would be protected against the ups and down of the cattle industry and the art market."

"And you suspected this gang of thieves at the time."

"Let's just say that the sophistication of the procedure put me to mind of the Gardner. A lorry starts out from its point of origin. It arrives within an acceptable time frame. Nothing seems amiss until the doors are opened, box after box is unpacked, revealing only rocks. The pots have disappeared without a trace. Virtually none of the Mimbres pots that have gone on the market—black or not—can be traced definitely back to the cache. Three might have been put up in an auction, and there was some recent activity on the internet, but again, we are not definitely sure they are from the cache."

Zoe flipped over the Mimbres material, held together with clasp. The next items were three photographs. Two were in color; but they looked as if they'd been blown up from, perhaps a three-by-five. They were grainy. One was obviously taken on a public street, from far away. "That is she," said Ferguson. "Jane Faulks, alias Cricencia Morgenhouse, alias Chris Morgen. The Paris auction house dinna' allow photographs inside, and I couldna' get in anyway because I dinna' have an invitation. I caught her as she stepped out at an organized break in the proceedings. You can see she's just about to draw the hood of her mackintosh over her head to hide her face."

The second photo looked to have been taken in someone's living room. Zoe was looking at a woman's face, turned toward the camera: a face sculpted in planes and angles, emanating strength, confidence, determination—but caught in a frown, with mouth half-open, framed by full sensuous lips. The woman's hair, brown with platinum streaks was long, but piled onto her head and held with silver barrettes. Strands of thin silver circled her neck. A broad-lapelled, pale blue suit jacket, buttoned, covered the bottom half of a white blouse embroidered in four vertical parallel lines framing the buttons. She was obviously saying something not complimentary to the photographer. She was striking; not exactly pretty, more handsome than anything, but hard to forget. That face would be hard to disguise. It could not be definitively matched, thought Zoe, with the face of the woman on the street, but it was not inconsistent with it either. The final photo was actually two: a face and a half torso, front and side, a black label with white lettering plastered across each: "Cricencia Morgenhouse, 10-19-1949, X-5621049." "Her mugshot," said Zoe. She thought, *she looks about thirteen. Short, unruly dark hair, grim expression. Yes, it could well be the same person as in the living room photograph that was taken, perhaps, twenty years later?*

"Precisely. She was arrested once, when she was nineteen. Numerous counts: shoplifting, breaking and entering, theft, transporting stolen goods. Sentenced to eight months, but did only four. That other photograph, the close-up, was taken more than twenty years later. She was'n' using Cricencia Morgenhouse, but rather, the name Jane Faulks. I matched the photo I had against her 'mugshot,' as you put it, using the FBI database. That is not usually available to non-law-enforcement but let's just say I have my contacts."

"She was in the FBI database? For shoplifting?"

"No. For transporting stolen goods across state lines. Steal stuff, and maybe you can plead it down to a misdemeanor; transport them across state lines and it's a federal offense—a felony. The FBI gets involved."

"Oh. From where to where?"

"From Louisiana to Texas."

"So, this Cricencia person is from Louisiana?"

"Yes indeed."

"And this picture?"

"That third picture is from Lloyd's own files. That was a bit of a fluke. I searched for any cases in the files of Assurance Associates involving high-end items that were well-insured or over-insured and where there might have been fraud, and in which the perpetrators seemed to have simply melted away, vanished, gotten away with it. And I found the case. It was one in which a gentleman in California had been pensioned off from a minor contractor that had supplied the space program with guidance systems for the space shuttles. When it was clear that the Endeavor would be the last of the shuttles, back in the 1990s, the company quietly dissolved. High level employees, the engineers, were paid off with handsome pensions. The gentleman decided he needed something to do and he had a modest stamp collection. His idea was to go into the mail order business. Well, he answered an ad in a reputable stamp collecting periodical. Joy Stamp Shop in Santa Barbara, California, had gone out of business when its proprietors had become too aged and frail to carry on. They had tried to sell the shop but found no takers. At least, this was the story that he was told. So, a broker had been authorized to receive responses to a notice from parties interested in purchasing all or part of the inventory.

"Ye may recognize the strategy when I tell you what I have observed in Oswego, New York. At any rate, nearly twenty years ago, in California, the ostensible broker turns up in answer to the would-be entrepreneur's response. Now the broker brought the collection to the gentleman's home and made a very modest proposal: she would leave the collection with him, as they say in the trade, 'on approval.' He would have a week to look it over. It was apparently a very large number of mostly used but some new—'mint,' never used—postage stamps.

"Well. He plowed through the collection and found, by far, the most valuable items in the collection: a block of four of what are known as the 'Upside Down Jenny.' The Jennys were the first airplanes to carry mail. Those first airmail flights in 1918 were commemorated with the Jenny stamps. Well, some—nobody knows how many—were fed into the printer wrong and the Jenny is flying upside down! A printing error. Genuine ones are worth hundreds of thousands. A block of four, like this, would go for over a million dollars, probably a million and a half today. Now what he did was probably not altogether ethical, but it was certainly not illegal. He discovered the Jenny block of four in one of the many boxes of loose stamps but did not mention them to the broker when she returned on the Friday next. He eagerly and enthusiastically negotiated a price for the collection that required him to withdraw a substantial amount from his pension fund, at a penalty, along with a considerable tax burden. He promptly placed the Jennys in a bank safe deposit box, then contacted Lloyd's and wanted to ensure his inventory for $1.5 million. When Lloyd's balked, pointing out that he had only shelled out $224,000, he then sent along a photograph of the Jennys along with a clipping from a stamp magazine noting recent sale of one Jenny from a stamp auction for just under $500,000. Lloyd's issued him a short-term policy, good for six months, but for only $600,000, assuming retail would fetch substantially more than the wholesale price, but nothing like $1,500,000. Lloyd's then insisted on authentication from the American Philatelic Society. You can probably guess: the Jennys were counterfeit. There had indeed been A 'Joy Stamp Shop' in Santa Barbara, California, but it had gone out of business in the 1960s, not the 1990s.

"Now, you see, not only did the perpetrator have to have the stamps counterfeited; but also had to accumulate a substantial pile of stamps to make it look like it was an inventory of an entire shop and also had to trump up a story. The perpetrator also had to study the whole trade, get to know the relevant periodicals, learn the trade lingo. You can also bet she scoped out the folks who responded. Who knows how many others she fooled, who were too shy to come forward! A very carefully forged—pardon the pun—plan. She was not merely a fly-by-night thief peddling counterfeits.

"It so happened the gentleman's young son was an in-your-face ten-year old with a point-and-shoot camera that he had gotten for his birthday. He was tearing around pointing and shooting at just about everything—snap, snap, snap—including the elegant lady who brought along the stamp collection. Lloyd's sent out an investigator who got a hold of the negatives. This was in the very last days of film so he was able to get this one print into the file. He did extensive interviews with the gentleman who now really did have to go back into business and he eventually was able to recover his loss with aggressive marketing and by acquiring more lots from auctions. But o' course he couldna' sell the Jennys.

"It was the cleanness, the cleverness, the neatness of the operation that put me in mind of the Mimbres case sixteen years later. It's got Jane Faulks' signature all over it: plausible deniability; the investigation goes off on a tangent and the perpetrator gets neatly away. For the Mimbres scam? One looks at the ranchers and the gallerists. For the Upside Down Jenny fraud? One looks to the stamp collectors and dealers. For the smuggling of illicit Native art circumventing US Customs? One looks to a couple of shady antiques dealers, willing to impersonate legitimate ones."

Zoe studied the photograph again. "Was there any way you could follow up on her possible involvement in the Mimbres case?"

"I trotted that second picture from the postage stamp fraud around to every gallery in Santa Fe, Sedona, and Scottsdale, asking if anyone resembling her had been around. But o' course we're talking six or seven years ago. Everyone I asked claimed to not recognize her. I suspected at the time that some of the gallery personnel were just playing mumchance. But I had basis on which to press. Finally, I found a young woman in Sedona who thought she did, indeed, recognize her. She said it had been her first day on the job and there had been a terrific thunderstorm. She dashed out just as it broke to wind back the canopy sheltering the entrance. Just as she did so, a woman ran up to shelter under it so the young lady shooed her inside; the two of them were alone in the shop for ten minutes while rain poured down. The salesperson chatted up the serendipitous visitor, as you might imagine she would in the circumstances. She was face-to-face with her. She thought, indeed, it could have been the same person, fifteen years older. So, there is not a link directly with the Mimbres goods; but there is reason to think she was, as you might say, in the right place at the right time. And this surely smacks of being the same sort of scam."

Zoe nodded. "But this is not the person I'm going to follow."

"No. Leave that to me. I will journey back up to Oswego on the morrow, and I may have to do the first leg of the tailing. That would mean you would have to meet me somewhere quite far down the road. But I dunna' think they are going to leave tomorrow, after all. There were a number of comings and goings late today: trip to a bank, another to a Price Chopper for supplies, finally to a Jiffy Lube. But that wasn't all; what made it so easy for me to track 'em was a wee device I attached to their vehicle when it was parked underground in Manhattan. Well, I should 'a'e known. The garage personnel must have alerted them. Or maybe the male member of the team simply hung around and looked up, while the van was on the Jiffy Lube lift. The device was discovered, I presume. It suddenly stopped transmitting. Smashed, probably. I canna' attach another; they will but look for it again and I'll be trackin' a trash bin.

"But when the van returned Ah sauntered around to where the garage gives out onto the alley; there was no packing of the van. Ah'm assumin' they will no' be leavin' tomorra. But Ah will be in surveillance mode tomorrow beginning at eight a.m. Ah will be in touch with you." He dug into his trouser pocket and withdrew a flip phone. "My phone number is programmed in; it's the only one in there. Can you call me? Then Ah will have this one as well as your personal phone number. Use this one to get in touch with me." He drew a charger out of his pocket and handed that to her too. "Ah've downloaded two maps: one to a Marriott closest to the target residence and another from there to the residence. This flip phone doesn't have browsing capacity so I'll have to send them to your personal smartphone. If they do run tomorrow you may have to do a lotta' driving to catch them up. But otherwise, you'll drive up to Oswego at your leisure. When you arrive, you give me a call and we'll meet in the hotel parking lot for some tips on how to tail. Then we'll drive over to the target residence; next morning you're on your own. Get there by eight. Watch the alley. At some point a venerable old green van with pink trim will exit the garage. That would be them. Then off you go."

"OK. So, I follow them. They're going somewhere southwest—Santa Fe, Sedona, Scottsdale, Phoenix, Tucson—and when I get there, I figure out how to keep following them until they hook up with a gallery where they peddle their mask. Then what do I do?"

"You'll check in with me whenever you need to do so. They may stop along the way, as you say, to pick up the full complement of items."

"Meanwhile you follow this—Cricencia-Jane person?"

"Aye. And if my intuition is correct, she will not be far behind. Probably by plane, then by rental car."

"And your intuition has been pretty good, so far."

"Aye. I was indeed thankful for it when I followed Jane to the museum, then switched and tailed those two, first in the museum, then up to what turned out to be their actual place of residence. If I'd gone back to following her, I would ha'e lost the whole caboodle. I was sore puzzled at the time until I found "Cannings'" on line with the address and talked with your good employers the next day. And your observations were indeed crucial in putting the last piece of this puzzle into place. But my intuition said, 'Keep your eye on Cricencia' and once again, it paid off, when she and her friend went off on the train with her precious luggage."

"Which you saw them carry in and not carry out, therefore leaving it with the imposters."

Ferguson nodded. "Aye. Which they left with the imposters. And which my intuition says they will transport to one of the Mimbres miscreants. The imposters are now fronting for Cricencia, and are going to try to flog the mask to them."

"So, you're staking out Cricencia's place on Long Island until she makes a move."

"Which I expect she will do shortly after she gets word from the imposters that they are on the road."

Zoe decided she would have to drive back to Connecticut tonight; she would pack up, then drive back tomorrow morning before daybreak, pick up Ellie's Honda, and load everything into it.

11

ZOE STOOD AT THE WINDOW, with curtains open, that looked out on the patch of weedy grass that the management ludicrously, she thought, described as the apartment building's interior "courtyard," invisible now in the night's dark. She mused on the significance of how she intended to change her life. She needed to give herself a little pep talk. *For five years you've done what other people told you to do. And more than that, she thought, you've basked? No, wallowed in the attention that he thought he was showering on you. But really, you were showering attention on him, mistaking his sanguine acceptance of it as approval of you. Now, there's a chance of slipping away from all that, from him. Not so much overthrowing him and his priorities and the life you've thought you've built with him but actualizing the life you've built for yourself using him as a willing prop. He doesn't see that you've been building a launch pad, extending out from him into another world, another universe, another dimension. Yes, you have to change your life.*

So physical movement translates into spiritual, emotional, intellectual movement. He'll go on as he has always been doing, or at least as I've known him to have been doing. Or, more to the point, as I haven't known him to have been doing, but only surmised he was. Now I know.

She turned away from the dark window that only partially reflected her image back to her. Would she, should she, leave him a note? Write an outline of what she would say? Fix a cup of coffee so she could stay up until he eased his way into the apartment, assuming he was also easing his way back into her, their life, at midnight or one or two in the morning when she knew he would return?

No, I've tried that. I've tried to talk to him. He always shut me down. So why would it be any different this time? Tadpole grows legs. Egg hatches chick. Butterfly emerges from its chrysalis. All these stupid analogies. How about soul accomplishes lift-off and takes body with it?

She turned away from the window, then sat down at the small desk and hand-wrote the letter. She knew it would be a long one:

Dear, Dear Nick,

Yes, you know what this letter is going to say. I'm leaving: you, the flat, Weston, Croton Corners, Cannings', the Murrays. Well, maybe not quite the Murrays, but physically I'm leaving the job. You can have what's left of the weed. You can have everything that I haven't taken or shipped out to Washington. You knew this was going to happen. Maybe even wanted it to happen, made it happen by goading me into making a choice: continuing to be your ever-faithful, unquestioning companion, your loyal fan, your appendage, your "girl Friday," or to do something else.

It's not that I don't love you. Or at least I love what you've been to me and represented for me.

Now Zoe couldn't help but start sobbing; tears flowed freely.

So much of those early times when we were together you made me feel radiant, sexy, erotic, sensual. I was a little bit of a chunker, wasn't I? You were athletic, elastic, firm. In Paris—was it in the Pompidou?—when we saw the Degas dancers, the little girls, with their strong, beautiful legs, you said I looked like one of them. But I didn't! I wasn't quite a Rubens, but I resolved I would look like a Degas dancer. Kung Fu tightened me up, gave me form, balanced me. I thought, "Well, good. I'll become what he beheld. We'll be such a great team!"

And the more I learned from you, the more it seemed I was getting more in balance: What I was beginning to know was getting piled on one end of the scale while what I was beginning to know how to do was getting piled on the other. The more I learned, the more pleased I got with the moves I could make with my body. And the more I fell in love with you. At least, I thought I was falling in love with you.

Our trip to what you called "the high points of art," to study brush strokes of all things, was what really cinched me to you, plastered me right up against you, made me want to be your herbal rub. For me, looking at the art and looking at you were the same thing: I looked at you and I looked at the art and I felt the same violent restlessness and awe, a change in rhythm, a deliberate altering of lifeline that was wild with desire, with endless possibilities, with passion that brought shocks, tremors, a kind and protective carnage that spewed destruction over all the mundane, functional, ho-hum robotics of the hamburgerism, the macmansionism, the wonderbreadism of the everyday American life that I'd experienced up until then. You brought me to different countries, different dialogues with new characters from the daring world of art, edgy even in its canonical classicism: cherub pissing on Venus, men's faces made of vegetables, madonnas with swelling boobs, teeny future queens with jowls like prize-fighters, Zorah-faced heroines of shipwrecks, celebrations of women with butts the size of barrels. It was like a certain kind of dream lay waiting among the messages conveyed from those actions, those faces, those emotions welling out from the paintings. There were doors to be opened, adventures to be had behind them in the stories of the making of the paintings. Those stories were passionate, dangerous, enticing, seductive, all engulfing. That's what you introduced me to.

When we got back, it was that academic year that really launched me. I mean, you really launched me. Do you remember? That was the year we read Justine together. You said Durrell probably modeled her on a combination of his second wife, Anaïs Nin, and June Miller. But I always was thinking secretly, "That's me. That's the way I want to be." Except for all that political crap she got herself into. But then we got really naughty and read Henry and June! I'd stopped wearing bras but then you gave me a whole set for "Happy Solstice" day and said, "Let's do what June did. Cut the tips out of them so your nipples show though like June did for Henry Miller." And we did. And you had me go around the flat like that.

Zoe's tears gave way to giggles.

We had easy companionship; we relaxed into a really pleasurable place. You gifted me those tattoos for Valentine's Day! "Everybody needs a birthmark," you said. "But all you have is vaccination marks!" So, were those tattoos my rebirth?

But then you started periodically disappearing. To where? At first, your vanishing for a few days, the frenzy of your preparations, the grandiose schemes you hinted at were exciting. You would often return long after I was asleep from weed and wine, late Sunday night or in the wee hours of Monday morning. Sometimes you even cancelled class or arranged for a guest discussion leader—sometimes it was me. I was so flattered, so jazzed, so thrilled to be your substitute while you went off somewhere important.

But you would never say where to, even when I got hot under the collar, teary-eyed. Even when I was belligerent and started calling your absences your "trips to your other wife," you kept so cool. You always just smiled and said, "Hey—I'm consulting!" But you would never share with me where or with whom, and wouldn't tell me until almost the last minute, no matter how much I fumed. Sometimes I felt like I wanted to smash a plate of tomato and mushroom pasta over your head!

Nick, I began to feel you pulling away.

Hot tears assaulted her cheeks again.

We have more to reveal to one another. But that can't happen if I'm only your little thing on the side, providing cover to you as you go your merry way authenticating. You'll tell me all about it once I have my degree? and we're out of this two-bit town? and you know you have a commitment from me? give my commitment to an enigma? Hah! Hardly! You take life too cavalierly; you crash around with too much recklessness. You have your secret inner self that's tied to your career as the yay-or-nay-sayer of authenticity for the paintings with the stories that were so passionately dangerous, enticing, seductive for me. Now, you quash those stories.

I need my independent life, too. I can't pretend that my passivity is a good fit for your bravado. You say you want me to be your collaborator. But, then, who is my collaborator? Isn't it fair that I take a position from which I can keep pace with you? I can only do that if I set about building my own life. If I'm only your girl Friday, I can't do that. I won't ever do that. I'll never know how to have my own life. So now I have to say goodbye, now. Now.

I have a three-year fellowship in the PhD program in art history at University of Washington, with the possibility of applying for funding to travel if I need to do so for my dissertation. I also have an opportunity to do some work in connection with Cait and Robb Murray's business, beginning right now. It involves travel. So, I'm leaving now to do that and to get on the road to Washington state. I can't let you set a course for both of us, I'm sorry. I have to set my own. Life is filled with unrevealed possibilities, with unknown, unidentifiable notes vibrating somewhere and I want to find them and tune into them. I want to see all that might confront me as wild, metamorphosing, unknown mysteries to be entered and explored.

Dear Nick, you launched me and now I want to do the rest myself. You can text me, or not; phone me or not; email me or not. But please, please know that what you have shown me a kind of love that enters through the eyes, something that overwhelmed me, and has stayed with me, and that now I must engage that magical process on my own.

Love, truly, in every conceivable way, but also, firmly, Goodbye. Zoe.

She knew the letter was idiosyncratic, even perhaps slightly incoherent in spots. But was he going to grade it? No! Would he understand it? Hopefully. Would he appreciate it? Well, hard to say. *He must know he and I are living in fragments, illuminated in the distorting mirrors within ourselves,* she thought. *Can I continue on in those mirrors, another fragment? No!*

She doused her face in cold water at the kitchen sink. She left the note on the table, with a fat rolled joint and a wineglass beside it.

12

WHY COULDN'T THEY HAVE SPRUNG *for a nice, comfortable motel?* grumped Zoe.

She had arranged the boxes so that she could crawl into the back seat and just about stretch out in her sleeping bag with her head in the corner and her feet on a box in the other corner. But she hadn't counted on their barreling along without even a visit to a drive-thru since three o'clock; she had watched one of them pop out of the van—the woman—and go into the Walmart; return; pop back in, so her companion could do the same, which he did. She suspected it was a potty break.

Zoe had heard from Ferguson Saturday mid-morning, just as she was bringing the last of her two papers to a close. He told Zoe he had watched as Jen and Thad had taken turns carrying suitcases, a box of paper towels, a vintage picnic basket, a cooler, two sleeping bags, a couple of blankets and pillows, a hanging wardrobe, a couple of boxes with who-knows-what in them into the garage; presumably they all went into the van.

"You were that close, to see all that?" Zoe had queried.

"No, a very powerful telephoto lens on a camera brought me close."

He had told her to meet as soon as she could do so. She had quickly packed all her worldly goods into boxes, then trotted over to Tess's place, leaving her the key. She promised to ship whatever she found still in Zoe's apartment to the Department of Art and Art History, University of Washington. Then she had piled as much as she could into her little VW, including a sleeping bag and satchel with clothes for the road, driven to Ellie's, transferred everything into the Honda, signed the transfer ownership papers, bid a quick goodbye to Ellie, and driven to Oswego, stopping at the Marriott. She had phoned him on the burner when she arrived at the Marriott.

Ferguson had insisted she meet him in the restaurant at five thirty for a quick breakfast the following morning. Then they went out to the parking lot and he gave her a short course in tailing: always stay a few cars back; do not pass unless you absolutely have to do so; if they exit and take a right turning, you take a left turning and figure out how to circle and follow up; if they park, you circle, hover, but don't let them see you.

Now, an exhausting seventeen hours later, in the Walmart parking lot, she would have to retrace her route to the Burger King back out on the interstate for yet another burger and fries and for her potty break and return; she would have to hope that they were planning to overnight in the parking lot.

⟋

MONDAY, 5:30 AM

Zoe roused herself at first light; she could do nothing but sit in the car. She thought about entering Walmart to use the bathroom, but decided she couldn't risk it. They could easily spot her, even though she thought they would not know she was following them unless and until they spotted her entering Walmart and then somehow noticed her in the car. She decided she had to risk it. She had slept in her clothes. She scrambled out of her sleeping bag in the back seat and into the front, started the car, and drove slowly, cautiously down a lane far removed from where the green van was parked. She stopped at the entrance on the other side of the building.

When she emerged, got back into the car, and again drove to her surveillance spot, she was relieved to see there was no activity at the van. It was another two hours before their taking turns to the bathroom from the previous night was repeated. Then it was back on the interstate; but at Hays, Kansas, they turned off onto a two-lane secondary road, taking it south. Zoe took the same exit, but headed north; after five minutes she turned around. This would be trickier; they could be the only people on the road, or close to it, except for local traffic. But fortunately, nearly all roads in Kansas were arrow-straight and the terrain was all but flat; she spotted them as she came up on a small rise. She fell back, certain she would have no trouble tracking them. She popped a Bee Gees CD into the player.

⤴

MONDAY, 8:35 PM
KANSAS

The vanners ended up on US 50 and stopped just outside Garden City, Kansas, at a rest area. It was pleasant, green, warmish. The intermittent rain had been left behind at Lawrence and now the skies were clear. A sign proclaimed, "Overnight parking permitted" and "Camping permitted." Zoe continued past it; the van was parked in a space. Only one other car was at the rest stop: a peculiar boxy little car, but long. It reminded her of a package of Rollos. It was yellow with a brown top. *Is it a Mini—maybe an old one?* she wondered. *A station wagon?*

This would be a problem. She could not stop at that rest area; it was too small. *If I stop here, I'll be spotted, for sure,* she thought. But she now thought she knew where they were headed. There wasn't much traffic; Zoe opened her smartphone and consulted Google maps. She knew now they would stay on

50 for a while; and either they would, at some point, head south on I-25 to Santa Fe, or continue on to Albuquerque, then head west on I-40, and then go south again to Scottsdale or Phoenix, or possibly Sedona, on 17. But what if they fooled her? Turned off again at some dinky road? Whew!

She could go on to the next town, get a room, ask for a 5:00 a.m. wake-up call, and lie in wait at the next lay-by until they passed, then follow. The next town was Granada, Colorado. She parked in front of the Holly Inn; it would do.

~⟳

TUESDAY, 6:30 AM
GRANADA, COLORADO

She parked on a side street and chose a café on the main street, which was US 50. She sat at a table facing the large window. She ordered her first decent meal: coffee with half and half, eggs over medium, breakfast steak, hash browns, English muffin with butter and jam. Then suddenly, in a space right outside the window, there it was! Not the van, but the funny little car. And it was indeed a Mini. Out of it climbed a slender young man, with full hair that looked a little like hers except all brown, and a trimmed brown beard to match. He was dressed in Levi's jeans and a Levi's jean jacket over a turquoise shirt with pearl snaps, not buttons. He came through the door, closed it, surveyed the dining room. His eyes locked with Zoe's. *Hell*, thought Zoe, *two days with not a single conversation with a living soul except harried servers at drive-thrus and several thirty-second conversations with Ferguson?* She smiled at him. He smiled back. He came over. "Is this seat taken?" he asked.

~⟳

His name was Phil—Phil Backstrom. He was two years older than she, a graduate student pursuing a PhD in anthropology at Indiana University, and described himself as an "ethnologist, doing a comparative study of the designs on the contemporary pottery of eight artists at three Pueblos." Zoe itched to ask him about prehistoric Mimbres pottery but decided that would just be too much for what was turning out to be a pleasant "this-is-who-I-am-who-are-you" conversation. He was, in fact, on his way out to the Pueblos for his second season of fieldwork.

Before she knew what she was doing, she was spilling everything about herself that was now self-affirming: her thesis that she needed to finish before August, the fellowship to continue that research at University of Washington, the highlights of her coursework. He had originally enrolled at Indiana to do linguistic anthropology, was fluent in German and competent in French from a year abroad, and his professors had recognized the talent Phil had for languages. But a funding opportunity for research with the material culture of Native Americans had turned up and Phil had suddenly switched his interest. Now he was hooked. "Have you ever been to Europe?" he asked.

That question led to her lyrical recounting of the eight weeks of traveling, eating, learning, and—yes—loving with Nick in Europe. She thought she was over it; but she wasn't. When she mentioned Nick, her voice wavered and she recognized hot tears starting to well. "Excuse me," she said, standing quickly, throwing her napkin on the table, turning heel. "I've got to go to the bathroom." She realized when she sat that she really did; it was finally a relief after two days. But the tears continued to spill. *What a mess*, she thought. When she splashed her face with water at the sink and looked in the mirror, she realized she was not so much a mess: roundish face with a nose that she now thought was a bit Kim Kardashian-like: blond highlighted frizzy hair that looked okay even when mussed, pretty good curves up top, latte colored skin. And she'd been holding her own in terms of "interesting conversationalist" until just a few minutes ago. She took a deep breath. She would tell him about her breakup with Nick; it would underscore the independence that she was now honing.

She bracketed the Nick breakup with a sort of "daily life" run-down of life as an undergraduate, living with a knowledgeable, worldly, popular teaching assistant who could make art and artists come alive in the classroom, with whom she shared mutual interests and the savoring of shared tastes, who was easy to live with but who, as she explained, had moved farther and farther from constituting a significant part of her destiny. She talked about her weekly commutes to Croton, about the generosity and sturdy dependability of Cait and Robb, about the unique, quirky food she served at the Cat and Custard, about how she had considered a career in the antiques and collectibles field. She told him about Ellie and the car.

And that led her to what in cartoon art was a "light bulb" moment. He could help her. He could help her tail. Yes, he would stand out like a sore thumb. But in that underpowered Mini, trundling along behind the green van would not seem untoward; meanwhile, she could pass them both, speed ahead, and disappear, rendezvousing with Phil someplace and sometime later, after he had tracked the vanners to their next stopping point. But how much could she, should she tell him without telling whopping lies or coming across as suspiciously secretive? She decided a slightly varnished truth was her best bet.

"And actually," she continued, "I'm doing more than just meandering out to U Wash."

"Well, yeah, I thought so. You're not exactly making a straight shot. You're obviously planning some detours. To some of the monuments? Sand Dunes? Mesa Verde? Chaco Canyon?"

"Well, no ... I'm kind of, like, keeping an eye on a couple of people, as a favor to the Murrays—the people I told you about."

"Who run the shop."

"Right. Who run the shop." And she told him about the incident at Cait's and Robb's, casting it as so distinctly peculiar it had come to the attention of a private investigator. The insurance investigator, in turn, had fingered the mysterious burglars as suspicious. Here she had to embellish a bit: he thought the burglars had probably somehow hacked the Murrays' computer files and were now on their way to an unknown destination to wreak some havoc on one of their suppliers from the Southwest. It was them that she was following, a couple in a van. She told him about the insurance investigator's short-lived surveillance of the couple that had turned up, only the revelation that they were leaving, and that they probably had a Native American ritual object with them. Well, she was leaving too, so, she told Phil, she had decided she might as well take the same route as they. She told him about seeing them turn into the Garden City camping lay-by.

"They stole this ritual object from your employers? And so, you're like, tailing them?"

"No, no." She shook her head. "I mean, yes, I'm tailing them. But they didn't steal the ritual object from my employers. My employers would never, never traffic in something like that. Having something like that would actually contravene the Native American Graves Protection and Repatriation Act."

"Ah!" interjected Phil. "NAGPRA!"

"Right. Anyway, they got it from someone they met at the American Museum of Natural History, someone that my employers were going to rendezvous with, but which never happened. They … the vanners, the couple in the van, more or less, like, kind of hijacked the rendezvous, and impersonated my employers, Robb and Cait Murray. Then the person they met brought this ritual object to them, to their home in upstate New York. But anyway, my employers, Cait and Robb, might be kind of implicated in some kind of underhanded dealings with this ritual object. So that's why I'm tailing them, to kind of, like, get the full story." She could tell he was not exactly buying it, but that he could not think of a credible objection her tale.

"But isn't it dangerous? If they're criminals?"

"Nah! It's a doddle. It's a lark. These people aren't dangerous." She could see he was skeptical, to say the least. Then to take him away from what might be yet another objection, she conjured up her letter to Nick, again sparing him details, but presenting it as her "dear-John-goodbye" letter to him. Tears welled. Her lips trembled. Her voice quavered. "Besides, this tailing … it, like, takes my mind off…"

"Ah!" said Phil. He nodded. "I get it."

She thought he probably really didn't, but that he thought she was a good-looking enough thing to go along with her non-explanation.

"So … so, once you track them to their destination, then what?"

Zoe shrugged. "I don't know. Maybe see what they do, where they go. Like I said, it's a lark, a diversion."

"Will you file a report?'"

She grinned. "Yeah. I'll call Ferguson—that's the investigator—and tell him. Then that'll be it. Hey—you could help. You want to?"

"Huh? How?"

"Well, like, I'm getting kind of tired just dawdling along. Like, this car I've got—it's a pretty new Honda Civic. You know, gifted to me by Ellie. I'd like to really *drive* it, not just pedal along behind *them*."

"Yeah…"

"And, well, your Mini—what year is it?"

"It's a 1968, and it's a real one. An Austin Mini station wagon. It's kind of rare. It was gifted to me, too, from my uncle. He bought it in England, had it shipped over. He stopped driving it ten years ago but kept it in mint condition. Actually, he was my father's uncle, conked off at age ninety-five three years ago, left it to me in his will—along with a lot of books."

"Okay. Well, it really can't go very fast, right?"

"It *shouldn't* go real fast."

"Yeah. Well, their old van doesn't go very fast, either. You could poke along behind them and they wouldn't think anything of it. While me, sooner or later, they're going to notice me. But I speed ahead, pass both of you. You know how many meals I haven't had? How many cups of coffee I haven't drunk because I can't afford a potty stop, have to keep on their tail? I thought this game would be easy, but it's got its downers. I could use a day off! If you need a break, I could probably figure out how to spell you without getting caught."

"Okay, so let's say we do that, then what?"

"Well, once you track them to where they stop, you and I rendezvous somewhere." She could have merely said, *we'll be in touch by phone, but I really wanted to actually see him again.* "You go back and keep an eye on them. You've got a really good car to sleep in; I don't. I've gotta cram myself into the back seat. It'd be nice to have another night in a real motel."

"Yeah. Okay. I see. Yeah, I'm sleeping in my car anyway."

"You'll do it?"

He shrugged. "Sure! Why not? I'm up for it!"

"Great! I'll give you my phone number." She gave him her smartphone number, not the burner number. Phil reached around and took his phone out of his jacket pocket. "You wanna take mine?"

"My phone's in the car. But text me, and then I'll have yours."

They had spent nearly two hours in the café. Now Zoe glanced up. "Ooops! There they are!" Zoe spotted the green van coming to a slow halt at the stop sign. "Let's boogie!" She stood up, took her billfold out of her back pocket, threw a ten down on the table. Phil did the same but threw a twenty. Zoe found a five and threw it down. They charged out the door. "Thanks!" they yelled to the wait staff.

"Okay. There they are."

"Got it," said Phil. "See you on the road!"

13

ZOE HAD INDEED SPED AHEAD. She and Phil talked by phone a couple of times, but there were no surprises. Zoe stopped for a burger in La Junta, where she also made another potty stop and picked up four turkey-and-cheese sandwiches plus two bags of BBQ chips and four fizzy lemon waters at a Kum-and-Go. It was sunny and warm. She was quite sure that the vanners would go on to turn south onto I-25.

She was not in a spot where she could really see or be seen from the highway but, just to be safe, she pulled around where she would be out of sight if, by chance, the vanners had the same idea she had had. She was sure they would turn off 50, undoubtedly to a feeder road, route 71, which would take them to Trinidad and the junction with I-25; then on to Santa Fe. So she was surprised when Phil called and told her they had indeed turned off 50, but onto a road that was even smaller than 71: route 10. She waited another ten minutes at the junction, then turned onto 10. She whizzed along until suddenly, she saw Phil's Mini a few hundred yards ahead; she fell back and followed a couple of miles behind.

The vanners stopped in Walsenburg. Zoe consulted her smartphone. *They're most likely going to continue west on 160, then go over La Veta Pass and come down into Taos*, she reasoned. *So, Taos is the destination! Not Santa Fe!* Phil phoned. "They're stopping in front of a little restaurant. The woman went in; the guy is still in the van. They must be getting take-out." But five minutes later Phil reported that the woman was still in the café. There was a park more or less across the street which was where Phil was.

"Hey—is there someplace I could park without them seeing?" asked Zoe.

"Sure. You can park a block or two away. There's a park more or less across the street from the restaurant."

"Then why don't I do that. As soon as I see your car I'll circle and find a spot to park. I bought some sandwiches and chips. Are there tables? We could picnic. They wouldn't see my car. Can we sit at a table where we can see them but they can't see us?"

"Yeah—I think so. Sounds good! See you in the park."

1:10 PM
WALSENBURG, COLORADO

Thad came out of the restaurant and handed Jen a menu. She looked at it for less than a minute. "Okay," she said. "You go on in. Have yourself a nice meal. But bring me out a doggie bag first: the enchilada combination plate with red sauce, with the side of sopapillas. You can tell them I have this bad cold and I don't want to infect everybody."

"Right. Good. Be sure to slide the bar on this side and lock it."

"Get me a side of cole slaw, too. And a large coke."

Thad came back fifteen minutes later with Jen's take-out. She rolled down the window. He handed it in to her. "Enchiladas, fried, sopa—whatever they are, cole slaw. My chicken should be up soon."

Twenty minutes later Thad returned. "Sorry. I had the broiled half a chicken with po-something. It took a while."

"Posole. That's okay, but hey—I have to pee. And I can't go in there if I've got this bad cold and don't want to infect everybody."

Thad turned in his seat and pointed. "There's a porta-potty over there in the park."

"Ah!" said Jen, hopping out of the car. "I'll be right back."

Zoe and Phil polished off their sandwiches and a bag of chips each and shared a 55 percent dark, non-GMO fair trade chocolate bar; Ellie had loaded her down with a dozen of them, four different flavors, three each. They chatted some more about themselves; Phil told her more about what he called his "fieldwork."

"The Pueblos are like little oases from the nineteenth century. Most have electricity and piped water—although some don't—and TV antennas and all that, but the houses are all one or two stories, the roads aren't paved, and there's nothing commercial—no neon signs, no billboards, just some little curio and craft shops and a couple little grocery stores. In some villages, there's not even that. The one where one of my pottery ladies lives, once you get into the village itself, away from the road, there's no electricity. Everybody has propane refrigerators and stoves, although some people still prefer to cook and heat with wood. There's no plumbing—outhouses—and not even what you could call roads. One day after it'd rained, I saw a woman with a couple cooking pots in one of those little red wagons kids used to have; she had a ladle and was ladling water from some holes in a huge rock outcrop into the cooking pots! I mean, like, that was her water supply!"

"Wow! That's unbelievable! In the twenty-first century!"

"Yeah. Even my pottery lady has to go out to a stock pond once a week and fill a garbage can with water. She and her husband then wrestle it back into the house."

"Is it okay to drink? The water"?

"Well, when I visit, I always bring a six-pack of pop, offer her one, drink one, leave the rest."

"They must be really poor."

"No, not at all. Not really. It's…"

Zoe noticed Phil staring past her. She started to turn around to see what he was staring at.

"No, no! Don't turn around!"

"What?"

"It's one of the vanners. She's heading this way. Uh-oh. Oh … no, wait— she's heading for the port-a-potty."

"Oh, shit," said Zoe. "She must have seen us."

"Just sit tight. Don't look."

"Right. Okay. Let's just keep chatting. We'll be really into each other and our conversation."

The woman exited the port-a-potty and made strides toward the van. She glanced over at the table where Zoe and Phil were sitting. When the woman had gotten back into the van and Zoe Phil were hastening to their respective vehicles, Phil confided to Zoe: "I hate to tell you, but that woman's gaze lingered just a little longer than mere curiosity would warrant."

As they parted, Zoe admitted, "Okay, so maybe we've been spotted. But there's nothing we can do; you've got to keep on them. I'll meet you somewhere in Taos. But I'll take a different road, if I can figure one out." Her smartphone showed a road from Cimarron. *I'll have to backtrack to I-25,* she thought, *then take it south until it hits the turn-off. It'll probably take me longer than it would take the vanners and Phil. And will there be cell towers? Might have to wait until she was actually in Taos to get in touch with Phil.*

4:40 PM

She had just come through the ski resort of Eagles Nest and was coming down off the mountain when "Respect" sounded. "They're not staying in Taos," said Phil. "They went into the La Fonda Hotel, separately—first she went in and came back out about twenty minutes later and then he went in and came back about fifteen minutes later. Now they're back in the van. They were only in there thirty-five minutes total."

"Huh?"

"Don't ask me!" said Phil. "But I guess I'll follow."

He did call her again an hour later. "Weird," he said. "They just came into Española and went through town, and now they've turned back north heading for Abiquiú. But hey, this is my stomping grounds! Two of the Pueblos I'm studying are right here."

"What do you think they're doing?"

"Don't know. I'll call you when they finally settle."

Also now coming into Española, Zoe decided to wait in a Walmart parking lot until she heard again from Phil. In the meantime, she decided to google the La Fonda Hotel. She got four hits, but they were all for a La Fonda in Santa Fe. She amended the search for Taos. She got ten hits. She chose the Trip Advisor. It got good reviews. *Why aren't they staying there? And what did they do there for thirty-five minutes? Were they meeting their contact—the Jane person? Aha! The La Fonda has a historic collection of "erotic" paintings by D.H. Lawrence. So, they made a detour for dirty art! Amazing!*

Her phone insisted. It was a text: *pulld into campgrnd looks lik ther staying I will 2*

Zoe texted back: *ok I to friend coco sf call u when ther*

TUESDAY, 9:15 PM
SANTA FE, NEW MEXICO

As soon as Phil had given the vanners' location, Zoe called Coco. Zoe followed the directions given her by Ellie, who had told her Coco would be expecting her sometime that day or the next. "Come right along," Coco said. "I'll have crackers and hummus and baba ganoush. Are you vegan? ... No? All right, I'll have Neil's yard cheddar and turkey pepperoni as well. And hot cocoa! And also, some pleasant Chablis." Coco and Zoe were not strangers; when she had lived with Ellie for nearly seven years in Massachusetts, Ellie and Coco had had an art-and-frame shop together; they also sold some pieces of twentieth century art on consignment for clients. Zoe had been in and out of the shop on an almost daily basis and frequently Ellie, Coco, and Zoe took their evening meals together.

Now, she gratefully munched the snacks.

"I know some details of the kerfuffle with your employers—what are their names?"

"The Murrays."

"Yes. I got the potted story of why you're here, and what you're doing, and what it has to do with the Murrays' unfortunate experience, and why you're going out to Washington early and that she has given you her Civic. But Ellie was a little unclear on exactly what you were going to do once you got here."

Zoe thought with nostalgia of her tired, old, very used Jetta; somehow it seemed a more appropriate vehicle, teamed with Phil's Austin Mini, for this part of the adventure and this part of the world than Ellie's Civic. "Well," responded Zoe, "it's kind of a complicated story. And now it's even more complicated since I've met Phil and he's volunteered to help."

"Phil?"

"Yeah. Yes. He's ... he's a friend that I've ... I've kind of met on the road, like, and..."

"Oh! He could have stayed here, you know. Where is he?"

"Well, that's what I mean. He's helping out. He's giving me a break by keeping an eye on the couple—you know, the ones we think did the damage to the Murrays. He's at the same campground they are; we're keeping in touch by phone. Oh! Which reminds me. I've been charging it from the car battery but I should really plug it in and check in with him—and also with the guy I'm working with. Or for. The investigator."

"Yes, and you need a shower and a good night's rest. Why don't we pick up the details of the story tomorrow? Over a good breakfast? Say, nine thirty? We'll go out. I'll phone Pascal's and make a reservation."

She rose and led Zoe though the living room, past a little kitchen, and into a very small room, a kind of conservatory, with what looked like a potted lemon tree and several schleffleras, with French doors giving out, probably, onto a garden. Zoe picked up her suitcase, slung her rucksack—it was a real one, partially leather, that she had gotten in Bavaria—over one shoulder, and dragged her sleeping bag behind. "You won't need that," said Coco, gesturing to the sleeping bag. Zoe saw there was a small day bed in the conservatory. "And this is not luxury but there's a tin shower, sink and toilet just through there."

14

A FIGURE DANCED IN PLACE, its knees high-stepping, fluttering a
dress or kilt decorated with marks—some sort of symbols? The figure raised a
stick in its left hand as it danced, a wand with something—feathers? yarn?—
attached to the top. As the stick was raised, slowly—more slowly, it seemed,
than the figure's knees going up and down, up and down, a long, slow, high-
pitched "woo-woo"-ing sound emanated from its mouth. But it was not a
human mouth; it was an animal mouth, surrounded by a face speckled with
dots, topped by a mop of feathers. The figure danced and flapped its kilt and
raised its wand and issued its cry, that rose to a high pitch then subsided,
then rose again.

The figure danced at the corner of Jen's vision, just out of reach of full
view. Then she blinked. She realized she had been dreaming. The figure
was gone. But the sound remained. Jen stirred in her bag. She was aware
of warmth: not the kind of warmth that she felt on most mornings in the

big, decaying, drafty house on Lake Ontario that made her want to revel in snugness, to drift back into a doze while heat gradually wafted up from the ancient furnace's octopedal tentacles up to the second floor. No, this heat was more like the beginning of a toasting, a slow almost-burn, accompanied by a pinkish white light that whispered, "Get up! Rise and shine!"

Jen opened her eyes. The "woooo" cry rose and fell. She struggled to the window on the other side of the van, her elbows stumbling over Thad, who grunted. Jen shuddered despite the warmness. She drew back the curtains—curtains that she had cut from muslin, stitched, and mounted onto tension rods—that lined the van's windows all the way around.

Thad grunted "hmff." Jen squinted as she peered out into the bright sunlight apparently radiating from an as-yet-invisible sun. Blue and red lights flashed on and off, round-and-round, on and off, round-and-round; emergency vehicles, several hundred yards away, going up the paved road down which they had come the night before—how many hours ago? "Oh!" she exclaimed quietly. "Garrgff" said Thad. The vehicles and their sirens disappeared.

She slumped back, half way out of her sleeping bag, and rolled to the other set of windows on *her* side, propping chin in hands, moving back the curtain with her head. Sky. She saw sky, sky and mountains, or at least hills, dark shadows over which the sun's rays were just beginning to stream. Fluffy layers of pink topped the shadows: globs of strawberry marshmallow cream that had escaped their container, floating away from a mound of fudge into which somebody had stuck tufts of green sugar crystals, dipping dots. And then, between the pink marshmallow and the dark fudge appeared the blazing sun. It made her think of the blues song about the house of the rising sun in New Orleans, also of Conrad's trite metaphor of the wafer pasted in the sky, so ridiculed by Mr. McCafferty, her high school English teacher.

The van's interior really was heating up. She leaned toward the third wall: the van's rear windows. Here, when she drew back the curtain, she saw clear forms: a picnic table perilously close to where they had parked, the red-dust road they had driven in on, and another, much smaller form which bore no resemblance to fudge and dipping dots but looked like just what it was: a hillock with tufts of grass and miniature cactuses on its flanks, some with yellow flowers, some with magenta. Wedged into the hillock were horizontal layers of rock, varying from yellowish through red to deep brown. Jen thought they resembled somebody's attempt to shove pizza dough into a too-small oven: the layers were crumpled and folded like elephant skin.

Marshmallow? Fudge? Wafer? Pizza? Jen realized: *I'm hungry!* She briefly reflected: *What was the figure that had danced and dipped, gestured and gyrated, accompanied by a soundtrack from reality? It was the mask! The thing's emerged from the portmanteau, acquired life, and has entered my mind! But no—of course, that's impossible! It was just a dream.*

They had pulled into the campsite so late and so fatigued that they had not even bothered breaking out the now stale bread, ever hardening cheese, and increasingly greasy sopressata; they had just slid the bars and locked them, gotten out, crawled into the back, secured the backdoor lock bar, slid into sleeping bags, and instantly fallen into comatose slumber. The van was equipped with three sets of interior lock bar: one each on the driver's and passenger's doors and another two across the span of the back doors. They had had them installed, (reasoning that car alarms were useless; nobody paid any attention to them) before settling into Oswego, when they were itinerant antiques dealers, moving from fair to fair, from flea market to flea market, and had to store their wares in the van. The bars swung up on hinges and normally rested against the ceiling. They could lock them all with a single key, then shut and lock the doors. Anyone prying open the van's doors might be able to wriggle into the van if they had the body of a ten-year-old, but they would not be able to extricate the items stored in it through the bars. And as often as not, the goods would be piled on the two seats, and on the floor, and stored in the boxes, with plywood hinged tops, that formed the bed on which lay the sleeping bags from which Jen and Thad were just emerging. When locked into place, one of the back lock bars blocked the cabinet doors that gave access to the boxes from the rear when the van's back doors were open.

They had not used the lock bars for years, not since they acquired occupancy of the huge house as entrepôt, courtesy of Louie-the-landlord. But now the lock bars came in handy—more than handy. They were a necessity for peace of mind, now that the portmanteau with its $10,000 mask was stowed in the boxes underneath them.

"Jonathan!" she snapped sharply and elbowed the lump next to her.

The mound sat up "I told you never to use that name ever again!"

"Got your attention, didn't it? And it's fun to tease you. Hey—let's get going. Salami and cheese on stale bread is getting old. I want a real breakfast when we get to Santa Fe. We've always done the restaurant at lunch. But today I want a nice, good, real breakfast. Or at least a brunch with good coffee and nice eggs and crispy bacon."

"Okay, okay," said Thad. "And we've got to find a motel—even a flea-bag—where we can get spruced up before looking for Mr. Glenn Woodard."

"It's Mr. Woodard Glenn," corrected Jen. She slid out of the sleeping bag, pulled on her jeans and top, unlocked the rear lock bar, slid it down, opened the back doors, and dropped out onto the ground. Thad followed her. She slipped into the driving seat turning the key; Thad took the passenger side, hefting the old picnic basket onto his lap. "But for now, you want a liverwurst or a salami?"

The van started up with a roar. "I had a dream," said Jen. "I had a dream about the mask. It came alive. It was a real—what would you call it? A real spirit…"

But Thad had other things on his mind. "Hey," he said, as they exited the campground. "See that bearded guy loading that tent into the back of that Mini station wagon? I'm sure I saw him at that rest stop we slept at in Kansas." He frowned, turning around to spot the classic little Mini slowly also taking the turning south. Jen did not turn around to look. She was silent all the way into Española.

They wound slowly down a two-lane highway through the Rio Grande Valley, which occasionally narrowed to high, pinkish cliff walls on one side and the river on the other, then widened to farmland that seemed to be mostly orchards, then narrowed again. Every few miles there was an outpost of some sort—sometimes just a single house, at other times a little village, not infrequently a closed-up fruit stand. Huge trees, delicately swathed in light green leaves, lined the riverbank. They drove through Española, announced by billboards advertising Indian casinos. Traffic picked up once they were through the town and so did the speed limit; a four-lane highway took them up a moderately steep, long grade where first "flea market," then at the hill's crest, "Opera" were announced. They came down into Santa Fe without encountering any of the sleazy motels they were looking for; just the Sheraton Hotel, which Thad noted "couldn't be the only hotel in town? There must be a motel row, maybe on the other side of town."

Without knowing exactly where they were headed, they found themselves driving up a street that took them past a theater, a bar, five galleries, and an incongruous old-fashioned general store with a diner; it looked like they were going to circle a four-sided plaza with some sort of monument in its center. Jen turned right, then right again. Thad turned in his seat. "There was a restaurant back over there," he said, motioning with his hand behind Jen. But Jen was already continuing down the street. "That looks like a neat place." She pointed straight ahead of her.

One way street signs directed them several blocks out of their way before they could circle back to the restaurant Jen had spotted. "La Fonda Hotel," said Thad, pointing to his right. "I wonder if it's the same owners as the one in Taos."

"Doubt it," said Jen. "Remember the Taos La Fonda guy—Sacki, Thacki?—was a friend of Lawrence."

"It was a nice little detour," said Thad, settling back into the seat. They had circled back around. The "neat place" was on their right.

"Oh, look," said Jen. "There it is: Pascal's."

"Well, yeah, but look at the line coming out the door!" objected Thad.

"That means it's a really good place. I mean, it's not like we're starving now with that standard fair, ho-hum snack we had. It's worth standing in line for a really good breakfast. Look—if we find a parking place, let's do it." And they did so: a car was just pulling out of in front of a shop with the unlikely name of Doodlet's. Jen did a highly illegal U-turn and parked.

"Okay. It's your turn. Don't forget to feed the meter. I'll stick here," Thad said, pulling the bar into place and locking it. Jen exited. Thad undid his seat belt, leaned over and did the same to the driver's side lock bar, rolling down the window. "Bring me back some of those sopa things but something else that's not too messy. No congealed eggs."

Jen joined several people who were standing outside. A retired-looking man half turned to her and said cheerily, "Good morning!"

Hmm, thought Jen. *This could take a while.* "Is this the only place in town for breakfast?"

"No, but it's the best place; the breakfast is great," he said. "The home fries are homemade, nice big chunks with just the right browning and the chili rellenos are better than you want them to be: big Anaheims fried in egg batter on a griddle but without all that grease that they get coated with in other places. Coffee's fresh ground, fair trade, organic. Espresso or latte; cappuccino or regular. And it won't cost you the price of a five-course dinner. You should have been here ten minutes ago; the line was around the corner." *Indeed*, thought Jen. *A bunch of diners must have finished up and gotten a move on. More people let in.* But the line was still half a dozen deep.

As Jen resigned herself to a stomach-growling, still-too-long wait, she noted a young woman in black silk skirt, white linen jacket and ruffled blouse, wearing, of all things, a thin, red-striped necktie and a wine-red beret, who, accompanied by a much older woman decked out in what Jen could see was high-quality turquoise and silver, a gray raw silk jacket and an almost-hip-pie, full-length skirt decorated in multi-colored fish on a black background, squeezed past the line and entered the restaurant. "Hey—how come they get to jump the line?!" exclaimed Jen.

"Probably have a reservation," said her new-found friend. "I come here every day and I always get a table—except Sundays when I do make a reservation. But I'm usually here about 7:45 a.m. when there's a lull and today I just didn't get over here in time."

"Hmmm," said Jen. "Is there any other place nearby?"

"Yeah," said the man, "there's the Santa Fe Café." He gestured. "Just up the street, turn right, another block, and then left—it's right on the plaza. It's a big place so you'll get a table for sure. Greasy chili rellenos and stringy fries out of a package. Coffee's either watery or sludge."

9:29 AM
SANTA FE

The wait person sat them at a small table near the entrance, where they could see out a window.

Just then, Zoe's phone grumbled; she had put it on vibrate. Zoe dug in her left-hand jacket pocket. "Hey, Phil, where are you? … Yeah… They did? Holy moly… Why do you think so? … Oh … I'm at a place sort of around the corner, Pascal's… Just a sec; I'll check."

"Excuse me just a minute, Coco. I have to check on something." There was no line now; she walked outside, looked up and down the street, then took a few paces up the side street and there it was, parked: the green van. She thought she saw someone in the driver's seat; she nipped back into the restaurant.

She picked up the phone. "Hi … Yeah … I think it was her, actually on line when we arrived. We squeezed past her… I don't think so. I look really different—I mean, I'm not in tee and shorts and I'm wearing a beret. I think you're right; she got a really good look at both of us while we were sitting at that table yesterday in that Walton place … yeah, Walsenburg, at least good enough to recognize familiar images, like a young slim guy with a nice little beard and a short brown nut with frizzy brunette hair with blond bozo ends, chunky in a red tee, white shorts … I'm not? Thanks! Yes, well, they are pretty good. Didn't think you'd noticed… I don't know. This kind of blows it unless you can keep an eye on them and somehow, we can—I mean, Coco and I—that lady I told you about—can get a bead on them and tail them without them noticing… No. I'm in a different car—Coco's got a yellow VW bug… That's good, but it's going to delay you. Do you think she spotted you? Oh! You saw her in line here? Oh boy! And you decided to opt for the one a couple of blocks away and suddenly there she was walking in the door. Well, I don't know which is luckier or unluckier: that she didn't recognize me or that you did track them and she *did* see *you*! Okay, okay… Yeah. Stick with them, whatever. Their van is parked really close. At least one of us might still be incognito. Talk to you soon."

The wait person had brought them menus. To read the menu, Coco took a pair of glasses from an antique maroon glasses case that she had fished out of a woven bag, snatched up quickly as they were leaving the house—a bag remarkably like the one Zoe carried. In between giving Zoe a series of questioning looks she perused the menu and now the wait person, with a black apron, thin facial hair and a black, frizzy afro, stood at the side of the table, his stylus and tablet at the ready. "We'll start with coffee," said Coco. "A large double latte for me and…"

"Uh, actually a … just a regular coffee for me, with milk."

"Good," said the waitperson. "Half and half okay?" Zoe nodded. "I'll get those right out to you. Have you decided or do you want a little more time?"

"Oh, no," said Coco. "I'll have the chili relleno with green, bacon, home fries and sautéed mushrooms."

"The same," said Zoe. The wait person poured Zoe her coffee, then departed. Zoe took a deep breath, then a sip of her coffee. "I think Ellie told you about this couple that are impersonating my employers at the antique shop, apparently so they can get in on fencing some Native American art that they have in their van. The van is parked almost right in front of this place. My friend Phil followed them last night and they and he stayed in the same campground just outside Abiquiú. I told you about Phil, right? He followed them here and saw them park and figured they were headed for Pascal's and decided to head for another place he knows where he can get menudo, just kind of around the corner."

"Ah! That would be the Santa Fe Café," chimed in Coco.

"So, there he is, sitting right near the entrance, in a booth, and he had to park kind of far away so he thinks they didn't spot his car. He spotted the female half of the couple we're following in line here, just before we arrived. He thought she would stick here. BUT—there he is, sitting there at his table, chowing down on his menudo, reading Stieg Larson, and guess who walks in! Yep. Like, it's her! So, she was here, on line, when we first got here, but then she left; obviously she opted for the café where Phil's having his breakfast. Like, she's heading for a table kind of in the middle of the place and he looks up and she looks over and there they are suddenly making eye contact. He thinks she may have recognized him: the guy with the beard who's the same guy with the beard who was sitting with the chick at the table in the park across the street from where they had lunch last evening in Walsenburg, Colorado. Because, like, we were sitting there in the park, and we kind of thought, well they're in the restaurant, they're not going to come into the park or even look that way. But, like, then she pops out of the van and sprints into the park and over to the port-a-potty."

"And you were the chick."

"Right. It looks like they're going to try to interest gallery owners here in what they have so unless I stay housebound, there's some chance that we just might bump into them. I'm going to have to look as different from the chick sitting at the park bench or driving the silver Civic as I possibly can. Ergo the linen jacket—thanks for the loan—and the skirt, even if it is a bit rumpled. But now I've got to get my hair dyed totally dark. And now they've spotted him, Phil and I shouldn't be seen together. I just hope he can get out of that café and into his car and follow them without them catching on. Soooo—is there a hairdresser that can do me a dye job and straighten my hair? Get rid of these blondie tips?"

"Well, that's different," said Coco. "Usually people go from dark to blond. Not the other way around. But even if they do catch on, what would be the consequences?"

"I'm not sure. But I don't want to find out. Anyway, I'm counting on them not recognizing me, even though they might have recognized Phil."

"Maybe you can get the jump on them. Get one step ahead of them. At least narrow down the number of galleries they might be going to contact to do their sacrilegious act. Imagine! Trying to sell a religious object that is sacred? When Ellie told me that, I thought, now who in this town would be foolish enough to take on that task? But then I thought, well, maybe discretely offering it to select customers, that's a possibility. One that any number of gallery owners here might entertain."

"Yeah. That's all I know. They've got this item of Native American cultural patrimony and they've got some contact here that they're going to fence it to."

Coco held up her hand like a traffic cop and said, "I can help. I'm known here. After I sold the shop in Concord and Ellie moved to Croton Corners, you know, I had already inherited all that money from poor, dear Charlie, so I continued to dabble in brokering fine art. And I continued to do so after I moved here. There are a lot of people here who've come from someplace else and they're only superficially charmed by all the Pueblo and Navajo décor and accoutrement. They want just what I can supply for their Italianate villas tucked away in the hills here: tasteful oils by competent, but not well-known Italian and occasionally French artists working in the eighteenth and nineteenth centuries: a Venetian gondola-on-canal scene for their guest bathroom; a scene of the ruins at Agrigento for the entry hall; a Roman agora for the guest bedroom. I've gotten to know a lot of the gallery owners and dealers whether I wanted to do so or not, just because I wanted to assure them that I was not poaching on their territory, although there are one or two of them that also handle European antiquities, including pictures. You said your people are probably marketing pottery? And definitely a sacred mask."

"Yeah," said Zoe. "The people I'm working for are pretty sure they have at least one mask—maybe a couple-—in the van, and maybe some pottery, stolen a few years ago. Or maybe *they* don't have it, but they're going to hook up with the people that do."

"Well, my guess is unfortunately they're probably going to contact some black-market person. But on the other hand, the masks—if they were auctioned publicly, and you say they were—they are legal, if not legitimate."

Zoe nodded vigorously. "Exactly."

"So if it's the masks they're marketing they might well contact any number of legitimate galleries. Now some years ago, I was told, there was a gallery owner who got egg all over his face when he hung and advertised for sale a mask that he thought—or claimed—he had legitimately bought from another dealer. It turned out the mask had been stolen and a very elderly Pueblo man—I forget where from—was brought in and he identified it as a mask that he had seen used in ceremonies when he was a child. Apparently, the FBI was brought in and the gallery owner was never charged with receiving stolen goods, but only on condition that he give the mask back, which he did. He's since moved to Arizona, is my understanding. So I don't think any of the galleries here are going to risk displaying a sacred mask for sale. That's why your friends are going about this so hush-hush. But technically, legally, as long as nobody gets wind of their having these auctioned masks for sale, there's probably no crime committed, unless they got them through customs without declaring them."

"Ha! Which I'll bet they undoubtedly did!" interjected Zoe. "And my— the people I'm working for—aren't actually after the masks; they're only hoping there's a network of people who are involved in this that'll lead them to the stolen pottery."

"Ah!" said Coco. "Well, let me propose something: if it turns out these two—the people you call the van people—contact legitimate gallery owners, let's figure out how to get either you or me or both of us in there as spies. Now there are several possibilities: if it's really the pottery they're costermongering, they might contact Kevin Gilchrist. He runs a small shop specializing in historic and prehistoric pottery. You say this pottery might be Mimbres." Zoe nodded. "But I doubt he would give them the time of day. He wouldn't want to even touch stuff that was dubious. There's also Woody Glenn. He's a possibility for the masks. Woody goes in for the high-end: turquoise-embedded pottery, Fonseca, Namingha, Old West, Romantic Indian stuff—Russell and Bierstadt, but also more recent stuff like Joe Bieler. Then there's Gregg Neal, or was." Coco nodded.

"Gregg Neal!" Zoe exclaimed.

"Yes," continued Coco, without seeming to notice Zoe's surprise. "He does—or did—sort of underhanded deals, an operator, an opportunist. I'm given to understand he got the Indians to agree to arrangements obligating them to make a certain number of baskets or pots or whatever, but with vague references to prices such as 'market value at the time' and then 'at the time,' that is, when the time came to collect the craft items, he always paid less than what they'd get if they peddled them themselves to the various shops and trading posts, and far less than they'd get at Indian Market—that's here in August. But by that time, they've put all the work into it so what can they do?"

"Gregg Neal! Where's his shop? Let's go there."

"Doesn't have an actual shop. He's had one on and off, I'm given to understand, over the years, but as long as I've been living here, he's been dealing out of his home. He actually kicked the bucket about a month ago but I knew him and his partner and I've got his number in my rolo. I can call the partner—Plumm—and leave a message."

"Yes," said Zoe. "Yes, he did indeed kick the bucket." She lowered her voice. "And under suspicious circumstances. The coroner decided it was heart failure but there's something else to it. Like, why was his hand bandaged? Why were there two glasses on the scene? Who was the visitor he'd had with him? It was written up in a short newspaper article that … that the person I'm working for showed me."

"Well. I'll see if we can get over there this afternoon. I'm not sure you'll get any answers to those particular questions. But we can see what we can see. Plumm is selling off the inventory slowly, piece by piece, although I understand at some point, he'll have a big general sale or maybe an auction.

"But we should also go see Woody Glenn; I know him much better. I really doubt he'd be involved in something like this directly, but he may be a contact point for your van people, a way for them to get introduced to collectors. It wouldn't hurt for you to make contact. We don't have to make an appointment; he's got a gallery. We can just walk in. His wife runs a gallery too—a fine art gallery: Galleria Cavaletto. I worked with Nelda a lot when I first came here; she handles the Taos Painters and the Santa Fe School but also European Impressionists and some of the Avant-Garde. I think maybe Glenn is your best bet. Something tells me the clientele for ceremonial masks are, if perhaps willing to look the other way in terms of provenance, at least discerning and probably not show-offs. These masks—if it is the masks—were offered at legitimate auction, right?"

"Right."

"Whereas the pots were actually stolen, correct?"

"Correct."

"So, the only dicey thing about the masks is their, say, publicity liability. High-end, discrete collectors might well want a real mask to hang next to their Namingha or their Kabotie, and would be completely satisfied with an international auction being the latest provenance, while not wanting to try to go hunting for such a thing on the black market. Why don't we visit Neal's place first, then Woody? Woody hasn't seen me in a while but he knows me through Nelda and I can introduce you as my young assistant who's doing my legwork in response to a request from one of my old clients who now wants to move into Indian art, that I don't really deal in. Well, Zoe, with a short respite back at the house, what say we go there this afternoon, if you can accommodate this serving as lunch."

"Sure!" said Zoe. "Let's go! This will give me a chance to change appearance a little, and what do you say to a change in name? How about Claudine—Claudine Trilling. Claude, instead of Zoe."

Coco frowned. "Well, if you think it's necessary. I can see why you want to darken your hair to throw them off the scent, but why assume a different name?"

"We—I—don't know how much the imposters know, about Cannings', about Robb and Cait. They may or may not know they employ—or employed—a college student named Zoe. But just to be safe, since we're now all at the same destination, it's not unlikely we will tread the same paths. If the imposters do contact Plumm, or Glenn, or some other gallery that we've already been to and start asking questions, the less they can trace me to Croton Corners the better; and a name and hair change are a start, even if I can't do anything about my cocoa coloring!"

11:45 AM

Zoe shook her head and said almost defiantly, "But right now, I have to do something about my hair!" She consulted her phone. After a few minutes, she found a hair stylist in Pen Road Shopping Center.

"Oh, Pen Road is right around the corner. But you'd better do it now; I think we should try to catch Woody before three and that means getting to Mr. Plumm around one or one thirty."

Zoe changed into jeans and a tee and was on Pen Road in ten minutes. At City Different Stylers, the sign in the window said, "Walk-ins welcome," but in this miniscule half block of storefronts masquerading as the Pen Road Shopping Center, a "walk-in" was laughable. You could really only get here by car.

"Do you want it 'total Goth'?" asked the girl. She was about eighteen, with what looked like a real tattoo on her neck, a thick silver ring in her nose, jet black hair with just the hint of a dark blue streak that fell around a face that Zoe thought she might have seen on ancient Zapotec effigy pottery. The girl ushered her to an old-fashioned barber's chair, wrapped a blue-striped barber's smock around her shoulders, turned around to a sink, and began to run water and unscrew bottles.

"I don't want any of it shaved; I just want it dark, dark, dark especially at the tips, and totally straightened," responded Zoe.

"How about a streak of magenta? And some pomade to make it stick up? I'll have to clip it just a bit; otherwise, it'll flop into a Liberace."

"Okay, yeah—sounds good, put the pomade on one side but absolutely no magenta."

Forty-five minutes later, Zoe emerged with clipped, pomaded, well-darkened hair, as well as a re-do of the heavy mascara she'd applied earlier, in the morning. She wondered what poisons were seeping into her body from all the dye.

Phil had texted and now called just as she entered the house. He had tailed the "Pimpmobile," as he was now calling it, all over the east side of town, then to La Posada and Garrett's Desert Inn, then finally to Cerrillos Road and the Golden Saddle motel. The vanners were apparently ensconced there, although the woman had quickly come back out, climbed into the van again, and was still in there. He was pretty sure they now knew he was tailing them; the woman had probably recognized him at the Santa Fe Café and now, although he had driven up a side street and parked it, around the corner from a Ketterman's Automotive, it was hard to hide the Mini on these stop-signed, unjammed streets. He had taken refuge in a laundromat, to which he had quite legitimately trudged several blocks with his sack of laundry, churning in one of the machines, from which he was now watching the Golden Saddle, on the other side of the street. The man had gone into the motel office; the woman had stayed in the van and not emerged, although the man had entered the motel room that presumably they had rented. He texted Zoe, *watch golden saddle motel they sleep can u take em now.*

Zoe called him. He would follow them to wherever they went next, if she wanted him to do so, but from here on out he thought it was advisable that

"Claudine" take them. Did she have the "new" car? Yes, she did: Coco's old VW. Did she think they had recognized her when she barged past them at Pascal's? She didn't. So, could "Claude" meet him where he was parked if he gave her directions? No, she said, Coco had plans; they were going to make the rounds of galleries to see which ones might front the masks. Zoe/Claude told Phil she would get back to him after that. For now, he should follow them to wherever they went when they left the motel.

Sitting on the sofa in the living room—darkened by blinds drawn to keep out the intensifying late spring sun—Coco removed the *Harper's* magazine where she had laid it while awaiting Zoe's return as Zoe entered the house and patted the now vacant spot. "Sit, dear, and tell me what we do next. This is so exciting!"

Zoe sat, but on the edge of the sofa. "Let's make a beeline for these galleries, the ones that are likely to fence the masks."

"Well let's take our time getting to Canyon Road—let Woody recover a bit from his undoubtedly liquid-fortified lunch," responded Coco. "We'll tackle Plumm first. I think tomorrow we can make more gallery rounds—go to those I mentioned. We'll have to just hint about what we might have that their clients might want but I'll leave that to you. But if we get to the gallerists first, then when the miscreants turn up with whatever they have, the gallerists may just notify us, or me, rather, and tell the taradiddlers something like, 'Oh, we might know someone who might be interested' and … and … what's that phrase?"

Zoe furrowed her brow. "Ah! 'Bob's your uncle'!"

"Right! The important thing is, we have to set ourselves up as the contacts that the gallerists will think of first if the shameless peddlers start making the rounds. Then you can plunge right in and charge right ahead as my assistant. Then you can … well, you can… What actually will you do?"

"I don't know," said Zoe softly. "I really don't know." *Call Ferguson?* she thought.

15

JEN HAD ORDERED SOFT BOILED EGGS ("Make them a little on the hard side," she'd said) with bacon, hash browns and toast, with sides of a jalapeño corn muffin and sausages and a double side of sopapillas. She brought a doggie bag to Thad with the one of the eggs, sausages, the corn muffin, and the sopapillas. "Good luck with the egg; maybe you can peel it without it popping and spilling all over the place. Little heavy on the carbs, but you've got the sausages." They had driven around and into the hills before driving back down and finally finding two hotels: La Posada and Garrett's Desert Inn, both of which quoted rates beyond their budget and advised them that no rooms would be ready until three o'clock. But there were plenty of motels down on Cerrillos Road, they were told; just go down a few more blocks and turn left. Luckily, they were good directions-followers. "I never would have connected 'Sir-Rios'" with C-e-r-r-i-l-l-o-s," remarked Jen.

They saw several motels on the left-hand side of the road but had to go down to a left-turn signal and do a U-turn before being able to access one-two-three, all of which announced they wouldn't know about rooms until also, yes, three o'clock, until, at the fourth one—a particularly venerable-looking one called the "Golden Saddle"—the bald man at the desk, grayish-white shirt barely covering his paunch over which red suspenders clipped onto brown, much-washed trousers, nodded and affirmed that yes, he had a room that they could occupy right now.

"Okay," sighed Jen. "I'll stretch out here with our friend while you take your shower and primp; then it's my turn. But don't be too quick. I need a couple hours of kip."

"Well, if you insist," piped Thad cheerily. "I'll 'primp' as you put it and knock off my own set of Zs. Knock on the door when you're ready."

Jen climbed into the back of the van, slotted the lock bar into place and sacked out on top of the sleeping bag.

1:25 PM: Coco and "Claudine"

"Claudine" navigated Coco's yellow VW bug into the heart of Santa Fe; they parked on a quiet street not too far from the Capitol, across the street from a modest pale orange pseudo-adobe, or maybe, thought Zoe-Claudine, it was a real adobe, hard to tell. Dark-colored round beams protruding from the front wall supported a ceiling over a porch. "As far as Mr. Plumm goes," said Coco, "we'll just hope he's the talkative type and will tell us if Mr. Neal had plans to branch out from contemporary crafts and prehistoric pots to sacred masks. Maybe we'll spot some of your Mimbres pottery!"

"I also want him to talk about Mr. Neal's mysterious demise. I don't know if it has anything to do with anything, but the guy I'm working for—Ferguson—must think it does; otherwise, he wouldn't have clipped the obituary about Neal's death and stuck it in the file he showed me." They pressed the bell; a tall, thin, willowy man with an unruly shock of light brown hair and a furrowed, worried look, dressed in a very unstylish polo shirt and dark flannel slacks opened the front door. Zoe could not help noticing his Christian Louboutin shoes; Nick also had a pair. He swung the door open. "Come, come," he said, gesturing. They entered a comfortable room that clearly doubled as a gallery, although it was not immediately clear what was and what was not for sale. Zoe's eyes roamed the space. *Maybe everything is for sale at this point*, she thought. "Hello, Mr. Plumm. We've met, although you may not remember me. I'm Coco Vanderjagt, and this is my assistant Claudine Trilling."

"Just Claude," said Zoe.

Plumm nodded at both of them but made no move to shake hands. "How nice. Come through." He led them into the middle of the room but remained standing.

When they expressed regret at Mr. Neal's passing, he heaved a sigh full of pity and sorrow. "Yes. It was horrible, tragic, totally unnecessary." Zoe noticed tears beginning to well. *Clearly*, she thought, *Sebastian Plumm had been more than Gregg Neal's business partner and renter*. "And you know, you have to know," he leaned toward them slightly and looked from Coco to "Claudine," and back again, "that I have not lived one moment since Gregg's death without blaming myself, feeling shame, guilt, intense sorrow. If only I had been here. I could have helped him. I could have saved him. I could have given him my breath until the EMTs got here."

"But the newspaper said it was heart failure," noted Coco. "What could you have done?"

"Given him artificial respiration, called 911; at least I would have been here for him. My only consolation is that he died here at home, surrounded by the things he loved."

"You were not here at the time?"

"I was away, on a buying trip. To the Hopi villages. Gregg usually went himself, or sometimes we'd go together. He'd go when they were in greatest need—in the spring, when tourists are non-existent, seasonal fire-fighting jobs have dried up, there aren't any fairs or pow-wows, stores of corn are running low, and snow's still on the ground. He'd buy whatever they had, even some items that were not the best and that he knew he couldn't sell. They know me, as well, and they were happy to see me; I brought back some of what you see here." He swept the room with his hand. "But of course, what you see here is the last."

"You're not going to keep the gallery going?" asked Coco.

Plumm shook his head. "No. It's too painful. I can't. Besides, it doesn't belong to me. He didn't make a will, so his nearest of kin inherits the premises. His sister. She doesn't get the inventory because that belongs to the business and we did have the good sense to incorporate as one. That was only last year."

"So, you've been his partner for only a year?" queried Coco.

"Oh, no. Much longer. The issue was taking me in as a *business* partner." Plumm heaved another sigh. "He'd been burned. Actually twice. I couldn't blame him. Years ago, he went in with partners on some Curtis prints. You know, Edward S. Curtis? Who did all those marvelous portraits of Native Americans?" He gestured to the walls. "The partners, as he told it to me, sold, so to speak under the table, to finance their other projects. They didn't have galleries. They more or less flooded the market and he was stuck, so to speak, having shelled out *beaucoup* dollars into the partnership on the basis of a valuation of each print that didn't hold up. But that's when he decided that he had to branch out into everything Native American and make contact with the actual people; he even found a couple of the women still around who were the subjects of the photographs! He gave them each the print of themselves."

"You said he was burned twice?" asked Zoe/Claude.

"Yes, yes. This was just a few years ago—another partnership! I find it so vexing that it happened twice! This is just about the time I met him." Plumm stared into the middle distance, a half-smile appearing on this face. "I was more or less homeless, a distraught waif, cast up on the shores of a world of incredible magical beauty in its adobes, its light, its art, but constructed on an underbelly of drudge and grind and servitude. I'd managed to get what I was told was 'only a seasonal' job at the Sheraton—you know, it's out of town? —and was living in my car. You know the people who do the dirty work—the cleaning of the galleries, the waiting at tables, the laundering and straightening and mopping up at the hotels, the people who make it all work; they're paid a pittance. I was one of those. Well, as the season was coming to the end, I was having less and less work days. So, I started making the rounds of the galleries. Gregg was having one of his seasonal open-house sales. Well, long story short: he recognized my talents."

"You're an artist in your own right, aren't you?" asked Coco.

"Yes, I craft ceramics. My works don't really fit here, but Gregg got me into a couple of galleries that don't cater to Native arts. I show at the Cavaletto Gallery and at Karen Ruhlen." He addressed Coco. "You said on the phone you had clients that want Native art that will fit with European post-impressionist and avant-garde? Items that are, say, understated, or perhaps complementary?"

Coco nodded. "That's it. You wouldn't have anything of that sort? Or would you. Maybe some items that have only recently come available."

Plumm shrugged. "I've taken myself out of those loops, deliberately. But feel free to look around. There's some good items in the basement, too. Larger items—sculpture, some more weavings." He pointed to some weavings, perhaps blankets or perhaps garments, richly colored bands of solid yellow, orange, red, black, folded and draped over what looked like an old-fashioned wooden clothes-drying rack. "These weavings were packed around the pots that Gregg was going to be selling for Stan Joiner. I don't know anything about them. I can show you around the basement, if you'd like."

"Would you trust me to look around up here and make a few notes into my phone while Claudine accompanies you downstairs?"

"Certainly! I don't think you're likely to stuff a pot under your blouse and make off with it! Feel free to make notes, take pictures."

Coco laughed. "Very good, then! Claudine—you'll give me a report."

"Sure."

He led Zoe/Claudine through a door into a smaller room, a parlor, that was obviously part of the living quarters. It was accessorized much like the front room, with built-in and free-standing cases of shelves of pots, baskets and carvings, more Curtis prints and weavings on the walls. But this room was clearly also workspace: a corner held filing cabinets, a mahogany desk with a laptop computer on it, and a swivel chair. They went through another door, lace-curtained, into a large kitchen with dining nook, and then through yet another door into a mudroom. He opened another door. There Plumm cautioned Zoe/Claudine: "These stairs are narrow and steep and they twist." The ceiling was low. They came down into a cavernous space, also with a low ceiling, crisscrossed by large and small pipes visible though a heavy double sheet of clear plastic. A half wall of what, Zoe surmised, was probably asbestos encased a large furnace on three sides.

Plumm glanced up. "The plastic is a fail-safe in case a pipe leaks or heaven forbid, bursts. We change it out every six months. Pain in the butt, but makes more sense than a false ceiling." Zoe did not see exactly why. Plumm waived his right arm around expansively. "This is what you might call the overflow." Zoe saw three four-foot-high cases with glass fronts. On their shelves were piles of rolled weavings, baskets nested in baskets, and some pots. A deal table held six boxes stacked on top of one another, and a half-dozen seven-foot-long primitive lances placed across it. Two large wooden crates, one on top of another, stood in one corner. "What's in the crates?" Zoe asked.

"Nothing," said Plumm. "They're empty. Those beautiful Shipibo pots in that case and the ones upstairs came in them. We need to get them out of here. The crates, not the pots! There are more in those boxes on the table. Actually, only one or two in each since they're fragile and it's mostly packing."

Zoe looked at the spears. One of them was broken in three places. She walked over to the table and glanced, she hoped nonchalantly, at the spears. She felt a frisson of realization settle over her; she hoped she didn't visibly shiver. But at least one thing, maybe more, was becoming clear. Then she walked into the center of the space and turned her head slowly from one side to another, eyes wide. She took out her phone and began talking into it, she hoped convincingly, giving a short overview of the inventory. She pressed

End. "Wow," she said. "This is a lot of stuff." She glanced again at the spears, pointing, and turned her gaze to Plumm. "What are those?"

"The spears? They're labeled 'Shuar,' 'Achuar,' 'Siriono.' I have the feeling they may have come from someone else's collection, maybe refurbished; the points look new, or at least more recent. I don't know anything about them or even why Gregg had them. They came along with the crates of Shipibo pots, from Peru. I don't really know why Gregg agreed to take them—we really don't handle anything outside of North America, although the pots are a good addition to our inventory because we do handle Native ceramics. Stan Joiner brought them up from Arizona. He called the day after I'd gotten back, after I'd found … found… Anyway. He was wondering if Gregg was going to keep them. Apparently, he left them here on consignment and Gregg was meant to send him a check for a certain amount—ten percent of the value, he said. I told him what had happened and of course he was shocked. I guess when he left, Gregg was perfectly fine. He drove straight back to Scottsdale. Well, of course I sent him the check but I told him he was free to come back up and get them since I was going to have to put them into the fire sale."

"When is that going to be?" asked Zoe/Claudine.

"Whenever I get word that Rachel—that's Gregg's sister—is about to swoop down and take custodial possession. It has to go through probate but she's applied to the court to be appointed executor."

"What did he say?"

"Stan? Oh, he was devastated to hear. As far as the pots go, he said he'd think about it."

"This … Joiner … person hadn't known that Mr. Neal was … was…"

"No, no. As I said, he told me there was no hint of Gregg having difficulties. He said Gregg was fine when he left. It was a heart attack, you know."

Zoe/Claudine nodded her head. *Heart* failure, she thought.

"He and Gregg had gone for an early 'good-to-see-you-again-celebratory' dinner at the Coyote. Stan said Gregg invited him to stay over but Stan told me on the phone he'd wanted to be in Scottsdale to open up shop next morning and thought he could make it to Holbrook or Flagstaff at a reasonable hour, get up early, and then get to Scottsdale by ten to open up."

"So that's what he did?"

Plumm shrugged. "I guess."

Zoe went over to the table and looked again at the spears, at the boxes, which were closed.

"I unpacked a couple of the boxes that were in those huge crates," said Plumm.

Zoe darted one more glance at all four corners of the cellar. She spotted a potter's wheel, a table, and sacks of what were probably clay in a corner opposite from where the crates reposed, but took her gaze back over to the crates and let it rest there. She noted the wheel and table formed its own work space. "Surely you didn't get those huge crates down the stairs?" she said.

Plumm gestured to the right of where they were standing, to a contraption that reminded Zoe of a gigantic version of the luau grill that her father used in his backyard. He had thrown a little party for her, his buddies grilling chicken, pork, mango, papaya, and small, hard, red bananas over a bed of palm wood coals on the only occasion on which he had sprung for her to come out to see him in Hawaii: her graduation from high school. The contraption here in the basement had weights and wheels and chains and pulleys; an overhead gantry spanned its length. Plumm pointed to a set of large double doors, slanted, just above the contraption. "That was a coal chute," he said. "We took out the chute and expanded it and had those double doors set in. We had that lift made from a giant grill that came out of a defunct Hawaiian restaurant in Albuquerque."

So, it really was a luau grill!

"We lowered those cases, the table, and that sculpture over there…"—Zoe noted two large carved wooden pieces that vaguely resembled birds—"and I presume Gregg and Stan lowered the cases down on the lift and then trundled each one over there using that dolly." Plumm pointed to a four-wheeled flatbed leaning against the wall. "I wonder if that strain was what did it." Plumm's lower lip trembled and again, tears welled in his eyes. Zoe couldn't help feeling sorry for this displaced, misplaced middle-aging artist who would now once again be cast adrift. She noted some of his "ceramic creations," resting in a corner near his work station. She wondered what this Stan fellow was all about.

"Do you mind if I take pictures?"

Plumm waived his hand. "Please. Go ahead. Feel free." Zoe/Claudine made sure she got all four corners, including the crates and the spears on the table. "I'd like Ms. Vanderjagt to see all of this but I'm not sure she should negotiate the stairs."

"Of course. That's fine. And she might as well be up front with her clients and tell them they should wait for the big sale. They'll get bargains." He heaved a big sigh. "It'll be in the next couple of months. I'll find a space to display the Shipibos upstairs. I'll get those sculptures up there too."

They made their way back upstairs and she and Coco bid Sebastian Plumm adieu. He shook both their hands, clasping Coco's in both of his. "A pleasure! Nelda Cavaletto has mentioned you in glowing terms a couple of times when I've brought my poor offerings into her gallery, to the effect that she hopes you'll get back into the trade, or at least loan her your rolodex." Plumm giggled.

They got into the car. Zoe started the engine and put it into gear. "Well, I don't think he's a candidate for fencing the masks. He says he's getting out of the business and I believe him. On to Woody Glenn's?"

Coco nodded. "Absolutely! And yes, I believe him too."

At least some of the pieces are indeed falling into place, thought Zoe, *as Ferguson hoped they would do, but perhaps not quite as he had intuited them doing.*

3:10 PM

Jen had awakened, popped out of the van and knocked on the motel room door. "Out in a minute," responded Thad. But it was more than that.

Jen grew impatient. Finally, twenty minutes later he had emerged in Tony Lama boots, Levi's, a Hudson's Bay leather vest, and a heavy, L.L. Bean hurricane shirt. Jen had then entered the room, emerging fifty minutes later, showered, combed, modestly cosmeticized, in Bottega Veneta shoes, a Veronica Beard Rae Dickey jacket over a cream-colored, silky top, and brown suede Hermès riding pants, all of which she had gotten from Amazon (except the pants—eBay).

The comings and goings from and to the van were observed by Phil, who sent a short text to Zoe.

"You look spiffy," Thad said to Jen. "Quite a change."

"So, do you and equally. Changed I mean. Shaved and all that." She banged the door shut and reversed the van, heading out of the parking lot, right, onto Cerrillos Road. "By the way," she said, "I think we're being tailed."

"Yeah."

"That scruffy-looking guy at the park. I don't know if you noticed him. He was sitting with a girl at a picnic table right across from the place where we—you—ate. He had a beard and she was in shorts and a tee. I couldn't see much of her because she had her back to us and her head turned when I walked by."

"Yeah. That's the same guy who was just pulling up tent stakes when we pulled out of the campground this morning. Drives an elongated vintage Austin Mini."

"Hm-hm. Well, guess who was sitting at a table in the café where I ate this morning."

"Yeah. I'm not surprised. I'm just surprised if he's really tailing us, why he's so bad at it. I actually spotted him in the rear-view when we were still in Kansas. He was at that campground, too. I didn't think anything of it at the time. But he's definitely watching us. He's definitely tailing us."

"So, what do you think is going on? Do you think he's in cahoots with Dahlia? Or is it something else? FBI?" Said Jen plaintively. "And what can we do about it—I mean his tailing us?"

"Don't know," responded Thad. He heaved a sigh. "Not much. He doesn't seem to be around right now. But I'll bet anything there's a Tonka toy Mini parked somewhere around here. We can't wait around for him to go away. If he really is FBI all we can do is hope he—or they—finger Woodard Glenn for receiving stolen goods … if they really were stolen at some point."

16

ZOE/CLAUDINE NAVIGATED Coco's yellow VW bug through town and, on Coco's directions, onto Paseo de Peralta. She was wearing the mid-calf black dress she had worn to Pascal's, but without the shirt and tie and linen jacket; the dress had spaghetti straps and a nice deep décolletage from under which her large, firm breasts swelled up and out, from under a light-purple and gold scarf tied at her neck, creating (Zoe hoped) a peek-a-boo, now-you-see-them-now-you-don't effect. Coco had changed from her colorful and slightly flamboyant outfit into a pale lavender-colored suit that looked to Zoe/Claudine to have not experienced many wears but nonetheless have witnessed a couple of decades of hanging in a closet. Zoe surreptitiously sniffed for napthene and gratefully found none.

Coco gestured to their left. "Galleria Cavaletto. That's Woody's wife. Nelda. Handles only non-Native fine art. She's got two rooms—one for modernists, avant-garde, post-Impressionist, including the Santa Fe and Taos artists; another for everything else, including some of the lesser-known Italian renaissance painters, mostly small works. I helped her find a couple of them."

They turned left onto Canyon Road, parked in the gallery's parking lot and entered through the overly broad, glass gallery doors. A stunning young woman, with dark honey complexion and twinkling eyes, jet black hair wound around her head and secured with a heavy silver-and-turquoise burette, in black skirt, black turtleneck, and black sweater popped up from a desk positioned a few yards into the show room. "Can I help you?" she asked as she came around the desk toward them. *We must look like real customers*, thought Zoe.

"We'd like to see Woody. Is he here?" said Coco.

"Do you have an appointment?"

"No. But please tell him Coco Vanderjagt would like to chat. We haven't seen each other in an age."

The woman nodded. "Let me see if he's in." She turned and walked on half-heel pumps toward the back, disappearing behind a door which she opened with a key. Zoe crossed her arms and hugged herself. She realized why the young receptionist was wearing a turtleneck on this brilliantly blue, sunny, eighty-degree day. "It's cold in here," she remarked.

"To keep the art stable," said Coco. She gestured toward a gallery to their left. "Those in there are a Bierstadt and a Bodmer. And over there," she gestured behind them "are some mid-century Katsina dolls that are probably fragile in terms of their glue and their feathers. Why don't you stroll around—it'll keep you a little warmer—and I'll make the pitch to Woody. When we've had our chat in his office, I'll tell him about you, and we'll come out and find you."

"Fine. Remember, though I'm Claude—Claudine Trilling."

"Right."

The stunning young woman was walking resolutely toward them. "Come this way, please. He'll see you in his office."

This gallery is like a museum, she thought, *with each painting labeled with a long paragraph of explanatory text.* Zoe turned to find Coco marching toward her, a tall, slightly disheveled but amiable looking man with a full, wavy head of brown hair, dressed in a short-sleeved shirt, beige slacks, and bolo tie in tow. *His office must have a barrier membrane against the air conditioning in office*, thought Zoe, *or its own separate thermostat.*

"Claudine, this is Woody Glenn. Woody, this is my assistant I was telling you about, Claudine Trilling."

"Claude," said Zoe, shaking Woody's hand.

"Well, well, well—so Coco is branching out into Indian art and you're going to do all the work for her! You can see the items we have here—pretty great stuff, I think. I've also got what you might call a private gallery out of town, where I live. I'm having a get-together there Friday afternoon. Why don't you and Coco plan on coming? We'll start with drinks and canapés around three o'clock. Come any time after that. I'll give you directions." He smiled and looked back and forth from Coco to Zoe, but his gaze settled on Zoe. She smiled, thinking, *I wonder if it's the cleavage or if it's the whole package.*

"Well, I think I'll bow out and let Claude have the pleasure of getting to know the territory on her own, so to speak," said Coco, turning her head slightly as her attention was grabbed by something in her peripheral vision. It was the receptionist, giving a high sign, obviously to Woody. Woody and Zoe also turned. Zoe had to keep herself from violently starting, almost falling, gulping, coughing. She managed to recover before Coco or Woody noticed.

"Be right there," Woody said to the receptionist. Then, turning to Coco and Zoe, he said, "You'll have to excuse me. Today is busy! But ask Hilary for the directions before you leave." Zoe/ Claudine turned to go, but lingered just long enough to allow the woman who had just walked in to move deeper into the showroom guided by a chattering Hilary. "Claudine, we can talk some more about your plans on Friday and you can meet some of the folks who might also be interested in Coco's wares. You know, themed accessorizing is kind of *passé*. Eclectic artisan designing is in."

WEDNESDAY, 3:23 PM

Jen and Thad turned right onto Paseo de Peralta, then again right onto Canyon Road. There it was: Woodard Glenn Gallery. She parked in the parking lot. Thad stayed in the van and watched as Jen hastened into the gallery. An older woman accompanied by a woman in her post-teens walked out of the gallery and toward a lemon-yellow VW parked in the lot. They climbed in and quickly drove away.

Within a few minutes Jen emerged from the gallery. "He says bring it in." Thad got out of the van and opened the back door. Together, they eased the portmanteau out from under the wooden box structure. They walked into the gallery.

When they were on the road, Zoe/Claude led out her breath. "It's them. The van people. The people I'm tailing! One of them came into the gallery, just as we were ending our conversation with Mr. Glenn."

"What do we do?"

"I guess I'll turn up to the Friday afternoon soirée and see what happens. I'll bet anything they'll be there."

Thad propped the portmanteau against the wall. They shook hands with Woodard Glenn. "We're Thad and Jen," said Thad, handing him a "Suwanee Antiques" card that had everything on it except their names. They had decided to use their real ones, or at least the ones they were now using, rather than confusing the situation by trying to pass themselves off as the Murrays. Woodard Glenn did not have to know they were not. And Dahlia—wherever she was—would keep herself in the background, so there was no risk of her finding out they were Jen and Thad and not Mr. and Mrs. Murray or Mr. and Mrs. Canning.

"Good to meet you!" enthused Glenn. "I'm Woody, Woody Glenn."

They followed him into his office. Woodard Glenn walked behind his desk, took a seat in the swivel chair, studied the card, looked up and said, "You're a long way from home!" Thad smiled and shrugged. Glenn set the card on the desk, leaned back, and folded his hands behind his head. Jen and Thad took seats in the two hard-backed chairs in front of the desk. "I really don't have much time. This is a busy week. But show me what you have."

Thad took out his billfold with the little key attached to the chain. He unlocked the portmanteau. He unzipped it, letting the case cover fall to the floor. Woody instantly sat up.

"Whoa!" exclaimed Glenn. He stood, walked around the desk to the portmanteau, bent down and spent nearly a whole minute carefully look at its contents. "Whoa!" he said again. "And you got this … where?"

"Well, it came from an auction in Paris."

Woody went behind the desk, sat down again, placed his elbows on the desk, and fixed them, first one, then the other, with his stare. "A year ago. You bid on it."

"Not exactly. Someone else bid on it. On this one and on others."

"And got them."

"And got them." Thad nodded.

Woody folded his hands in front of him. "So, how many items like this do you have?"

Thad and Jen looked at each other. "We can't really say," said Jen. "But if you're interested, we can get more."

Woody Glenn stared at the mask. "Well, you know… You see, items like this are … sensitive."

Thad nodded. "We know. We understand."

"I can't just buy this from you and hang it on the wall."

"Yes, exactly." Thad nodded again.

"Although, in fact, I think items like this would appeal to a very special clientele You ... we ... might want to identify this clientele before we ... I take any definite action. And, you ... you're brokers, sort of like?"

"We have, what you might call, silent partners."

Woody Glenn nodded. "Let me propose something. I'm having a little get-together at my place out of town this coming Friday. A number of people are coming in from out of town. Collectors, art connoisseurs, people who might ... who would be interested in items such as this one. Why don't you come along to the gathering? Bring that along. I'll introduce you to everyone and whenever I get a chance, I'll mention the availability of this and others like it to this or that person on an individual basis. Almost everyone will be staying the weekend; you can do so, too. I have several guest rooms and a number of guest houses. I can get you together with those who express inter-est over the weekend. They can view it and—don't take this wrong—verify it. I know how much you—and your partners—most likely paid for this and others like it. Not everyone would want to spend that kind of money but I know some that can and would do so." He stood up. "But you will really have to excuse me. I have a lot to do to prepare for the end of the week. Ask Hilary—she'll give you directions and a map of sorts. Once you get out of town it's easy to find. Pleasure meeting you!" He came out from behind the desk and shook their hands again.

Thad zipped up the portmanteau, took out his wallet and key, relocked it. They found Hilary and got their directions and a Google map printout. They exited the gallery, opened the back doors, and slid the portmanteau inside. Thad slammed the door. He relocked the padlock. He got into the driver's seat. Jen got into the passenger seat. "Crap!" (Thad) "*Merde!*" (Jen) "Shit!" (Thad) "Bollix!" (Jen) "*Puta!*" (Thad) "*Madone!*" (Jen) "Bugger!" (Thad) "Piss!" (Jen). Thad heaved a sigh. "So, we're stuck with this thing for two more days! Why couldn't he have said, 'Gee, this is great! Let me take it and look at it and contemplate and lock it away in my safe-hold'?"

"Yeah, really," agreed Jen.

Thad started the engine. "So back to the Golden Saddle. Want to toss a coin for who gets to sit out here with our friend?"

"Don't you think we can just bring it in with us? I mean, we're so close…"

"Exactly why we can't do that. We're so close."

"You really think Dahlia is going to pop out of somewhere, crowbar in hand, jimmy open the motel room door, barnstorm in, and nip out with the goods before we can get our shit together? Why would she—or her Adrian guy—do that? Isn't this what she hired us to do?"

"Yes. We've transported her goods. We've made the contact. We've set everything up. Who says she doesn't already know about this little get-to-gether with all the ready-made clients ready to be hit up and she'll just turn up with what we've got in the back?"

"But unless she blows us away or ties us up and locks us in a closet, if we turn up without the portmanteau, Woody Glenn would have alarm bells going off in his head," objected Jen.

"He might. And we've got to make sure that she and her minion *don't* tie us up and throw us in the closet, and show up Friday saying, 'Oh, Jen and Thad sent us. We're the silent partners.' If that happens, we're out $10,000, and we're out of the picture. We can't very well go to the police or to Woody Glenn complaining that Dahlia took back something that was already hers."

"But that doesn't make sense. Why go to all the bother? She told us she can't show up around here, at least not to Woody Glenn's! That's what she told us. And it's probably true. Otherwise, why hire us? That's why we're doing this and not her! She had to remain incognito."

"Well, maybe you're right," admitted Thad. "But still, better to be safe than sorry. I mean, Dahlia did say we were being—what was her word?—surveilled? We *know* we're being tailed. So there probably *is* an unknown third-party out there ready to pop up and hie off with the goods. Or, Woodard Glenn could decide to take matters into his own hands and cut us out. If the thing disappeared sometime overnight, all we could do would be to report it stolen. Truth to tell, a hefty pair of bolt cutters could slice through our lock bars."

They had pulled into a space at their room at the Golden Saddle. Thad shut off the motor, turning to look at Jen. They continued to sit in the vehicle.

"But Woodard Glenn is Mr. Good-Upstanding Citizen," said Jen thoughtfully. She wrinkled her brow. "He was very gracious. I mean, he's invited us out to this grand gathering."

"Yes," agreed Thad tentatively. "Having us there will give him and his clients opportunity to check us out. I'm sure some—or all—of the potentially interested clients will be there. With that super gallery, he's gotta be well connected and his clients have gotta be well-heeled."

Jen nodded vigorously. "If he really did have dealings with dubious Dahlia, however many years ago, he's come a long way since, don't you think?"

"Definitely." Thad changed the subject. "Look," he said, "it's almost five o'clock. We didn't have any lunch. I'm starved. I could use a good meal and a class of wine or two. I wonder what this Guadalupe Café is all about?" He started the engine and maneuvered the van back to the parking lot entrance, and after a short wait for a break in traffic, turned right. While they drove the short distance to the café, Thad speculated: "What about the scruffy little guy who's been tailing us? Where does he fit in all this?"

Jen shook her head vigorously. "He could be that unknown third party. But his turning up could also be just coincidence. He just knew the back routes like we did. And how many cheap places to eat are there around here?"

"Well, maybe you're right. But I still say, stick to our paranoid routine."

"Okay," sighed Jen. "You chow down. Take your time. I'll sit here in the van with our friend and catch up on email. Cell towers should be all over the place. Leave the Dahlia phone with me. I'll call Dahlia and tell her we're more or less in. But tomorrow I want to find a chamber of commerce or tourist bureau or something and find out what's to see here. I mean, even taking turns at a couple of museums beats sitting around in the room with the boob tube or sitting around out here reading Jo Nesbo."

~◯

WEDNESDAY, 7:14 PM
ZOE, PHIL, COCO

When Coco and Zoe/Claudine exited the gallery, Zoe had texted Phil: *meet us at cocos call 4 directions*. Phil called and said he would keep tabs on the vanners just to make sure they were going back to the motel.

"Come over when you're sure," Zoe told him. "Here's Coco. She'll give you directions."

Now they sat in Coco's kitchen. "Well, Phil, you'll have to tell me all about your adventures in the Pueblo villages. I see why you had no trouble getting here and following those two bandits. You probably know Santa Fe fairly well." Phil nodded. "But first, I think Zoe wants to do a—what did you call it—a…"

"A kind of run-down. I've figured a few things out. Or I've got a theory. I've got to call Ferguson right after this." Coco had set out sesame crackers, Stoned Wheat Thins, Stilton, a dish of dried chick peas and another of mixed olives, "homemade" pork and poblano mini-empanadas that were not really homemade, but were from a bakery more or less down the street in a mini-shopping mall, and a bottle each of Côtes du Rhône red and Kono sauvignon blanc.

"Okay," began Zoe. "Let's go over this whole thing." Mainly for Phil's benefit, she included her conversations with Ferguson that tied the theft of the Mimbres pots from nearly seven years earlier with the scam that brought the sacred mask into the hands of the vanners. Or rather, that did not tie the pots to the mask, but might tie the people who had thieved the pots and orchestrated the insurance scheme with the people who were orchestrating the Murray imposters and their masque behind whom they were hiding in order to peddle the sacred masks.

Phil shook his head. "That sounds really complicated."

"But it's beginning to make sense. Here's why: first of all, the imposters are on a phishing expedition. They went into the gallery with the portmanteau that I'm ninety-nine- and nine-tenths sure had the mask in it. They came out with it, which means that Woody Glenn wasn't interested."

"How do you know they didn't take the mask out and came back out with the porto- whatever empty?"

"Because you don't just leave a thing like that sitting around. It's got to be stored safely. Why take it out of its packing? No, I think they're going to try to peddle it elsewhere—probably to those other galleries you mentioned to me, Coco." Zoe was counting on her fingers.

"Second, and separately, there's something really fishy going on at the Gregg Neal gallery. That's something that's really going to interest Ferguson. Gregg Neal was the one who offered Mimbres pots for sale online and Ferguson said at first, he thought they were from the stolen cache but then the techies at Assurance Associates, based on their analysis of the photos, said they weren't. So, you know what they were? Imitations! Made by none other than our Mr. Plumm!"

"Oh!" said Coco.

"Yeah. I spotted a potter's wheel in the basement when I was down there. And remember he said he showed his pottery at a gallery?"

"Yes. At Woody Glenn's wife's gallery. Galleria Cavaletto Fine Art."

"What would be simpler for him than to knock off a couple of fake Mimbres?'

"Ah!" said Coco.

"And! Here's really something: There was a bunch of spears in the basement. They all had wooden tips. And Gregg Neal died after just getting a cut, or a puncture, in his hand. Those spears weren't for hunting animals. Wooden points aren't effective; they'd break off when they hit the animal's hide. Those were fishing spears. You wade into a slow-moving stream or pond or shallow lake, spear the fish, wait a few minutes, and the fish stops thrashing. You know why it stops thrashing?" Zoe did not wait for an answer from her perplexed but rapt audience. "Because the wooden spear points are coated with a slow-acting poison. Curare. It's a poison made either from the gland of a frog found in the Amazon: Dendrobatidae, or from a really common Amazonian vine. Learned this in a course I took in Peoples and Cultures of Native South America, in case you're wondering. Native people tip their spear points in it; the poison enters the fish's bloodstream when the point penetrates the flesh. A single person can spear a half-dozen large fish that way, then just wait. After about five or ten minutes, depending on the size, the fish are so docile they can be fetched ashore with a net. Doesn't affect the fish's flesh at all; it has to enter the bloodstream to be effective. In the gut of a person or animal that eats the fish, it just passes right out with no effect."

"So, you mean, somebody charged Gregg Neal with a spear, hit him in the hand, then just stood there while he slowly expired?" asked Phil.

"Something like that. My guess is somebody stabbed him and then left. It would have been a few hours before he expired—maybe longer than that. The poison slowly paralyzes. It's pretty bad. The person is aware the whole time; just immobilized. Eventually the lungs stop working and that's that."

"Oh! That's awful!" said Coco.

"It is, indeed," agreed Zoe. "The question is why and who? It probably or maybe even definitely wasn't Plumm; he was away."

"But we only have his word for it," objected Coco.

"Too true." Zoe nodded. "But the newspaper article said he'd had a visitor. I'd bet anything that visitor was this Joiner person, the same dude who brought the pots and the spears."

"So Joiner, whoever that is, smears the spears with the poison? Then jabs Neal?"

Zoe shrugged. "Or it could have been an accident. Could be Joiner didn't know the poison was on the spears. Could also be that Neal was playing with them, grabbed the wrong end, something like that. But no, I think it was deliberate. I think Joiner—Stan Joiner—is one of the people who was in on the theft of the Mimbres pots. What if Neal was all set to pull a scam similar to the Mimbres scam—get a bunch of people to put up earnest money for x number of sacred masks. He's about to approach Woody Glenn about fencing them. Then somebody—maybe Joiner, maybe not—maybe a rival, maybe somebody who smells a rat, offs Neal? The scheme falls apart. The scammers have to scramble to recoup their losses. They decide to send the Murray imposters to Woody Glenn because Neal's no longer around."

"Well, so, it's gotta be Joiner who did it … who offed Neal?" suggested Phil. "Maybe in cahoots with this Dahlia-Jane person that you said Ferguson's been tailing?"

"Yes. Maybe. Because here's thirdly: Ferguson's identified the Dahlia-Jane person Faulks as being at the Paris auction a year ago, bidding on a number of masks successfully. Then she disappeared, popped up again just recently, and met with the imposters first at the museum, then at their place in upstate New York. And they've got one of the masks that Dahlia-Jane got from the auction. Obviously, the imposters are meant to be the conduits for the money coming from clients that Woody Glenn sets up and going to the Jane person. But I think this whole scheme has been in the planning stages for a while. My guess is that Gregg Neal was intended as the original middleman and therefore the guarantee of integrity, because he's also a dealer; but Coco here says he's kind of shady, and maybe he tried to do an end-run around Faulks. Maybe this Joiner person was—is—in on it too, and he got spooked when Gregg Neal started peddling fake Mimbres pots on the internet."

"So, he offed him? By stabbing the poisoned spear point into his hand? Then, the Jane person contacts the Murrays to use them as middlemen. But would the Murrays have gone for that?" asked Coco skeptically.

"No, they wouldn't. So that was just a ploy. She sends in the imposters and sets up this elaborate sham of getting them to be the brokers. They may just be semi-innocent dupes brought in to double-cross this Joiner person."

"Who double-crossed Neal. Wow! Crooks double-crossing crooks! What a conspiracy!" said Phil. "So how is this going to work now?"

"The imposters may be as much innocent patsies as perpetrators," responded Zoe. "They oversee the loading of a dozen or however many portmanteaus with a mask in each. They sign some sort of notarized statement to the effect that the portmanteaus really do contain the masks. Their van is too small to fit all the cases. So, separate shippers are arranged. The shippers drive off. The imposters drive off. Once they get Woody Glenn to secure the clients who are going to buy the masks, they rendezvous with the Jane-Dahlia person and/or the shippers and deliver the goods."

"So why doesn't Jane-Dahlia do all this herself? Why have the imposters in it at all?"

"Ferguson speculates that if Dahlia-Jane was involved in the Mimbres scam, there was some kind of falling out. Neal was probably involved, as well, and maybe this Joiner guy. So, Dahlia-Jane needs them to masquerade—no pun intended—as legitimate brokers because Neal, whom Glenn trusted, is gone, and she doesn't want to show her face." Zoe was jazzed, stoked, riding high on all her clever theorizing. "Wow! I'm really glad Cait and Robb didn't get hooked into this but you know something? I'm really glad I did. The important thing here is that Woodard Glenn is about to become complicit in this scheme to profit by selling sacred objects in the shadows of the legitimate art market even if he wasn't before."

Coco shook her head. "I'd be very sad to learn that Woody is part of something underhanded," said Coco. "But I'm afraid you're right." She shook her head. "Even though I must say you've kind of lost me in all the possible twists and turns to this mystery," she lamented. "I only get that you think Gregg Neal's demise has something to do with a scam with regard to the sacred masks, but maybe also to do with the Mimbres pots business from some years ago."

"Right, right," said Zoe. "And Woody Glenn *could* be an 'innocent' in all this, yes, but not for long."

"Wild!" said Phil. "So, what do we do now?"

"I call Ferguson and tell him all this." She waved the burner in the air. "You guys chat." She stood, stuffed a couple of Stilton-piled crackers in her mouth, scooped up a handful of olives, and headed for the back of the house with her phone.

"Well," said Coco to Phil. "You're probably wondering why I'm called Coco. You probably think it has something to do with Coco Chanel. It doesn't. My birth name is Cheryl. Cheryl Cocroft, pronounced 'kuh' plus 'croft'. Cheryl Tilden Cocroft. Well, in college, at Smith, I loved hot cocoa, with a dash of brandy. While everybody else was tanking on red wine or Budweiser, I sipped cocoa spiked with brandy and got a lot more potted a lot sooner than they did. Well, cocoa-Co-croft—I became known as Coco. It's ironic that it's Ellie who ends up with the chocolate rep."

Phil, in turn, fortified with several glasses of wine, introduced her to the mysteries of Pueblo dances (non-tribal members are banned from most of the sacred ones, but some allow them for masked dances, he noted), and their meanings, and the ambience of dance days in the villages and communities, often punctuated with the sharp scent of burning piñon pine and the enticing smell of roasting corn.

After 45 minutes, Zoe emerged. Ferguson, she said, was actually nearby. He was astounded at her sleuthing and her theorizing. She told him about Phil. He okayed Phil's continued participation.

"Philip Marlow to your Miss Marple," chuckled Coco.

Zoe addressed Phil: "You're to keep on shadowing them, while I stay in the background, until Friday. Then, I suggested you show up with me as my 'significant-other-of-the-moment,' and he thought that would be all right."

"Oh! Good! That means you and I can do the museum rounds, Zoe," said Coco. "There are a lot of them here. And not a bad art museum in Albuquerque. We can take the train. In the meantime, maybe after some fortified hot chocolate, I'll bid you good night. Phil, do you have a sleeping bag?"

"Sure..."

"Well, you can throw it on that couch right there; or on the floor if you like a hard surface. Or ... or you can make other arrangements. But do stay here tonight."

Zoe looked at Phil.

17

THE VANNERS HAD NOT MADE THE ROUNDS of galleries. Jen and Thad went first to the Museum of Indian Arts and Culture, using the same strategy they had used as long as Phil had been trailing them: first one went in, leaving the other in the van, then the other. Phil had gone across the road to the Laboratory of Anthropology and the Folk Art Museum. When he maneuvered the Mini into a position where he could see the van, Phil parked. Soon, the man returned, got into the driver's seat. Now they were headed for him; Phil drove partially down the hill and stopped. He did a U-turn, drove back up the hill in time to see the woman entering the Folk Art. Phil drove across the street, parked, entered the Museum of Indian Arts.

He texted Zoe, *vanners to bkfst then to motel then to tourist buro now museum hill.*

After hearing from Phil, Coco and Zoe had decided it was safe to visit the New Mexico State Museum and then the Georgia O'Keefe, more or less around the corner, and of course, the Palace of the Governors, where the

Indigenous people selling their art, sitting on blankets under the portico, were of more interest to Zoe than the museum's interior. There was no danger of Zoe and Coco colliding with the vanners, since they were on Museum Hill. While Coco and Zoe were strolling under the Palace's portico, Zoe's phone brumped. Phil texted: *vanners go down hill maybe to town*. Now, Zoe and Coco would be forced to change plans. They drove back to Coco's house for a late lunch of smoked turkey sandwiches with tartar sauce on bakery rye with a simple salad of greens, Kalamata olives, and tomatoes with an olive oil and mustard dressing, followed by oranges. Zoe looked at Phil's latest text, sent at 2:15: *lunch at casa sena fed meter walking i park side street follow at distance now into nm statemus i to burrito co & library where parked.*

2:30 PM

"Poor Phil!" Zoe said. "I feel like we should feed him a banquet tonight. Obviously, they aren't going to galleries. I'm going to tell him to meet us back at the house—when?"

"We'll do that," Coco agreed. "The museums on the hill are a substantial tour; let's say five just to be safe."

Zoe texted Phil: *We to museums on hill meet us house @5.*

Phil texted back: *library small ho-hum sure they go back to motel after no need to hang w/them.*

"Would he want to come with us to the museums on the hill? Or I guess he's already been here, hasn't he?" Coco asked.

Zoe texted again: *or meet us here museum hill?*

They parked and stood outside the car as the Mini came chugging into the parking lot. He strolled toward them. Stopping he said, "Actually, been here, done that. Would it be possible to return to the house, your house, Ms. Vanderjagt? I could really use a shower."

"Please. It's Coco. And yes, of course," she said, fetching a key ring from her pocket book. She slid two keys off the ring and handed them to Phil. "Make yourself at home! We'll see you there about five."

After the tour of all three museums, Zoe and Coco arrived back at the house. The door was unlocked. Coco declared herself exhausted but after a bathroom stop, insisted she would go to Kaune's, pick up pork shoulder and fresh green beans, shove the pork in the oven, and collapse for a nap. Zoe headed for her small bedroom. She heard the shower. She went back into the main part of the house and used the bathroom. She went back into the bedroom, sat down on the bed. The shower stopped. "Phil?" she called.

"Hi," he replied. He emerged from the bathroom in just a towel around his loins.

"You've been in the shower this whole time?"

"No, I asked at the library if they had any archives and discovered the New Mexico State Museum Library was just across the street. I accessed their catalogue to see what they had that might interest me. Sorry." He nodded at a pile on a chair. "Those are my clothes…"

He had shaved off his beard, but kept his mustache. Zoe took in the rest of Phil's body. She was surprised that his chest and legs were almost as tan as his arms. Not a lot of muscle, but a lean torso; almost no body hair. She couldn't help comparing. Nick was also lean, but with rolls and mats of black hair on his chest, stomach, back, surprisingly contrasting with his clean-shaven face. Did men try to strike some sort of balance in their hair displays?

The previous night they had each spent in chaste solitude, she in her bed, he in his sleeping bag thrown on top of hers on the floor. Each had disrobed awkwardly under their respective covers. "Pajamas?" Zoe had asked.

"Sleep naked," Phil had replied.

"Me too," she'd responded. They had reversed the process in the morning, or almost, Zoe emerging in panties and top, into the bathroom and the shower. Phil was gone. A note on the kitchen table told her he had "gone tailing." She had concluded he must not even have stopped for a bowl of granola; she'd hoped he'd grabbed a donut and coffee somewhere.

But now Zoe made a decision: she'd kept on with the morning pill ritual out of habit more than anything. It was time to do a final Nick exorcism. She approached Phil. "You don't need your clothes," she said, reaching down and pulling the towel free of its knot. "We don't have to do anything. I just thought maybe it might be nice to explore."

And it was. Phil undid her blouse slowly. She wore a light half-chemise underneath; she hated bras. She drew it up over her head and off. He undid the buttons on her jeans; she shoved them down and off her feet. Then she slid down her panties. She looked at him appraisingly. Nick was a good six inches taller. That should have translated roughly to a 10 percent advantage. But it wasn't. Phil was bigger. "That's a nice one you have there. Can I try it out?"

Phil took her breasts in his palms, then gently pinched her nipples. "These are pretty nice, too," he said. She looped her arm around him, led him to the bed, gently pushed him down onto it. She kneeled over him. She liked to straddle, liked it best. She liked all the other preliminaries too—the licking: the licking off the honey, the whipped cream; getting pieces of chocolate sucked out. But they didn't have time, space or place for that now. She was beginning to feel just the beginning of cramp. Tomorrow this would not be possible.

"Phil!" she said. "That was great!" She looked intensely at him. He was grinning the proverbial ear-to-ear. She kissed him fiercely on his bristly mustachey mouth. She usually was not for mouth kissing, but she wanted to show him it was more than just an impetuous, vehement, aggressive shaft.

18

IT HAD BEEN JEN'S TURN TO SLEEP in the van. She awoke, sleepy. She had watched television in the room until eleven, leaving Thad to shiver in the van. She had eventually found semi-entertaining back-to-back *Seinfeld* re-runs, then a Discovery Channel program on mummies, and finally a channel showing a good old Sean Connery movie, *Russia House*. They had arranged that Thad would rise no later than seven, shower, dress, and relieve her no later than 7:45 a.m.

Now she activated her phone and accessed email. Message from Louie. Wow! She could not believe this! They had left Louie in charge of Suwannee Antiques and Collectibles in a kind of default arrangement: he could open up if someone called. Someone had done so and he had done so. Whoopeee! She couldn't wait to tell Thad! And here he came. He knocked on the side. She slid aside the curtain. Yes, it was Thad. She opened up the back. "Okay, shower time for me. And have I got a surprise for you!"

"Huh?"

"Uh-uh. Wait 'til I come back. But we're going to have a whopping cele-bratory breakfast and we're going to find out some place interesting to go today besides museums, before we journey out to the soirée!" She had slept in her jeans and top and popped out and into the room, emerging twenty minutes later, to take her place shotgun. Thad took the driver's seat. "Don't start it yet. Just look." She showed him her phone, but only for a few seconds, then said: "That gigantic monstrosity brought $16,000? That nineteenth century French buffet with all those carvings of deer and curlicues? We thought we'd never unload it! Well, Louie unloaded it for *$16,000*! The buyer brought around a certified check, and Louie transferred $3,000 into our account! Boy, am I ever glad we told him to run things for us while we're gone! I mean, Louie's kind of a sleazebag, but he knows what he's doing; and he may be a bit of a crook, but he's an honest one."

"That's all?"

"What's all?"

"That's all we get? Three thousand dollars?"

"Well, remember we owed him ten thousand plus 10 percent interest, and also remember that when he sells something of ours from his barn, he gets a 15 percent commission. Yeah, it's not a lot, but now we have a cushion."

"Ah, right! And so now we can let Dahlia keep the $10,000 and we can…"

"Ah—ah-ah, no, no, no, no, no, no, no," objected Jen. "No, we can't. Nothing doing. You're thinking we can keep the thing and figure out how to sell it on our own. Nope. You were the one who insisted that Dahlia was out there, lurking, ready to swoop down on us for whatever reason. Well, if we do something stupid, like not following through with Woody Glenn, we're toast. Don't even think about it!"

"Yeah, you're right. It was just a thought. Let's go get you some breakfast and me a doggie bag and figure out how to kill another day, or half-day."

The decided to explore the big, busy-looking street that crossed Cerrillos near the motel. They found a café there, Celebrations Village West, where Jen had breakfast and got a doggie bag for Thad and asked the wait person about what to do besides galleries and museums. "There's a drive you can take," she said. "Up to Sandia Peak—that's a ski resort with spectacular views. Or go down Cerrillos to Rodeo Road and then to La Cienega. That's a nice scenic drive along the Rio Grande. Then pick up the old highway, route 85 down to Albuquerque. But don't go all the way to Albuquerque—stop in Corrales."

Jen told Thad about the wait person's recommendation when she returned with his doggie bag. "So … potty stop back at the motel, then let's do it. Then we can go straight to Woody Glenn's."

They did not go up Sandia peak in the interest of time. They took the scenic drive to La Cienega and then to Corrales, where they found a curious structure a block off of the highway: a concrete teepee and painted on its side, a masked dancing figure. *Spooky*, thought Jen. *It's the figure from my dream days ago! I wonder what it means?* Thad stopped the van. Behind the teepee was a cavernous, rambling structure, part house, part shop, with what looked like original adobe walls and tin roof jammed onto an early twentieth century neo-Victorian addition. A large "For Sale" sign was posted in the neglected front yard. They did not get out, but Jen hurriedly jotted down the phone number in a little notebook that always sat on the engine compartment dash between them. Thad turned the van around. "Let's head back."

2:30 PM

Zoe and Coco had, indeed, taken the train to Albuquerque and spent a pleasant mid-morning at the art museum. Zoe was surprised. It had some sappy religious art by minor South American and Mexican artists but a good, large "modern room" with some O'Keefes, Piet Mondrians, a Berthe Morisot, a Judy Chicago, several Jackson Pollocks including an unusual piece from his early, Western "realistic" period, several colorful acrylics of local scenes—mostly churches—by a local artist named Tom Noble, a huge avant-garde canvas by another local artist, someone called Tommy Macaione, and several pieces from someone called Susan Rothenberg, also apparently local.

"Phil's texted a couple of times," said Zoe. "The vanners are just kind of meandering around the area. I wonder what their next move is going to be. You think they're going to show up to Woody's party?"

"I wouldn't be surprised. Will that be okay with you?"

"Yeah. One of them may have spotted both of us at that park in Walsenburg, like I told you, and might recognize me. Maybe my new hair will throw them off. But I think it's Phil we have to worry about. He's the one that the woman got a good look at. He shaved off his beard yesterday, so maybe if they happen to run into him while he's spying on them, as long as they don't spot his car, maybe we don't have anything to worry about."

"But so what? Even if they do recognize you, what can they do? I mean, hiding right out in the open is sometimes the best strategy. In fact, it would probably be a lot less suspicious if Phil actually showed up at the party, too, with you. That would explain his presence here, wouldn't it? He's your friend; you came into town together and the only reason you're not palling around with him is, well, something like you have to entertain your fussy old aunt who takes a dim view of young ladies cozying up to scruffy anthropologists! Nobody has to know he's staying with us. In fact, why *not* show up with Phil at the party tomorrow? Woody knows I'm bowing out, so it would make sense. The lid is off, so to speak. You can show up with your beau."

"That's exactly what Ferguson suggested, so I guess, why not. I'll drop you at your place, change, get the Honda, and then text Phil and go get him." Zoe called the Glenn Gallery; Hilary answered. Would it be all right if she brought along her beau, Phil, in Coco's stead? Yes, was Hilary's answer, accommodating if not effusive.

19

GOING OUT TO LOS PAJARITOS;
WOODY GLENN'S HOME IN WALDO

JEN AND THAD

Jen had selected a burgundy long sleeve casual baby doll dress she'd found on the internet for $9.95. It was a half-dress, letting most of her thighs show—which were still good, thanks to the elliptical cross-ramp exercise machine in their basement—and a JC Penny high neck, short sleeve blouse that let her tits shifted subtly, occasionally with some nipple-hardening as they moved against the fabric, noticeable only if one really—well, took the effort to notice, set off by two delicate necklaces: both silver, one with a heart-shaped setting of amethyst and the other with a square of sparkling garnet. She'd girded the dress with a tightly-cinched, very wide black belt that would prevent the dress from riding up too high, in case she had to bend over. She would be comfortable in the warm weather that had suddenly blown in, and fetching for Mr. Glenn and his guests.

Thad wore a blue western snap-button, long-sleeved shirt and a bolo tie with turquoise pendant, also found on the net. Jen hoped the turquoise was real. He had gone back and forth between a pair of light tan Stafford pleated slacks and spanking new Levi's. "The Levi's are itchy," he'd objected, but finally agreed with Jen that they were more appropriate here and would offset her baby doll look nicely. They both wore cowboy boots: he a pair of modest Tony Lama boots; she a pair of light burgundy fringed Dingo JuJus: stylish and comfy. Comfy was what she wanted for this close encounter. Thad could play the starch.

⌐⌐〇

3:35 PM: CLAUDINE/ZOE AND PHIL

The directions, printed on the verso of a reproduction of a colorful eagle dance scene by Tonita Pena (noted as now housed in the Museum of Indian Arts and Culture), emblazoned with bold black lettering announcing **VIEWINGS BY INVITATION ONLY,** took them on a state highway southeast of the city, then onto various named roads until they were twisting and turning along a wide, dirt-and-gravel road, just out of Santa Fe, that paralleled the Rio Grande. Phil and Zoe were in Zoe's Civic. The unforgiving harshness of April, with its alternating rain, hail, and piercingly sunny cold had given way to the soft warmth of May. Roiling clouds, tinged with a touch of orange filtered a golden light that made poplars and cottonwoods sparkle with yellow. Occasional clusters of houses and outbuildings threw purplish shadows as they rounded one bend, then glowed brilliantly as they rounded the next. A large arched doorway, flanked by open blue doors rimmed in red and a hand-painted sign, "Los Pajaritos," announced their destination.

They stopped just inside the entrance. A man in a fringed leather jacket, Stetson hat, and Levi's with a large silver-and-turquoise belt buckle approached them. He carried an old-fashioned clipboard in his right hand, a pen in his right. Zoe rolled down her window. "Good afternoon," he said. "Welcome to Los Pajaritos. Name please?"

"Claudine Trilling," replied Zoe. "And this is Phil." She could see the sheet on the clipboard; it was a printout with names, some with ticks next to them. Next to her name was a handwritten name, "Phil" and the initials "HL" within a circle. "Ah! Yes, Miss Lowe asked that your name be added, Sir." He looked into the car, beyond Zoe, to Phil. "Park anywhere."

They parked, then walked over to a large, rambling adobe building, bermed into a low hill; the front door was open. They entered a slim airlock; Zoe noted a second door, a sliding one, nested in the thick wall. The walked along a red-tiled hall, a half wall on their right, with a shellacked pine panel in the middle of it separating it from a large open area. Two large pots occupied up-lighted niches at either end of the hall. The wall curved, sending those who were entering the house down three broad steps into a sunken room with a stone floor. To their right Zoe noted several large skins—she supposed they were deer or elk—tacked to the wall against which stood a wide buffet table, obviously meant to be accessed from three sides. To their left a deep banco with woven rugs and pillows lined the other portion of the wall; another banco on the wall opposite complemented it.

Zoe sent her gaze around the walls of the house, taking in as much as possible. Partial walls and half-walls that seemed more purposed for displays than for creating closed-off rooms divided, but did not totally separate, three sections of one huge room. Numerous posts and beams supported an only slightly gabled ceiling, which reminded Zoe, inexplicably, of a sauna where she and Nick had spent a dreamy, drifty, steamy late afternoon following several hours of hard skiing in an Adirondack winter three years previously. Hundreds of rough-hewn, narrow, reddish, squared-off sticks made chevrons, herringbones, cross-hatchings, parallel lines, and diamonds that transformed the ceiling into a piece of art.

Zoe's head started to swim. She lowered her gaze, flicking a glance in front of her long enough to register tableaux of two, three, four people, arranged but not clustered, in the three sections of this gigantic room: welcoming, magnanimous cocoons of space colored in reds, pinks, yellows, turquoise.

She swiveled her head swiftly to left and right, making sure she had seen what had flashed in the edges of her vision: on either side of her, to the left and to the right, there were wall niches with half-globe Plexi-glass display cases, softly up-lighted, with mirrors at the back so the entire pot could be viewed. Zoe glimpsed enough of the design of the two pots they contained to trigger recognition: a little lizard, with a diamond pattern on its back, crawled up the inside of a perfectly rounded deep bowl. In the right-hand one, its little digits—its hands—were broken off by the ragged scar of the edge of a hole. She looked to left: this vessel was the mirror image of the other one, except that the lizard's little hands grasped something: a feathered something. A stick? There was no hole in the pot. *Yes, indeed*, she thought. *Just like the ones pictured in the photographs in Ferguson's folder. These are Mimbres pots. Grave goods.*

Two plastered pillars rose from the room's center, separated by about thirty feet, holding huge beams that supported smaller beams that in turn supported the latticework ceiling. Across the room, three more steps, not as broad as the ones they had just descended, led up to another open room with another beam-and-lattice ceiling supported by immense plastered pillars. Zoe noted two more niches in two corners, also displaying pots—Mimbres pots. All the walls except the one behind the buffet were hung with colorful weavings, some quite large, interspersed with modernist paintings with vaguely Native themes: ceremonial dances, coyotes decked out as dancers, very large, dark-skinned women in colorful blouses and skirts. A huge picture window on the far side of this section of the room gave a spectacular view: a mountain range capped with lightly snowed peaks. Another half wall separated this section of the room from yet another section; the middle of the wall was broken with a large archway. Another large window gave out onto the same view.

A table in the room into which she was looking held sturdy paper plates, glasses and wine glasses. The tables, Zoe noted, had adzed wood bases and tops of some sort of laminated hides. All three sections held clusters of men and women, almost all of them at least twenty to thirty years older than Zoe and Phil. Zoe thought the space in which they were standing held about twenty people; another ten or fifteen people milled about the second space. Zoe thought the third space probably held about the same number. Nobody was sitting on the bancos or at the tables. *Standard*, thought Zoe. *That always happens at parties: everybody wants to mill, nobody wants to sit, people balance drinks and plates of food on their fingertips, and everybody wants to head for the kitchen.* Though it wasn't clear to Zoe just where the kitchen was.

While they were looking around, taking it all in, a young woman, definitely the youngest person in the room aside from themselves, sporting a skirt that reminded Zoe of one of the Mondrian paintings she had seen the day before, reaching to her ankle on one side and completely open on the other, revealing thigh clear up to her hip, lace-up leather boots clack-clacking on the stone floor, trotted smartly toward them. A blouse secured closed with a large knot just above her navel, and a large silver clasp at a plunging neckline, was obviously meant to accentuate the rhythm; her breasts danced artfully behind the blouse, unencumbered by bra or halter.

Zoe recognized Hilary, from the gallery. Her eyes were marked with kohl; eyelids fluttered turquoise. "Hi!" she greeted, "So glad you could come! And this is Phil, right?" She held out her hand. Phil took it; she immediately slid it out of his grasp. "Please help yourselves to the buffet. And there's drinks set up on the banco in the other room." Hilary pointed. Zoe saw that a movable bar had been set on the banco. It was cleverly designed. A dozen shallow concavities held bottles; another half-dozen held various sorts of glasses. Under the bar was a metal trough filled with ice. Six of the bottles had their bottoms nested in the trough; Zoe supposed these were bottles of white wine. A hose drained ice-melt into a bucket at the far end, underneath the banco. Next to the banco, closer to the steps, was what looked like an old-fashioned ice box. She saw a distinguished-looking gray-haired man in a suit bend down, open the ice box's door, and draw out a beer. "And of course, you're staying the night? We have oodles of room—guest bedrooms and houses all over the place."

"Sure," Zoe replied. Phil nodded. "That's very kind of you, of Woody…"

"It's better that way. Nobody goes driving off the road! You know, I'd introduce you, but I don't know where to start. I don't know where Woody's gotten to, but he's somewhere."

"That's okay," said Zoe. "I think we'll start with someone I know." She had spotted Sebastian Plumm in a twosome with a woman. "But I think first we'll visit the buffet and the bar."

The buffet had plates and steam basins piled with small bites. Signs held by little stanchions in the shape of hands announced the fare: lamb shanks; bacon-wrapped prawns; tiny purple and red new potatoes roasted in *pico de gallo*; *iberico* ham; dates, some stuffed with Stilton cheese, others with pieces of serrano pepper; chunks of sea wolf marinated as ceviche; strips of prosciutto wrapping bite-sized chunks of grilled steak or, if you preferred, cantaloupe balls; three kinds of vegan wraps—mashed carrot, pepper hummus, and shredded cabbage with capers and pimientos; chorizo pig-in-the-blankets; mini-quiches; mini-tacos, pinched at both ends—grilled chicken, beef, sweet red pepper, or hominy-filled; mini-margherita pizzas; and the standard chunks of cheese—Emmenthaler, cheddar, jack, and manchego—as well as a chevre-tartar dip for broccoli flowers. Three carafes—olive oil and vinegar with rosemary; mustard with capers; and creamy pine-nut pesto—were available to dress offerings from a huge glass bowl of baby spinach leaves and arugula salad, garnished generously with cherry tomatoes and marinated baby artichokes and a few garbanzo beans.

"Wow!" said Zoe. "What a spread!" They loaded up their deep-dish cardboard plates, then headed for the bar; Zoe for a glass of pino grigio, Phil for a Corona from the ice box. They made their way toward Sebastian Plumm. He was saying something about a lone wolf. When they approached, he did a sort of double-take, then said, "Oh, hello! You're…"

"Claudine. And this is Phil."

"Yes, yes—you're Coco's new assistant." The woman with whom he was talking, dressed in a well-cut blue suit, with minimally gray-streaked brown hair and, for jewelry, only a one-strand silver filet raised her eyebrows. "This is Nelda Cavaletto." Nelda nodded her head ever so slightly.

Ah! Thought Zoe. *Woody's wife. His bankroller, at least in the beginning.*

4:15 PM: JEN AND THAD

Meanwhile, outside, the last of the guests were arriving: Jen and Thad, in their very quaint green van, were in line behind a Chrysler Le Baron and a Mercedes 257. When it was their turn, they watched as a man in a fringed leather jacket, Stetson hat, and Levi's with a large silver-and-turquoise belt buckle approached. He carried a clipboard in his right hand, a pen in his right. Thad rolled down his window.

"Good afternoon," the man said. "Welcome to Los Pajaritos. Name please?"

"Jen and Thad Pritchard." The man consulted his clipboard. There was a notation beside their names Thad could not decipher. "Ah!" said Mr. fringed and Stetsoned. He pointed to a small cottage on the far side of the compound. "Park over there." He fished a piece of paper out of his fringed jacket pocket, handing it to Thad. "Here's the code. Just punch it in, then push the door open."

Thad parked. Thad opened the van's back doors, retrieving their two suitcases. Jen punched in the code, opened the door, then returned to the van. Together, Jen and Thad eased the portmanteau out from under the boxes and carried it into the cottage. Thad returned to the van, closed the back doors, returned to the cottage, and closed the door. Jen had shifted the suitcases inside. "Whew!" he said. "Finally, we can just leave Mr. Mask here and forget about it for a while."

"Right," agreed Jen. "If anybody makes off with it, it'll be Mr. Woodard Glenn who has to answer to Dahlia. Here. Put this in your wallet." Jen handed Thad the piece of paper.

They exited the cottage, pulling the door to, and made their way to the main house. Inside, they were met by Mr. Woodard Glenn, dressed in tan Dockers, holding a drink, pepper-and-salt bare arms crossed in front of an un-logoed t-shirt; a wide smile broke across his symmetrical, tanned face. "Welcome! Welcome!" He set his glass down on a wide, slightly rounded half wall—*a precarious perch*, noted Jen. He took both their hands in both of his in succession. "Let me introduce you to a few folks; then you can visit the buffet and the bar." He led them into a large sunken space, then up another few stairs into another space, introducing them to clusters of men and women as they went, never letting them spend more than a minute at each cluster. Jen knew she would not remember anybody she was meeting, but that it was somehow important for everybody to whom she was being introduced to be aware of her and Thad. She caught names: Diane, Joe, Larry, Christina, Penny, Dean (was he dean of a college or was that his name?), Doris, Dick, Martha, Rudy, Sarah, Tracy, Bill, Barbara, Helen, James, Deborah, Duncan, Melanie, Kurt, Stan (or was it Dan?), Joan, Mark, Kay (or was it Kate?), Dennis, Madison, Molly (or was it Polly?), Julia, Jedda (or Jetta? or Jenna?), Matt, Gareth, Orson, Loren, Abby, Toby, Geoff, Eric, Rachel, Walter, Nelda, Sebastian—but she would never be able to match face with name. Jen could tell that Thad was equally flummoxed. Finally, he led them back out of the smallest of the three rooms and over to the bar. "Please, help yourself. The buffet is over there." Woodard Glenn pointed to his right, as the fringed and Stetsoned greeter approached them. "And this is Art. Art Tatum. He runs the place! Gates closed?" he asked Art.

"Yes sir. All guests accounted for."

"Art will be your guide through the drinks in case you need one."

"Pleasure," said Art.

"You're not *the* Art Tatum, surely?" asked Jen.

"Well, not quite. But that's what people call me so, please, you do so too!" Art Tatum helped himself to two fingers of Chivas Regal, added ice and a spritz of tonic. "'Scuse me," he said, "Ah'll just see if Mr. Glenn needs anything."

Jen and Thad passed the next 45 minutes in pleasant conversation with some of the people they had met in their whirlwind tour; their end of the conversations always went the same way: *We handle antiques in upstate New York… Yes, we really like it out here… Thinking of relocating… Yes, this is quite a collection… We had a bit of a windfall… Have something more along the lines here… Yes, might set up here… Have to see how we could maybe provide a service to folks out here… Yes, so we understand… Not everybody accessorizes with Native art….*

After a suitable interval of socializing, Jen and Thad set their glasses of wine on one of the low tables, made their way to the buffet, and returned with loaded plates. They sat on the settee. "Don't look now," said Jen, "but he's here."

"You mean the scruffy guy who's been following us."

"Precisely. Except he's shaved off his beard. And he's with a gal," observed Jen. "I'm pretty sure it's the same gal who was sitting with him in that park in that dismal place where we had lunch—where was it?"

Thad shrugged. "Who knows. What do you think they're doing here?"

"Beats me," said Jen. "I wonder why we weren't introduced."

"Because obviously they're not players."

"Then what are they doing here?"

"Do you want to saunter over and find out?"

"No." Jen shook her head. "Best we don't show particular interest. We're confident. We're in control. We're dealers in art. We're interested in customers. We have nothing to say to a post-teeny-bopper and her teddy."

"Maybe relatives?"

"Of Woodard Glenn's?"

"Well, that might explain it. And yeah—maybe it is all just coincidence. It's really her who's the connection, not him. I'll bet she's in college somewhere in the east; comes back out here for the summer—bet Woodard Glenn's her uncle or something—meets the scruffy along the way, drags him along… He does the Santa Fe trots just like we did."

"So what was she doing in the meantime? Why wasn't she with him?" objected Jen.

Again, Thad shrugged. "Like you say. Let's just hang loose. Play it by our favorite instrument. Wait for things to develop."

After filling up on snacks, they drifted from this cluster to that cluster, but had only one memorable conversation, with a couple—he in a suit, with a shock of white hair, she with probably a dye job in a black skirt and red sleeveless top. Jen remembered they were Tracy and Barbara. They spent some time talking with them; he taught economics at the university. They collected art. Barbara said right out he was some kind of genius. "Thanks to his genius we've got a Chagall and a Picasso. Just a drawing," added Tracy nodding. "He's like the rain man," continued Barbara. "He counts cards. You know the rain man?"

"Oh, Dustin Hoffman?" Jen had said.

"Right," Tracy said, "except I'm not autistic."

"He made a fortune for us at the blackjack tables," continued Barbara.

"Yeah," said Tracy, nodding, "but now they bar the doors when they see me coming."

"He has a photographic memory," added Barbara. "We love our moderns. We got them through Nelda, of course, but we're thinking of branching out into some of what Woody handles."

Ah! Thought Jen! *That's why we were introduced. And evidently, they've already been told about us and what we've brought.*

As the hours passed, Zoe and Phil roamed the huge room; Woody Glenn appeared briefly, glanced in their direction, but did not approach to say hello, circulated, then disappeared, re-appearing only a couple of hours later. As he approached Zoe and Phil, Zoe noted that he looked fit, rugged, relaxed. Zoe realized his head of hair was either a toupee or must be dyed. As he approached, seeing Phil, a puzzled look briefly crossed his face. "Hi!" he said. "Good to see you! Where's…?" But just then his trouser pocket beeped. "Excuse me," he said, clomping up the steps and disappearing through an arched doorway. *He probably expected me show up with Coco,* mused Zoe, *not with a strange man!*

At several points, a woman who looked to be Native, in what looked like Native dress appeared, renewed the bar, and replaced some of the steam basins; one held, so said the sign, grilled portabella mushrooms. A plate of grilled asparagus also appeared. Several people, almost always in twos or fours, men and women, approached Zoe and Phil, almost systematically, it seemed, to learn who they were; after several of these encounters, Zoe and Phil had developed a kind of back-and-forth routine—*art history, Western Connecticut, fakes and forgeries, University of Washington, really interesting place here, helping Coco Vanderjagt; Indiana, Pueblos, potters and pottery designs, met on the road...*

Their conversation with Plumm had been a non-starter. Nelda Cavaletto drifted away as Plumm held forth on much the same theme that Zoe and Coco had heard at the Gregg Neal gallery. They drifted as well, they hoped casually, to the up-lighted niches holding pots; sotto voce, Zoe noted they were Mimbres. Phil nodded. They tried their best to drift away from the vanners, who did not seem any more anxious to encounter them than they were to be encountered. They learned from Hilary that the couple they were tailing were called Jen and Thad, from upstate New York. Zoe found that puzzling. *So why aren't they impersonating the Murrays from Croton Corners?* she thought. Maybe all the trouble she had gone to, to be not who she was, was unnecessary, if there was a possibility that "Murrays" and "Croton Corners" would be meaningless to everybody here—except, of course, to the vanners.

The longest conversation they had was with a man who introduced himself as Stan from the Concho Gallery in Scarsdale; he seemed to be the only one there besides Plumm without a mate. Stan probed her, it seemed a little too assiduously, about her and her presence in Santa Fe. *Was this Stan* Joiner, *person of interest in one of the multiple layers of the masquerade, but now showing just a little too much interest in her? Who knew what he was phishing for?* She mentioned working in a restaurant-bar, but she was very conscious of not mentioning its name nor of course its actual location nor anything about Cannings' or antiques. Stan probed about her thesis and seemed to challenge her about why and how she was going to spend the summer learning about Native American art in order to help her aunt Coco when she was planning to disappear into the rainforest of the Northwest. But she managed, she thought convincingly, to talk about a long-term situation, a fail-safe in case she could not get a teaching job with her PhD, and after all, there was a lot of Native art on the Northwest Coast...

Finally, Stan withdrew his antennas and sauntered off to other conversations. For most of the time they had real conversations only with each other and with Hilary; they were by far the youngest people there, and could talk about bands they'd seen and music they liked and college and courses and art. Hilary turned out to be surprisingly well-informed. It turned out she also had a degree in art history, from UNM.

This was obviously a sort of open house; people seemed to stay a couple of hours, then depart, except for a couple of dozen holdouts. At nine thirty, Art Tatum appeared and announced, "Anybody going into Santa Fe? I can take up to nine in the chariot." A half-dozen people murmured and nodded and followed Art Tatum to the door.

He turned around. "All the rest of you have your quarters. Oh—I'm sorry—you two." Art detached himself from his crowd of passengers at the door, some of whom were visibly weaving, and approached Zoe and Phil, who were off by themselves in a corner. He led them through the room with the bar, into the next room, and to a door in the far side, which he opened with a code. "Just a sec. Oh—pardon me—you two *are* together, aintcha?" They both nodded. Art Tatum retreated back to the bar, took a cocktail napkin, retrieved a pen from an inside pocket of his fringed jacket, wrote something on the napkin, and handed the cocktail napkin to Phil. "That's the code for the door. You have luggage?" They both wagged their heads back and forth. "Well Mr. Glenn specifically instructed me you're to have this bedroom. We lay on breakfast at seven thirty over on the buffet. And don't feel like you've gotta go right to bed; feel free to have another glass of wine or two. There's still the cheese board—I think Lupina's put out some melted fig-jam brie."

"Thanks. But I think we'll call it a night." *I wonder why we've been offered a room*, thought Zoe-Claudine. *The vanners—Jen and Thad—also seem to be staying somewhere on the property. Is there something afoot that we don't know about?*

～ↄ

9:35 PM JEN AND THAD

Art Tatum departed with his flock of Santa Fe-bound revelers, who were now looking somewhat deflated. Only three other people were left: the willowy, somewhat stressed-looking man that Jen was pretty sure was called Sebastian; the somewhat disorganized-looking man with a salt-and-pepper beard who was either Dan or Stan; and Hilary. Woodard Glenn had disappeared again.

"Well, I'll toddle off as well," said Sebastian Plumm to Jen and Thad. "Nighty-night. I'm in Sansouci. We share a wall, but it's thick. You're in Edge of Taos Desert, right next door."

Thad furrowed his brow. "All the cottages have names?" Plumm nodded.

"Don't worry; we're not loud," said Jen. She looked around for Nelda, or was it Nilda? Or Gilda? But she had quietly slipped away.

The man named Dan—or was it Stan? She couldn't remember his second name—approached them. "Well, I don't know where Woody's got off to and Nelda seems to have disappeared like the wind in the willows. So, I guess I'll play substitute host. Care for a sit-down and a drink?"

"Actually, thanks anyway," said Thad. "I think it's getting on towards ten—we've had a long day! Excuse us if we just—what's the phrase—toddle off?"

"Sure, sure. I think I'll sit up for a while. Usually there's a couple of recliners in here but Woody had them moved out for the party." Stan moved through a small arched doorway to the right of the buffet table from where they were standing; a heavy gray, red, and black weaving covered the doorway. He emerged dragging a vintage green canvas-and-steel deck chair, set it next to the buffet table, fixed himself a Chivas Regal with no ice and flopped into the chair. "I imagine we'll see a lot of each other tomorrow," said Stan. "I'm intrigued to examine your goods."

"Great," said Thad. "I'm looking forward to tomorrow!" He reached out for Stan's hand, grabbed it, and pumped it. "Well, good night."

Now ensconced in a king-sized bed in the guest bedroom, with its own private bath facility attached, Phil said to Zoe: "So now we're—you're done, right?"

"Right. I guess tomorrow after breakfast we'll just go back to Santa Fe. I'll call Ferguson and tell him. I feel a little bad taking advantage of Woody Glenn's hospitality. Besides Hilary, you and I were the youngest people there! I wonder how he explained me. He seems so nice, generous. I can't believe he's be involved with anything like insurance fraud and stealing pots."

"What will you tell Ferguson?"

"Well, just what we've done. We know the vanners are here. They're going to negotiate something with Woody Glenn. Now it's up to Ferguson."

"Then…?"

"Then, then … I guess I go on to Seattle. Well, maybe I'll stick around here another few days and see some more of this area."

"Yeah—I'll give you the conducted tour of San Ildefonso and Santa Clara. Maybe we can go to Nambé and Tesuque, too; they're not quite as interesting—oh—except there's a neat picnic area near Nambé Pueblo—Nambé Falls. Maybe we can drop in on a couple of my pottery ladies."

"Sweet! We'll do it."

A pen stood next to a little sign on the dresser: "We would like breakfast at (Circle please) 7:30, 8:00, 8:30, 9:00, 9:30, 10:00 and hang me on the outside door handle."

Breakfast okay for eight?"

"Sure."

Zoe was in her panties; Phil was unbuttoning his shirt. She filled in the sign, went to the door, opened it a crack, hung the sign on the clinker, closed it. "But you know, I wonder if all this disguise business, the false name and all that was really necessary. I'd like to get together with this Jen and Thad couple and just ask them: 'Did you know? *What* did you know? *When* did you know it? What did you do? Why did you do it? What did you think?'"

Phil drew off his trousers. "Are you sleepy?"

"No," said Zoe, tumbling onto the bed. "But I really did finally get it. I hope I can sleep. I should take ibuprofen. My period."

"Oh."

⁓つ

Inside their cottage, Thad immediately took a cocktail napkin out of his breast pocket and a pen from his jeans pocket. He wrote on the napkin: *could be bugged. Just chit-chat.* Jen formed an "o" with her lips, then nodded. As they prepared for bed, they kept up a realistic banter: *Nice wall hangings—wonderful spread—did you have the mini-quiches—I really liked those prawns—great stuffed dates—did you check out the pots in the corners?—That buffet table is an antique—how many of the guests will you remember tomorrow?—Hope we'll have a chance to mosey around here tomorrow—looks interesting.*

Throughout the banter, Jen felt increasingly mellow, ripe, for the first time in days—or was it weeks? She wanted him to gently part her thighs, enter her, kiss her mouth as he moved in her, kiss her slowly, taking his time, bringing her along until she shrieked. *Surely, if there was a bug in the room, such sounds would dispel any suspicion...*

20

ZOE KNEW SHE DIDN'T HAVE TO GET UP at eight o'clock just because it was the time their breakfast was set for; in fact, as she and Phil stepped into the shower, she felt a bit chilled. When she and Phil emerged from the room, Zoe in bare feet, she realized the stone floor was heated. Had it turned cold?

The buffet was once again laid with steam basins, three of them; from the smells, Zoe thought they must hold potatoes and sausages or bacon. A four-slot toaster stood beside two large plates, one stacked with large squares of corn bread and white and brown rolls, the other with three stacks of bread slices ranging from white to very dark. A small dish held a mound of soft butter, six small bowls held jams, honey, and red and green chili, and a shallow bowl held tangerines, apples, and pears. Two very large coffee urns labeled "coffee" and "water" along with several boxes of teas, a jar of Nescafé, a bowl of brown sugar, and two pitchers holding, Zoe speculated, milk and cream respectively had replaced the wine and liquor bottles on the bar.

They mounted the steps and saw that the pine panel in the half wall had been opened and the elk hide had been drawn aside to reveal a huge fireplace with a fire now roaring in it. From somewhere, a heavy, dark table with a half-dozen chairs that reminded Zoe of a monastery, even though she'd never set foot in one, had been hauled in. As they approached the table, a short, young woman emerged and stood next to the long, dark table, which was set with eight places. She was dressed in a long-sleeved green blouse and freshly pressed jeans that looked brand new. A necklace of small, irregular turquoise stones encircled her neck.

"Good morning! I'm Lupina. The buffet table is down there. That's potatoes au gratin, home fries, and sausages and bacon over there." She looked over at the buffet. She spoke with a distinct clipped accent. "Come up and take a seat! Get your plates and help yourselves, or if you want cereal or eggs, I'll bring 'em out. Would you like granola? Or fresh raspberries? We also have Cheerios if you like 'em or shredded wheat. And we can do eggs any way you like them. We can also do you a half-grapefruit. By the way, we eat in shifts here. I know Woody and Stan won't be in until around ten. That other new couple are coming at nine. There'll be a big rush at ten with Mr. Glenn—the Crosbys, Mr. Plumm, the Motts, Mr. Joiner."

They sat. "What about … uh … Nelda?"

"Mrs. Glenn has already left, gone back to town. She has a gallery, too you know. And she has to open today. What would you like?"

Zoe asked for soft-boiled eggs; Phil for easy over. "No cereal?" asked Lupina.

"No, thank you," replied Zoe. Phil shook his head. Lupina disappeared behind a bead curtain just as Hilary appeared coming the other way. Incongruously, she was dressed in extremely short shorts, huge fluffy slippers, and an oversized cardigan. She hugged herself. "Brrr! It's cold! They're saying it might even snow."

"How can it snow?" asked Zoe querulously. "It was sunny and warm yesterday…"

Hilary sat down. "That's the way it is here. Did you hear the wind last night? The weather blows in and the temp can drop, like, forty degrees in twenty-four hours." Phil smiled a half-smile and nodded.

Lupina returned holding a tray with a small covered plate and two egg cups. She set them down in front of Zoe and Phil, removing the cover as she did so. "What will you have, Miss Lowe?"

Zoe nodded silently in her head. *Yup!* She thought, *Nelda Cavaletto Glenn is definitely a figurehead, a used-to-be, but not quite tossed aside, because she's still a player. But day-to-day, she's out; Hilary's in.*

"Oh, I guess, the usual, granola with raspberries on top, and I'll go get some of that au gratin. Oh!!" She moaned. "I have to leave soon!"

"Why?" asked Zoe.

Hilary sighed theatrically, wiggled her eyebrows, and shook her head. "I have to open the gallery! Meanwhile Woody sleeps in and I have to handle the whole gallery all day—and Saturdays are always super busy; mostly meandering tour-a-touralae—but somebody still has to be there. Woody has important business that he has to stick around for here."

Lupina appeared with Hilary's granola. Hilary took the bowl, rose, and went down to the buffet. Lupina hovered. "We're Claudine and Phil," said Claudine. "Pleased to meet you."

"And you." Lupina nodded.

"You from around here?" asked Phil.

"No. I'm from Honduras. Me and my family came here as refugees from the earthquake in 1999. I hardly remember it. I was just a tot. But Mr. Glenn sponsored us."

"So you live around here."

"We did for a while but now we live in town. My father's a journalist. He covers Mexico and Guatemala, and Honduras, but from a distance, for *The Guardian.* My mother's getting her teaching certificate from College of Santa Fe. She's paid her dues! She spent most of her life raising me and my sister and my brother."

"And you were serving last night, right? I think I saw you topping up some of that food for the steam basins. That makes for a long night!" remarked Phil. Zoe nodded. She remembered the very pretty, dark-skinned girl dressed in a black Native dress who periodically appeared with covered trays and periodically refurbished the drinks bar.

"No, that was my sister. She's started a catering service and this is her first big gig. I think she did pretty good! She had four people working in the kitchen last night!"

"She sure did do good!" said Phil.

"Did you get that fire going? It's actually beginning to get hot in here!"

"No, that wasn't me. That was Art."

"Does he live on the premises?" asked Phil.

"Oh, yeah," replied Lupina. "He lives in the go-down. Mr. Glenn offered him one of the cottages when there're no guests in it but he says, no, he likes the go-down. No plumbing in there! But he likes it anyway. Well, I should get back and see if Lorencita needs anything; she sent her crew off after they set all this up so she's doing everything, from now on, on her own."

"You know," said Hilary, returning to the table. "It's too bad it's so stinky out today. You should really walk around and see some of the places people have built and also the museum. Woody's set it up like it was 900 years ago; like people just left."

"Yes. This is quite a place. Did someone design it or did it just sort of grow?"

"Oh, no. It was designed. Three of the cottages were done first; they're supposed to be solar efficient. I mean, on good sunny days they heat up all by themselves. Designed by Peter Van Dresser. Then when he passed away, Bill Lumpkin took over. He designed this, the main house. Can you stay over? Tomorrow's supposed to be better weather."

Zoe and Phil looked at each other. "We'd like to. We really should be getting back today, but it would be great to look around," said Phil.

"But we didn't bring warm clothes." objected Zoe/Claudine.

"I can find you some warm woolies and coats," said Hilary. "Okay, me for some of that au gratin." She pronounced it "oh-grattin."

"Me too," said Phil. All three of them filed down to the buffet, Phil and Zoe popping pieces of bread into the toaster and filling plates with "oh-grat-tin;" crisp, slightly blackened home fries; red chili; bacon; and for Phil, sausage. They glanced up as another couple came in from the direction of the kitchen. "Look who's here," said Zoe, sotto voce. "Well, we finally get our chance. Or I do. I guess 'an honest tale speeds best being plainly told' and 'honesty is the best policy,' or at least unavoidable."

They followed Hilary back to the table. Jen and Thad had already sat down. "Hi! I'm Hilary! You remember, from the gallery?"

"And we're Claudine and Phil. I don't think we met last night."

"No. We're Jen and Thad," said Jen. "How do you know Mr. Glenn?"

"Oh," said Zoe, "we don't. Not really. My aunt—well, she's not really my aunt, she's a good friend of my aunt, er, well she's not really my aunt either, but she's like an aunt, a family friend, she—my aunt here—her name is Coco, Coco Vanderjagt, she sort of, like, deals in fine art and she knows Mr. Glenn, or maybe more, his wife. Anyway, my aunt, that is, Coco, has clients that mainly want European art, but now her clients are wanting some Native art, and, well, she called my aunt back home and said, hey, does Claudine need a job for the summer? She can come out and help me, help me get familiar with Native art, and so forth." Zoe knew she was babbling but thought it rang true and, well, it almost sort of was, if you left out a lot. "How do you know Mr. Glenn?" Zoe piled au gratin onto a piece of toast.

"Ha! We don't either," said Thad.

"We're on a sort of vacation, maybe looking to relocate," said Jen. *Nice bullshit!* "In fact, we found a sort of run-down ramshackle place yesterday down in—down in—what was the name of that place?" she turned to Thad.

Thad did a double-take at Jen. "Corrales. We deal in antiques—mostly furniture."

"Where are you from?" asked Zoe-Claudine.

"Oswego. Oswego, New York. Worst climate in the world. Nothing for anybody to do but shop big-box stores and go to large screen movies," said Thad.

"And go looking for antiques," added Jen. "We just sort of meandered out here. We'd heard of New Mexico for years and we even have some people out here who are our customers, but more in Arizona."

"We kind of just stumbled into Mr. Glenn's gallery," said Thad. "We had a kind of windfall that we don't exactly know what to do with. So, we thought we'd bring it out here and combine it with a holiday, see what the market is like out here for antiques or see if we'd like to go into Native arts if it … if it works out for us to … to do something with this … this piece of art that we don't really know what to do with."

Oooohh, sliding uncomfortably close to the truth, thought Jen. *But maybe we'll find out a little more about this gal's truth.* "And I gather you're not from out here either?" asked Jen.

"I'm just finishing up a master's at Western Connecticut College, going out to University of Washington for a PhD, in art history, and thought it would be good to get some real experience in the art world through Coco. I'm really grateful to Aunt Ellie for setting it all up."

"And you?" asked Jen, looking at Phil.

"I'm also in a PhD program. Indiana. Anthropology. I'm really just along for the ride—a temporary ride. Z—Claudine and I met, sort of on the road and, well, she's really out here to sort of do an internship with her aunt, sort-of aunt, and so it's kind of awkward, I mean, for us to get together, so this is kind of nice. I can't hang around very long—I mean, I shouldn't. I'm studying Native pots and pottery design and potters and I've gotta get some progress done on my dissertation, so … I guess we, I don't know exactly how it's going to work out."

Nice save, thought Zoe. *Did they notice? Did it matter?* Now another, much older couple emerged from what Zoe assumed must be the entrance not only to the kitchen but also an access to outside. "Well, I guess we should get ready to take our leave," she said.

"Hey—I've gotta leave too," said Hilary. "But let me go find you some nice warm coats. You can wander around outside until you need to go."

~∽

9:15 AM

They did, indeed, take a self-guided tour. As she had handed them their coats—a quilted thick sheepskin one with fuzzy ruffs and cuffs for Zoe, but overly large, and an equally over-large fur-lined Canadian Air Force coat with hood for Phil—Hilary explained that the compound, and the three rooms in which the party had been held, were used periodically as conference space for small professional archaeological conferences and once a year for a writer's workshop. The guests that were not chauffeured back to Santa Fe or lodged in the cottages were, she said, actually residents in several two-and-a-half-acre estates on what had originally been a fifty-two-acre ranch that Woody bought years ago.

"I'll bet it was his wife's money," said Zoe as they walked the path. "According to Coco, she financed his gallery so probably this too."

The gravel path wound around six small adobe cottages, built back-to-back, or maybe tandem would be a better way to describe the common wall that embraced them. The path meandered around the cottages and down into a natural hollow where they encountered a small ruin, built of close-fitting stones.

"So those are the imposters!" declared Phil.

"Yeah. Jen and Thad. Did you see how they avoided us all evening? Strange, since they haven't kept up the pretense of being the Murrays."

"Well, we kind of avoided them too," noted Phil, "because we're pretty sure they tumbled to the fact that we were following them, right? Why do you suppose we were suddenly ushered into the guest bedroom?"

"Well, maybe Jen and Thad let Woody know about us tailing them and he decided we were suspicious characters and needed to be kept an eye on. Or maybe he bought Coco's story about me and thinks I need to be mightily impressed with his setup and credentials so I'll drum up business for him through Coco. Hilary's insistence that we go on this tour is probably part of that."

Now they encountered a very low wall that enclosed a plaza; the wall made a half circle and intersected with another wall with a doorway shaped like an old-fashioned keyhole.

"But you know, they seem kind of nice. I mean, likable. Jen and Thad do."

Zoe nodded. "I agree. But remember, they're in the same business as Cait and Robb—antiques and collectibles, legit and otherwise. They deal with the public and also with wholesalers and collectors when they have what they want. They have to put on a good face—affable, sincere, ingratiating, ready with a good story. And what they did to Robb and Cait was only semi-nice— nice if you don't mind being tied up and pantsed."

"I can see that," agreed Phil.

More keyhole doors led them into a number of rectangular rooms, one after another, around the ruin's periphery, then into a round room that a painted wooden sign announced as a "Kiva. Used for ceremonial purposes." They noted that several of the rooms had broken, undecorated pots in their corners; another had what seemed to be a corner hearth. The kiva had a banco on its interior periphery. "This one is pretty small," said Phil. "But the people would cram onto the benches and dancers—maybe four or six with a couple men on a drum—would perform in the middle here."

"You've been in one of these?"

Phil nodded. "Kivas are still used in the Pueblos for ceremonies."

They exited through another large keyhole door into a rectangular plaza that gave onto another circular structure, free-standing, and much larger than the interior one. "I'll bet there's another little pueblo around here somewhere," said Phil. "But here's something I don't get about the Jen and Thad puzzle," he said. Why *aren't* they passing themselves off as the Murrays?"

"Probably because they don't need to do so. They don't need to be Mr. and Mrs. Well-established-Shopkeepers-from-a-Respectable Address. All they need to be is people with the goods—the goods that Woodard Glenn will broker to his clients. Who were, I'll bet, basically all the people who were at the soirée."

They entered this kiva through a doorway that was not a keyhole. "I think this entryway is artificial. This structure would have had a cover, with a hole and a ladder, for entering." They walked around two rectangular depressions, about two feet deep. "I'll be these are foot drums," said Phil. "They would have been covered with slabs of wood. Dancers would stomp on the foot drums and the sound would resonate through the whole kiva." A banco also circled this kiva's interior periphery.

They exited the kiva and walked up a slight incline that leveled off, over to a plastered wall, just short of head-level. On tiptoes, they could see over it; on the other side was a road. "That must lead to all the other, uh, 'estates,'" noted Phil. "So Woody Glenn has this whole little compound here with grateful sycophants for neighbors who bought from him, after he did the right thing and had this pueblo properly and archaeologically excavated, and now he can play slick operator hiding behind the mask of respectability."

"I wouldn't say hiding," Zoe temporized. "He *does* have respectability. But if Ferguson is right, that he was one of the recipients of what was essentially looted grave goods—the Mimbres pots—and then also participated in the subsequent insurance fraud, then he also embraces the labyrinthine paths that let dealers navigate legal technicalities enabling archaeological artifacts and cultural patrimony to be redefined as collectible, displayable accessories and sacred objects to be redefined as art."

"For a profit."

"For a profit," agreed Zoe. "Well, I guess we should get back. I've got to have a long conversation with Ferguson and see what all this has really led to, if anything."

SATURDAY, 11:00 AM

Jen and Thad made their way across the graveled courtyard from the side door of the main house; Jen noted a perfect square of cultivated earth in its center. She supposed it was planted, or would be so soon, in vegetables or maybe flowers. Pots of blooming red and white geraniums lined the path. "So, they turn out to be just what they seem to be," said Thad. "And it's her, not him. And *she* turns out to be a non-starter, a non-entity, a non-player."

"Yeah, yeah, yeah," said Jen. She stopped in her tracks. "But we've got to call Dahlia."

"Not before we have the *tête-à-tête* with Woody and that other guy—what's his name?"

"Stan. But that would be sometime this afternoon. We're to meet them back in the big house at one."

12:50 PM

Thad carried the portmanteau across the graveled compound yard; Jen opened the door to the big house. They went through a sort-of tunnel, noting the double swinging doors to the kitchen, now open, which revealed a cleaning crew working with sour-smelling liquids that they spread on the floor and, given the open doors, in the ovens of a large Aga stove. Thad carried the portmanteau down the steps. The settees had been moved and were now lined up in front of the bancos; the low tables had disappeared. Two imitation leather recliners now sat in the middle of the room but Woody and the man called Stan were seated in two Herman Miller Aeron chairs in the far corner; the heavy curtains on the windows had been rolled up but the day was still overcast and the light was muted. "Bring it over here, if you would, please," said Woody.

"Now open it up and let Stan see what you have." Thad did so, and with Jen's help, held it open. Woody slid off the chair onto his knees. "Okay, let's look at this thing carefully." He rose, walked to the banco, plucked one of the two long cushions from it, dragged it over, and placed it in front of the portmanteau. He then kneeled on it and scrutinized the mask, craning his neck to take in the mask's top, then moving his head slowly down, from side to side. "We need better light here and some aids."

He rose again. "Can you give me a hand, Stan?" Stan rose and followed Woody, punched a code into a door to the left of the now empty buffet table. He emerged with two large magnifying glasses in one hand. In the other he carried an old-fashioned goose-necked desk lamp. He plugged it into a baseboard socket, then carried it over to the portmanteau, set it down, and turned it on. Stan carried an easel and two black bags that looked heavy. He placed the easel behind the open portmanteau and dumped the weighted bags behind two of the easel's three legs to steady it. The portmanteau rested easily against the easel. Woody handed one of the magnifiers to Stan. Stan took his seat, but Woody knelt again on the cushion. He scrutinized the mask again, this time through the magnifying glass, craning his head to look at what he could of its back. A full five minutes passed while he emitted various comments: "Ah! Hmmm. Interesting. Okay… Yeah." He particularly examined the feather fringe lining the mask's "face" and a kind of cloth tunic which looked somewhat the worse for wear.

He rose, then sat back down in the Aeron chair. He nodded. "It's genuine. It's been ceremonially used, at least several times. It's not a museum piece." Stan nodded. Woody looked at him. "I can't see any sign of an accession number."

"Good," remarked Stan.

"And there are holes in the tunic; some of the feathers have been chewed; others have been replaced."

Jen and Thad stayed mumchance; they had no idea how much they were supposed to already know.

"And I'd say it's at least sixty, seventy years old. Probably older. Probably from the nineteen-thirties, or maybe even the twenties. And you have how many more of these?"

"Well," said Thad. "I think that depends on what kind of arrangements we can make."

"What kind of arrangements do you want?" asked Stan.

"Well, probably some sort of guarantee that you really want items like this one."

"Exactly what kind of guarantee are we talking about here?"

"These items, as you note, are the real thing," said Jen. She was trying to remember everything Dahlia had told them. "Some of them might be deaccessioned from museums, but that shouldn't diminish their value."

Woody nodded. "Can you give us a figure?"

"I should think somewhere in the thirties would be appropriate," said Thad.

"But you can't think that we—I—could cough up enough to buy more than one or two?"

"Maybe not. But maybe some of the folks we met last night might be interested."

Woody nodded. "Tell you what. Why don't you let me put this item on … on show, more or less, for some folks who might be interested and … and I'll be able to give you a more realistic idea of just how… how many of these items we might be interested in."

"You mean, leave this with you?"

"Well, more or less. What I'm proposing is that you and this item be our guests for say, a week, and we bring some folks over to have a look…"

"But I think we would have to insist that you not disturb it. It is carefully situated in its case, here," said Thad.

"No, no, of course. We'll keep it here. We'll secure it so it doesn't have to leave the case. I'll roll the curtains back down and leave instructions that no lights are to be turned on." He bent down, and turned off the lamp. "In the meantime, you will be our guests. But, of course, you don't necessarily have to stick here if you don't want to. I think you'll be interested to visit our little museum out back but I'm sure you'll want to take advantage of the many fine galleries in town. There's much more than Native art here—some fine examples of Western art, very innovative sculpture and ceramics, almost every sort of modern represented. Fauvists, expressionists, abstract … also the impressionists and even some old masters."

"Will you excuse us for a moment?" Jen gave Woody and Stan a bright, winning smiles. Then she tugged Thad off to the room's farthest corner. "Do you think it's okay, to leave it here with them?"

"Well, isn't that what we were instructed to do?" temporized Thad. "If Woody plays crook and steals it, didn't we agree that doing that would pretty much let him out of a lucrative deal? He's got to trust us to come up with the rest of the trove; we're going to have to trust him to keep it, keep it safe, and not make it disappear."

Jen nodded. They returned to Stan and Woody, who had made themselves busy examining the mask.

"Well, okay. If you keep us apprised of your … progress. Actually, I think we'd like to go into town this afternoon; maybe you can give us a list of those galleries and a map? So we can find where they are?" said Jen.

"Sure, sure," said Woody. "But first let's see what kind of sandwiches Lupina can make for us. What would you like? Smoked turkey? Ham and cheese? Egg salad? Tuna? Liverwurst? Salami?"

SATURDAY, 2:30 PM

They drove slowly up Canyon Road, noting the galleries as they went, until they arrived at, literally, the top of the road. Thad parked. "Okay. Time to call Dahlia." He punched the burner. The call went to voice mail. "Dahlia? Cannings here. Your Mr. Glenn is interested. Tell us what's next. We'll sit tight 'til we hear. Call us ASAP." He hit *End*. "Let's sit here a minute; see if she calls. Ah!" The ring tone went off.

"Yes… Yes… He's interested… Yes, we left it with him… You have thirteen besides this one… But how can we ask them to pay for something they can't even see…? Why can't you get the rest of them to us so we can show them…? Yes, we can show them the catalogue… Just a minute…"

Thad hugged the phone to his middle. "She wants us to get what she calls down payments for all fourteen of them. I don't see it. Who's going to cough up money for what they're not even sure they're going to get?" Jen nodded vigorously.

He spoke into the phone again "Dahlia! How can we collect money from people without the goods…? All right. So maybe the clients trust Woody and cough up. But why does Woody trust us…? Okay, yes, he does have the one. But is its value equal to the amount of the down payments…? Half…? Yes, yes. Fifteen per cent is usual. Fine. But you want us to collect *50* percent of the assumed sale price of all fourteen, calculated at $32,000 per each, minimum…? That's $224,000. Okay, okay, but what about Woody Glenn? He'll get a commission too? We split it with him…? What if he doesn't go for it? Incentive for charging more! You mean, like, if he soaks them for an average of, say, $38,000 each, you get—let's see—a minimum of $26,600 on each sale and then that's $5,700 on each sale for Woody and $5,700 for us, or maybe more on one or two if the clients are going to go for higher prices… Yes, $80,000 is nothing to sneer at… Yes, I guess, and Woody gets $80,000 and good will and solidifies the client base and so forth… But where do we rendezvous with you to pick up the goods…? I guess you're right. We have no choice. Are you nearby…? All right, all right… Ten days, max." He rang off.

"Well, you heard the gist of that." Thad shook his head, then put his head in his hands.

"How are we going to convince Woody Glenn to hand over $200,000 in what Dahlia calls 'negotiable securities' for nothing more than a picture in an auction catalogue?!"

"What does she mean by 'negotiable securities'?"

"Bank drafts, blank cashier's checks, money orders. No personal checks. Cash is okay too, so says she. She says that's why we're working through Woody Glenn; because he has a solid rep and his clients know he's not going to run off with their money."

"What if Dahlia runs off with their money?" objected Jen.

"Exactly. If she does so, she runs off with ours too."

"What if we just leave."

"Hah! She's probably got us in her sights right this minute. We wouldn't get away with it. We have a max of ten days to get all this together."

"Do you suppose we can stay with Woody Glenn that whole time?"

"I'd say we're more or less Woody's prisoners for the next ten days. A gentle incarceration. Count of Monte Cristo."

Thad punched in Woody Glenn's number.

SATURDAY, 3:30 PM
WOODY GLENN AND STAN JOINER

Stan sat in one of the Aeron chairs, now in Woody's office, post-brunch brandy in hand. Woody sat in a recliner. Stan chewed on a pipe. *With his salt-and-pepper beard and tonsure and his large but sturdy frame, he's maturing into an Edward-the-Seventh doppelganger*, thought Woody. An hour or so later Thad had called with their terms: 50 percent of anticipated purchase price, for fourteen items.

"You don't think it might be a sting?"

Woody sipped, shook his head. "I don't know what to think. I'll admit, it's coincidental to the point of being pretty quirky. This couple shows up with goods from the Paris auction, but they weren't there themselves; they just somehow seem to know that I—we—had our eye on those masks, from a year ago, coming from an antiques store in upstate New York at just exactly the same time that Coco Vanderjagt turns up with another couple in tow who are going to help her clients accessorize with high-end Native American art!"

"The girl's going to do it; don't know what the guy's role is."

"No. We don't really know what the real story is with Jen and Thad either. But what they told me is, they're keeping a low profile because this is where the market is but it's also where the Natives are who made the things in the first place and, as we well know, the Natives are restless. But the gal's beau is an anthropologist," added Woody, "working with exactly some of those tribes where some of the masks in this catalogue originated." He leaned over and pounded his right-hand index finger on the catalogue that lay open on his desk.

"And," said Stan, "the gal—or your friend Coco—want *us* to help them do the accessorizing and the New Yorkers just *happen* to turn up with goods that just *happen* to fill the bill." He shook his head. "I just don't like it." He sat back. "I wonder if we can put a wire on them?"

"I'm way ahead of you on that." Woody rose and stepped over to the desk, opening the middle drawer and pulling out a small, flat object. "Recorder."

"Ah!" said Stan. "And?"

"I had it in their cottage. Voice activated, so we have everything they've said from last night through this morning." He shook his head. "Nothing. Just chit-chat. What you'd expect. The house, items on display, the food, the wine, the place… Nothing suspect. Far as I can tell, they're just who they say they are. No conspiracy. No sting in the offing. So, if we don't jump, they might just go on to the next gallery—there are plenty of our good friends and competitors who wouldn't hesitate to fill the void. We don't even know that they didn't mention what they have—even in very general terms—to the gal. She wasn't shy about telling everybody about how she was helping Coco who has clients who're bored with European art and want something different."

"Hell, they may even have talked directly with your better half," growled Stan. "They might be planning to play us. If we don't jump for it, Jen and Thad go to your friend Coco. They may have even made some arrangement to that effect at the soirée last night. Maybe they're there at your friend Coco's right now. You should have wired that room the gal and her friend were in, too."

Woody shook his head. "Didn't think of it."

"You should have asked Art to follow them into town."

"The gal and her friend?"

"Yeah."

"Didn't think of that either."

"Well, at least let's keep track of the Jen and Thad couple."

"If you insist. Art could do it, but I gave Art the day off. What makes you think Coco's gal and the anthropologist might be in cahoots with Jen and Thad?"

"Yesterday. At the party. They studiously avoided each other. I mean, you know, everybody was circulating. Except every time those two couples came anywhere close to colliding with one another, they headed in the other direction. But when one of them wasn't looking, the other one was darting furtive glances. They were both doing it. They know each other. I couldn't keep an eye on them the whole time." Stan gritted his teeth and shook his head. "They could have gotten together and made some arrangement. Maybe we should stick with what we have and forget the mask masquerade. It went well yesterday morning, with the pots, didn't it? That couple—what were their names? And the other ones? We got more than we thought we would."

"Carters, Kay and Walt Carter. And the Motts. The other ones were— ah—I forget. Mack or Matt and Julie or Julia. Hilary's got their info. But that's because they're newbies. And the price included the case and the up-lighting along with installation. But we'll be getting to the bottom of *that* barrel pretty soon. And there's been some degree of market saturation there."

Stan guffawed. He rose, walked over to a low, squat cabinet that looked like ones that hide mini-fridges in motel rooms (and actually was) on which stood five different bottles. He selected one, poured two fingers into his glass, opened the mini-fridge, stuck his hand in, removed two ice cubes, plopped them into his glass, and returned with it to his chair with an "umph."

Woody frowned. Why did people out here seem to think it was okay to add ice to brandy?

"Yeah!" said Stan. "And we wouldn't even have what little's left of that market if fate had not intervened. If Gregg had continued to compromise the market with his fakes, we'd have been hawking our goods for sixpence."

"Well, not quite. But his fakes were good. He even managed to not completely pop the bottoms out of them."

"The little shit! Where was he getting them from?"

"I have my suspicions. Mr. Sebastian Plumm, his 'business partner.'" Woody made quotation marks in the air. "He's a potter. Shows at Nelda's gallery. His signature work is very good."

"So he's been doing fakes! But he doesn't show the fakes at Nelda's gallery!"

"No, no. Those are very fancy-schmancy avant-garde stuff. Little pockets on the sides. Rims popped up in little knobs and snake heads. Inlays of onyx, turquoise, even diamonds, undoubtedly industrial quality but the fans won't know."

Stan slowly wagged his head. "What a sneak! Did you ever talk to Gregg about it?"

"Tried. But all he said was, 'They're not from the stash.' He wouldn't admit to their being fakes."

"Well of course they weren't from the stash! How would he even have gotten in there!"

"You know it was a sore point with him. Gregg wanted free access whenever he decided he could peddle a pot to somebody. He didn't like the idea of paced release. Anyway, it's a moot point now."

"So, what do we do about our mysterious-masque-mask-masqueraders?"

"Why do you call them masqueraders?"

Stan wagged his head. "I don't know. I just think there's something about them that's not on the up-and-up."

"In sharp contrast to us."

"Well, okay. What do we do with them?"

Woody shrugged. "Either we tell them our suspicions, and risk scaring them off, sending them to Coco, or we say nothing. If they're here to pull off some sort of sting, we get our lawyers on it. It would be entrapment."

"Yeah—and we not only loose the opportunity but have our resources drained in years of litigation to boot."

"No, no, I don't think so. I think you're right that Jen and Thad have already been in contact with Coco and … and … what's her name?"

"Claude. Claudine. I had quite a long chat with both of them."

"And…?"

"There's a kind of conspiracy there but it's a conspiracy of entrepreneurship and opportunism. It makes sense. So, what's the bottom line?"

"We go ahead with the deal. But we just very politely—naively—ask Jen and Thad if they know Coco. Or the gal, Claudine, given Claudine's summer job as Coco's assistant and Coco is branching out into Native arts."

"And if they say yes?"

"Then we know we have to act, and act quickly. Okay. So then let's make up the list."

"The list?" queried Stan.

"Yeah. Means and interest. We put the thing on show right where it is and bring people in to see it who are interested and hope we can get commitments. We get them to commit to shelling out, let's say, $32,000, on average, per mask, by putting up $16,000. I'll have the catalogue right there."

"But we don't know which items from the catalogue are actually on offer."

"That's true." Woody shrugged. "Can't be helped. Unless we can force the Jen and Thad people to tell us which ones they have. They're demanding, or the people they're brokering for want to strong-arm us—or rather, our clients—for $16,000 apiece as 'good faith down payments.' But if there's something really good and they can get more for it, well, then our commission goes up. So, let's say $16,000 is the minimum each client puts up on the assumption that they're going to be paying a minimum of $32,000 for any one piece, but more like $35,000; and I'm going to try to bump that figure up so altogether the average tag is $35,000. In a way, we've got the Jen and Thad people by the short hairs. They need us and our clientele. We can't scare them away by trying to screw them but we can get them a fair price while we split the 15 percent with them for our trouble and theirs. I'd really, really like to know who they're brokering for; who the owners of these things actually are. I really don't think it's them, themselves."

"So we get our friends and clients to fork over a total of over $224,000? And then we just hand it over to these Jen and Thad people? What if they walk away with it and we never hear from them again?"

Woody was silent.

"Ah!" said Stan, nodding. "I think we can take measures to assure that that doesn't happen."

"Well, anyway, okay—let's make up our 'show' list…"

When the list was at the point they wanted it, Stan said, "Well, let me know. I'll Be getting on the road." He rose to leave. "Maybe I'll stop at one of those casinos out west. Don't have to get the mice back on the treadmill 'til Tuesday. Wish I had a Hilary."

"You've had three of them."

"Those were wives. Not the same thing."

5:00 PM
SANTA FE

"Ferguson hasn't called back. I wonder why… Ah!" said Zoe. "That's him. Yeah," she said. "So, what do we do now…? Nothing? Really nothing…? I didn't spend it all… Okay, and the fee too…? When? You're nearby? So how did you follow them…? As a *woman*? You were disguised as a *woman*? Well, yeah, when you buy tickets at the last minute you pay two, three times as much… Yeah, you can come here but how do you know *they* won't follow *you*…? They don't…? You're sure…? Okay… We'll probably be having dinner …" Coco mouthed, *invite him.* "We'll save you some."

"I'm going to make lamb stew with tomatoes and garlic and lima beans and couscous and turnip greens," said Coco, after Zoe ended the call. "And before you turn up your nose at turnip greens, you should know they don't taste anything like turnips and I throw in some shredded golden beets—just about a quarter cup—and some Chablis, so it's kind of sweet and takes away the bitterness of the turnip greens. There'll be plenty for us and your friend Ferguson."

They sat at the kitchen table; the savory scent of the stew hovered everywhere. Zoe smiled a little ironic smile. It was *déjà vu.* Just a scant two weeks ago she and Ellie had sat around a kitchen table with Mr. Ferguson. Except Phil had not been there, of course. The first thing Ferguson did was to present Zoe with a cashier's check for $1,000. "Your fee," he said.

"But I hardly did anything."

"You did enough. Now it's in my hands. But I still may request your assistance."

"How so?"

"Well, for one thing, I need to know just when the best time would be to confront them. I'd like things to proceed a bit further, to know the details of just how the Pritchards—that's the Jen and Thad couple—by now you've met them, aye?"

"That's the people you call the vanners," affirmed Coco.

Zoe nodded.

"So now I need to know how they are going to be presenting the goods, where they have them stored, or where Cricencia-Jane has them stored, how they're going to arrange and orchestrate the whole thing. And at what point I offer Faulks-Morgenhouse the *quid pro quo* of telling all she knows about the insurance fraud in exchange for not calling down the FBI on her to investigate her being complicit in receiving stolen and illegally deaccessioned ritual objects."

"Maybe we can see if we can, as you say, get in on the proceedings," suggested Coco. "I can call Nelda. That's Woody's wife. Surely she'll know what's going on."

Zoe stifled a smirk and addressed her question to Ferguson. "And then you're going to—what? —approach Woody Glenn with Morgenhouse's—Jane Faulks'—confession and sort of make him do a plea bargain? He admits to the insurance fraud and you let him go ahead with buying the masks and reselling them? I thought you were going to blow the whistle on them and get them to return the masks to the tribes." For the first time, Zoe seemed to sense some hesitation, an uncertainty, or was it as a bit of dissemblance on Ferguson's part?

"Well, yes, I don't see why I can't do both. Insurance fraud is a crime."

"So Woody Glenn gets a double ding: he loses out on getting a stash of rare, one-of-a-kind sacred ceremonial masks that he could peddle to his upscale clientele, and he also has to cough up millions for the insurance. In fact, he basically loses his business."

"He made the choice to take that risk with regard to the insurance fraud some years ago," objected Ferguson.

"So, you're going to—what—confront Jane-Cricencia with the possibility of publicity to the tribe about having the masks as well as shame her into giving them up? And make her say she was part of the Mimbres pots scam? Threaten her 'til she agrees to give you an affidavit fingering Woody Glenn and whoever as the Mimbres thieves?"

"Something like that."

"And Woody Glenn? Confront him and say, 'Hey, I know you and whoever committed insurance fraud because Jane Faulks/Cricencia Morgenhouse says so'?"

"Something like that."

Zoe mentally shook her head. She did not see how this was all going to work. "And what are you going to do about Jen and Thad?"

"Look," said Ferguson, folding his arms and placing them on the table. "What I want to do is make a bargain with all of them. I want all of them in the same room at the same time. And I want as many of the other partners in the Mimbres scam as I can get there, too. I think one of them is Stan Joiner, from Scottsdale, and that another is Jackson Kane from Phoenix."

"Oh," said Coco. "I think he's the one who had the mask that got returned those many years ago. Good luck on getting him!"

"Precisely," said Ferguson. "Quit the gallery business after that, but he still deals in Native art part-time. No longer has a gallery. I think at least Joiner and Glenn will apply pressure on Kane; surely, they'll not want to shoulder the entire burden of blame themselves. And I now know that Gregg Neal, deceased, was also one."

"About which I have a theory," said Zoe.

"Aye! Another of your theories!"

"Yes. But before I tell it to you, I want to hear more about your strategy for getting the masks back to the tribes and trapping Woody and his partners into admitting to theft and insurance fraud. Weren't there also a couple of ranchers?"

"Three," said Ferguson. One of them is also deceased."

"And the other sold his ranch to the Archaeological Preserve."

"Correct."

"Okay. So let's hear it. How are you going to finesse all this?"

"I will hold over Jane Faulks' head the possibility of an FBI investigation into her receiving and possession of stolen and/or illicitly deaccessioned religious items covered by the Native American Graves Protection and Repatriation Act, and also that she may be subject to investigation and prosecution from ICE for evading customs regulations. I will propose to Jane Faulks that an affidavit affirming her knowledge of, and involvement in, a conspiracy to thieve and defraud, with the names of her co-conspirators as well as a recitation of how the theft was done, could get her off the hook from the FBI and ICE because of her cooperation in her willingness to turn state's evidence."

"But you're not ICE and you're not the FBI," objected Zoe.

"No. But I have connections with persons in both. I will hold over the heads of the ranchers and the gallerists the possibility that they could be charged with possession of stolen goods on the basis of Jane Faulks' affidavit, or at the very least, have their assets attached and their businesses tied up for, perhaps, years on end by Assurance Associates' attorneys, and that once their clients take possession of the masks, their 'good customers' could also be charged with the crime of being in receipt of stolen goods, to the ruination of their businesses and reputations. With these considerations, I will suggest Assurance Associates' willingness to negotiate so that they can avoid these embarrassments if they a) turn over what's left of the thieved pots; b) agree to repay amounts pro-rated on the assumption that if Rosenstock and Faulks are one of the partners and another is deceased, Rosenstock has probably absconded with his share to Mexico and can't be touched, Faulks has squandered hers, and the deceased's share is not recoverable; and c) they agree to a payment plan to do so over the next ten years. That means their liability is no longer ten million dollars, but rather, only seven million. Divided among gallerists, dealers, and the two ranchers, that's probably less than a million dollars each, and over ten years, that's only $100,000 a year. I would venture to say each one can afford it."

"And they and Jane Faulks will have to agree to repatriate the masks to the tribes."

"Correct."

"Okay," said Zoe. "I guess I get it. Now here's another little thing you may be able to hold over at least Stan Joiner's head." She told him about the spears and her idea about the curare. "And I'll bet anything that the last person to see him alive was Stan Joiner."

Ferguson rose and began walking around the kitchen in circles. "Verra interesting. Verra, verra interesting." He rolled his *R*s. He sat down again. "That changes the leverage issue. I think your participation is not yet over."

"You mean you want me there, when you bring all these folks together? Why? And what about the vanners, Jen and Thad? Are they going to be part of this too?"

"Yes, indeed. As I said, I want all of the players in the room together. And Phil—I think you need to be there too, because you are, as an ethnologist, for our purposes, the resident expert. If someone protests that these items are not used for ritual purposes, you will be there to gainsay them. And, to Mr. Joiner, I'll only suggest what might actually have happened: that somehow, Mr. Neal grabbed hold of the spear point, it pierced his skin, he died of … whatever—you say paralysis, Miss Zoe? But that Mr. Joiner was witness to that event and that he was responsible for putting the poisoned spears into Mr. Neal's hands, or hand."

Zoe nodded. "So how will we—I—know when you're ready to make your move?"

"I dunna think our Jane is going anywhere until she completes the transaction. And, of course, she has no intention of doing that in person. I know where she's settled. So, I think the green van people are still the key to it. But I dunna think it's a good idea for either of you to resume your surveillance. At some point they will have to rendezvous with Jane to make arrangements and do the transfer of the goods. Whenever Jane leaves her hotel in Albuquerque, I'll follow along. I dunna think they will notice if I keep changing rental cars every day or two, which I can easily arrange to do. And there's my prompt: off I go!"

"What do we—I—do in the meantime" asked Zoe.

"Whatever ye like. Ye have several days—maybe a week or more free. It will surely take Mr. Glenn some time to arrange buyers, show them the sample, so forth. We'll be in touch."

Zoe nodded distractedly, "We'll be in touch."

6:30 PM

Nelda Cavaletto stretched, sighed contentedly, and rummaged in the drawer of the night table. She found a little bottle, opened it, shook a pile onto a sheet of rolling paper, which she secured at both ends, then lit, drew, held, exhaled. "Here," she said, offering it to her partner.

"Nah. One a day is my limit." He sat up. She ran the fingers of her other hand over his bare torso. "You know whiskey and brandy are my poisons."

Nelda sighed again. "Can you stay for another round?"

"Sure. Woody's preoccupied. You got something for supper?"

"Sure. But what's the rush?" Nelda took another toke, reached under the covers with her other hand.

~⌒~

10:30 PM

They couldn't make love because of her period, or at least, chose not to do so, and were now contemplating sleep. "Hey," said Zoe, "before we fall into nod-land, I want to run a couple things by you."

"Okay, but only if you first tell me about this." He threw off the covers, put his arm on hers and pulled. She fell over on her front. Phil dug his finger into the bottom of her left buttock.

"This?" said Zoe. "My tattoo?"

"Yeah. I get the other one—this one." He leaned over. "It's a woman's red lips and a smoking reefer." Zoe flexed her right leg a couple of times. The woman's lips appeared to move around the joint and take a drag, then release. Drag, release.

Phil moved his head down to her where his finger had been. "It looks like … it looks like … uh … this one, is a man, a bearded man, but wearing a skirt … and he's … he's moving something toward a … a doorway?"

"Right."

"The square thing he's got his hands on—it's a rectangle…"

"Yeah. It's hard to make out. She did a really good job, but there's just so much you can do with a needle."

"These are really complicated. Three colors! They must have cost a fortune!"

"My … my boyfriend, my then-boyfriend paid for them. Birthday present. I had to get really stoned to have them done. It took a long time. The dude is a cross-dresser; he's in drag. And he's hauling—dragging—a painting into a room. In honor of my interest in the making of art."

"Huh!"

"So, you put the two together and I'm the girl with the drag-in tattoo…

"Ahahahahahahaha!" Phil laughed loudly and long.

"Shhhhh!" said Zoe. But Phil kept laughing. "That's … that's … incredible! I get it! I get it! I get it!" He laughed some more. "But nobody sees it."

"Well … it's just barely partially visible depending on how I move my ass in summer shorts and it's totally out there in a bathing suit. Okay, so before we fall into dreamland, two things: First, could we go to your Pueblo village? Talk to somebody who might know something about stolen masks? Not to get their hopes up about getting more back, but some have already been returned, right?"

"Right."

"So, I mean, like, stolen masks and the auction and all that are kind of, like, common knowledge?"

"I wouldn't necessarily say common knowledge," responded Phil. "But yeah—when I was there last summer some of the masks had just been returned. Yeah. A lot of people talked about them."

"So, if we got some, like, oral history, some testimony, about how important they are and maybe when and how they disappeared, that could help the case for returning these."

"Help Mr. Ferguson."

"Well, yeah, I suppose, maybe. But that's the second thing."

"Huh?"

"There's something not quite right, fishy, rotten in Denmark," replied Zoe. "Doesn't it seem peculiar that Ferguson was able to just hop on a couple of airplanes and end up sauntering along in Jane Faulks' footsteps? No missed planes, no fuckups, no having to take the next one standby, no lost trail? I mean, if you don't already have your ticket and your boarding pass and you have to go through security and all that—it all takes time. And, like, aren't the airlines always telling you, *we've got a completely full flight today, yada yada yada*?"

"Well, yeah…"

"So, isn't it, like kinda weird that Ferguson just saunters on and off the same planes that Jane Faulks is on? And she doesn't tumble to it?"

"I thought you said he was in disguise, as a woman?"

"Well, yeah—how realistic is that? That's what he says. As a woman? He gets a driving license with his picture as a woman? And TSA and everybody just goes for it? And he just happens to be able to get on a flight from Atlanta to Albuquerque, just like that?"

"Well, he probably had an inkling that's where she was going to go. And you can get a fake driver's license pretty easily."

"How did he know she was headed for Albuquerque? Why not Phoenix? Or Tucson?"

"Well, he just… Well, he probably… Well, I don't know. But you said he told you himself how easy it is to get fake IDs."

Zoe shook her head. "Yeah, right, exactly. Call me cynical, skeptical, say I have a suspicious mind. But I lived for almost three years with a secretive guy and I think I know the signs."

"Yeah?"

"Yeah. But let's meander out to the Indian villages. There's nothing we can do now, with or without Ferguson. And it'll be a week or more before Jen and Thad bring in the remaining masks for Woody's clients to buy, or bid on, or whatever. Coco's going to get herself into that by asking to be one of the viewers. We'll keep in touch with her when we're on the road."

21

ZOE AND PHIL DECIDED TO SEE the rest of the Santa Fe sites: more museums, the "oldest house," Palace of the Governors again. Monday and Tuesday, they spent visiting some ruins: Bandelier, Puye. On Wednesday they headed for the Pueblo where Phil had done his ethnological research on potters and pottery.

They set up their tent in a nearby campground and then drove to the Pueblo, which operated a restaurant featuring Native foods. They savored a meal that Phil promised would be as delicious as it was unusual: mutton, hominy stew, roasted chili peppers, blue corn muffins, and flat beans in their pods that resembled lima beans. "These beans are native to here," said Phil. "Tomorrow we'll go to visit some friends of mine and see what we can learn."

THURSDAY, 10:00 AM

They drove to the village and stopped in to visit with Betty, one of the potters that Phil was studying. Betty offered them coffee and watermelon. "It's from the store so it's not as good as one of ours but ours aren't ripe yet." She laughed. After about an hour, Betty directed them to Marie-Claire's house. "She knows everything that's going on around here," Betty explained.

"Do you think she's at home?" asked Phil.

"Yeah, yeah, yeah. She's there." Betty nodded.

They found Marie-Claire's house. Like Betty's it was on the edge of the village, but unlike Betty's, it had no electric line serving it. Zoe was surprised that, although Marie-Claude turned out to be a woman in her seventies, she could still be described as pretty. She wore her largely silver hair medium-length and permed. She was dressed in black pants, a baggy brown sweater, with a colorful shawl around her shoulders. She invited them in as they knocked on the door; Phil introduced himself and Zoe. They entered the house. "Sit down!" she said. "You like coffee?" Zoe noticed that she wore a beautiful heavy silver overlay bracelet.

"Actually, we're kind of coffee'd out," said Phil. "But do you have any fizzy water?"

"Ohhh," said Marie-Claire. "Fizzy water. No, I don't think so."

"Ah! Well, I've got some in the car."

Marie-Claire laughed. "Betty says he always brings them some when he comes."

Phil had picked up a case of it in Flagstaff. He explained to Zoe that people appreciated gifts, and also that it was wise not to drink the local water; tap water in the villages that had plumbing was likely to be contaminated with sewage leaking from old pipes that had been laid side by side with the equally leaky water pipes. And where plumbing had not been installed, people periodically hauled water in garbage cans from stock wells. "If nobody in the house was sick—hey, no problem, if somebody dips a cup into the garbage can full of water. But it's better not to take a chance. It's nothing dangerous," said Phil. "It's just different bacteria that we're not used to." They had left a dozen bottles with Betty.

He exited the house, then returned quickly, bringing in a dozen bottles of water and set them on the round table at which they were all seated. In the meantime, Marie-Claire had brought out an already opened package of Bashas' donuts. Phil and Zoe each took one and opened bottles of fizzy lemon water. Phil told Marie-Claire a shortened version of what they were trying to do: they had become aware of a mask from the Paris auction of a year earlier and it was now with a dealer in Santa Fe. They were going to try to get it and another dozen returned to the ceremonial leaders.

"Yeah, that's good," said Marie-Claire. "What you're trying to do. We know about that. You know that lady, Sacky? Or something like that, she got some of those masks from that place in Paris and turned them over to the Cultural Preservation Office. I guess they still have them down there at the Tribal office. I think they gave some of them to the priests but we didn't get any in this village 'cause we can't do those ceremonies anymore. We don't have enough mens."

"But do you think any of them, or other ones from the same auction, might have been from here? That they might have been stolen?"

"Yeah, yeah. I think so. I wasn't here when it happened; I only came back a few years ago. I was living with my husband at his place. I had a daughter by another guy and she was staying here with my mother. And then I had one with him. But then you know I had two more kids with him, my husband, and so I asked my mother if I could bring my little boy to live with her too. My mother said, 'Why don't you stay here for a while?' So, I came and stayed with her a while, and helped her out. One time she came back once from her father's house—that's down in the village and she hadn't been down there for a while, I guess, but it's where all those sacred things are stored, you know, from my grandfather's time. He was a ceremonial leader here and so he had all those things. But then he died and so did all those other old men who'd been initiated, so all those things were stored in his old house.

"My mom used to go down there to feed them, to feed the masks. You have to feed them, you know. They're alive. You feed them with cornmeal. So that time, my mom came back and I could tell she was upset about something. So, I ask her, 'What are you upset about?' And she says, 'Oh, somebody's been in there again, been stealing.' Then she told me: every time she went to her father's house, something else was missing. It was mostly masks but some really old things, like from the altars? You know? I guess you call them statues."

"How many things do you think had been stolen? What happened to them?" asked Zoe.

"Well, I don't know. But you know I had a couple of uncles. One of them was an alcoholic. I think he probably got in there and got some of those masks and sold them for that. But the other one, my other uncle, he had a kid that needed an operation. I think he got those things and sold them so his kid could have the operation. I think they were the ones going in there and taking things. But there was a lotta stuff happening, that time. Another one of my uncles had an accident, they said it was an accident. He fell off the cliff, broke his neck." She shook her head. "Lotta stuff going on, that time."

Zoe wondered about this. "But surely his child, your cousin, could have gotten the operation from the Public Health Service?"

"Yeah, my mom said they put him on a wait list but he just kept getting worse and worse so I think my uncle just decided to get it done himself and that's why he took those things and sold them. That's why my mom wouldn't say nothing, you know."

"Do you know who they sold them to?" asked Phil.

"I don't know. But you know sometimes a guy would come around asking if we had any old things to sell. He goes around the other villages too. So it might have been him. Or maybe some of those anthropologists, you know, from the museums? There was a man from here, went on a trip

254

back east. He went to a museum someplace, maybe Chicago? And he saw some of our sacred things, secret things, from the men's societies, you know, that nobody should see except them, those mens, there in the museum. They were behind windows, but for anybody to see. I think maybe years ago, maybe before my time, somebody got into my grandfather's house and sold those masks to a museum."

"But now with NAGPRA, those sacred items have to be returned," observed Phil.

"Yeah, yeah. Some of those leaders got some back from the Heard Museum. And you know, when all those masks got returned from that auction, I wonder why they didn't all get returned? Isn't it illegal to have those things?"

"Well, unfortunately, NAGPRA doesn't apply to other countries, like France," said Phil.

"But if the masks were sold, or resold here, and it could be proved they originally came from museums, or if they were stolen from you folks in the first place, you could eventually get them back," said Zoe. "We're pretty sure that that's going to happen pretty soon and when those masks turn up, then we—or, not me, but a guy who's investigating all this—can maybe get those masks back for you."

"Ohhh," said Marie-Claire. "How will that work?"

"We don't know exactly. But we're pretty sure that dealer is going to broker them to wealthy people in Santa Fe who want to hang Native American art on their walls," replied Zoe. "And we're going to try to interrupt that."

"But they're not art," said Marie-Claire. "They're sacred. They're important to us."

"Exactly," said Phil.

FRIDAY-SUNDAY
AT THE PUEBLO VILLAGE AND ON THE ROAD

Friday, they spent touring some of the nearby ruins. On Saturday, at Marie-Claire's urging, Phil and Zoe stayed for the first rounds of the masked dances before lunchtime. Now, at the dance, Phil was telling Zoe what to expect. "There'll be clowns at this one, too," Phil told Zoe. "They're the basest aspect of the human condition. They do everything bad as examples to the people of how not to behave. But they're also funny, entertaining, so it's also a kind of release, kind of like, you know, our comedians. They'll come in between the dances. The dancers will do three dances, then the clowns come."

They arrived in the plaza, a dusty place surrounded by what looked like ordinary houses of native cut stone, with gaps at each corner, just as the dancers filed in through one of the gaps. The pungent scent of pinon, fueling the cooking of hominy stew, pervaded the atmosphere. Two men clad only in buckskin kilts led the dancers in; Zoe counted 47, all dressed identically in woven cloth kilts adorned with what Zoe thought must be symbols. All wore identical masks with evergreen ruffs. The masks resembled the ones Zoe had seen pictured in the auction catalogue, but only in being made of leather, with wooden structures mounted on each dancer's head, adorned with feathers, that Zoe later learned were eagle, hawk, and parrot. Each man's torso was painted brown and marked with white symbols. Around his waist was a broad red and white sash, and behind his right knee was a rattle made of turtle shell. A fox skin attached to the sash cascaded from the middle of each dancer's back. Each man also carried a rattle; many were painted with a large cross, turquoise and black, but a few were plain.

"See the cross on the rattle?" said Phil, sotto voce. "It's not Christian; it symbolizes the four directions." The headdresses, said Phil, were painted with designs symbolizing clouds and bolts of lightning.

The dancers arranged themselves on three of the four sides of the plaza. A line of nine women in long black woven dresses, very much like that worn by the server at Woody Glenn's shindig, also entered, carrying large painted gourds in one hand and some sort of wand in the other, and danced alongside the line of men. *Ha!* thought Zoe. *So even though Lupina and her sister are Honduran, Woody had them dress in traditional Pueblo garb for events! Guests are to assume they* are *Puebloan! All part of the ambience. Cultural appropriation!*

Later, Phil insisted that those were also men. "Then they must have been wearing wigs," said Zoe. Each "woman's" hair-do resembled Carrie Fisher's—Princess Leia's—hair style in *Star Wars*. Each also wore a colorful shawl.

Apparently on a signal, the men began a subdued chant, striking the right foot against the ground in unison, in a rhythm different from the cadence of the chant. Every now and then, the dancers shook their rattles; Zoe thought this might also be some sort of signal, as the entire line turned, faced the opposite direction, then turned again. She mentally chuckled to glimpse a patch of polka-dot boxer shorts under one dancer's kilt; several, she noted, wore socks, but most wore their moccasins over bare feet.

At some point, Zoe thought in the middle of the whole proceeding, the dancers stopped their chant, turned to face the interior of the plaza, and each other, and the "women" knelt on the ground. Each "woman" took a flat object out of "her" gourd, laid the "wand," which turned out to be a ratchet, across the opening of the gourd and, in unison, drew the edge of the flat object across the ratchet. Later, Phil told her the flat object was the bottom of a turtle shell. He was uncertain about what the sound was meant to signify: the roar of a lion in the mountains? Wind howling through the trees? While the "women" "roared," the men were silent. The dancers/chanters then filed out.

Now, seven clowns entered the plaza. Three were painted white with black circles on their torsos and were dressed only in G-strings. They were unmasked, but wore caps with two pointed peaks. Four more clowns, three of them clearly little boys, were masked, each rigged with a domino with knobby brown protuberances where there should have been ears. Another brown knob protruded from the head, like the topknot on a bobble hat. The clowns did indeed act out lessons about how *not* to behave. The mask with the knobby protuberances was meant to represent a product of incestuous sex, Phil told her later; rules prohibit marriage or sexual relations between one member of a clan with a member of the same clan, as well as with the individual's father's clan, he explained. Zoe was somewhat taken aback by the clowns' antics: they made gestures that Zoe interpreted as "up yours"; "suck cock"; and "masturbate." They wasted food, throwing watermelons to each other but failing to catch them, so that they landed on the ground and burst. They shouted obscenities and one of them approached an older non-Native man watching the spectacle with folded arms, challenging him, "You know mixed plate? You don't know mixed plate? That's where you put everything together and mix it up." Zoe thought it must have some sexual entendre. Another clown approached the same man and shouted, "Are you watching the *Katsinas* through your eyes?" Later, when she asked Phil about the possible meanings of these challenges and who the man was, he shrugged his shoulders. "No clue," he said.

But Zoe did think she understood the overall meaning of the performances. *This isn't just boisterous obscenity! The clowns are pointing to self-centeredness, self-indulgence, selfishness, disregard for cultural and social norms, public exposure of things that should be private, irreverence, commodification of culture (well, if you recognize tourism as a kind of commodity). Clowning, comedy, is meant to instruct people about the baseness and ridiculousness of human nature. It shows us the defects and vices of us ordinary people. And therefore, clowning makes us examine all aspects of life more closely. Truth revealed through the depiction of the world as, hopefully, worse than it actually is.*

In the midst of these antics, a masked figure with what looked like an owl's head came dancing animatedly into the plaza. He took a position in a corner of the plaza and, dancing in place, raised a decorated lance, and emitted a long, drawn-out "Woooooooo." The figure then danced to another corner of the plaza, and repeated the gesture, again dancing in place and again crying, "Wooooooo." After two more such performances, the figure danced out of the plaza. The clowns also departed the plaza, having paid no attention to the owl. They stayed for three more rounds of dances, interrupted by forty-five-minute breaks. It was now one thirty. "This is lunch break," said Phil. "They'll come back at three o'clock. You want to stay for the afternoon?"

"Sure!" said Zoe.

They did not stay for the final dance, departing shortly after six. As they walked back to the car, parked on the edge of the village, Phil explained that the masked dancer they had seen emitting the long, drawn-out cry was indeed an owl, giving warnings; if the clowns did not mend their ways, they would be punished. "The climax of the performance is punishment by the women," said Phil. "That'll be tomorrow, late afternoon. They bring in buckets of water, douse the clowns, slap them around, and sometimes even pull off their G-strings."

"Wow!" That'd be worth sticking around for!" quipped Zoe. But they did not do so.

SUNDAY, MOTHER'S DAY
ON THE ROAD

The following morning, they enjoyed a breakfast of blue corn pancakes at the Cultural Center. "I'd like us to see that punishment by the women," said Phil. "What I was telling you about. Is it okay if we stick around for the grand finale—the clowns' punishment? That'll happen around seven thirty this evening."

"I'd like to, too," said Zoe. "But with things about to pop, I think we should get on the road. And especially if you insist on making yet another stop."

"Hey—like I said, you can't tell when you'll be in this part of the country again. You've *got* to see Petrified Forest; it's one of the wonders of the world, or at least of North America."

Cell service was sporadic; Zoe had not been able to raise Ferguson on the phone at all, and had had only a broken-up conversation with Coco, who had told her that Woody was having "viewings" of the mask at his place in Waldo all week. Coco thought it likely that Woody would secure pledges from his clients to purchase the remaining thirteen masks, and the process would get underway shortly. Zoe told Phil: "Even if I'm not there for all the fireworks, I'd like to at least be around for the aftermath."

They returned to the campground, packed up, and departed.

On the road, Zoe reflected on what she had experienced and seen. "You know, talking with Marie-Claire and learning about the pressure that people are under to keep a way of life going that has at least as much, if not more legitimacy than our Euro-centric indulgences in false luxury and phony, smug superiority, and seeing the masks like the ones in the catalogue come alive in a real expression of what we call religion but that's really a way of life, really makes me even more steamed about how places like Sotheby's can callously commodify another people's sacred objects and symbols and just not care about the living people and—if you believe in it—the spiritual beings behind the masks, and how other people can scoop them up for a few pieces of silver and pretend they're just pieces of exotic art."

"Right. Yeah. That's exactly it. Wow! What a mouthful! But that's a good statement! You should write that down and put it into your thesis or make it into an op-ed piece in the *New York Times*!" Said Phil.

"What did I say? Was it that great? It sounded to me like I was just going on and on."

"No, no," said Phil. "I mean, like, what we saw today: that's the real religion of this continent. I mean, Jesus Christ and all that is just fine, it's an okay religion, but it's not a way of life. And it's from someplace else—not from around here. I've been told that Jesus Christ appeared here right after he resurrected, but here he appeared as a medicine man. So even Indian Christians aren't all tied in knots about sin and redemption and forgiveness and all that because Christ didn't come as a savior of sinful man, but rather, as a healer."

Zoe nodded. "Ceremonies to bring rain: it's like, these people are really connected to the life forces. If you're doing all these elaborate rituals as prayers for rain, you really show respect for water and its life-giving force. It's like, they have environmental responsibility built into their culture. And the masks are part of it."

"Right," said Phil. "Like Marie-Claire told us, the masks are alive."

Monday, 7:50 AM
Petrified Forest National Monument

After hiking around the monument, they had a supper of salami and cheese on crackers and an orange each. The experience, Zoe reflected—the trip to the various now-ruined pueblos, archaeological sites, and the dances, and now the Petrified Forest, had been exciting and instructive, but also exhausting. Before setting out on their sojourn around the monument, Zoe had called Ellie to wish her happy Mother's Day and they had had a nice long chat.

Now, emerging from their sleeping bags and dressing in Phil's little tent, they were assaulted with the unbearably seductive smells of perking coffee and sizzling sausages and bacon. The smells came from a Coleman camp stove set up on the table in the campsite next to them. Zoe looked over and immediately locked eyes with a young woman, about her own age, she thought, or maybe a few years older, in overalls and a quilted coat.

"Hey! How are you?" the woman shouted over to Zoe and Phil. "Have you had breakfast yet?"

"Uh, no..." said Zoe.

"Well come on over! We've got a pot of coffee and we can put more eggs and bacon in the skillet, toast too."

"Not really toast," said her companion, a man slightly older than his companion, Zoe thought, very tall, in a heavy plaid Pendleton shirt, Levi's, and a plaid hunting cap. "More like bangers and mash."

They were Mitchell Johns and Jessica Keegan. "I design logos, mostly for people who have blogs," said Mitchell. "People who have something to sell. You can get sort of standard logos from the people who run the blog but they're limited and they're not very creative. I give them a lot of tools to get creative with. They choose the images, then I put them together. You know, you can do your own marketing."

"And believe it or not, I'm a photographic artist," said Jessica.

"Why believe it or not?" said Phil.

"Because she works with film," said Mitchell.

"Real film?" asked Zoe.

Jessica nodded. "Real film. Black and white film."

"You can still get it? And have it developed?"

Jessica nodded. "You can still get it. There are actually a couple of manufacturers. There's a guy in Eureka, Nevada I get the paper from. He's an analog photographer too. I develop the prints myself."

Mitchell, still at the stove, loaded cardboard plates with eggs, bacon, sausage, and slices of whole wheat bread that he had swabbed around the frying pan. He poured coffee into four enamel cups, set two in front of Jessica and Zoe, then retrieved their plates and went back for the plates and coffee mugs for himself and Phil, balancing one plate on his forearm like a seasoned waiter. Jessica brought out real silverware from a small hamper. "I'll show you some prints afterward if you're interested."

"Yeah, sure," said Zoe.

"Hey, we've got some rolls—our friends at one of the pueblos loaded us up with a couple dozen. We can't eat them all—they'll go stale. I'll go get 'em and bring 'em over," offered Phil. They fell to their meals.

"Oh, Great!" said Mitchell. "We'll douse them with jam. Canned milk for your coffee okay?"

"Yeah, please," said Zoe. "But no bacon or sausage for me. Just toast and eggs." Jessica retrieved a can and a can opener from the hamper, shook the can, and opened it, setting it on the table.

"We saw you pull in last night," said Jessica, "and put up the tent. We said, 'yay, somebody to talk to tomorrow.' You know" she said, lowering her voice and looking around, "almost everybody in these places—this time of year—is kind of old."

"Yeah," added Mitchell. "They're all in RVs. And then along comes summer and everybody's still in RVs but they've got a million children, running around, yelling."

After they had finished breakfast. Jessica invited them into the tent and pulled over a portfolio.

Phil looked around. "This is a nice big tent."

"Bean's Wall Tent," said Mitchell. "Can sleep six in a pinch. Got it at L.L. Bean's in Maine, last summer. You know they're open at midnight in high summer?"

"I think they're open twenty-four hours in peak season, honey," said Jessica. She set to portfolio on a folding table standing against one wall of the tent. "I take pictures of ruins," she said.

"Oh, yeah—we've visited a few of those in the last few days."

"But not these ruins," said Jessica. "These are historic ruins." She showed them sharp, 12 by 10 prints: a pair of glass-bell gas pumps, a piece of nine-teenth century farm equipment, a caving in teepee-shaped curio shop, a series of unpainted, rough-hewn plank structures in various states of disrepair, an old mine shaft opening, a dilapidated large building that might have been a dance hall or a lodge. Jessica told them she and Mitchell enjoyed taking off about three times a year, usually in spring, late summer, and fall, to photo-graph all over the West.

"The nice thing about what I do," said Mitchell, "is I can do it from anywhere."

"The classic place for photographs is Bodie. It's a real total ghost town.

People just walked away from it in, I don't know, maybe the '40s? or the '60s? It's a state park now, or is it a national monument?"

"State park, I think," said Mitchell, "on the border of California and Nevada."

"But I've photographed some places hardly anybody every gets to. Most of them aren't total ghost towns, but they're really depopulated. Palisade, Nevada; Austin; Gold Hill; Virginia City; Silver City, Idaho… And before you go away still wondering, no, I don't make a really good living at it, but yes, I do sell enough to keep me going. Mitchell helped me design the web site!"

"Do you ever show in galleries?" asked Zoe.

"I've got some pieces in a few galleries—Sedona, Georgetown, Denver, and in Guerneville, where we live."

"That's in California," said Mitchell.

"Oh, and in Jerome. That's in Arizona," added Jessica. "I was urged to take a lot of photos there because people like to come up from Phoenix and they want a souvenir. Jerome's been cutsey-pooed up, like Virginia City. But there's lots of places that aren't ghost towns but they still have some good, tumbling down buildings. Which way are you headed?"

"Albuquerque, Santa Fe."

"Ah, too bad," said Mitch. "If you were headed west, I'd recommend a detour to Bodie."

"Where is that 'Indian curios' teepee place? Is that in Arizona?" asked Phil, examining one of the photographs.

"It's actually in New Mexico. And it's kind of on your way. You could take 85 up to Santa Fe instead of I-25. The tumbling down teepee place is right on the old highway, in Corrales." She shrugged. "There's not much to see, but it's a piece of history that hasn't been scraped yet and replaced with an Applebee's or a Days' Inn."

"Good," said Phil. "We'll do it. We're not that far, so we can sort of meander."

They packed up, said their goodbyes to Jessica and Mitch, who declared they were going to have a leisurely morning. On the road, Phil drove; Zoe phoned Coco. Yes, Coco had been to one of the viewings and had seen the mask. Yes, it looked like the final "pledges" would take place soon, maybe even today, but probably not until tomorrow, and it seemed that there might even be a sort of mini-auction, with people offering more than the projected 30,000-plus benchmark price for each item.

She hit *End*. "So," she said to Phil, "Ferguson will make his move soon." She called him, but it went to voice mail. Her message said only that she was checking in.

22

SATURDAY, 7:30 PM-MONDAY, 11:44 AM

Santa Fe; Oswego; Elsewhere
in New Mexico

NELDA VICTORIA CAVALETTO SAT at her office desk. She was working late. She wore a white Sahalie butterfleece open cardigan over a blue lace-
trim long sleeve crewneck with teal polyester pants; like all gallery owners,
she kept the temperature at no more than 68 degrees, preferably lower. Good
for gallery-goers on the move; not so good for sitting. Her mobile rang. "Yes.
Hi, Stan.... right... On the road...? Not headed for Scottsdale...? Ah! Will
you do blackjack...? Maybe...? Hmmm... Slots for sure...? Well, as long
as you win, right...? Dana Andrews...? Oh! So, why is staying at El Rancho
so much better than just staying at the casino...? Ah. Yes. You are indeed a
creature of habit.

"Uhhh ... a favor ... for old times' sake. Those were very old times, as you
well know... Why can't you do it? What's to keep an eye on...? Well, I don't
know ... yeah, yeah, I suppose I could take in a show. You don't have to do
that. I can take it off my taxes, since I'll be visiting an antiques store... How

far…? Oh. Okay. Why don't I pay for the air tickets and the car and you pay for the hotel room in NYC. That's going to cost you! Oswego. Do you have an address…? Okay … I can Google map it… Why do I have to tell Woody anything? You know we've been living separate lives for … a while."

SUNDAY, 4:17 PM
OSWEGO, NEW YORK

Nelda Victoria Cavaletto stood in front of the pink Queen Anne mansion. It was drizzling. Two loose dogs were sniffing at a privet hedge fronting the yard; their owner marched along a half block behind them carrying a leash with a baggie tied around it. Two cupolas and an outside second story balcony made the house look a little the worse for wear; the cupolas needed painting and the balcony sagged. A sign identified it as Suwannee Antiques. No hours were listed; only a phone number. She mounted the three stairs and rang the bell. There was no response. She got back in her car and called the phone number. "Yes, I'd like to…You're sure it's no trouble… Okay."

Ten minutes later a Subaru Outback pulled into the driveway adjacent to the house. She got out of her rental car and met a disheveled-looking man with rounded shoulders and a potbelly, dressed only in a blue down jacket unzipped over what was probably a XXL t-shirt and cargo pants. He mounted the steps and stuck two keys into two locks in the door. He turned around as she came up on the porch. "You must be Vicki." He stuck out a meaty hand. "I'm Lou, Louie Delassandro. Come on in."

"So, so … this is your place?"

"Yes, indeed! And If you're asking, can I sell you anything you see here, the answer is yes."

"But normally you're … you're somewhere else."

"No, no, sometimes I'm here, sometimes at the warehouse. This time of year, it's not really worth it to open up the house. Brrr! Cold! Sorry! But it's usually like this, this time of year. Not really tourist season yet. You can see why! Now, I can give you the grand tour or just sit down here while you go through the house. I'll trust you're not going to nick the silver! You said you have a gallery of your own?"

"Yes, in Santa Fe. They told me at my hotel that if I was really interested in antiques, there were two places—Croton something and Oswego. I guess I can take a commuter train to Croton but I thought I'd start here and then I can get rid of the car."

"Right, right. Okay, so why don't you wander around. As I said, everything's for sale—oh, except for that big monster buffet over there and the four Chinese Chippendales upstairs in the spare bedroom. They're already spoken for."

She walked over to the buffet. "Wow! How much did this go for?"

"Eighteen thousand. A real antique. Eighteenth century. There's a basement with some things, if ya wanna see 'em. Feel free to take pictures."

She wandered around the room, then headed upstairs, noting that the red stair carpet had some threadbare spots. She found the chairs in the spare bedroom; one bedroom was closed, presumably where Louie slept.

She thought she could probably get away with not visiting the basement. After all, she'd learned what she needed to: there was no Jen or Thad having any association with Suwannee Antiques. *If there were,* she thought, *wouldn't Lou have mentioned them? Wouldn't their names be on the sign outside? Wouldn't the phone number be* their *phone number, rather than Lou's?* She came back downstairs. She would have to admit that maybe Stan was right: *if Jen and Thad from Woody's party had told him they were proprietors of Suwannee Antiques in Oswego, New York, and they were not so, then they were indeed masquerading as something they were not and there had to be a reason.*

"Well, Lou, thank you so much. I understand there are a dozen shops here so I guess I'd better get going."

"Hey—my pleasure. Here's my card." She looked at it. It did not say Suwannee Antiques, but it did have his name and the same number as on the sign outside. She tucked it into her pocket. She'd phone Stan and tell him all this and let him make what he wanted of it.

$$\sim 9$$

7:35 PM
ARIZONA

Stan was speeding down I-25; he would drive straight through to Flagstaff, maybe have a bite; a couple of hours on I-15 would get him into Scottsdale shortly after midnight. But he was really fuming; Woody held the "partner" card once again, even though the goods that had gotten the "partners" to be "partners" were just about gone. But Woody had called each and every one of the folks he had brought up for the almost-final distribution of the pottery—some of them brand new clients—and brought them back out, paraded them in front of the mask-in-a-poke, and now actually had commitments from three of them. So, yes, he had been roped in. Plus, Woody had insisted that Stan also put up "earnest money"—$16,000—for the sake of maintaining clients' confidence; Woody had done the same. "And then I'll have one and you'll have one—just in case you get another client who didn't jump when the jumping was good," he'd said.

But now I've gotta do something, and do it fast, he thought to himself. *We're being bamboozled. We're gonna collect the money from the clients and hand it over to those imposters—and our money's in there, too—and those phonies are going to disappear and all we'll have is one lousy mask, a quarter mill to make good on, one hell of a legal headache, and our reputations shot.*

He called Woody. "I'm telling you. We need to call it off."

"But that's absurd!" objected Woody. "I've had about twenty people come through here to view it and Hilary's already collected the earnest money from three of them! I'm doing the last showing tomorrow afternoon and evening and I expect to get another ten commitments, maybe more. We'll have the money by next Monday end of day!"

"Look," said Stan. "I'm telling you, they're phonies. There is no such thing as 'Jen and Thad's Suwannee Antiques.'" He was almost shouting now. "Suwannee Antiques is run by a slobby old fat guy. He lives there, works out of a warehouse someplace else, opens up Suwannee Antiques only in tourist season or when somebody calls and wants in. We've been had, Woody! We've been taken for a ride!"

"But what kind of ride?!" Woody was now shouting too. "They have a mask from an auction. I have the auction catalogue. The mask is identical to its illustration in the catalogue!"

Stan said slowly and carefully, "How. Do. You. Know. It's. Not. A. Clever. Replica. A FAKE!!"

Woody responded equally slowly and emphatically: "Because. I. Know. My. Indian. Art! Don't you think I can spot a fake when I see one? How do you fake dermestid damage—nibblings and poop!? Age!? What do you want us to do?"

"Confront them!"

"With what? The word of some mysterious person that you so stubbornly refuse to identify who draws conclusions from a one-time visit and our suspicions that they're crooks, based on zilch?"

Stan was silent for nearly a minute. "Okay. You go ahead and be complicit with the bilking of a coupla hundred thousand dollars from some of our most loyal customers—friends!—and see what your reputation's like when whoever gets that mask—and all the rest, for that matter—calls in an expert, an authenticator, and they sue you for fraud. But I've taken steps to see that your Jen and Thad in their disintegrating, leaky old van are not going to get far with their scam."

"Good. It never hurts to take precautions," he said, fuming, and rang off. Woody sat back, sighed. "Let's just hope you're wrong," he said, meant for Stan, but now of course to himself. Woody had had it with Stan trying to take over everything. "If not," he said to himself, I'll take the loss, make good on everybody's money if I have to. Hang the thing here if I have to. Wait around 'til somebody takes if off my hands."

Stan continued fuming as he raced down the highway. He hardened his resolve. *He'd* take action, if Woody wouldn't. He'd get those guys in Miami, the guys from the Colombia-Amazon job. When he got home, first thing tomorrow morning—or maybe even when he walked in the door—those guys probably stayed up late? Right? He'd phone them. It would only be around eleven thirty or twelve back there.

~~~~

SANTA FE

Jen and Thad had spent the week wandering slowly through every gallery on Canyon Road, every gallery not on Canyon Road, craft fair booths at a "pow-wow" at an Indian school, three archaeological ruins, Sandia Peak, "Old Town" Albuquerque, and two museums there and in Santa Fe that they had not visited before. They were tired of wandering; they would have preferred to be involved in showing the mask. Why had Woody insisted on pushing them out the door every day before the "viewings" would take place? "Control," Jen said. "He wants control."

A WEEK LATER: SUNDAY, 10:12 AM

Sunday morning, Jen and Thad embarked on what they were determined would be their last thumbs-twiddling, time-killing, tedious tourist undertaking to the "Oldest House" and Christo Rey Church (the largest all-adobe church in the world, so the tourist brochure said). They did not notice the late-model white SUV that had turned off a dirt road onto the two-lane highway taking them into Santa Fe. Thus, they also were unaware of the two men in the SUV, and their agenda, who followed their trail keenly but discretely, two miles distant, to their various destinations and ultimately back to Los Pajaritos. Thus, they were also unaware of the SUV turning right onto the road just short of the entrance, onto the road paralleling the wall separating Los Pajaritos and the other "Galisteo Legacy Estates" from the mundane world, parking on the verge. They were unaware that one of the men opened the back of the SUV, removed a crate, carried it over to the wall, mounted it, and took up watch until he saw Jen and Thad turn off the lights in the cottage, exit it, and crunch along the gravel path to the big house. The man then vaulted over the wall, accomplished what he needed to do and returned to the wall, and, reaching his arms above his head, was hauled back over the wall by the second man. Taking the crate, both men quietly got into the van, turned it around, headed back to Santa Fe, and parked in the Sheraton's underground garage.

"Well at some point Woody's going to have to give over the cash," said Thad. "And if she wants it, Dahlia's going to have to come through with the other thirteen masks." After getting instructions from Dahlia, the phone had gone dead every time they had called; the burner showed "no service" or went to voice mail, hosted by a disembodied voice announcing only that "the party you have called is unavailable at this time…"

Now back in their adobe bungalow in Los Pajaritos in Waldo, they resolved to give Woody Glenn a deadline: 5:00 p.m. tomorrow, Monday. But the ultimatum turned out to be unnecessary; just a few minutes ago, Hilary had knocked on the door and told them drinks were on the buffet table along with grilled cheese toasties with portobello mushrooms and bacon. She handed them a folded printout announcing a late dinner at quarter to eight: a merguez sausage and couscous stir-fry with sides of pork tamarind, water chestnuts, green mango chili, roasted potatoes, lightly braised long beans, peas, and asparagus with a safflower curry drizzled over them; they would end the meal with rum raisin ice cream over baba-au-rum as desert. Woody would have news for them following dinner.

~⌒~

LOS PAJARITOS, WALDO, NEW MEXICO

Following dinner, Woody did indeed tell them: he had fourteen clients lined up (he did not mention that two of them were himself and Stan Joiner), each of whom had each put up earnest money in anticipation of all fourteen items assembled in Woody's great room in Waldo in what would amount to a mini-auction to facilitate who got what. He would schedule the auction (he did not call it that, but rather, labeled it a "collective viewing") just as soon as Jen and Thad delivered the thirteen additional items to him.

Thad went back outside to the van and retrieved his smartphone: *well, this is it,* he typed.

good can we try to get away some time tomorrow and call Dahlia? Jen typed. *how about going to see the cathedral? Say, we meet her there at ten?*

how do we explain suddenly getting religion?

we read a tourist thing about Bishop Lamy just for the experience to see the cathedral.

sounds good.

MONDAY, 9:30 AM

Again, Jen and Thad were unaware when the SUV again appeared on the parallel road and parked discretely, or when it once again made maneuvers taking them in the wake of their green van, now also leaving a barely discernible trail of vital fluids that would have marked their progress if they had been able to notice.

10:10 AM
SANTA FE

At the cathedral, Thad called Dahlia. She would be ready with "the goods" as soon as she heard from them that they had "the securities." They wandered down a cross street; the first few bars of Beethoven's Fifth sounded. Jen opened her purse and took out her smartphone. It was Hilary. "We have what you need," she said. "Come by the gallery."

They did so. As they walked in, they noted Woody, talking with a customer. He nodded at them. Hilary trotted up, took each by an arm, and steered them to the office. She opened a vault and retrieved a long, flat lock box, secured with a tiny padlock, which she opened with an equally tiny key. She lifted the box's lid and removed a brown inter-office envelope and handed it to Jen. She motioned to the desk. "Here. Count what's in there, then sign this receipt." Jen sat at the desk, Thad peering over her. She counted fourteen items of immediate negotiable securities: bank drafts, cashier's checks, money orders, each in the amount of $16,000. Stan's and Woody's "earnest money" was included. The last item was a receipt for $224,000. "Both sign, please," instructed Hilary. They did so. Hilary put the securities back in the lock box, secured the padlock, locked it, and gave the key to Thad.

"You'll make all the arrangements tomorrow? I'd suggest you go right back to Los Pajaritos and put this in your cottage. It'll be safe there," said Hilary.

Outside, in the van, Jen and Thad locked the doors; the lock box sat on Jen's lap. "Whew!" she said. "That's, that's a lot more than we thought they were going to cough up! Woody Glenn is our friend!"

"Or he's Dahlia's friend. She'll be ecstatic!" said Thad. "But why don't we take that dinky padlock off. Put it in your purse. We don't want to chance losing that teeny little key."

"Right, right," agreed Jen, and did so.

Thad called Dahlia again on the burner. It went to voicemail. He left a message: "I think we'll have what you need tomorrow. How do we get it to you and pick up the masks?" Dahlia called back a few minutes later. Jen answered. She would not meet them at the cathedral. They were to meet her at Gran Quivira, a ruin to the south, halfway to Albuquerque, between eleven and eleven thirty. "I'll give you directions," she said.

"Tell her no need," said Thad. "We've been there. We've been to every ruin within a hundred miles! What time?"

"She says eleven," Jen replied. "If she's not there when we get there, we're to wait."

GRAN QUIVIRA,
SALINAS PUEBLO NATIONAL MONUMENT

As it was, as they turned south onto the two-lane highway, then east onto a more major highway, then south onto minor road, and finally entered Salinas Pueblo National Monument, parking at Gran Quivira, Jen and Thad were as yet unaware of their vehicle's imminent disablement.

"What do we do now? Just wait?" said Jen as Thad cut the engine.

Thad nodded. "Just wait." They did so, for nearly fifteen minutes; then the Dahlia burner phone rang once more. "Adrian should be pulling into the parking lot any minute. You'll give him the envelope with the securities."

"What!?" exclaimed Jen. "You're not coming??"

"No."

"But Adrian will have the goods."

"That remains to be seen," said Dahlia.

Thad grabbed the phone. "Wait a minute, wait a minute! If he doesn't have the other thirteen, then there's nothing doing. Nothing doing! The deal was, we give you the cash, you give us the goods."

"And so we shall. But we have to make sure the cash is good. Our bank people will know within a few minutes if the securities are immediately negotiable. If they are, no problem. We'll call you and arrange the transfer." The call ended. A red Nissan Maxima entered the parking lot, moving past them to the far end of the lot. Adrian, dressed incongruously in a greatcoat, exited the driver's seat, closed the door, and stood by the car. Jen and Thad exited, Jen slinging her cross-body bag over her neck and resting her right hand on the clasp. They took positions standing beside the van. *A stand-off,* thought Jen. *Do we wait until he caves and approaches us? Or do we just suck it up and go crawling over to him? No. We have what he wants. He can come to us.*

But that proved not to be the case. After a good five minutes or more, Thad muttered disdainfully, "Okay. Let's go. Clearly he's not going to budge."

Jen slid the lock box out from under the passenger seat, unlocked it, took out the manila envelope, and placed it in her bag. Thad exited the van and began walking slowly toward Adrian and the red Nissan; Jen followed. The only other vehicle in the lot was a white SUV, apparently unoccupied. As they walked slowly, Jen idly imagined who might have come in the SUV: *a clutch of oldsters, quietly exploring the ruins? A couple with baby and toddler? Where are they? How simple life once was!* Suddenly, Jen felt very, very weary.

As they approached, Adrian assumed a kind of Dahlia-like demeanor. "Good of you to come," he said. "I assume one of you has the collateral?" He looked from one to another. Jen nodded. "Good," he said. "Mrs. Canning, why don't you and I sit in this spacious back seat and do the transactions. Mr. Canning, you can take the front passenger seat." Thad did so. "Naturally I'll give a receipt for each deposit. Those will be your units of exchange for each of the goods. I'll write the number of the check or m.o. on the receipt in the place for a person's name. Presumably each client has kept a receipt with the number." Adrian closed the front passenger door. Jen took her seat in the back. Adrian got into the back seat and closed the door. He took a receipt book from an inner pocket of his greatcoat. "You hand me one, I'll hand you one."

Jen opened her bag and took out the 4x11 manila envelope. She removed fourteen money orders, bank drafts, and cashier's checks. As Jen handed him a check, on the line where a name was meant to be written, Adrian wrote the nature of the deposit and its number. He tore the receipt out and handed it to Jen. Jen noted that it, and the one underneath it, and she guessed all of them were pre-signed with an unfamiliar name. "Who's Jane Faulks?"

"Surely you didn't think 'Dahlia' was a real name that someone would actually go through life with? Who wants to be the equivalent of a big purple bloom?"

"Oh," said Jen. "Why didn't she use her real name from the very start?"

Adrian shrugged. "Just for extra security."

"I suppose you're not really Adrian, either." Adrian shrugged. *And of course, we're not really the Canings, or even the Murrays.* "When all is said and done, when we're all finished, can you pay us our share in cash?"

Adrian nodded. "If that's the way you want it."

The whole transaction, the handing over of $224,000, represented in fourteen pieces of paper, was over in ten minutes. If Adrian was surprised at the amount, he didn't show it. They all exited the car. Adrian gave a little bow. "Thank you so much. We will be in touch."

"Just a minute," objected Thad. He grabbed Adrian at his elbow. "Why don't you have the other thirteen masks?"

"Because as Dahlia—Jane—told you, we have to make sure these securities are … are what they seem to be. Rest assured, you will be informed about the next step—where to pick up the remaining goods. Now … please … uh … unhand me." Thad did so. Adrian opened the driver's door, slid into the seat, slammed the door shut, secured the locks, clicked on the starter, and moved slowly through the parking lot to the exit, then roared away.

Jen and Thad stood for another minute, then walked slowly and silently back to their van. "Have we just been had?"

"If we've been had, then so have Woody Glenn and thirteen other people. And he's not going to be pleased." Jen opened the driver's seat door. "Shit! What's that?"

Thad came over to her side. "Oh, oh. That's a leak. A gas leak."

"I thought I'd been smelling something."

Jen climbed, inserted the key, started the engine. "Shit! The gas gauge says 'empty'!"

"Shit, shit, shit!" said Thad bending over with his head in his hands. They took up their standard swearing duet: "*Merde!*" (Jen) "Crap" (Thad) "Bollix!" (Jen) "Fuck!" (Thad) "*Madone!*" (Jen) "Bugger!" (Thad) "Piss!" (Jen)

"Hey—that SUV!" Jen leaned on the horn, then got out of the car, shouted, waved her arms in the air, jumped up and down. But the SUV was already out of the parking lot. She slumped against the van. "How did they get out of here so fast? Where were the people? Did you see them?"

"No."

"They just materialized out of nowhere and were suddenly in that SUV!"

"Well," said Thad. "We can wait around for somebody else to come along, or we can try to get to that little town, where we turned off. I mean, on a weekday? It could be hours before somebody comes along, and even if they do, what could they do? They'd just give us a ride into town where we wait around at a gas station for a tow truck. Drive slowly. Maybe we can make it to that junction—that little town—I'm sure I remember a gas station there."

"Eeewww," said Jen as she pulled up to the stop sign at the parking lot's exit. "The brakes are mushy!"

"Crap!" said Thad. Drive *REALLY* slowly."

But only halfway up highway 55, and still a good five miles from Mountainair, the van chugged to a halt. Jen pulled onto the verge, barely. Thad pulled out his smartphone and looked up AAA in Santa Fe and in Albuquerque; Santa Fe gave him voicemail, but Albuquerque answered. "They say at least an hour, hour and a half; that'd be one, one thirty. But she says allow until three o'clock to be safe."

"That's almost three hours from now!" wailed Jen.

"What else can we do?" said Thad. "This is not our day. Could we have kicked up a rock or something? Or scraped bottom?"

"Hard to do that in this thing. It's pretty high off the ground. I wonder…" Jen said reflectively.

23

SHORTLY AFTER ADRIAN HAD DEPARTED in his red Nissan
Maxima, two men rose from their prone positions in the front and back seats
respectively. The man in the back seat quickly exited the SUV and took the
passenger seat. The driver flipped open his phone and punched in a number.
"Hey, Chimmy here."

"I know," was the reply.

"Yeah," said Chimmy, "well the guy in the fancy red car got the other two in
that ratty green van to come over, then they all sat in the car and they did something for about ten minutes… Huh…? Pansy-lookin' guy… Well, it was kinda
hard to see, ya know, peeking over the back seat… You think…? Yeah, could
have … okay. Yeah, right, right. Okay." He flipped it closed, pocketed it. "Change
o' plans, Horace," he said to the man in the passenger seat. "We follow the money."

It was easy for the men in the white SUV to almost catch up to the red
Nissan and to follow it to Mountainair, then through Bernalillo, and back up

the interstate to Albuquerque and to the Doubletree Hotel. The man in the passenger seat, known as Horace, jumped out in time to see the man park, exit the Nissan, and enter the Doubletree. Following, he noted the man enter the elevator. The elevator stopped on two floors: 4 and 12. The man called Chimmy (Jimmy), panting, joined him. Chimmy flipped open the phone. "Hey," he said, "This is Chimmy."

"I *know*," came the reply.

"He's either on the fourth floor or the twelfth… Okay … okay … How do we do that…? No, I don't have a white coat, just a, you know, long-sleeved white shirt… Yeah, no… Okay." He flipped the phone closed and addressed his companion: "We take off our jackets and stow them in the vehicle, then take up watch, you on the fourth and me on the twelfth floor. Wait for them to come out. They're prob'ly gonna have, like, a lotta luggage with 'em."

Ten minutes later, Horace, on the twelfth floor, lurking around first one corner, then another, noted a tall man in a bowler hat, with what looked like the start of a thin mustache, exit the elevator and knock on the door of room 1215. "Ferguson," he said. The door opened. He entered. Five minutes later, Horace noted he and a prim-looking older lady in a plum tweed skirt and matching jacket exit room 1215. They called the elevator. Horace quickly pulled out his phone, punched in a number.

Exiting the elevator, Ferguson and Dahlia walked quickly across the lobby, through the hotel's revolving door, and turned to the left. For the business they were going to transact together, Ferguson had donned a beige twill sport coat and clipped a bow tie onto the collars of a pin-striped shirt with midnight-blue agate buttons; he wore 501 Levi's held in place with a dark brown leather belt and a pair of vintage black Acme cowboy boots. Dahlia wore a powder-blue pants suit. They did not notice the man in suit trousers, and a long-sleeved white shirt but no tie, following them.

After walking three blocks, they entered a bank. The man in suit trousers and a long-sleeved white shirt waited a few moments, then also entered the bank. He stood just inside the entrance for perhaps thirty seconds, then exited. He rounded the corner of the bank, flipped open his phone. "Yeah… Yeah… Yeah, some kinda transaction. Okay… okay. What do we say to them? Should I just stop 'em now? No, back to the hotel, I think… Okay…" He called Horace, still in the hotel lobby: "We take action. Meet you there."

Chimmy watched the two marks walk quickly out of the bank. They stood together just outside the revolving door. Around the corner, Chimmy was not noticed. He heard the woman say, "Well, Mr. Ferguson, I won't say it's been a pleasure doing business with you, but it seems we should cap this mutual venery with some sort of minor do. We have to vacate our room soonest, but it's several hours before we have to leave for the airport. Care for a libation back at the hotel?"

"Och, why not." Ferguson unclipped the bow tie and put it in his pocket. He undid the top button of his shirt.

Chimmy walked back to the hotel, a half block behind Ferguson and Dahlia. He gradually reduced the distance.

"We're done," Chimmy heard the woman say. "We're all set to go. Our luggage is packed. It was instructive to come to a mutual understanding."

"Aye. Well. You know my part of it is not quite over so I'll be visitin' a gallery tomorrow with that certain document. I hope never to encounter you again."

"And I likewise. And remember, I not only have your word but I also have some prima facie information with which I could go to the authorities, so…"

"As do I," Chimmy heard the man reply acidly.

As Dahlia and Ferguson entered the hotel lobby and then the elevator, they took no notice of two men, both in suit trousers and long-sleeved white shirts, no jacket, entering the elevator with them. When they exited the elevator, the two men exited as well, walking briskly in the other direction, but then turned around, stopped, and peered behind the corner.

The door of room 1215 opened. Two suitcases were shoved into the hall, followed by the young man who, Chimmy noted, had driven the red Nissan. Chimmy flipped open his phone. "Yeah… Yeah… They're makin' tracks.

They're outta here. Okay… Yeah. We can do that… No… You'll have to. No time." He flipped his phone closed, walked quickly to the now closed door of room 1215 as the young man picked up both suitcases. "'Scuse me, 'scuse me," he said. "I'm from management. I'm Chimmy and this is Horace." He took out his phone. "We'd like to just ask you a few questions about your stay here and our service."

"I'm sorry," said Dahlia. "We don't really have time…"

"Maybe we can just adjourn back into the room? You still have your key card?"

Dahlia and Adrian and Ferguson all assumed equally confused, even consternated expressions. Chimmy said again, "Yeah, could you please open up the door again?"

"No, no," said Dahlia. "Move aside. We don't have time for your survey, or whatever it is."

Horace let something drop from his shirt sleeve into his palm. Dahlia and Adrian and Ferguson stopped speaking as they heard a soft "snick." Horace showed them what he had in his palm: a stiletto.

"Yeah," said Chimmy. "Let's just go back in the room."

Dahlia extracted the key card from her handbag and opened the door. Adrian hefted the two suitcases back inside. They all entered the room.

"What do you want?" said Ferguson stonily, all his reflexes and senses now on alert.

The door swung shut. "Sit on the bed," directed Chimmy. Adrian, Dahlia and Ferguson sat. Chimmy and Horace planted themselves in front of them. "Now, we have it on good information that when youse went to the bank just now, youse did a little transaction, a deposit. We'd like to 'company you back to the bank so youse can undo what you did. Make a withdrawal, in the exact amount o' that deposit. Waddaya say?"

Their request was met with stony silence. Horace opened his palm so that the stiletto was visible. Now Chimmy fished in his trouser pocket and withdrew a stiletto. Ferguson stood. Dahlia stood. Adrian stood. Suddenly,

Ferguson pivoted, grabbed Horace' elbow, twisted, and at the same time gave Horace as much of a body slam as he could do at such close quarters. Horace yelled in pain, lost his balance, and fell against Chimmy, the stiletto flying out of Horace's hand. Ferguson head-butted Chimmy in the stomach. Chimmy let out an "oof" and he and Horace toppled to the floor. "Run!" yelled Ferguson. Dahlia ran. Adrian collapsed.

Dahlia kicked Horace in the shins and dashed to the door but could not get it open because it was blocked by the two suitcases. Horace rolled over and pushed one of the suitcases into Dahlia. Dahlia and the suitcase slammed to the floor. Horace, on hands and knees, dragged Dahlia by her ankles away from the door. He rose to his feet and kicked her savagely in the lower back. She let out what would have been a scream if her face had not been plastered into the thick carpet. Horace went over to the door and threw the bolt.

Ferguson used the diversion to get up off the floor. But Chimmy rolled, grabbed Ferguson's ankle, and pulled hard. Ferguson went down again. Horace, now standing, grabbed Ferguson by his jacket, pulled him up, and swung a fist hard at Ferguson's jaw. Chimmy, back on his feet, had come around behind Ferguson, who slammed into him from Horace's blow to his jaw. Chimmy grabbed Ferguson around the throat and, with his other hand, was trying to twist Ferguson's arm behind his back. But Ferguson twisted and drove a fist up between Chimmy's legs. Chimmy yelled and took his hand from his throat but did not let go of Ferguson's arm. Horace found his stiletto, and now charged at Ferguson, ripping it up Ferguson's jacket sleeve from wrist to shoulder. Ferguson shrieked with pain; Chimmy balled a fist and struck Ferguson savagely on the jaw, then boxed him numerous times around the head. Ferguson, his back to the bed, slumped over, his right arm and jacket soaked with blood.

Dahlia, slowly, painfully, had risen and was standing, hunched over, breathing hard. Both panting, Horace and Chimmy stepped back, each with stiletto in hand. "Now you went and complicated things." He nodded at Dahlia. "Go into the bathroom and get some towels and clean him up. And *DON'T TRY ANYTHING OR THIS GUY GETS IT!*"

Ferguson's arm wound turned out to be largely superficial but required a towel wound around it to absorb the blood. "Hey, you," Chimmy barked at Dahlia "unpack one o' them suitcases and get out a new shirt." Ferguson watched as Dahlia slowly walked over to the suitcase that was still standing, picked it up, plopped it onto the bed, and sprang the latches. Ferguson had mightily hoped Dahlia could have had it in her to swing it out against Chimmy's head, but clearly, she was winded, in pain, and did not have it in her. *We've been bested*, he thought resignedly.

Ferguson wriggled painfully out of his jacket, then out of the shirt. Dahlia extracted a shirt from Adrian's suitcase and handed it to him. Ferguson put the shirt on; it did not exactly fit because Ferguson and Adrian were different sizes, but with a jacket over it, the bulging, shirt and the bloody towel might go unnoticed by the casual observer. Chimmy wadded up Ferguson's bloody shirt and threw it into the suitcase.

At the foot of the bed, Adrian sat up. "Ow!" He put his hand to his head. "What happened? Was I knocked out?"

Dahlia sighed. "You fainted. You hit your head on the bedpost."

Horace stood guard with both stilettos, one in each hand. Chimmy picked up Ferguson's jacket from the floor, felt in its pockets, extracted a phone, then patted Ferguson's trouser pocket. "Looks like you got two phones. You reach in that pocket nice and slow and take out that other phone and hand it to me." Ferguson did so. "Okay. Grandma—I'm gonna look in you' purse. I ain't gonna take any money or credit cards, just you' phone." He did so. "Hey, you got two phones too. Everybody got two phones? How 'bout you?"

Adrian was standing now. "I have a headache." Chimmy patted Adrian's trousers. "Okay, you gimme that one too. Where's you other one?"

Adrian shook his head. "I've only got the one."

Chimmy shoved the phones into his shirt and back two trouser pockets and extracted his own—a burner. He made a call on it. "We got 'em... No, we had a little difficulty but it's all taken care of now... Okay. So, we take 'em to where we were gonna take the others...? What about the others...?

Yeah, they're probably still there. We can find 'em... Yeah... I've got it. Yeah, yeah, we've got everything—tape, rope, fishing line. We gotta improvise three more bandanas but we'll manage." He rang off. "Hey, you," he nodded to Dahlia. "You ladies always got scarfs, right? Now, lady, you walk over to youse suitcase and put it on the bed. Don't try nothing or Horace lets go with one o' them li'l clam openers. You open up that suitcase and get me out five scarfs." Dahlia did so. Chimmy grabbed them and stuffed two of them into his trouser pocket. He handed the other three to Horace. "Here, put those in youse pocket."

"Now we gonna take a little trip." Chimmy walked over to the mini-fridge, opened it, and took out a small bottle of whiskey. He opened it and doused Ferguson's head and shoulders and soaked Ferguson's jacket sleeve on the injured arm. "So, Horace is gonna put one arm around you and the lady is gonna be on your other side and the other gentleman will walk with me right behind you. If anybody down in the lobby asks, you had a little accident with a bottle and fell down so we're takin' you to the doctor's. Now you know we got some very persuasive hardware in our hands."

Reddish-purplish bruises were beginning to bloom on Ferguson's swelling jaw.

"What about our luggage?" asked Dahlia.

"You won't be needin' it," replied Chimmy. They exited the room. Chimmy let the door swing quietly shut. They walked to the elevator, took it down to the lobby, and walked out of the hotel and into the parking lot without incident, to the white SUV. "Now, Horace is gonna drive and we four are gonna get into that seat all the way in the back, four across. Horace is gonna be our chauffeur." He addressed Horace. "'Nother change in plans, Horace."

1:45 PM

Horace drove them back to the highway and to the turnoff for Gran Quivira. They soon came upon a disabled green van on the side of the road. They stopped. A woman who had been sitting in the van walked briskly to the white SUV while Chimmy opened the door and got down from the driver's seat.

"Hi," said Jen, "Thanks for stopping! This is a really lonely, desolate road! Nobody's going to Gran Quivira on a weekday! We called triple A and they're coming out so we've got to stay here 'til…'"

Chimmy palmed his stiletto and opened it toward Jen. Jen looked at it in his hand, then at his face, then back to his hand. Thad appeared by her side. "What's going on?"

"I'll tell you what's goin' on." He walked to the back of the van and opened the door. Then he returned to where Jen and Thad were standing. "Yous're goin' for a little ride."

"Huh?" said Thad.

Chimmy pressed the stiletto ever so lightly into Jen's side. "*We're goin' for a ride, ain't we,* little lady?"

"Oh," said Jen. She peered into the van; she gasped, as she saw Dahlia and Adrian and seated between them, a man that she didn't recognize. He seemed quite the worse for wear, with cuts and bruises on his face. And he stank. All three passengers turned their heads and shot quick, sullen glances at their new captive companions.

With his other hand Chimmy prodded Jen on her back. She looked at him. He nodded toward the SUV's open back doors. "Oh," said Jen again. She walked toward the back doors, Thad following.

"First you give me your phones, nice and slow," instructed Chimmy. Thad gave him his smartphone and the burner Dahlia had given him.

"Mine's in my purse, in the van," said Jen.

"Okay," said Chimmy. "We're not gonna worry 'bout that one. Now." Chimmy reached into the back of the SUV and took out a red tool box. He set it on the ground. "You're gonna turn right around, both of you. That's right." Chimmy took a reel of fishing line and tinsnips out of the tool kit. Cutting two long lengths from the fishing line, he told Jen and Thad, "Now youse both put your hands behind your back."

"Hey," said Thad.

But Chimmy already had the fishing wire wound tight around Thad's wrists. He tied it. Then he did the same to Jen. "Don't go nowhere." Then he took out a coil of plastic rope and cut two lengths, winding each around first Thad's, then Jen's wrists, binding them together. "Now youse sit right down on the tailgate here. That's right." He repeated the procedures with their ankles, pushing their socks down so the fishing line bit into their legs. "Now youse scoot as far back as ya can and squeeze in." Chimmy shut the door.

Chimmy went around to the passenger side of the van, opening the double doors. Horace jumped out, then reached in and dragged Ferguson out, knocking his legs out from under him and cuffing his head as he did so. Horace leaned down and poked Ferguson between the ribs with the stiletto. "One false move, one word outta you throat, I stick this in you," said Horace.

Ferguson was still on the ground. Horace grabbed both his legs and yanked them. He then tied them first with fishing line, then with plastic rope. He turned Ferguson roughly onto his belly, yanked his arms behind him and tied them, again with fishing line and plastic rope. Ferguson yelped with pain. Then he yanked him to a standing position. "Youse." He motioned to Dahlia and Adrian. "Out!" They climbed out. "You!" He yanked Ferguson to a standing position and prodded him. "In." Ferguson tumbled into the SUV, situating himself on the seat as best he could. "You!" He nodded at Dahlia. "Sit on that seat."

After tying up Dahlia and Adrian in fashion similar to Ferguson, Jen and Thad, he remounted the driver's seat. Horace slid into the back seat beside Adrian. Not a single car had come by. Chimmy wished he could have blindfolded their five captives but once they got on the highway, even through the SUV's tinted glass, an alert motorist, or an alert passenger might have found it curious to note that a vehicle held five blindfolded people. *The last thing we need*, thought Chimmy, *is the New Mexico State police pulling us over 'cause o' some upright citizen makin' a call to 'em.* Chimmy turned the SUV around, retracing their tracks, but bypassing Albuquerque and turning off at a sign that said "Ski Sandia."

After a couple of miles, he turned off onto a rocky dirt track that eventually snaked up the side of the mountain, then into a canyon. He stopped the vehicle, hopped out, opened the back doors, and beckoned Jen and Thad out. They butt-slid out, standing as best they could. Chimmy took out the red tool box again, opened it, and pulled out a roll of duct tape and two red bandanas. From his bulging trouser pocket, he pulled the three scarves that he had gotten from Dahlia. He placed one of the bandanas around Thad's head, covering his eyes, and tied tight in back. Then he snipped off a two-foot length of duct tape and wound it around Thad's head, covering the bandana. "There," he said. "Don't think you're gonna be able t' see outa that." He did the same thing to Jen, then, using the scarves, to Ferguson, Dahlia, and Adrian.

"This is barbaric!" objected Dahlia.

"That's why youse is all gonna have this tape over you' kissers, too, so you can't mouth off." He slapped a length of duct tape over first Dahlia's, then Ferguson's, then Adrian's mouth and then did the same to Jen and Thad. "Okay," he said, youse two scoot back in, butts first." He slammed the back door shut.

Jen noted the SUV's speed diminishing as, it seemed, the road or track they were on became rougher and rockier. She was trying not to sob. Eventually, the SUV came to a halt. Doors were opened. The hapless passengers were herded out of the vehicle and were shuffled through a low doorway by Horace and Chimmy. Ferguson went first, banging his forehead sharply on the low lintel. "Umpph!"

"Yeah. Youse might wanna duck down a little." The rest of the passengers shuffled as best they could into a tight space. One of their captors opened a second door. The captives heard a crackling, as if a stiff, heavy curtain might be being pulled aside. The captives felt themselves being shoved into yet another small space, perhaps behind the stiff curtain.

One by one, the captives landed on a cold, hard, dirty surface. Their captors ripped first the duct tape, then the blindfolds off, one by one. "I'd o' just as soon leave youse mum and blindfolded but them ain't our instructions."

Chimmy slowly rotated the flashlight around the space. "See them crates there?" said Chimmy. All eyes, slowly growing used to the dim light provided by the flashlight, fastened on stacks of wooden crates, leaning against one dirt wall of the space. But Chimmy was specifically talking to Horace. "Get four, five o' them crates and line 'em up in a row in front o' that curtain there." Jen followed the flashlight's beam. A series of hides hung from a wire at the back of the space.

Horace moved to take two of the crates from the stack, stepping on Ferguson's hand, Jen thought, probably deliberately. "Ow!"

Horace threw the crates toward the curtain, then retrieved three more, then lined them up in a neat row. "Now youse scoot you' selves w' yer backs up against them crates," commanded Chimmy. The five trussed and hobbled captives did so. "Now, you, Horace, you get four, five more o' them crates an' put 'em in front o' our friends there." Horace did so. "Okay. Don't go nowhere." Chimmy exited the chamber, leaving the door ajar. He returned shortly heaving along a plastic picnic cooler. He opened the lid, took out a package of cardboard plates, which he opened, placing five of the plates on the crates in front of the five supplicants. Then, he took out two small tubs of cubed cheese, opened them, and tumbled them out onto the five plates. Next, he opened a package of sliced salami and repeated the move. Finally, he opened a box of crackers and sprinkled them on top of the cheese cubes and salami slices. His final act with the contents of the cooler was to lift out two quart bottles of water with straws.

Omigod! thought Jen, *what goes around, comes around.*

Then Chimmy cast the flashlight beam and his gaze around the space once again. "Ah! There they are." He fetched three paint cans from the wall with the crates, took the stiletto out of his trouser pocket, and without open-ing it, slid the sheath between the rim of each can and the lid. They popped open. "Good. Almost empty." The rancid smell of old paint filled the space. He shoved the paint cans in between Ferguson and Dahlia and Jen and Thad. "Now youse got lots t' eat and some water and youse can use them cans for

… ah … bodily needs. Sorry we don't got more water but we only planned for two, not five. Change in plans. Now don't go away. We'll be back. We're gonna bring somebody here who wants to talk to you."

"How do you expect us to be able to eat with our hands tied behind our backs?" Dahlia demanded.

"Oh, you just stuff your face in the dish and scarf, like in a doggie bowl. Snuff, snuff, woof, woof."

"And go to the bathroom?" spat Jen.

"You never unzipped your boyfriend's fly with your teeth?" chuckled Chimmy. As Horace and Chimmy exited the space, Chimmy threw a roll of toilet paper into their midst, then pulled the curtain back into place and pushed the door shut. The hostages heard another door slam. They were back in total darkness.

A Disused Mine, Sandia Peak, New Mexico

"Disgusting," said Dahlia. "I'll pee in my pants first, thank you."

"I have a headache," said Adrian. "Where are we?"

"Ye have a headache? A headache! Ah've got bruises and aches all over me body," complained Ferguson, "And Ah've been stabbed!"

"And I've been kicked in my kidneys!" declared Dahlia indignantly. "Who kicks little old ladies in their kidneys? Who's pulling the wires on these hooligan puppets?"

"Do you think you have internal injuries?" asked Jen softly.

"Don't know," replied Dahlia. "Hopefully not."

"Ah canna say these accommodations are conducive to improving the bodily condition," stated Ferguson.

"Ha! Understatement of the day!" squeaked Adrian.

"Achoo!" Jen sneezed. "And it's musty in here!"

"At least it's dry," commented Thad.

"I think we're in someone's cellar," said Dahlia.

"Maybe a root cellar, but I think it's more likely were in an abandoned mineshaft," said Thad.

"We saw several of them when we were driving around," offered Jen.

"But who has done this to us? And why?" complained Dahlia, obviously exasperated. "I think there's a third party that's got wind of our goods and at some point, we're going to be made some sort of quid pro quo: we'll let you go if you give over the remaining masks to us. It's either someone from long ago, when I was the dupe for that bunch of pot-hunters—which did include Woody Glenn—and someone who is acting just as unscrupulously now as they did then—or someone completely unknown to us who somehow got wind of our plans—ours and the Cannings' here—but doesn't know exactly who holds the cards, who's actually in charge. I can't think that it's in Woody's interests to imprison us here like this."

Ferguson guffawed. "I thought *you* were in charge, Miss Jane. Or at least you thought you were."

Dahlia/Jane sighed. "So I did; so I did."

They all fell silent.

Jen could not see but the vaguest shapes, but she ran her mind around the room as it had appeared in the shadowy light of Chimmy's torch. *Crates: in back of them and in front of them. More crates: stacked against a wall. A door, that Chimmy had opened with a code, now shielded by—not exactly a curtain. A stiff piece of—hide. Hides were hanging in front of them and, yes, in back of them. Elk hides!*

"Yes," said Jen, "I'm sure we're in an old mine shaft, converted to a storage chamber. Secured by two doors, no less. And you know who likes to hang elk hides all around the place? None other than Woody Glenn. And we've got an elk hide in front of us and one in back of us. It's Woody Glenn who's done this to us."

"No, no, that makes no sense," objected Dahlia.

Ferguson agreed with Jen. "Aye. You're right. And unless I'm mistaken, there's some storage space right in back of us. But if not Woody Glenn himself, then it has to be someone who is very thick—thick as thieves as the saying goes—with Woodard Glenn. And ye may be right, Ms. Jane, that the culprit is one of those from the Mimbres heist from long ago, who was cheated out of what he or she regards as his or her rightful share. If that is indeed the case," continued Ferguson, "then I'm pretty sure I know what's behind that elk hide in back of us. Rows and rows of shelves and on those shelves, rows and rows of ancient prehistoric pottery of the Mimbres culture."

"Good God!" exclaimed Dahlia, then quietly said, "Dan Rosenstock? Couldn't be! Or could it?"

"Who's Dan Rosenstock?" asked Thad.

Ferguson sighed. "It's a long story. And maybe it ends right here unless we get out of here. And Ms. Faulks, it would be ironic indeed if your husband has resurfaced to claim his share of those ill-gotten gains, and you have ended up his victim!"

Dahlia gnashed her teeth and spat, "Well if that's the case, I will surely seek my own day of reckoning with *him*, even if it takes me the rest of my life! We will have accounts to settle!"

"Well, I'll bet I know what else is behind that curtain, too. I'll be it's a stash of thirteen items from an auction in Paris about a year ago," said Thad

After a moment, Jen said, "No, Honey. That can't be."

"Huh?"

"If Woody Glenn is behind this, and he already has the masks, well, then, why would he be behind *this*? I mean, sending thugs to kidnap not only us, but *them*?"

"*Somebody* disabled our van while it was parked at Woody Glenn's. Those hooligans must have done it last night while it was parked at Woody' place," said Thad. "Put a pin prick in our gas line so it slowly dribbled out; put crimps in our brake lines so after a while they developed pin prick holes and voilà! Leaky brake lines, leaky gas line, van no go. All they had to do was follow us, then pluck us up. And who besides Woody Glenn could they be working for?"

"I think Ferguson is right. I think it's some, as he put it, 'third party,' and I wouldn't put it past my double-dealing husband, that skunk, to perpetrate this horror. And I do think you're entitled to some sympathy from us, Mr. and Mrs. Canning," said Dahlia somewhat grandly. "You do seem to be the victims of … uh … a mistaken culpability. But our captors must be planning to do something more with us. They must somehow know that money has changed hands but they must also be somewhat in the dark about who has access to what, and are hatching a plan to get their grubby mitts on our money *and* the goods. Otherwise, they wouldn't have left us all this food and water and…"

"Yeah. Potty. Food. Water. Rope. Duct tape. Déjà vu," said Thad.

Husband? Thought Jen. But she was too fatigued for her mind to follow out the implications of this little morsel of information Dahlia had dropped. All she could think of was, *as ye sow, so shall ye reap*. She uttered the aphorism quietly.

"If this is a mine shaft, then there are probably other abandoned mines around here and that means old roads, to get the ore out. There just might be people out there—you know, hikers, off-the-road bikers, ATVers," said Thad. "Why don't we try yelling?"

"I have a headache," said Adrian, as if that vetoed the yelling idea.

"'Tis worth a try," said Ferguson. "Let's do it." He, Jen, and Thad all began yelling as loudly as they could do, for as long as they could do so, probably, reckoned Jen, a good five minutes until first Jen, then Ferguson, and finally Thad quit.

"I was getting hoarse," croaked Jen in the silence.

"Do you think it's nighttime yet?" asked Dahlia. "If so, there's not going to be anybody out there until tomorrow morning."

Jen started to nod off, then shivered and started, awake. "Oooo. I hate to say it, but I have to pee."

But now they heard noises at the front of the space. They heard the door open. Chimmy drew back the elk hide curtain, but very little light spilled in because he had closed the latter, coded door. "Here." Chimmy and Horace appeared with arms full. They threw two thin sleeping bags and three heavy coats at the hostages. "We don' want youse to catch you' death or get sick or nothin'. Look what we went and got for ya. Army surplus." Doors slammed shut, first one, then another.

"Looks like they're keeping us long-term," lamented Thad.

"Thad," said Jen. "I need your teeth. And the paint can."

"Teeth?"

"Zipper?"

"Oh."

"I'll do the same for you."

24

ZOE AND PHIL FOUND THE CURIOUS STRUCTURE, a block off the old highway, that had been in Jessica's photograph: a free-standing plaster teepee with a painting of what Zoe now recognized as a *Katsina* dancer in motion, shaking a rattle, and the notice, "Teepee Curios." An arched doorway was shut with a half-sheet of plywood, held in place with a structure of two-by-fours. In back of the teepee stood a second structure, a cavernous, rambling building, with what looked like original adobe walls and tin roof jammed onto an early twentieth century neo-Victorian addition. It looked as if someone had started to build a house, then thought better of it, and had slap-dashed tin sheets that sloped from a second story almost to the ground, covering a cinder-block series of rooms that jutted out to the front and sported two plate glass windows framing a door, clearly meant to be a shop. The house itself was surrounded on two sides by a roofed portico-porch, reached by buckling and racked steps. The front door to the house was Eastlake style, Zoe noted. The overall result was a confused and derelict effect.

They parked, got out of the car, and walked around it. A sign announced it was for sale, with a name and phone number. The several sheets of tin had been nailed over the pink adobe walls, Zoe thought, to prevent the whole thing from melting away.

Zoe and Phil walked up the crumbling steps to the covered porch running the length of the building, which they could not fully access because of the sheets of tin. The solid Eastlake door, padlocked, was curtained from the inside. Zoe peered through the tiny gap between the two halves of the curtain. She glimpsed a dirty, gray, wooden floor littered with broken jars, bunched filthy pieces of cloth that could have been garments or curtains, and three pieces of furniture: what looked like an old wind-up Victrola, a chest of drawers with one leg missing, and a sofa spitting out its stuffing.

As they walked around the structure, a slightly portly, middle-aged man with wispy gray hair blowing around a balding pate emerged from a small RV parked at the house next door in front of a garage on a weed-infested driveway that had, at one time, been graveled between two cracked cement pads. "Interested?" he asked.

"Curious," responded Zoe. "What was this?"

The man introduced himself as Carl Larsen. "A trading post, for a good many years. It went bust in the seventies when the new road went in—the interstate. Before that, some professor from Albuquerque owned it. Chemistry professor, what I heard tell is, some of his experiments got out of hand and the place halfway burned down, him with it. Then another professor—friend of his, anthropology professor—bought it. He's the one put up the phony teepee. He opened the place up as a trading post. He had a little dig, too, an archaeological excavation, in the back. Couple years in a row, every spring and summer nice big girls would show up in white shorts and T's and sit there in the dirt, sifting more dirt through big screens sitting on cinderblocks. Don't know what they was lookin' for or if they ever found it. Then, in the 'nineties, a couple bought it, opened it back up again—handicrafts, jellies, hot sauces, some antiques."

"You know a lot about this place."

"Yeah. I own it and I own the place next door, too; grew up there, rent it out now. I live in Albuquerque, but come up here on weekends, stay in that there RV parked in the driveway or take it up to Sandia, bunk in it."

Zoe looked over at the driveway next door where a Land Rover was parked behind a RV just large enough, she thought, to accommodate a small kitchen arrangement, toilet and shower, with a double bunk bed over the cab.

"I've got a real estate license so I handle a few properties here and in Sandia. You know Sandia?"

"No, no, not really," said Phil. "We're just looking around."

"Well, Sandia's kind of interesting. You might wanna check it out. It's fun t' poke around in those hills, find old abandoned mine workings, especially now that ski season's just about over. There's not many tourists. But don't go int' any o' those old mines unless you know it's not gonna cave in on you. Lotta times, the supports are old, rotten. I poke around in 'em but I always make sure it's safe afore I do. The state makes the owners put doors on them and signs and so forth but the doors are a joke—you can get in pretty easy if you really want to."

"Do you ever find anything?"

"In the mines, you mean? Yeah." He shrugged. "Sometimes some interesting junk, a few pieces of turquoise, a nugget of copper. I bring some of it back and pile in a corner of the yard there." He nodded in the direction of the house next door. "Well, if you're interested, the price on the old trading post is $189,000." He handed Phil a card, holding out his hand, which Phil took.

"Thanks," said Phil.

A woman, much younger than Carl Larsen now emerged from the house next door carrying a picnic hamper. "You ready to go?" she asked, addressing Carl Larsen.

"Oh, hi!" She addressed Zoe and Phil, approaching them. "Hi. I'm Sarah, Sarah Konopinsky." She held out her hand first to Zoe, then to Phil. "But I go by Sarah Kono. Konopinsky's a mouthful, so I'm Sarah Kono. You're interested in the property?"

"Well, not really," said Phil. "We're … kind of vacationing, more or less, staying in Santa Fe…"

"Oh, where have you been?"

Zoe explained, as succinctly as possible, their trip out to the Pueblo and to various archaeological sites.

"That's quite a trip!" exclaimed Sarah. "What do you do when you're at home?"

Zoe and Phil found themselves giving the same recitations they had given at Woody's party. But Sarah seemed really interested.

"Have you been up Sandia?" asked Sarah.

"No, no…" said Zoe.

"Would you like to go?"

"Umm…"

"Why don't you come along? Come with us? We love exploring the old mines, the ones that are safe to go into."

Phil shrugged. "Well, I guess we have time. But it'll be cold up there, right?"

"I'll get you some woolies." She turned on her heel and re-entered the house.

Zoe sensed that Sarah liked Carl, but was eager for younger company.

"She's a great gal," said Carl Larsen. "Kind of got handed a raw deal. Aunt and uncle live in the house; I give them as much of a break on the rent as I can. But she's a full-time, twenty-four-hours-a-day caregiver and the only time she gets out is on our little spelunking trips up Sandia. She arranges for a private caregiver to come in one day a week, Mondays if she can manage it, but this week it had to be Tuesday. Mondays or Tuesdays are best to go exploring during winter. But now the skiers have all gone home, and school's still in session, there's a few weeks when the peak's nice and quiet and empty."

Sarah returned with two heavy sweaters and two slightly old and seedy looking coats. "We'll have to go in my Land Rover," announced Carl Larsen. "Your car wouldn't make it; it'd bottom out. I'll pull out the Rove and you can park it behind my old RV there in the driveway."

On the way, Zoe and Phil talked more about their trip and Carl told them about his hobby. "I bring along bolt cutters so we can get into the mines that are sealed off. The only reason they do it is to keep people like us getting in, breaking a leg or tripping a cave-in, and then suing them! I think it's a federal law. But I've been doing this for thirty years and I know what I'm doing. After we've explored, I put a new padlock on the door; I have a whole bunch of them. The people that put the locks on originally have probably forgotten all about them or they're long gone. The locks are to keep people out! But hell, we don't do any harm. Sometimes we find a little copper nugget or two, or sometimes a little lode of silver and turquoise. Sometimes I can heat them up and get a little bit of this and that out of it; but mostly I just put 'em on a shelf in my basement in my house down in Albuquerque. Sometimes I find interesting junk like that ore car there in the front yard you saw that's got the clematis in it."

Cait and Robb would love poking around like this, thought Zoe.

They followed the highway to the turnoff, then turned off the metaled road on to a dirt track that got increasingly rougher; Carl put the vehicle into four-wheel. Zoe, Phil, Carl and Sarah bumped up, down, and along old mining roads that were little more than rough, rocky tracks.

Carl showed them one mine that he had visited before. Grayish dirt, scree and boulders, kettle-sized to human-sized, formed an embankment at the sides of the slope out of which a tunnel had been hollowed. A squared doorway framed the shaft's entrance, constructed of rough-cut logs and scrap lumber. Low, scrubby green vegetation struggled to take back the hillside. A path, strewn with reddish-brown pebble-sized stones led to the shaft. A gray metal door, secured with a padlock, closed off the entrance.

"That's one of my padlocks," he said. "See where they pounded that four-by-four in? That was to close the gap between the door and that upright. And see where the door hinges is screwed into that upright on t'other side? I coulda yanked those screws outta that rotten upright and just pulled the whole thing way. But then I might o' had a cave-in on my hands. And anyways, I like t' do as little damage as possible."

Zoe's attention was drawn to the hillside opposite the mineshaft, separated by a shallow arroyo oozing reddish-brown water. A three-story tumbling-down wooden structure loomed. *It must have once been a handsome dwelling*, thought Zoe. It featured a bay window and the remnants of a partially wrap-round porch. *The mine owner's mansion?* She wondered. Now she noticed a rubble of rotted planks that had cascaded into and down the arroyo. *The remains of outbuildings? Shops? Little stores? Mine-workers' shacks?*

Carl's voice took her out of her reverie. "See what I mean? Nobody even bothers to come around to discover they can't get in! This is a pretty interesting one." He stopped the Land Rover, pulling on the handbrake. They climbed out. Carl cut the padlock with his bolt cutters. He drew open the heavy wooden door and shined his flashlight in, revealing a surprisingly large cavern. Carl walked in; Sarah, Phil and Zoe followed.

In Carl's flashlight beam they saw rail tracks leading into the shaft, which appeared to descend deeper into the mountain. Three battered ore cars stood on the rails. "Neat!" said Zoe.

"First time I came here I took a good long time examining the walls. Know what I found? Little dried out pieces of food. Evidence of Tommyknockers."

"Now he's going to tell you a Carl Larsen tall tale!" said Sarah.

"It's not a tall tale!" objected Carl. "It's miners' lore!"

"Tommy what?" asked Phil.

"Tommyknockers," responded Carl. "Tommyknockers were thought to be the ghosts of miners that'd died in the mines. They stuck around, and if you heard a knocking noise, well, that was them. Them and their knockin' could cause a cave-in. Know what you did if you was a miner and you heard knocking? Or even if you didn't hear knocking?"

Zoe and Phil shook their heads. "Unh-unh," said Phil.

"Well, you'd open up your lunch bucket, take out your cornbread or tortilla or pasty, break off a piece, and push it into the side of the mine shaft, as an offering to the Tommyknocker."

"Cool!" said Zoe.

"Yeah," said Carl.

"How far in can we go?"

"Well," said Carl, "You can follow the rails a little way, but when you go a little way in, you can see there's been some fall-in from the ceiling."

"Was this a copper mine?" asked Phil

"Not that I can see. Everything says coal, to me. There's chunks of it around and lots of black dust. But let's take you to a mine that was copper—copper and turquoise."

They exited. Carl closed the door, took off the broken padlock, took out a new one from his pocket and fastened it. "There!" he said. "Good as new!"

"He loves this breaking and entering." Sarah raised her voice and drew out "loooves" like it was taffy, vocalized. "It gives him the secret panache of being a burglar without the risk of getting thrown in the pokey."

"Don't do no harm to no one," Carl commented plaintively.

They climbed back in the Land Rover and bumped along the track for another fifteen minutes. Zoe felt her stomach beginning to growl. Breakfast—two Cliff bars, a couple of going-stale rolls they had been gifted at the pueblo, and a bottle of fruit water—had been a long time ago. They had been doing this mine-spelunking for more than an hour; it was getting on toward noon.

Sarah proposed stopping to "have some nosh. It's too windy to sit outside; cold, too. We can just sit here in the car. We didn't plan for guests but we always bring more bottles of fruit water than we need. And I always pack two sandwiches for Carl—liverwurst and goat cheese. We can spare one of those, can't we Carl?"

"Oh, sure."

"And," continued Sarah, "we've got a whole unopened tube of Pringles, a huge bag of tortilla chips, and one bag of dried figs and another of mixed salted nuts, plus grapes. That'll do us, won't it?" Carl stopped the vehicle, opened the windows, and cut the engine. Sarah reached down between her legs, drew up the hamper, set it on the consul, and opened it.

Following their vehicle-bound picnic, Carl suggested they take off on foot. "We'll make better progress than driving and we can get to some out-of-the-way places." Soon they came upon another mine. "Turquoise and copper mine," noted Carl. This mine had no locked door, probably because it was obvious that a cave-in had sealed off the shaft a few yards in. It was much narrower than the other mine they had visited, with a lower ceiling; they could not really get very far in without crawling. The shaft's floor was damp in some spots, muddy in others. The plunk-plunk-plunk of one or more drips from the ceiling made Zoe aware that she would probably come away with black ooze coating her hair.

Carl aimed his flashlight beam all around the space. "There's some uranium 'dog holes' around here too, but this isn't one of them. They're always locked up, but…" He bent down to take up a chunk of something his flashlight beam had fastened on. He picked it up and rubbed it against his thigh. He showed it to Zoe and Phil. Sarah leaned her head into the huddle. "You see? It's a little bit shiny and it doesn't crumble, and it's heavy. Copper. Here." He plopped it into Zoe's hand.

"Oh, yeah!" she said. "Awesome!"

They exited the mine. The wind had stopped and it was warm now. They walked back and left their coats in the Land Rover; Zoe put the copper slug into her jeans pocket. "You know we can leave the Land Rover here and walk around some more," suggested Carl.

To their left was another track and another mine; they climbed down the rise, sidewise, so as not to slip. They stopped in front of a door with a padlock that looked at least as substantial as the first one at which they had stopped. The door seemed to be several inches thick. "Oh, yeah," said Carl, panting a little to catch his breath. "Yeah. This one is still used, at least for something. See that padlock? That's not mine. Whoever owns this one still works it, or maybe uses it for storage or something. I got in there once and there's another door on the other side of this one. And get this: it was armed with a code. Well, I felt a little bad. I'd already cut the padlock. I came back out, put on another one, locked it. The guy must have been mad as hell! Knew his vault had been violated! He'd o' had to use bolt cutters to get back into it."

"So, we're not going in," said Phil.

"Nah," said Carl.

They turned and started to walk away. "Wait!" said Sarah. "Did you hear something?"

⌒

They had been dead tired. In between fits of wakefulness, they had passed the night managing to get at least some sleep; at least, they thought they had passed the night. In the dark, they could not be sure. They had been so exhausted they could have slept on and off for twenty-four hours. But Jen didn't think so. Biorhythms would have declared another potty break. When potty time had come around, Jen and Thad and Adrian had figured out how to scoot around so that, hands tied in back were able to fiddle open buttons and zippers, cans were arranged, the necessities attended to. Most of the food remained unconsumed.

"Do you think it's morning yet?" asked Jen. "I'll bet it is. People might be hiking, roaming around now. Why don't we give the yelling another try?"

"Och, go ahead," said Ferguson.

Jen and Thad and Adrian bellowed "Help! Help! Help!" They listened. And listened. And listened. They heard nothing. Jen closed her eyes and tried to sleep again, or maybe meditate. At least, to counter an awareness of having to pee again.

⌒

"Do you hear something?" Jen cocked her head. No answer from Ferguson, who seemed to be dozing. No answer from, Dahlia who seemed to have migrated to a different space, seeming not to give credence to their circumstances.

Thad responded: "Yeah, maybe. Maybe I hear voices? Outside?"

Adrian began yelling: "Help! Help! Help!" Jen and Thad joined in.

Zoe, Phil, Carl, and Sarah stopped and listened. Sarah said, "Yes, voices. From in there." She pointed at the door. "I think they're crying for help." All four got an ear as close to the door as they could.

"Yeah, I did hear something," said Zoe. "But now it's stopped. Should we...?"

"Yes, I think we definitely should," said Sarah. "It sounded like peoples' voices. People could somehow have gotten in and got themselves trapped, like, if the door with the code was open but then a gust of wind blew in and that door with the code slammed shut. If people are in there, we've got to get them out. The worst that can happen is the guy who owns the mine has to buy a new padlock."

Carl had fetched his bolt cutters from the Land Rover and carried them with him, anticipating more mine exploring. Now, he used the bolt cutters to cut the padlock and wrenched open the door. He pushed back a stiff heavy hide curtain. He moved a few yards into the shaft, flicked on his flashlight. They all saw that the door was indeed openable only with a code. "Hello?" bellowed Carl.

"Yes, yes, we're in here. Hello. Please help us. Get us out of here!" The voices were yelling but faint; it sounded to them like two women and a man.

"Oh, boy," said Carl. "The only way to get that door open is with a couple of crowbars. We'll have to basically destroy it. I've got two in the car."

"I'll get 'em," said Phil. Carl handed him the keys to the Land Rover. Phil departed at a running pace.

"We're going to have to pry this door open with crowbars," yelled Carl. "This door is really thick. And it's metal."

"Do whatever you have to do," came a second man's voice. "Just don't use dynamite!"

Catching his breath, Phil returned with two crowbars, three screwdrivers, and a pipe wrench. "I found these in that big toolbox in the back." Phil handed the keys to the vehicle back to Carl. Carl shoved the keys in his pocket and looked at the pipe wrench. "Let's get going with the crowbars," urged Carl. They did so.

"Here. Let me try."

Zoe took the crowbar and inserted the tapered, two-pronged end between door and frame. She tried pushing the end further into the jamb while, at the same time, exerting prying pressure. But, time and again, the bar slipped out of the slot without accomplishing any noticeable alteration. A sheen of perspiration appeared on her forehead. Huffing, she withdrew the crowbar and set it on the ground. "I thought Kung Fu made me strong, but this is beyond me."

"Let's try a couple screwdrivers," suggested Sarah. "If we can dent the frame just a little bit and widen the slot, we'll have better purchase with the crowbar." Sarah took one of the screwdrivers and stuck it into the jamb, prying at it as Zoe had done with the crowbar. After several tries at it, she lurched as the tip of the screwdriver broke off.

Carl took up the largest screwdriver Zoe had ever seen. "This here is the mother of all screwdrivers. If this don't make a dent, in it, I don't know what will." He inserted it into the jamb and worked it back and forth. "Ha!" he exclaimed, straightening up. "I think that might just do it. I'm gonna make another dent down here and then, Phil, maybe you can get one of those crowbars and I'll try the other and we can pop this thing." Carl worked the screwdriver into the jamb two feet down from where he had managed to widen the gap. "Huh! Whew! Okay—let's try it. Phil, you stand to one side and I'll stand t'other."

They did so, Phil working the frame with one crowbar and Carl working the door with the other. Finally, with a groan of metal, the door came away so that the locking bolt was exposed. "Pluththth!" gasped Phil, laying down his crowbar.

"Now let's see what I can do with this blue-ox-sized screwdriver," said Sarah.

She's thinking of that legend, Paul Bunyan and his blue ox, Babe! thought Zoe. *It's a Paul Bunyan-sized screwdriver...*

Sarah inserted the screwdriver between the lockbolt and the frame and with a screech of metal she succeeded in popping the bolt free. "Uhhhh!"

Carl now inserted his crowbar into the jamb and gave it just a jerk, enough so that the door popped open several inches. Zoe stepped forward, took the edge of the door in two hands and, stepping back, pulled toward her. It was open! Carl took up the flashlight from the floor where he had placed it, stepped through the opening, and played the beam over the five hapless captives seated, in cramped positions, before him. "Holy...!" he exclaimed. "These folks didn't just wander in here and get trapped behind a slammed door; they've been imprisoned here!"

"You're darned right!" declared an older woman. Zoe noted she was dressed somewhat elegantly, in what had been a handsome pants suit, before it had gotten smudged and torn.

Zoe, entering behind him, realized as she did so that she could not help striking a classic cartoon pose: her jaw dropped. "Ferguson!"

"You know these people?" asked Carl.

"Who's this?" said Dahlia, turning first to Ferguson, then to Zoe. "You know each other?"

"Yes," responded Ferguson, nodding. "We know each other."

Zoe took in the scene: five people, in substantial disarray, leaning against crates and against each other like so many kingpins in a half-finished, abandoned bowling game. As Carl's flashlight beam roamed the space, Zoe took in the crates, pieces of cracker, cheese, and salami on plates and scattered on the ground, and the heavy hide curtain hanging in back of the people, trussed in bundles with plastic rope. An odor of must, mold, dirt, and humanity—sweat and urine—hung in the air. Recognizing Jen and Thad, she shouted, "And you're the imposters!"

"Oh gawd!" wailed Jen. "This is like Milady and Richelieu being rescued by the Three Musketeers!" Jen had developed the knack—*or is it my defense mechanism?*—of meeting the aftermath of a dicey situation with jokey repartee, sometimes only between herself and herself. She used it now.

"What?" queried Sarah.

"You're no Milady," spat Dahlia.

"Aye, but ye surely are," interjected Ferguson.

"Huh?" croaked Adrian.

"And I suppose that makes you Richelieu?" huffed Dahlia.

"Or more likely, Rochefort," Ferguson gasped amidst a coughing fit.

But the round of sparring was interrupted by the sound of motors. Zoe listened. Actually, there were two motors.

"Someone's coming," said Sarah.

"Mine owner coming?" suggested Phil.

"Trouble's coming," responded Jen.

Zoe turned and started out the door.

"Don't worry," said Carl. "We'll getcha outta here."

Zoe turned again. "No, wait," she said.

"The desperados," said Jen. "I'll bet anything it's gotta be the desperados coming back. Chimmy and Horace."

"Hold on," commanded Zoe. "I think we might have bigger priorities. They've survived this long; their liberation can wait. We don't know what kind of endgame is intended with these hostages here, or whose hostages they are. Bring those crowbars." Phil and Carl picked up the crowbars again; with Zoe and Sarah, they went back outside in time to see a white SUV pull up. The driver killed the engine. A man in white shirt and trousers, no tie, exited the passenger side; he took something out of his pocket. Zoe could see: it was a stiletto. As she watched, the man clicked it open. The driver, also in white shirt and trousers, no tie, now also was standing beside the SUV. He also took a stiletto out of his trouser pocket. "Who you?" he said. His gaze went back and forth from the open door to the tableau of four. He took two steps forward. The passenger man took two steps forward.

The two menaces stood, legs and arms apart, Zoe noted, *trying to gauge their next move.*

Zoe thought quickly. Her right foot was better than her left, her right arm, hand and fingers more responsive than her left. She would have to move quickly, kicking on the second step, body slamming the second man, then hope that, with both of them on the ground, she could punch two fingers just below the hyoid bone of at least one of them. She would then have to scramble to completely demobilize the other one, the driver man, maybe with a head butt to the stomach. She had never done anything like this before, but had read somewhere in one of the thrillers that counted for her recreational reading, that stomach-butts were effective.

Zoe looked at Phil, Carl and Sarah, who were standing just outside the mine entrance, crowbars, screwdrivers and pipe wrench scattered on the ground around them. She looked meaningfully at them. *Bluff it.* "I know you know how to use those, so why don't you each take up one of those and make sure our visitors stay where they are."

Phil, Carl and Sarah took up, respectively, crowbars and pipe wrench and moved tentatively toward the two men from the SUV. They were astonished to see Zoe quickly step forward, pivot, and deliver a swift and effective blow with the bottom of her raised right foot, knocking the blade out of the driver's hand. The move knocked her off balance, but as the passenger man moved toward her, brandishing the stiletto, Zoe threw her body into the air, arms folded, and slammed into him, connecting with him on his side and back. He fell to the ground on his back, emitting an "oof," but keeping hold of the stiletto. Zoe was on top of him in half a second and jammed two fingers into his neck. "Arghh, agga-ughh," gargled Horace. Horace dropped the blade and put his two hands to his throat, gasping and gagging. Chimmy, on his knees, halfway rose up, his right hand reaching out to grab Zoe, his left hitting out ineffectively. As he grabbed her, she wrenched away, tearing her blouse; Phil stepped forward but before he could intervene, Zoe, crouched, sprang, and rammed her head into Chimmy's stomach. He fell on his back.

Zoe stood, then took her left foot and kicked Chimmy's right temple with the toe of her boot.

She stepped away, leaning over, hands on knees, panting. "I … don't … think … I … killed him," she panted and repeated: "I. Don't. Think. I. Killed. Him." She straightened up, walked over to where Horace had dropped his blade and picked it up. She looked around, spotted Chimmy's blade where it had landed, a couple yards away, when he had flung it. *Ha! thought Zoe. When things don't go according to plan, the hooligans prove inept—especially when confronted by unlikely opponents!* Both men were now in various states of immobilization, writhing on the ground. "Okay. Now we can see about the others." But just as she said it, a bright red Jeep Wrangler with enormous tires stopped just behind the SUV. The driver cut the engine and stepped out.

"WHAT is GOING ON?!" shouted Stan Joiner.

Zoe eyed the new arrival warily. She recognized him from Woody's soirée. The thought sparked through her mind: *Clearly, he's connected with this whole scene somehow, maybe even orchestrated it.*

Jen and Thad, still in their bindings, had shuffled out haltingly to the mine shaft's entrance and were peering around the damaged door. "Stan Joiner!" exclaimed Jen. Then to Thad: "What's *he* doing *here*?"

Zoe watched Stan Joiner look wildly around, several thoughts seeming to animate his facial expression. He started toward Zoe. She decided he seemed to be trying to weigh assuming the role of detached, neutral observer, or making some sort of move. As he approached Zoe, he seemed to realize something, turned around, and quickly got back in the Jeep.

"Ha!" responded Thad. "Clearly, whatever he *was* going to be doing here, *now* he thinks it was a mistake!"

"Mistake or not, he's not getting away!" Zoe declared. She ran to the Jeep's passenger side with the two blades she had gotten from Chimmy and Horace and punched and tore savagely at the wall of the right front tire. The tire popped with the sound of a gunshot. Stan was now back out of the Jeep.

"WHAT DID YOU THAT FOR?!" shouted Stan, starting toward Zoe. "I'LL GET YOUR ASS IN A LEGAL SLING YOU'LL NEVER GET OUT OF! DISABLING MY VEHICLE, PUTTING ME IN DANGER FROM YOUR HOODLUM FREINDS!!"

Zoe brandished the two blades. "Stop the bluster. Stay right there," she told him. "Phil," Zoe was still panting, "Cut loose the younger woman." She flicked one blade closed and handed the other to Phil. "Bring the cords over here. Don't cut anybody else loose: just her. Then take up your crowbar again."

"I can't. I cut the cords but she's got some sort of wire around her ankles."

"Wire-cutters. That's what we need. I'll get 'em." Carl dropped his crowbar and loped back up the slope to the Land Rover. *He's surprisingly spry and agile*, thought Zoe. Phil took Carl's place guarding the would-be assailants. Moments later Carl returned with a pair of garden clippers—secateurs used for trimming grape vines. But they did the job.

Carl cut Jen loose. Jen staggered a few feet, hobbling with scraped and nicked ankles.

Horace and Chimmy were now each leaning on opposite sides of the SUV's hood, both panting and groaning. Phil and Sarah stepped closer to them, brandishing their automotive cudgels.

"Carl, hand that lady those ropes and the fishing line." He did so. Jen looked at the bindings that had so recently constrained her. Zoe handed Carl the two blades. One in each hand, he took up a stance on the other side of the SUV, close to Chimmy. Now, Stan Joiner approached her menacingly. "Please turn around and lie down on your stomach," Zoe told him.

"I WILL NOT!" he shouted. "YOU CAN'T INTIMIDATE ME!"

"No," said Zoe. "I suppose I can't." She sighed, then lowered her head and charged at Stan Joiner, ramming her head into his stomach. He emitted an "oof," then fell over on his back. Zoe pounced on him, taking him by his left arm and deftly turning him onto his stomach. She kneeled on his back and, pinning his arms with hers, raised up her body and came down on his back with both knees. "Aaargghh!" bellowed Stan.

"Bring that rope and fishing line over here," commanded Zoe. Jen did so. Zoe scooted down onto Stan Joiner's ample butt, then yanked his arms onto his back.

"Ow!" he yelled.

Zoe reached up; Jen handed her the fishing line and rope. She wound the fishing line around his wrists, then tied it off. Then she bound the longer of the two rope lengths also around his wrists. She tied a poacher's knot. Zoe turned around on Stan Joiner's back, facing his feet. The other piece of rope was not long enough to bind his ankles; she had to make do with a remnant of fishing wire.

Zoe rolled off Stan's back, then stood. "You," said Zoe, motioning to Jen with her head, "Come with me. Carl, can I borrow your snippers? Remind me to give them back when … uh … when all this is said and done." Carl handed her the secateurs. She jammed them into her back pocket.

Jen, grateful for being rescued but thoroughly perplexed as to how they had been discovered, and especially by this young woman, Claudine, who did indeed, after all, seem to have been following her and Thad ever since Jen had spotted her and her boyfriend sitting on the park bench at Walsenburg, followed Zoe back into the mine.

"Now will ye please, please cut us loose?" said Ferguson.

"No, I don't think so," said Zoe.

"Why ever not?" said Dahlia.

Zoe, Jen, Dahlia, Adrian, and Ferguson became aware of commotion just outside the mine's entrance. Sarah, Carl, and Phil charged in, caroming into Zoe. Regaining his balance, Phil said breathlessly. "They got into their vehicle. They weren't as bad off as we thought, I guess. They got it going and were headed straight for us. They were going to run us over."

They heard the sound of the SUV's engine fade as it wound its way back down the dirt track. "They're getting away!" wailed Jen.

Zoe stepped around the four and peered outside. They had indeed gotten away, but they had left Joiner behind. "Bastards!" he muttered through clenched teeth. Zoe reckoned they'd seen the last of them; they had all the hallmarks of hired hit men who had no particular loyalty to Stan Joiner, but obviously had been hired by him.

"Okay, let's get these clowns out of here. Oh—first, Phil, you can change a tire, right?"

"Sure," Phil shrugged.

"Use that crowbar to get that busted tire off and put on the spare."

"You need a jack? I've got one," said Carl.

"Can you get your vehicle over here?" suggested Phil. "Then if we need your jack, we'll have it. Also, we're going to load these folks into Carl's vehicle, aren't we?" he said to Zoe.

Carl went off. Phil gestured to the prisoners still in the mine shaft. "Are we going to cut them loose?"

"No," said Zoe.

"Why not?" asked an incredulous Ferguson.

"Because until we've got you where we want you, and can unmask this masquerade, I don't even want to take a chance that one of you might cuff us on the head or ram a fist into our sides and leave us to rot on the side of the mountain while you take off, scot free. I don't know what you're doing in here with this woman and these two imposters who smashed and crashed their way into Robb and Cait Murray's shop, but until I find out, I'm not letting any of the rest of you loose."

Hearing this off-hand reference to "shop" and again the word "imposters," Dahlia barely stifled a gasp. Something Adrian had said days ago, as they were about to pull away from Suwanee Antiques in Oswego came back to her: "Those aren't the Cannings. Those are Robb and Cait Murray, proprietors of Cannings." *My God!* she thought. *I should have listened to Adrian! This is revolting! How could I have been so cavalierly careless! Here I am trying to run a clever criminal operation and I don't even take the most elementary precautions! Have I fallen into another one of Woody Glenn's traps? Could this all be Woody's doing? Could these Canning imposters be hand-in-glove with*

Woodard Glenn? Collecting the rest of the proceeds from the sale of the masks but then absconding with the money? Smug and secure in doing so because they know we're forced to stay under cover? Then getting dumped into the mineshaft with us was just a ruse! And where does this chunky beardo fit in? Partner of Woody's? He comes to get us out but then this … this … girl and her boyfriend beat him to it? Who are they? Why are they?

"Heh, heh. What about her?" said Thad, nodding his head in the direction of Jen. "You cut *her* loose. How do you know she's not as good at karate chops as you are?"

"It's not karate; it's Kung Fu," said Zoe. "And you know what? Phil and Carl are going to drive the two vehicles and this gal is going to be sitting in the back of Carl's SUV between me and Sarah and I'm going to have this blade"—she brandished it, and clicked it open—"in my right hand and Sarah is going to have a crowbar sitting on her lap. So, I don't think she'll try any karate chops."

Carl departed and returned driving his Land Rover, navigating slowly in 4-wheel drive around the hummock, parking in front of Stan Joiner's red Jeep, where the SUV had stood. He emerged, opened the back, and retrieved a jack, which he carried over to Phil, just winding the last of the lug nuts off the disabled tire; he had the spare ready, leaning against the Jeep. "Okay," said Zoe, flicking the blade shut. "Excuse me, but, you're…"

"Jen."

"Right." Zoe nodded. "Jen, you go with Carl and get your hubby or boyfriend over to the Jeep." A moment later, Jen walked over to where Thad was standing and helped him hobble over to the Jeep. "Take him over to the Jeep and when Phil gets that tire on, dump him into the front pass." Phil was now jacking up the Jeep.

"Sarah, can you make sure Jen behaves herself? Carl and I will get the others."

Phil and Carl entered the mine shaft again. Adrian, Dahlia and Ferguson were standing, wobbly. "Could I ask ye a favor?" said Ferguson.

"What's that?" said Zoe stonily.

"Bring that torch back in here and draw back that curtain in back of us."
Carl fished the torch out of his trouser pocket. Zoe drew the stiff elk hide
curtain aside.

Carl shined his flashlight. "Good God!" he exclaimed. "There's a bunch
o' prehistoric pots back here! These belong in a museum!"

Dahlia and Ferguson twisted around, as best they could. Dahlia gasped.
Ferguson nodded. "Aha!" he said. "I thought so."

"So this is where they shifted them to!" exclaimed Dahlia.

"Could I ask a favor?" said Ferguson. "You've got your phone? They took
all ours."

"You want a picture. Here's your Mimbres pots. Or what's left of them."

"Right ye are, lassie."

Zoe stepped closer to the racks of shelves. She saw they were six deep.
A narrow space at the left gave access to each row. The racks were four high.
Most of the shelves were empty, but she reckoned they still held about twenty
pots. She didn't quite know if she was going to continue to help Ferguson
with his quest, but she decided having the data wouldn't hurt. She carefully
photographed: first a couple of general shots, then one for each pot. But she
was afraid she would soon run out of juice.

She went out and saw that Phil was finished with the tire. He was lowering
the jack. "Phil. Can you help? Do you have your phone?"

Phil re-entered the mine with Zoe, who directed him to the pots that she
was not able to photograph. Carl snapped off the flashlight and he shuffled
out with Dahlia. Then Zoe and Phil came first with Adrian, then finally with
Ferguson, hobbling between them. As the temporary mine dwellers exited,
they let sleeping bags and army surplus coats slide off, except for Dahlia, who
had managed to wrap the thin sleeping bag around herself and secure it, like
a coat, on her back side with her bound hands.

"Put one of these three into the Land Rover's front seat and throw the
other two into the back seat of the Jeep," instructed Zoe. "Maybe you should

put one of your padlocks on the door, just so nobody walks away with thirty or forty thousand dollars' worth of prehistoric ceramics."

"Will do." Carl went to retrieve a padlock from the back of the Land Rover. "This little adventure has sure taken the boredom out of a life of real estate rounds with sour-faced customers. More fun than resting turquoise nuggets away from Tommyknockers!" he chuckled.

Something occurred to Zoe: it would aid in the little drama she planned to stage once they arrived at Woody Glenn's estate. "Wait a minute," she told Carl. She had noticed that two of the cardboard plates were still scattered with remnants of crackers, salami, and cheese. She took them up carefully, then folded over the plates. She carried them over to the Land Rover. "Okay, Carl, lock it up. Sarah, can I put these in your picnic hamper?"

"Oh, sure. It's on the floor in the front." Zoe carefully placed them into the hamper.

"What about me?" growled Stan Joiner.

Zoe walked over to him. Thad was now seated in the Jeep's passenger seat. "Phil, Carl, can you help?"

The three of them got Stan Joiner up and got him more or less standing. "Ow, ow!" Stan groaned. "My back, *my back*! You'll pay for my hospital bed and my chiropractor, you little bitch!" he spat.

They got him into the back seat. Phil took the driver's seat. Stan Joiner had left the keys in the ignition.

"Okay, let's go. We're going to a place called Waldo. I'll give you directions as we go, Carl." Zoe shoved Jen into the Land Rover's back seat; Sarah took the seat on Jen's left, crow bar on her lap, and Zoe the place on her right. She opened the switch blade. Carl started the motor. Jen began sobbing great gulping gasps of woe. Tears flowed freely. "Sorry, I don't have any tissues," said Zoe. She tried to sound sincere but decided it came out sarcastically.

Sarah reached over Jen and pulled a wad of tissues from a box on the console between the two front seats and handed them to Jen.

Zoe was bone-achingly tired. When they reached the highway, suddenly, she could not keep her eyes open. But she knew she had to do so. She blinked and kept moving her head from side to side; she gave directions to Carl and kept talking, noting structures and businesses and even vehicles on the road. "Sorry I'm babbling but I'm still on an adrenaline rush," which, of course, was just the opposite of true.

She realized none of them had eaten, but decided doing so could wait. Woody could not be counted on to be hospitable. But if he was at the gallery, waiting for the call from Jen and Thad about delivery of the additional thirteen masks, the call that would never come. She assumed he and Hilary would come back home, that is, to Waldo after the gallery closed. *In the meantime,* Zoe thought, *we can probably count on a bewildered but gracious reception from Art Tatum and Lupina.* She decided Coco should be witness to the unmasking of the masquerade. She dug her phone out of her back pocket, then remembered it was out of juice. "Sarah, is your phone available? Can I use it?"

"Sure," responded Sarah, scrunching down in the seat and drawing her phone of the right-hand pocket of her jeans, quickly keying in the password. She handed it to Zoe.

Zoe punched in Coco's number. Coco answered. "Coco? Zoe here. Guess what…"

25

The two vehicles drew up to the bright blue doors of Los Pajaritos. Zoe disembarked the Land Rover, walked around to the passenger side, retrieved one of the stilettos and the secateurs from her back pocket, clicked open the blade, opened the door, and cut the rope and fishing line bindings on Dahlia's feet, then those on her wrists. Then she did the same for Ferguson and Adrian. "Don't get any ideas about trying to run away." She scowled at them. "There's no place to run to." She went round to Stan's Jeep, which had pulled up behind the Land Rover. Phil rolled down the window. "I'll cut Thad's bindings," she told him.

"Hey, what about me?!" barked Stan.

"Shush!" Zoe barked back. She handed the stiletto and the secateurs to Phil. "Cut this guy's bindings once all of us get inside the compound," she told him.

Zoe walked up to the blue doors and noted a rope attached to a bell that projected from the side of the adobe wall, just under an eve. The bell had an inscription on it: "El Camino Real." She had not noticed it on her previous visit. She pulled the rope. The bell clanged. She waited several minutes. No one came. She rang it again, several times. Again, she waited for several minutes. No one came. Then she noticed a button on the other side of the tall, wide doors. She pressed it and heard a buzz. Within a couple minutes a little door in the middle of the left-hand door slid open. Art Tatum's face appeared. "Yes?" he said.

"It's me," said Zoe. "Claudine. Remember? I came here last week with my friend Phil? For the party?"

"Oh, yeah," Art replied. The little door slid closed. The doors swung open. "Mr. Glenn is expecting us, at least some of us," said Zoe. "And I thought it would be okay if I brought some friends."

"Oh," said Art. "Well, yeah, folks from that party have been coming in and out all week. He did say some of those same folks might be coming back today or tomorrow, but he said that it would be happening at the gallery in town and he asked me to be on call to maybe come in and help. But I guess there's been a change in plans?"

Zoe nodded vigorously. "You could say that."

"Well, come on in. You can park anywhere." Art and Zoe swung the doors open and stood aside. Art took his phone from his shirt breast pocket, retreated to a corner of the compound, and made a call.

Carl and Phil drove the two vehicles into the compound and parked them. Zoe opened the vehicles' doors and instructed the occupants to get out. Phil cut Stan Joiner's bindings. "Don't try anything," Zoe warned him, sotto voce.

"I won't 'try anything,' right now, as you put it, but just you wait 'til I get out of your web, little Miss Muffat, and I guarantee you I'll try *something*."

Dumbass, thought Zoe. *Can't even get his nursery rhymes straight.*

Art Tatum closed the portal doors. He scrutinized them closely as they disembarked the vehicles. Tatum's eyebrows rose as he watched Ferguson, Dahlia, and Aiden shuffle dispiritedly across the courtyard to the doorway of the house, followed by Carl, Sarah, Phil and Zoe. "Say, are you … they, uh … Is everybody okay? Or…? What's happened to all of you? You look like you've spent the day camping out in a pig farm. And hey—what happened to *him*?" Tatum began walking toward Ferguson. Ferguson staggered a bit; Art Tatum reached him and steadied him by the elbow. He turned to the others following "He's got—is that blood? Dried blood on him? He needs medical attention." Then he said to Ferguson: "Here, sir, let me take your jacket." It was draped over Ferguson's shoulders.

Zoe answered Art: "They'll all need some water or tea. Mr. Ferguson would indeed appreciate some cleaning up and attending to."

"A wee bit o' medication and some sticking plasters would be appreciated," said Ferguson weakly.

Zoe nodded. "At least some TLC with a warm wash cloth and some bacitracin."

"Ah," said Art, nodding, having caught a whiff of the residual whiskey drifting off of Ferguson. "Maybe they've been celebrating a bit. Had a bit of a scrape and a tumble? Soon's everybody's inside, I'll fetch Lupina. Oh," he remarked, "there's our guests," as Thad and Stan disembarked the Jeep. "But where's their vehicle?"

"Broke down on the road, yesterday," said Zoe.

"We were kinda worried when they didn't turn up yesterday, didn't even call. But Ms. Hilary said they probably got caught up in touring around and decided to stay over somewhere and maybe figured it was too late to phone. Well, come on in." The clutch of visitors followed Art and Zoe across the gravel parking area to a small door in the main house, some of them requiring assistance from others, and Art continuing to help Ferguson. Art held the door open.

As Stan Joiner limped through the courtyard, Art greeted him: "Oh, hello Mr. Joiner."

Joiner stopped and glared at him. Sticking out his finger, not quite into Art Tatum's chest, he snarled, "I don't know why you're being so nice to these bandits, inviting them into the house. I don't think Mr. Glenn is going to be pleased."

Art stood scratching his head for a minute, then followed the visitors into the house and disappeared.

They were now all assembled in the hall leading to the dining area overlooking the great room. Art reappeared, accompanied by Lupina. "Well, come on through," he said.

"Art, can we all assemble down there in the sunken part of the room?" asked Zoe.

Dahlia continued to keep her sleeping bag wrapped around herself. Zoe noted that two massive leather recliners had been moved into the sunken part of the great room.

"Well, uh, I don't know…" said Art Tatum.

"Sure," said Lupina.

"We'll have t' rustle up some seats f'r ever'body…"

"Can we get those settees that were here for the party?" suggested Zoe.

"They're in the next room. We can bring them out," said Lupina.

"And those low tables?"

"They're in there too," said Lupina.

"Maybe we can set a couple of those tables in front of the folks once they get seated."

"Uh … uh … Miss, Miss?" Dahlia said, trying to get Lupina's attention.

Lupina turned around. "Yes?"

"Uh … um … I wonder … I wonder if you might have an extra set of … of lady's trousers?"

"Oh … well, I might have some shorts that would fit you but you know, I'm not exactly your shape," said Lupina.

Oh! She really did pee her pants! thought Jen. She motioned to Lupina, who approached her. Jen whispered something in her ear. "Oh!" said Lupina. Lupina then approached Art Tatum and whispered something in his ear.

"Sure, sure," he said, and followed her out. Dahlia remained standing.

Lupina and Art returned with clothing bunched in their hands. "Ma'am?" Lupina approached her. "Ma'am, would you like to come with me?" Dahlia did so. Lupina punched in the code and unlocked the room where the settees and low tables had been stored. Zoe saw that it was the same small bedroom where she and Phil had spent the night. Lupina led Dahlia, still wrapped in her sleeping bag, into the room. Lupina closed the door but remained standing in front of it.

"What's going to happen now?" asked Sarah.

"Now we'll wait for Woodard Glenn to arrive home, and when he does, it's going to be story hour," answered Zoe. "I'm going to tell a little story, aided by Mr. Brian Ferguson and perhaps also by Jen and Thad."

Ferguson must be in some pain, thought Zoe. *Or maybe feeling humiliated at being bested by a couple of dumb heavies. He's uncharacteristically laying meek and humble and low. And this Dahlia person—is she feeling disempowered after the same experience? And what's with the wrap-around sleeping bag? She's too old to have her period. Maybe trying to hold in the peepee so she wouldn't have to squat over the can didn't work? And she's peed herself? I guess that might give her some pause of some regrouping…*

She guided Ferguson to one of the recliners. Then she turned to Stan. "You can take the other papa bear chair, the recliner, for your back."

"Gee, thanks," said Stan sarcastically. "You're such a good hostess. A fake hostess, but so accommodating." He remained standing. "I don't know what kind of yarn you're going to spin to Woody, but I can guarantee you, if it's your word against mine, he's not going to believe you. How did you just happen to arrive at our storeroom just as we were about to get some answers out of those phonies and get everybody's money back for them?" He jabbed a finger in the air in Zoe's direction, then swept it to gather Adrian, Ferguson, Jen, and Thad into its arc. "I think you've been keeping tabs on all these folks because you are all in cahoots together, to pawn off a fake mask on Woody and me and make us think there's a dozen more out there be had when THERE AIN'T!" Stan was shouting now.

Zoe shook her head, then nodded. "I can sort of see why you might think that." Then she shook her head again. "But you've got it all wrong. And I think, yes, we will get some answers to questions, but not the ones you think." Zoe countered.

Sarah took her phone out of her pocket and made a call, then held it to her chest. "Carl! Lakshmi says she can stay the night and tomorrow, too, if I need her, but…"

Carl waved his hand at her. "That's fine. That's okay. I'll pick up the tab for her."

"Great!" Sarah returned to her phone.

Dahlia emerged from the bedroom, dressed in a pair of baggy Levi's, six-inch cuffs turned up at the ankles. "Thank you," she said as Lupina led her to one of the settees, following Zoe's indication. Art and Lupina carried out one of the low tables; Phil and Carl followed with another.

Zoe was grateful; she and Lupina seemed to have settled into an unspoken alliance, with Lupina smoothing hackles with hosting logistics.

Joiner eased himself onto the recliner and slid back into it. Everyone was settled now except for Zoe and Phil, who stood in the middle of the room, and Art Tatum, who stood against the interior wall. Adrian, Dahlia, and Carl were on one settee; Sarah, Thad, and Jen on the other. Ferguson and Stan Joiner occupied the two recliners, a low table beside each.

Clutching his head, Adrian croaked, "I have a headache."

"Can Phil and I help you get more chairs?" Zoe asked Art.

"Sure. Follow me." Art punched the code on a door by the buffet. When she and Phil entered, Zoe realized it was Woodard Glenn's home office. Art indicated two Herman Miller Aeron chairs, grabbing one; Phil grabbed the other. They placed them in the center of the sunken living room. Phil and Zoe sat.

Lupina disappeared, then returned some minutes later with a tray that she set on the dining table, then carried over to the guests. The tray held ten little dishes with two aspirins each. She set the dishes on the low tables and gave one each to Zoe and Phil. Then she retreated with the tray and returned a few minutes later with the tray now filled with small cardboard plates of two slices of white bread each, spreading knives, and little ceramic pots of jam which she distributed. Then she went up the steps to the bar, opened the mini-fridge, and withdrew ten bottles of water. Art quickly strode over to the fridge. "I can take some of these," he said. He and Lupina distributed the water bottles; Zoe and Phil set theirs down on the floor next to their chairs.

"Can I get you anything more?" asked Lupina.

"Hey, I could use a sandwich," said Stan.

"I'll bring you some baloney," responded Lupina.

"Would any of you like something more?" Lupina repeated. "We've got the makings for pita pocket bread sandwiches left over from when we had the viewings this past week."

Musical notes sounded. Art Tatum drew his phone from his pocket and retreated up to the hall where the dining table was located.

"Whatever you'd like to bring us would be fine," answered Zoe. "And maybe a little basin of water and a wash cloth, some iodine or bacitracin and some bandages so Mr. Ferguson can doctor up his little scratches."

Lupina seemed to be politely ignoring the disheveled, battered, and bruised condition of at least four of the persons in the room. Her gaze shifted from the back of Zoe's torn blouse to Ferguson. Now she came over to Ferguson and intensely examined his swollen and purple jaw, the bruise on the side of his head, his bloody arm, and his torn jacket, which Art Tatum had draped over his shoulders again. "Now that you mention it, did you all have an accident or something?"

"Something like that," replied Zoe. "At least, some of us did."

Lupina exited the room.

Art came down the steps, back into the room. "Mr. Glenn called. He and Hilary are on their way."

Lupina now appeared again with ten pita pocket breads on a tray along with a stack of small cardboard plates. Each pita pocket was stuffed with pieces of asparagus, pesto sauce, chunks of cheddar cheese, pickled pimientos, and tiny sliced cherry tomatoes. She and Art distributed the pita pockets to Adrian, Dahlia, Sarah, Jen, Thad, and Carl, and on the tables next to Ferguson and Joiner. Phil rose and took one of the cardboard plates from her as she approached; Zoe rose and took the other. They both balanced the plates on their laps.

"This is vegetarian?" said Stan. "How about some salami or pepperoni?"

Lupina smirked and threw Zoe a glance. "Anybody else want anything more?"

Zoe, Phil, Sarah, Carl all mumbled, "This is fine. Great. Perfect. Thank you."

"Oh, I almost forgot. I'll be right back." Zoe popped up and sprinted to the door through which they had come, leading to the gravel parking lot. She turned, "Can I get back in?"

"I've put the code on green. Just push the door open," responded Art.

"Carl, can I get into the Land Rover?"

Carl nodded. "I figured there's no need to lock it here."

Zoe quickly returned with two folded cardboard plates, which she set in front of Jen and Thad. They were the plates with the remains of the food from their mine shaft prison. "Just to jog your memory about some events of a couple weeks ago."

"Oh, oh, oh," mourned Jen.

A buzzer sounded. "That'd be the outside doors. We're expecting more company?" asked Art.

"Ah! that's my Aunt Coco," said Zoe. "You remember her. She came to one of the viewings."

"Yeah, yeah. Older lady. But lively, sharp."

"Right."

Art went to open the doors. A few minutes later Coco and Art stepped down into the living room. Art immediately departed again.

"Oh, my," said Coco. "Are these the customers?"

"No," said Zoe, "these are rogues, thieves, and innocent bystanders. You know Ferguson; just who these others are will be shortly revealed. We're here to raise the curtain on a theft from long ago; a recent crime against my good friends, the Murrays; a scam; possession of illicitly trafficked ritual objects; and at least one masquerade—probably two or three—and possibly a murder. But let's wait for Woody and Hilary."

Art and Lupina disappeared, then returned, Art lugging two folding wing-backed camp chairs and Lupina one, which they unfolded and set up. Art puffed, "For you, Ma'am, and for Mr. Glenn and Miss Hilary, when they arrive."

"Oh, how exciting!" said Coco. "And all the suspects are gathered in one place, right? Just like Poirot!"

"Power-what?" said Jen.

"*Pwa-row*," said Coco. "Hercule Poirot, Agatha Christie's detective. He always got all the suspects together and then one by one eliminated them or incriminated them."

"Oh, right, right," enthused Phil, "Movie: *Murder on the Orient Express.*"

"Exactly," responded Coco. "And also, a long-running TV series, as I recall."

"Here, take my chair," offered Zoe. "I'll sit in one of these camp chairs." Coco sat in the Herman Miller Aeron chair vacated by Zoe.

"Would you like anything?" Lupina asked Coco. "A pocket pita bread? Water?"

"Oh, no, dear, thank you. I'm fine."

"Uh … What should I do?" asked Art. He had mounted the steps again to the dining area and arranged Ferguson's torn and bloody jacket on one of the chairs. "Do you mind if I stick around? I mean, I'm kinda curious about how all this—whatever it is—got into play."

"Good. You'll definitely find it interesting. You and Lupina both." Art retreated up the stairs, hefted one of the Renaissance chairs from its place at the dining table, came back around the half wall, carried it down to the sunken living room, set it down, went back up to the dining area, returning with another and sat on it.

Lupina now reappeared, plopping a cardboard bowl with thin pepperoni slices onto Stan's lap. Voices and the outside door clattering open, then closed, announced more arrivals. Woodard Glenn entered, followed by Hilary Lowe. Woodard and Hilary stood in the dining area, behind the half wall, looking down on the assembled group.

"What is all *this*?" asked an astonished Woodard Glenn.

"Hey, Claudine!" greeted Hilary.

"This," said Zoe, "is going to be the unmasking of a masquerade, in which you and I and this gentleman here"—she indicated Ferguson—"Mr. Ferguson—have played central roles, and which you and this lady here"—she indicated Dahlia—"have partially orchestrated."

"This is an invasion of your house!" exclaimed an outraged Stan.

Dahlia broke her silence. "Greetings and *touché,* Woody. Maybe it will have been worth spending hours and hours cramped in a mineshaft to witness this unmasking!"

Woodard Glenn's gaze raked the room. He opened his mouth. "Jane?" he whispered, then clamped his mouth shut. Zoe thought he did an instant regrouping. He walked slowly down the steps into the great room, then down the additional steps into the sunken living room. Then he again assumed outraged bewilderment. "What? What! What *is* this! Art?"

"They came about forty minutes ago. Some o' them's kinda banged up." He indicated Ferguson, Dahlia, and Adrian. "They came in their vehicle"—he indicated Carl—"and with Mr. Joiner. And Miss Claudine here, said she's got some kinda presentation she wants t' make. And I figured you know the rest of 'em." His glance went from Jen and Thad to Zoe and Phil to Coco.

"Well! You barge into my home, bring in a bunch of strange people, make yourself at home, take over my household, and now you're inviting me to be a guest in my own place to listen to some presentation?!" blustered Woodard Glenn.

"Mr. Glenn. I'm sorry to bust in on you like this. But when you hear what's happened to some of us, you'll see that we need some answers to some hard questions. Not everybody is a stranger to you. You know me and Phil and Coco and at least three other people in this room and I'd guess also a fourth—the woman whom we know as Dahlia. Can I respectfully ask you to take a seat? And listen? I think several of us can offer some explanations for some events that we … uh … have been party to."

"Yes. Art told me on the phone we had some visitors. Visitors who might have an interest in the masks but not all of them necessarily clients. So, yes, by all means." He said sarcastically. Glenn glanced again at Dahlia, then looked at Stan. "I do want an explanation for all this. Whatever 'this' is. Are we supposed to sit in these camp chairs? Art, there's another recliner in my office. Can you bring it out here? These camp chairs aren't all that comfy."

"I don't mind," said Hilary. "I've done some camping in my life…"

Stan Joiner started wagging his head, pointing at Zoe/Claudine. "Don't mess with her, Wood. She's dangerous. When this is all over, we'll get her on so many crimes, she'll be in the slammer forever. She's going to try to fill your head with a bunch of whopping lies!"

"Hey, no, don't believe him," piped up Jen. "She saved us. She rescued us. She beat up those two bullies that kidnapped us and tied us up, tortured us. You should have seen her! She was great! She slugged them silly!"

Now Carl Larsen stood up. "My name's Carl Larsen. And this here is Sarah Magoffin. The only reason we're here is because the lady's right. We and these two"—he indicated Zoe and Phil—"we were riding around and just happened to stumble on the rest o' these folks imprisoned in a mine shaft." Now he pointed a bony finger at Stan Joiner, and declared in a loud, steady voice. "And I'll wager anything it's this guy that hired those two brawlers to throw five innocent people into that mine shaft, tie 'em up like goats goin' t' market, and make 'em piss int' paint pots! For what reason? That's what I wanna know!"

Stan Joiner rose, clenched fists balled at the ends of arms held at his side, and shouted back, "That's a goddam lie! That's an accusation you'd better be ready to take back because you can't make it stick! You can't prove I had anything to do with what happened to these people!" He gestured toward the settees holding Sarah, Dahlia, Adrian, Carl, Jen, and Thad and the recliner where Ferguson sprawled.

Woody exploded. "*Anything to do with* what *people*? Who *are* these people? And what's the '*anything*'? And what does it have to do with *me*?"

Art reappeared, slamming to the door of Woodard Glenn's office, dragging the recliner on wheels that he set in just about the only free space left in the room, in the middle next to where Phil and Zoe sat. He set the brake on the recliner's wheels. Woody settled into the recliner.

Hilary did not take the camp chair; she propped herself onto the recliner's ample arm, moving her hand over Woody's shoulder, stroking it deliberately. Then she placed her hand on his arm, leaned into him, bent her head down, and whispered something into his ear.

Carl spat at Stan Joiner: "If you didn't have nothin' t' do with getting those five people thrown int' that mine shaft, then you tell me why it was you pulled up right behind them two hooligans just when they'd come back to finish their dirty work?"

"What dirty work? You're crazy! You're talking nonsense!"

Woodard Glenn held up his left arm and freed his right from Hilary. "Stop! STOP!" He turned to Zoe. "If you've come here to stir up trouble, you can turn right around and walk right out that door. And bring all your friends along with you."

Stan sat back down in the recliner. Carl sat back down on the settee.

Art said calmly but forcefully, "Mr. Glenn, Ms. Claudine might know more about the … uh … situation here. I think it might be worthwhile to hear her out."

A thought crossed Zoe's mind: *Maybe Art Tatum knows about the shelves of pots in the steel-enforced strong room out on the side of the mountain?*

Woody frowned. Hilary placed her hand back onto his arm and shook it. "All right, all right," he said. "Let's hear all this. Lupina, can you get me and

Hilary each one of those sandwiches like they all have? But put some turkey ham in it. And one for yourself and for Art."

"Okay," said Zoe, finishing up her pita bread sandwich and looking around. "If everybody's ready, here goes. Let's begin."

26

TUESDAY, 6:50 PM

LOS PAJARITOS

"I'M ZOE DILL, AND THE ONLY REASON I'M HERE—and Phil
Backstrom is here"—she nodded in Phil's direction—"is because of some
nasty things that were done to my good friends and former employers, Robb
and Cait Murray." She looked pointedly at Jen and Thad. Jen pursed her lips
and looked at Thad. Thad looked down at his hands in his lap. "And because
the woman we know as Dahlia tried to involve them in conveying a sacred
ritual object, a mask, that was probably stolen from a Pueblo village thirty
or forty years ago, to Woodard Glenn."

Confusion distorted Dahlia's face into a grimace. She opened her mouth,
apparently to say something, then thought better of it, and clamped it shut.

Hilary screwed her face into a giant question mark. "*Zoe?*" she interrupted. "*Dill?*" But you said … You introduced yourself as … I thought you
were… You aren't? Your name's not Claude, Claudine?"

Stan Joiner exploded. "You see, you see, Woody! She's a phony!" He
jumped up and took a few paces toward Woody, then turned and started

toward Zoe. "You're a phony!" He turned toward Woody again. He waved his hand. "Just like her cohorts whose asses she hauled out of the fire!"

Woody leaned forward in the recliner but did not get up. "Stan! SHUT UP! SIT DOWN! Let's hear the tale!"

Stan limp-shuffled back to the recliner, holding both hands to his back.

Zoe nodded. "Yes. I'm Zoe; Zo-ee Dill; Damia Zoeller Dill. Otherwise known as Zoe. Not Claudine. Part of the masquerade. I created my own. And I apologize for the deception. But as will become clear, I didn't know what I was dealing with, who I needed to hide from. Me and my partner here, Phil Backstrom, got into this thing by accident—or, no, more accurately, under what you might call false pretenses. But let's start at, well, if not the beginning, at least at—what would you call it? A pivot point. Let's go back to about six weeks ago. Here in Santa Fe."

Zoe turned to look at Stan. "A cargo of pots and spears and fabrics arrives and is deposited with Gregg Neal. One or more of the spears are coated with curare, a paralyzing poison. Curare is a catch-all term for several natural substances, one derived from a vine growing widespread in the Amazon rainforest, another from a frog's hormone sack. The latter is much more potent. The poison is used in hunting, especially for spearing fish. It affects the fish slowly; the foragers haul the fish out, usually with nets, as they float to the surface. But for a human, it's, like, a slow process and a totally frustrating death. The vic is conscious the whole time and alert while the muscles slowly shut down. Curare's actually a muscle relaxant; the muscles just stop responding to the brain's messages. The last to go are the lungs, then the heart. Gregg Neal ends up dead, from blood poisoning by being stabbed with one of those spear tips smeared with curare. Stan Joiner is the one who brought those spears to Gregg Neal."

"Now wait a minute!" bellowed Stan. "Are you accusing me of stabbing him with one of those spears? Of *killing* Gregg Neal? You can't prove anything! He died of a heart attack!"

"Heart *failure*, brought on through paralysis, and I'm not accusing anybody of anything, yet. And you're right. I can't prove anything. I'm just stating known facts. You arrive. The spears are there. Gregg Neal is dead. And I think if we could play back the tape, so to speak, on that scene, just before Gregg Neal died, we would find you there, Stan Joiner, with the spears, and Gregg Neal's hand somehow coming into contact with one of those spears, and a wound resulting.

And I'll wager a chemical test would turn up curare residues on those spears. Curare enters the bloodstream; it works slowly, but it works. The ultimate result is paralysis: limbs, lungs, heart. That is, heart failure. *And* I'll bet those spears and pots and weavings, some of which ended up at Gregg Neal's, made their way from Peru along the Amazon River to Iquitos, Peru, and then from Iquitos into Colombia."

"So?" expostulated Stan dramatically, extending his arms palms up, as if in supplication for understanding of his situation.

"That's one of the preferred routes for cocaine smugglers."

"Oh, come on!" complained Stan.

"Growing cocaine is a staple of the economy for numerous Indigenous communities in countries like Bolivia. They harvest the leaves, bundle them tight, and sell them to middlemen, cooperatives, that sell them again to brokers who ship them, often secreted in shipments of other goods, to Colombia, where the bundles are sold again and manufactured into powdered cocaine, then shipped clandestinely, usually first by boat down the Amazon, then by plane to places like Florida and the Caribbean islands."

"How do you know all this?" asked Hilary.

"*Peoples and Cultures of Latin America*. We had a whole lecture on it and had to read an article, '*Coca Economy of the Bolivian Yungas*'."

"Awesome."

Stan placed both hands on the arms of the recliner, leaned forward and, popeyed, hissed, "Now you're accusing me of drug smuggling? Unbelievable!"

Woody cocked his head and looked at Stan questioningly.

Zoe continued. "Like I said, I'm not accusing anybody of anything. But maybe shipping stuff in crates of pots wrapped in antique textiles comes with some degree of risk. Perhaps Mr. Joiner has cultivated an appetite for risk and crime. Ergo, now along comes another opportunity for entrepreneurship, with the masks. Stan gets excited: he gets the Robb and Cait Murray imposters followed to the rendezvous point with Dahlia and Adrian, where they'll exchange the securities that Hilary gave them for the remaining masks that Stan assumes the imposters have. The stooges Stan hired are then meant to turn up at his storage facility in the mountains with the negotiable securities they stole from the Robb and Cait Murray imposters *and* the masks. Except they don't. And here, I'll admit, I'm conjecturing: his minions report back to him: no masks. The hooligans have goofed it all up."

"Those hooligan brawlers! Echh!" Jen shuddered.

Zoe continued: "The securities are gone and the masks are nowhere to be seen. Stan's stooges report back to him, so he tells the heavies to go into action, and he'll take it from there. He's got to find out where those masks have gotten to, but his stooges report two more players in the game: Dahlia and Ferguson. Who has the masks? One of them? Both of them? The original imposters? The only thing the stooges can do is to dump the folks that are supposed to have the masks and the holders of the securities into the strong room and wait for Stan to arrive. Stan drives up from Scarsdale, but it takes him awhile. The heavies have to keep the captives sitting tight."

"You were planning to double-cross us—me, the clients?" Woody glared fiercely at Stan.

"No, no. no, no, NO!" Stan hollered. "YOU ARE ABSOLUTELY, OUTRAGEOUSLY MAKING ALL THIS UP!! THIS IS THE BIGGEST COCK AND BULL STORY I'VE EVER HEARD!" he yelled.

"Maybe." Zoe cocked her head to the side. "But five people do end up kidnapped and in captivity in a renovated mine shaft. Would you care to explain that?"

"Yeah, yeah!" Thad rose from the settee. "But you're leaving out an important point. Those guys sabotaged us. They sabotaged our van: the brakes and the gas line. If we did get the masks, they were going to show up while we were stranded—which they did—clobber us on the head, and make off with the masks!"

"A good point," commented Zoe.

Carl now stood again and once again pointed his finger at Stan. "So, his henchmen go after Daisy here—or whatever her name is—and … and … whatever their names are?" He turned to Zoe. "To force them to tell them where the masks are and to get back the securities that are in the bank?"

"Oh," guffawed Stan. "That is so far off the mark! You've got it all so ass-backwards!"

"Something like that. It may be a bit more complicated," admitted Zoe, "because the four players in this scheme-scam get thrown into the same shit hole along with their supposed adversary, Ferguson."

Coco had had her hand raised for some time, like a student in school, asking to be recognized. Zoe smiled at her and nodded. "Remind us again, dear: going back to Gregg Neal. What was the problem there?" queried the puzzled Coco.

"Gregg Neal was the one marketing Mimbres pots, either from the stolen cache or very clever fakes, in any case promoted on the internet in photos doctored so as not to make them identical to the insurance photographs of the pots that we have," interjected Ferguson.

"You are absolutely, absolutely indulging in so much libelous, slanderous calumny!" Stan crossed his arms over his chest, wagging his head.

"Hey," objected Zoe. "Like I said, I'm not accusing anybody of anything. Yet. I'm just speculating, spinning out ideas, laying out scenarios. And yes, Neal was, so to speak, making a bid to—as you put it Woody—double-cross his partners: you and Stan Joiner. To take over the marketing of Mimbres pots. And if he couldn't get his hands on the real ones, he was going to market fake ones. Now there's a lead-up to all this that brings me in—and again, we have to go back a few weeks. Here it is: So, we're in Croton Corners, New York. Those two," she pointed at Jen and Thad, "break into Cannings' Antiques…"

Thad jumped up, addressing the gathering, wagging a finger. "We did not *break* in…"

"Sit down!" ordered Zoe. Thad sat. "So, these two *come* in, tie up my good friends, the Murrays…"

"The Murrays who own Cannings' Antiques," interjected Adrian, proud to contribute to the story.

Dahlia scowled at Jen and Thad and, leaning forward, scolded them as if she were their disapproving auntie: "Shame on you for deceiving us like that! And here we trusted you! With our valuable goods, no less."

"I *told* you that at the time! That they *weren't* the Cannings!" insisted Adrian.

Zoe stifled a laugh that threatened to peel forth, turning it into a hiccough. *Trying to redeem her dignity by throwing blame; him trying to redeem his by one-upping* her! "Indeed, they're not the Murrays or the Cannings but they do operate Suwannee Antiques, in Oswego, New York."

"No, no, no!" bellowed Stan. "They're not that either! That antique business in butt-fuck nowhere New York is run by an old fat guy who dresses like a bag lady!"

"You've been there?" asked Jen.

"Don't worry about it, lady, I've got my sources!"

"Louie's running Suwannee like it's his!" exclaimed Jen to Thad, but loudly so the whole assemblage heard. "He's ripping us off!"

"Well, what else is new," said Thad. Then Thad announced loudly, "Hey, everybody, Suwannee Antiques belongs to us! It's our place! We've had it for years!"

"You mean… But what about the shop on the Hudson? That's *not* yours?!" expostulated Dahlia.

Zoe held up her hand, constable style. "Hold it! Hold it! Let's roll it back and take this systematically and in sequence. No, they're not the Cannings. There are no Cannings. Cannings' is just the name of the shop. And these two are not the shop's proprietors. Here's what happened. These two happened to overhear a conversation in the shop that I used to work in, part-time…"

"You … you … work in that … in that shop?" It was Thad's turn to be bewildered.

"Oh God!" exclaimed Jen, rolling her eyes and wagging her head.

"These two overhear a conversation with someone on speaker phone—someone who says they have something really neat to sell them but they can't bring it to the shop so can they—my friends and former employers, Cait and Robb Murray—meet them in The American Museum of Natural History in New York the following Monday. So, what do these two do? They come back two days later just as the shop is closing, rough up my friends, tie them up, and leave them with this kind o' stuff." Zoe walked over to the low table in front of Jen and Thad, seized the two cardboard plates and held them up. "So Cait and Robb couldn't turn up to the meeting scheduled for the following day. They were tied up! Guess who shows up?" Zoe rose again and stalked over to the edge of the stairs, and pointed first at Jen and Thad, then at Dahlia. "It's Dahlia, because it was probably Adrian—Cait and Robb said it was a man—who's on the other end of the phone, who has something to sell. And guess who *also* turns up at the museum, sneaking around exhibit cases and hiding behind pillars?" She pointed at Ferguson.

Dahlia nodded, turned to Ferguson. "Ah, yes."

"Aye," added Ferguson. "And then I decided to keep tabs on Ms. Faulks here. I was having Zoe follow Jen and Thad and she roped in Phil to keep tabs on *them*. Ah couldna be in two places at once." He addressed Zoe. "Except ye dinna think there was any need to do so once ye'd tailed them here, leaving it wide open for someone else to take up the tailing: namely, hooligans number one and two. Ye had thought all ye'd need to do is confront them here—where ye would show up as they unveiled the remaining thirteen masks to the prospective buyers." Now he again addressed what he was clearly enjoying as his captive audience. "I was to join them. We assumed—uh—Ms. Dahlia and her companion would be at the event as well. Ah dinna know, as Ah know now, that Ms. Faulks had had a bit of falling out with everyone over the Mimbres scam, including her then-husband, Dan Rosenstock." Zoe noted Ferguson letting his Scots burr increasingly take over his speech.

"Your sleuthing, Mr. Ferguson and Ms. Dill's, leaves something to be desired, doesn't it?" smirked Dahlia.

"Oh," quipped Coco. "This is becoming awfully complicated."

"But wow!" exclaimed Sarah. "It's like a real mystery, an actual whodunnit!"

Zoe resumed. "So anyway, getting back to a couple weeks ago, Dahlia and Adrian over there visit Jen and Thad at Suwannee Antiques in Oswego, New York, except I guess you never tumbled to the fact that they're not Cait and Robb Murray, or that they weren't the legitimate proprietors of Cannings." Zoe paused, took a swig from her water bottle, then continued. "So now here's where I got bamboozled into playing the sucker. I fell right into your little web, didn't I, Mr. Ferguson? What would you have done if Robb and Cait had left it right there? Refusing to do your dirty work?"

"It wasna' dirty work…"

"But what would you have done? Maybe you and Dahlia, alias Cricencia Morgenhouse, alias Jane Faulks…"

"Aha! Yes," said Woody Glenn, "I thought so! I thought it was you sitting there all this time," continued Woody. "Yeah, you're a little different, a little older, but it's you…"

Dahlia laughed and stood up. Her gaze penetrated Woody Glenn. "Yes, I realized you'd recognized me. I saw the look on your face when we all trooped in here. Shock, then consternation. The person you'd cheated out of a proper share of your ill-gotten gains had turned up again like a bad penny! But if Mr. Joiner's henchmen hadn't pulled knives on us and pummeled us to pulps, Miss Zoe would never had been able to get us here! You would have never known."

"Hey," snorted Stan. "I object!" He stood and took two steps toward Dahlia, hunching over and staring at her menacingly. "You're laying *that* on *me* when you're the one who's committed fraud and theft! Yeah, you got your minions to front for you, these two who claim to be Suwannee Antiques, and now that you've gotten stopped in your tracks, you're trying to get off the hook by playing on everybody's sympathy for yourself and your poor benighted fellow thieves because you had to spend a few hours sitting in the dark! And your minions have *also* committed fraud and done bodily harm and burglary at your behest!"

"I had nothing to do with that!" screamed Dahlia. She also took a few menacing steps toward Stan. "I didn't know they were pretending to be who they weren't or what they'd done to be able to do it!"

Zoe held up her hand again. "Please! Both of you sit down. So, these four—Jen, Thad, Jane Faulks, Adrian ... that's probably not your real name, either, is it?"

Adrian responded: "My last name. I'm called Will. William. Will Adrian. And hey, can I ask a question? So, your showing up at the mine—you and your boyfriend and these two other folks"—he gestured at Carl, then at Sarah on the other settee—"was that sheer coincidence?"

"Believe it or not, it was indeed sheer coincidence. We'd met this couple at Petrified Forest National Monument..." began Phil.

"Hey, hon," Zoe said gently to Phil. "No time for those details. Let's keep the thread. Let's go back to the museum. So, Ferguson is tailing Dahlia, following, sneaking around..." She stopped speaking and looked at Ferguson.

Ferguson nodded. "Right. Ah'd caught up with the woman that Ah'd thought t' be Jane Rosenstock, alias Faulks, alias Cricencia Morgenhouse, who Ah thought t' be a major player in the theft of the Mimbres pottery and the subsequent insurance fraud. Ah couldna figure what she was doin'—in a disguise—in the Africa room at the American Museum of Natural History. But Ah wasna goin' t' let her go."

Zoe resumed her narrative. "Ferguson sneaks around and puts the pieces together: Jane Faulks picked up a couple dozen sacred masks, sacred to the Hopi, Zuni, other Native peoples, at an auction in Paris, a year ago. She disposed of some, but couldn't unload the rest because she knew they probably have murky histories: stolen from their rightful owners; illegally sold off by museums; smuggled out of the country for the auction in France, where US laws like the Native American Graves Protection and Repatriation Act don't apply. She knows she can't bring them into the country through customs; folks like the Native American Rights Fund and Tribal authorities and attorneys are watching out for these sacred items. So, she smuggles them into the country. Or maybe she doesn't; maybe she's already disposed of all of them except one. But she presents herself to Jen and Thad as having a whole cache of sacred items, just perfect for mounting on the walls of faux pueblos, McMansions kept by the global jet-setters for entertaining their jet-setter friends in what they regard as appropriate ambience. And she props up this masquerade by entrusting a sacred mask to Jen and Thad for them to present to dealer and gallerist Woodard Glenn, in Santa Fe, New Mexico, so he can convince his jet-setter friends to put up 'earnest money' to demonstrate their sincerity in wanting to purchase a mask from the cache. She plans not to show herself to Woodard Glenn because of their murky history together. That's why Jen and Thad were so crucial to her scheme."

"*My* scheme?" interjected Dahlia shrilly. "What about *his* scheme?" She pointed her finger at Woodard Glenn. "*He's* the one cooked up the insurance fraud! He and this Stan Joiner person and their gallery-dealer friends!"

Glenn looked around the room, his eyes coming to rest first on Ferguson, then on Zoe. He pointed to Dahlia. "Are you going to *believe* her?"

"Don't plaster *me* with that libelous accusation!" bellowed Stan.

"Why shouldn't we believe her?" Zoe retorted. "Mr. Glenn, weren't you perfectly willing to broker illicitly obtained sacred religious objects without asking any questions about how they've come to be available to you?" Zoe swept her eyes over the assembled gathering. "And now, in this, his latest scheme, once he's got the number of potential purchasers matched to the purported number of sacred items, he turns over the cash to Jen and Thad who will bring the items either here or to the gallery, and the customers will turn up in a gala like the one he had a week ago to put in their bids for this or that mask, with Woody Glenn as broker. And of course, for his services, yes, he'll gladly take a percentage. But now *he's* the target of a scam, because the masks are not supplied."

"Finally! *Finally* you've said the truth!" barked Stan. "We've been scammed! Woody and I and our clients have been scammed!!"

"Wait a minute, wait a minute," objected Thad. "There's some things I don't understand." He leaned over, addressing Dahlia, sitting across the room. "First of all, who was it you were so afraid of recognizing you when we were in the museum that you had to pose as a morbidly obese, eighty-year-old gray-haired lady with bad hips: grandma-with-the-canes? Was it Ferguson you were trying to hide from?"

"Ha!" replied Dahlia. "I didn't know! No, it certainly wasn't Ferguson at that point. I didn't know of his existence. Or let's put it this way: I was aware that somebody was on my tail but I didn't know who. All I knew was that somebody was tracking me at that auction in Paris. I didn't know if it was zealous Indian lawyers and their tedious wannabe do-gooder friends, or the FBI, or US Customs, or all of the above. All I knew was I was smelling something bad. So, I lay low for exactly a year."

More self-congratulatory back-patting! thought Zoe. *More repair to her tattered self-esteem by convincing us how clever she was!*

"Until you rented the house on Long Island," said Ferguson.

Dahlia nodded. "I knew I was definitely being watched when I surfaced on Long Island. But what else could I do? I thought there might be a chance I would be tailed into New York for that meeting, but I was hoping whoever was tailing would get off my scent and onto theirs—the Cannings, or Murrays—Jen and Thad, whoever you are. Indeed," said Dahlia, looking at Jen and Thad. "You two pulled off the masquerade very well, I must say. Anyway, that day at the museum, I didn't know if or who might have followed me in, but I decided to have Adrian—poor Adrian! He had to get out of bed at an obscenely early hour—get in position to get those forearm crutches to me as well as all the padding and the wig. That's why I was so late for our rendezvous. I went all the way to the Port Authority bus station, hoping I could disappear in crowds while I sequestered myself in a wheelchair cubicle in one of the toilets. Adrian had to stand around until he spotted me, then stand outside the women's until he found somebody willing to buy his story that his elderly aunt had gone off on a bus without her crutches but then had called him and asked him to bring them in when she found she couldn't get off the throne and hand the willing lady a bag of bulky sweater to boot. It took a while."

"Aye. And I almost lost you," affirmed Ferguson, chuckling.

"Then," continued Dahlia, "of course I had to make my way convincingly slowly back down to the subway, back up out of the subway, through the museum etcetera, etcetera. Once I was there, I did a recon and was sure I was being watched. Adrian was there too, and he thought there were two likely candidates for spy: one of them was you, Ferguson. The other was a man dressed like an Australian cowboy: outback hat, safari pants, clunker boots. He seemed to be following me, but had disappeared by the time I'd exited the ladies' room, having deposited my canes, and my padding, and costume with Adrian and heading for the rendezvous in the cafeteria. But then when we had finished making our arrangements and went our separate ways, I was thankful but perplexed that Adrian reported nobody apparently following me. I still kept up appearances, so to speak, but you followed *them*, not us, didn't you, Ferguson?"

Zoe now retreated to the Herman Miller Aeron chair and sat down.

"Aye. Well, I had to follow either you or the couple I thought was the Cannings. And there I just lucked out; I happened to make my second round of your rendezvous spot in the museum just as, apparently, you, Jane, had phoned them. That one," he nodded at Thad, "answered the phone with the name 'Canning.' So, that's how I knew who you were."

"But they weren't," said Zoe.

"No. But I dinna know nor care. All I knew was there had been some arrangement made. I must admit I was thinking, or hoping, more for whatever was left from the Mimbres pots than for the masks from the auction, or for both."

"Because these two and their gang," Zoe pointed at Stan Joiner and Woody Glenn in their recliners, "had pulled an insurance scam with those pots, what, seven years ago, and you suspected Jane Faulks, also known as Cricencia Morgenhouse, then married to Dan Rosenstock, of being part of it, but weren't sure if it was really her you were spying on?"

"Exactly."

"Now hold on!" roared Stan Joiner exasperatedly, rising again. "You don't know that and you can't prove it. You can't prove *anything*!"

"This is getting very, very interesting, to say the least," commented Sarah, "even if I'm not following everything. But aliases? Disguises? Spying? And a secret rendezvous in a museum? What a great story! And what are these pots, exactly?"

"We'll get to that," responded Ferguson.

27

"DAHLIA?" JEN PIPED UP. "So *that's* why you were so leery of dealing with Woodard Glenn directly! Now I understand that comment you made in the mineshaft about 'Dan Rosenstock my husband.'" *And that's what she was referring to back in Oswego with her obtuse talk about her basket being spilt all over the road and her goodie bag being snatched*, thought Jen. Dahlia said nothing, but she pursed her lips, then moved her head so Jen could not see the expression on her face. *Trying to hide a snigger? Finally giving Woody Glenn his comeuppance?*

Zoe also had her thoughts. *Stan Joiner's really losing it. He doth protest too much. This Jane/Dahlia person must have figured out that this confessional soliloquy on her part is not going to result in prosecution. She seems almost proud of having led Ferguson on a messy chase. And it's got to be because she knows she has him by the tail. These scenarios might unfold by themselves and we'll have True Confessions, but they still need a little prodding and poking and goading.* She turned to Ferguson. "But that story about how you wanted to nail Cricencia Morgenhouse red-handed with the masks so you could coerce her into leading you to these two, *and also* so you could return the masks to the tribes, that last part was bullshit wasn't it? You never did intend to return those masks to the tribes!" declared Zoe.

"It was *you* suggested that. You planted that idea, but I surely did and still do want to nail these three." Ferguson swept the room with his patched and bloodied arm.

"And that's where I played the sucker." Zoe took a tug on her water bottle. "I've got quite a bit of skin in this." She rose from her chair, strode purposefully over to where Ferguson sat and stood over him. "I'll bet there's a lot of bullshit in your story. Maybe you really are an insurance investigator, but I'll bet those IDs you showed Cait and Robb Murray were fake! You're not from Europol. You're not who you say you are or from where you say you are!"

Ferguson bristled "Ye have a right to be angry, I'll grant ye," he admitted testily. "But you're wrong, at least on most counts. My credentials from Europol are real. The Mimbres fraud case is real. My efforts to break it open are real. The masks from the auction are a different matter, but my name really is Brian Ferguson. The only thing you got right was that I'm not from Newcastle. I'm Scots, from Lewis."

Stan poked a finger at Ferguson. "See? See!? All a bunch of liars, Woody. Fibbers, imposters, fakes."

"I'm not so sure, Stan." Woody shook his head.

"Can we continue the story?" asked Thad. "So you, Ferguson, tailed us to Suwannee because you thought we had, or were going to have, or we were going to lead you to the Mimbres pots?"

Ferguson nodded. "It was a possibility. And ye did so—unintentionally."

Zoe prodded. "But my friends the Murrays said you turned up at their shop that same day. You charged all the way up to—where is it? Owego? And back in a couple hours?"

"It's Oswego. And yes and no. I did follow them to the garage where their van was parked. I always carry a kit in my saddlebag: lock pick, digital voice recorder, GPS tracker with a powerful magnet. I managed to be a few steps behind ye," he nodded at Jen and Thad, "then walked beyond and made as if getting into a car two spaces beyond. Then when I saw ye starting to get into the green van, I verra quickly attached the tracker to your back underside, then pretended to be tying my shoe at the back of the car in the next space over as ye pulled out."

"See, folks?" said Zoe with a half-smile on her face. "He *is* a real detective."

"Oh, yeah," said Jen, nodding. "I remember seeing somebody bending down, right by our van, but hadn't a clue what they were doing. That was you."

"Aye. That transponder enabled me to track you to your final destination and get up there again next day for a stakeout. Things were unfolding in ways that I could not predict. And then along comes Cricencia-Jane-Faulks-Morgenhouse pulling up in a limousine at your house! With what was obviously something that she was going to sell to you: maybe masks, maybe pots. I was gratified to see some things falling into place."

"But she didn't actually sell it to us," corrected Jen. "She made us pay what she called a bond-of-trust, $10,000! And told us to go see Woodard Glenn in Santa Fe, New Mexico, and offer him a bunch more masks from the auction; the one she 'loaned' us was meant to prove that we actually had them. But we were under no circumstances to mention her name to him, which she gave to us as 'Dahlia,' or even her existence."

"And then Ferguson spins his story and stupid little me, I play right into his hands. 'Oh, my, how dastardly of them!' says Zoe. 'They're profiting from someone else's sacred ceremonial patrimony and illicit prehistoric pots by mistreating the Murrays and masquerading as them! Oh, let me help,' says naïve little Zoe. Ferguson here wanted the Murrays to drop everything and run off and track those two and their boodle. They said nothing doing, ah! But naïve little Zoe says, 'Oh, please, pretty please, let *me* do it.' And stupid, naïve little Zoe stepped right into your trap. I joined all you other clowns in the masquerade. All part of the masque. Really, I was just a bit of diversionary fluff, wasn't I? We even had our own private, secret little phones. See?" Zoe continued, pulling the burner out of her left-hand back pocket and waved it around.

"You're not naïve little Zoe!" exclaimed Sarah. "You're fightem-punchem-teach-em-a-lesson-Zoe!"

"Maybe you were the owl?" said, Phil, so softly that he thought probably nobody heard him. "The owl at the Katsina dances that warns the clowns about their misbehavior."

Jen nodded. "We had our phones too—so we could communicate with Dahlia."

"Except the Mafiosi took ours. We no longer have them," said Dahlia.

"Probably binned them in the nearest rubbish skip," said Ferguson. "But believe me. No. You were not just diversionary fluff. Not at all. No, you were absolutely crucial. Once Mr. Thad-Not-Canning-Not-Murray discovered the transponder at the Jiffy Lube, I had to act fast."

"Yeah," said Thad. "We knew we were under surveillance. But we didn't know from who. We thought it was Dahlia."

"Ye must have smashed the thing; it suddenly stopped transmitting."

"I sure did!" said Thad.

Ferguson looked intensely at Zoe. "As Ah told ye, lassie, Ah couldna be in two places at once. Ah could ha'e followed the goods in the green van when I cottoned to the fact that they were indeed going to take the goods somewhere, but then Ah would ha'e lost Jane Faulks. Ah couldna' keep feedin' money to that local PI on Long Island. Ah couldna be sure that if Ah submitted a bill for an additional PI, Assurance Associates would make good on it, since Ah was operatin' on a hunch."

"Ha! As it was," said Dahlia, "that little creep was a joke. Adrian tumbled to his bumbling Fig Newton antics. Finally, we collared him and told him, 'Take us to your leader.' He took us to Ferguson."

"I thought so. So, you two were in cahoots from the very beginning!" said Zoe indignantly.

Ferguson wagged his head. "Not from the beginning. Only when she confronted me."

He's trying to shift blame, thought Zoe.

"We came to an arrangement," said Dahlia. "I finally convinced Mr. Ferguson that it was in his best interests for us to join forces. I had to promise him to share some of the, er, profits, in exchange for his promise to leave me out of it when it came to exposing the Mimbres scam. I gave Mr. Ferguson an affidavit noting the manner in which the items were diverted, once it was clear who at least *one* of the scammers was and who had custody of the pots." She looked meaningfully at Woody Glenn, raising her eyebrows.

"And they were diverted to Gregg Neal's place?" suggested Zoe

"No. We had scoped out the route. We had actually bought a van that was the same make and model as the vans used by the rental company the pot owners were going to hire. Got some iffy fly-by-nighter to paint it like the rental vans. Hired a drive-in storage locker to stow it in. When the time drew near, Dan, Dan Rosenstock, to whom I was married at the time, and I dumped rocks into the exact same number of crates, then hired some day-laborers to load them into my van. Dan went along with the driver of the other van, supposedly to safeguard the interests of the various parties that had ownership of the pots. Dan had a duplicate set of keys made for both trucks and by prearrangement, he dropped the set to their van in a potted palm just outside of the truck stop café where they stopped for coffee, at Dan's suggestion, of course. I was waiting in a lay-by off the highway in the van with the crates of rocks. When I saw them pass, I pulled out and followed them into the parking lot. I switched plates with the van with the goods, got the duplicate keys from the potted palm, and drove off. Dan had the duplicate set of keys for my vehicle. He offered to drive. The other driver promptly fell asleep in the passenger seat. I drove my van to a drive-in storage locker where I had parked our rental car. I locked up the storage facility and drove away. The van that turned up here had the boxes full of rocks."

So, he's got all this in an affidavit, thought Zoe. *No wonder he was willing to crawl in bed—at least figuratively—with she-devil Dahlia to go along with getting her and himself a little extra dosh on the side.*

"Aye." Ferguson nodded vigorously. "And the police turned up, checked with the rental company, confirmed the van that was rented and loaded was the same one that turned up full of rocks. But, of course, it wasn't. In the end, they said there was nothing they could do. The rental company took neither responsibility nor interest. I think the police probably thought it had been a scam from the get-go."

"Woodard Glenn, Stan Joiner, Gregg Neal, the rest of the gang, they were to divide the goods among them *and us*, that is, my then, uh, husband, Dan," continued Dahlia/Jane. "But when we said, 'All right, take us to the storage locker and give us our share of the pots, and we'll be off and out of your hair,' they reneged. Woody was in charge. He was our contact. He refused. He said, 'Oh, but what will you do with them? You're not dealers in art. You don't have a gallery.' You see, they were afraid we'd flood the market, the black market, and drive down prices that *they* could charge. So, then we said, 'All right, if you're afraid of that, give us the equivalent value of the pots that you're refusing to give us, and we'll call it square.' Again, he refused. 'You'll get your share of the insurance money when it comes in, so be satisfied with that,' he said. Imagine!" She looked around the room, fixing her gaze on Woody and Stan in turn.

"Yes, I was your contact," admitted Woody. "But I wasn't in charge. I was simply carrying out the wishes—the decisions—of others involved."

"Speak for yourself, Woody," said Stan. He shook his head. "I don't know why you're admitting all this."

I'll bet I do, thought Zoe. *I'll bet it's because Coco's in the room and he wants her to think better of him for confessing all. Otherwise, she could do it for him and there would go his reputation and standing with the Santa Fe art collecting crowd.*

"Well, when the money *did* come in, it all went to Dan. Typical male chauvinist pig, his argument was, 'Well we're married, aren't we? And I took all the risk showing up with the crates full of rocks, blah, blah, blah. Let's invest in a little art gallery. I know the perfect place, in Mexico.' Well, long story short, we had a parting of the ways. I've put all of this into the affidavit," said Dahlia. "My agreement with Ferguson was that once he had the affidavit, I could be on my way."

"Hooey and horseshit!" thundered Stan. "That story is preposterous! "That affidavit will never stand up in court!"

"A real affidavit, notarized and all?" asked Zoe. "That's amazing. That makes you culpable. That implicates you."

"Well," temporized Dahlia. "It's not quite a real affidavit. It's not notarized. But Adrian witnessed it."

"Mr. Joiner is right. It will not stand up strong in court," admitted Ferguson. "But it will stand up sufficiently in an investigation by attorneys from Lloyd's and the Assurance Associates to give prima facie evidence of fraud to warrant attachment of assets until the matter can be negotiated and settled. Those assets could be tied up for months, if not years. And now we know—which we did not know before—where those pots were shifted after they were moved from the storage locker to the mine shaft stronghold. That's the one good thing to come out of our trouble occasioned by Mr. Joiner's mafioso."

"That is total unmitigated slander! You can't prove I had anything to do with that!"

"Mafiosi," said Dahlia.

"Huh?" said Hilary.

"One mafioso. Two mafiosi," said Dahlia.

"Woody!" Hilary turned to Woody. "Is any of this *true*? You committed insurance fraud seven years ago and kept the pots that were insured? And you cut this, this Jane—Dahlia—whoever—out of the deal?"

Woodard Glenn shook his head. "They can't prove a thing, Hilary. Like Stan says, this is all speculation, and libelous speculation at that. Jane just admitted she and her husband *stole* the pots! Who's to say they haven't been selling them a few at a time on the black market this whole time?"

Hilary shifted off the arm of the recliner, walked over to the buffet table, folded her arms, and slouched against the wall.

"Because they're in an armed stronghold mine shaft that Mr. Joiner at least knows about, if not controls," stated Ferguson emphatically.

"Woody has more control over than I do," bellowed Stan. "It's in *his* neck of the woods, not mine!"

"So, you, Ferguson," said Zoe, "agreed to let the masks go as long as you got what you wanted—the affidavit from Dahlia. And she paid you off—part of the cash that Jen and Thad delivered to her as down payments on the masks that don't exist."

"I dunna' know if they exist or not," said Ferguson. "But aye, my focus has always been on tracking down the Mimbres fraud. And I must say that case is stronger now that we know where the remnants of the cache of pots are and the connection that Mr. Joiner has with it."

"Bullshit!" yelled Stan. "You can't connect me with that!"

Carl Larsen, his arms folded across his chest, answered Stan: "I'll wager we'd find that those two deadbeat hit men were gotten out here, and their car rented, on a credit card with Stan Joiner's name on it. Oh, yes, and of course we'd find, at some point, a transfer of title for a certain disused mining claim." He nodded.

"That's an outrageous accusation!" barked Stan. He rose, painfully, and hobbled up the steps.

"You've got the keys to his Jeep, right, Phil?" said Zoe. "So he can't get away." Phil nodded.

"I'm going to the bathroom," yelled Stan. A door slammed.

What's he up to? wondered Zoe. *More shenanigans? On the other hand, maybe he really does just have to pee.*

"So, Zoe and Phil really *were* following us," said Jen said to Thad.

"Yes," affirmed Zoe. "We *were* following you. But not Phil, at first. In my, like, incredible naïve hubris, I pulled him into it. I was paranoid that you'd spotted me following you on the road, then spotted me at the picnic table in the park in Walsenburg."

"We didn't spot you on the road," said Jen, "but we parked pretty close to the entrance in that Walmart parking lot in Ohio and I just happened to pull back the curtain to see how light it was and if the store was open yet and if we should be getting on the road and there was this young gal with frizzy hair marching determinedly into the store and it was you! Going in for a pee? Then I sure did spot you in the park! Then we didn't see you any more until you turned up here at the gala. But I also sure did spot Phil in the Santa Fe Café! We'd seen him in that campsite outside of Abiquiú, too. So, we decided that it was *him* following us, and then when Hilary told us your story—masters in art history, going out west for a PhD, yada, yada, yada, we thought, Oh, we're all wrong. They weren't following us at all. They have nothing to do with Dahlia. It's all just coincidence we were on the same roads at the same time! What dopes we were!"

"But why did you think it was *us* who was having *them* surveilling *you*?" Dahlia seemed truly perplexed.

"Well, you gotta admit, Dahlia, or Jane, or whatever your name is, you came off pretty secretive and sneaky with that whole story about how Woodard Glenn couldn't get wind of who you were and that you were a pariah and all that as far as brokering the masks, and so forth, and then that get-up you were in at the museum. I thought you were a total scammer," said Thad. "I thought that mumbo-jumbo about how you couldn't show your face was just so much BS. What I thought was, you'd gotten us to take all the risks in transporting it—I mean, what if you just made up that whole auction story? And you'd actually *stolen* the thing? What if the FBI was on to you and just waiting for the right time to pounce and come along with a charge of receiving stolen property? Or, maybe you weren't so much using us as dupes for the FBI as you were, plain and simple, just using us as dupes. Once you thought you'd gotten us safely away from whoever was tailing us, you'd follow us on the road, and at some point, bop us on the head and take back your 'friend' as you called it, then take it straight to Woody Glenn, and sell it to him for $30,000."

"We spent all those uncomfortable nights sleeping in the van, not letting it out of our sight, not ever having a meal in a restaurant at the same place at the same time, taking shifts sleeping with the thing, even when we were staying in that motel in Santa Fe!" Clearly, Jen was outraged.

Dahlia tsked, "Well, I'm sorry you couldn't have been more trustful."

Is that intended as irony? thought Zoe. "But once you and Jane-Dahlia-Cricencia went into cahoots together, you didn't need me anymore," Zoe complained to Ferguson. "Why did you go on with the masquerade? I mean, I didn't believe that story when I finally got a hold of you on the phone about how you got yourself tarted up as an old lady, fake driving license, rushing to ticket counters here and there! You and Dahlia, and I guess Adrian, just all got on the plane together and flew out here! So why didn't you tell me, 'I've tracked Jane Faulks to Albuquerque. You can relax now.' Just to use me as a diversion?"

"Something like that, I suppose. I didna want to risk exposure."

"Yes," sighed Zoe. "But why was it worth your while to tarnish your integrity—well, assuming you ever had any—by taking her blood money? How much did you get?"

"We split it half-and-half," interjected Dahlia matter-of-factly. "It would have been $112,000 for each of us."

"One. Hundred. Twelve. Thousand. Dollars!" said Zoe venomously, glaring at Ferguson.

"Do you know how much I made last year?" countered Ferguson. "Ah made $63,000! Ah dunna work on salary; only on contract. And I canna' call them; they call me. Sixty-three thousand dollars to keep body and soul together and pay child support for three bairns and alimony to ma ex-wife. And I was never after the masks, particularly. Ah've been chasing the miscreants in the Mimbres pots case for seven years. But now everything has changed, ha'n't it, Miss Zoe? You now hold all the cards. It's your game now. Ah only hope ye will see the justice in rectifying this insurance scam and help me persuade these two fraudsters to admit what they've done and let me draw up a plan for them to make rectitude."

"Yes, we do hold all the cards, don't we? It is our game now." Zoe cocked her head. "You want to tell the assembled multitudes why?"

Stan Joiner returned and collapsed into the recliner. "What rectitude?" he snarled. "You're not extorting any money out of *me*!"

Ferguson sighed, looking defeated. He said quietly, "Because you've got the photographs. The photographs of the remaining Mimbres pots on their storage racks in that fortified mine shaft where we were imprisoned."

"And photographs of everybody there, at the mine site—well, all except the hooligans and Stan Joiner," commented Phil. "They're on my phone— those photos. I've got the visual evidence linking the Mimbres material to the kidnapping and imprisoning of five persons and the linking of that to the place where the pots have been kept all this time, and therefore also to the insurance fraud. This means we have witnesses."

"And you've got us," declared Carl. "Sarah and me. We'll testify." Sarah nodded vigorously.

"Right," affirmed Zoe. "And also, Ferguson, we know about your and Dahlia's collusion to split the earnest money for the masks. That's outright theft, and something that Assurance Associates might well take a dim view of, especially when you submit your invoice for tailing Dahlia. If you want to pursue restitution of the insurance money, you can't do anything without those photos. Without them, without that evidence, your hope that Woodard Glenn lets you and Dahlia get away with nearly a quarter million dollars goes up in smoke, doesn't it? But if Woody makes good on the clients' earnest money, and if you coerce him into admitting the verity of Dahlia's affidavit with his agreement to an out-of-court settlement, with nothing said to law authorities, then you and Dahlia are going to have to give up your and little commission. Am I right?"

"Oh, Woody!" exclaimed Hilary. "Shame, shame." Her expression shifted from sadness and sorrow to anger and frustration. She shook her head. Woody grimaced but remained silent.

If storm clouds could manifest from a look, thought Zoe, *Hilary would have pelting hail raining down on Woodard Glenn!*

"Why should I be on board with any of this?" Woody had his arms folded across his chest.

If eyes could shoot daggers, thought Zoe, *I'd be perforated like a dart board.*

Now Coco was up, jabbing her finger at Woody: "Because if you value your reputation at all, if you still want to broker art in this town, and Stan wants to keep his Scottsdale gallery going, you'll admit your mistake and issue apologies. Apologies to your clients for getting them roped into a scam that you were too much of a sucker not to tumble to." Coco was adamant. "There's nothing else you can do. You can't make this Jane Morgenhouse-Faulks-Rosenstock—whoever she is—cough up thirteen sacred ritual objects that she probably doesn't have. And if you committed insurance fraud, even years ago, and have had anything to do with marketing Mimbres cultural patrimony, even just a rumor to that effect could finish you."

"Are you threatening me?"

"I. Am. Not. Threatening. You!" declared Coco fiercely, then more gently temporized: "I'm just warning."

Carl stood up. "What about getting the cops after those two goons and this guy here." He pointed at Stan Joiner. *He's* the worst criminal here. *He's* the one sicced 'em on them five people in the mine shaft!?" hollered Carl.

"IF YOU SAY THAT ONE MORE TIME, I'M GOING TO HAUL YOUR ASS INTO COURT FOR SLANDER!" shouted Stan.

Ferguson spoke up, raising his voice, "Ah dunna think there is much the police can do about any of this!"

Coco spoke up again. "Surely, Mr. Ferguson, that is a wantonly misleading assertion. The way I see it, there are grounds for making arrests of everyone in this room who had anything to do with the pots, the insurance fraud, the masks, the unlawful kidnapping and restraint, the deal-making and cover-up. That includes you, Mr. Ferguson, taking cover-up money. I'm sure the police would be delighted to perform arrests."

Instantly, Art Tatum stood up, and declared in an equally loud voice, "I'll tell you what. I agree with Mr. Ferguson here. But for maybe different reasons. Can I offer a perspective?"

Carl sat down. "The floor's yours, my friend. Go ahead."

"What do you know about any of this, Art?" said Woody acidly.

"I'm gonna tell y'all a little story," responded Art. "Back in the day—this was darn near half-a-century ago—I was just startin' as a Texas Ranger. Yeah, that's right. I was a Texas Ranger. Maybe y'all didn't know that. Anyway, y'all remember the oil embargo? Well, you wouldn't, I guess. Long time ago. Bad for consumers but real good f'r oil drillers. Price o' gas at the pump doubled in a couple months. Same time, there was a big oil strike in the Permian Basin."

As he talked, he lapsed increasingly into a thick, down-home Texas accent. "Some o' the drillers got together and did some price fixin', makin' sure nobody's undercuttin' 'em and drivin' the price back down. Illegal by US law, violates the anti-trust. But they did it anyway. They formed a secret association. Well, not all the oil drillers were party to this; just the big ones. And one o' the little ones got wind of it, through a mole. This little guy decided he'd throw the fear o' the lord int' the big boys so's they'd open it t'all the drillers. He hired a couple good old boys—mafiosi, brawlers, goons, stooges, whatever yaw wanna call 'em—t' bust in on one o' these secret association meetin's, in a back room o' one o' the bars. So, they did: guns drawn, hands up, all that. Held 'em there two hours at gun point 'til this little guy and some o' his buddies showed up and put the screws to 'em: let us in on this too and we'll letcha go and won't report ya t' the Securities and Exchange Commission. Well, they said okay, then turned around, called the sheriff, and reported a bunch o' crimes: kidnapping, extortion, trespassin'—I don't know what all. Sheriff didn't know what t' do so he called in the Rangers.

"Well, 't'weren't no matter f'r the Texas Rangers, neither, but me—just green, wet behind the ears, new kid on the block—the Rangers reckoned I needed 'sperience with the public. So, they called me in from Fredericksburg. I listened to everybody's complaints against everybody else, and ya know what? I just threw up my hands! I told 'em straight out, I couldn't figure out who t'arrest first: the guys violating the anti-trust laws, the upstart oil driller that got 'em corralled against their will and made 'em promise to let him int' the association, or the good old boys what claimed they was only havin' some fun and they'd all got license t' carry anyhow.

"So's, I told 'em that. Told 'em, 'You boys figure it out between yerselves. Texas Rangers got better things t' do.' Well, I see this here situation as bein' the same, if ya git ma drift. Ya git Ms. Daisy and Mr. Woody on stealin' pots and insurance fraud; ya git Mr. Ferguson on extortion and takin' cover-up money; and ya hit Mr. Stan with kidnappin' but ya can't prove a dang thing 'cause the ones done the *actual* kidnappin've flown the coop! Ya maybe get an accusation against Jen and Thad here for misrepresentin' what they actually had and who they were, and hell, maybe ya even get Carl and Sarah here for breakin' and enterin'! Where does that leave y'all? In a big mess. Sheriff's not gonna touch it with a ten-foot pole."

"Bah! You just said it! There's no way you could pin anything on me and make it stick!" barked Stan.

Art nodded. "I'll grantcha that." He looked first at Coco, then at Zoe.

Carl, clearly disgruntled, shook his head. "Yeah, I see what you mean. Who t' arrest first. That's a good one."

Hilary clapped her hands slowly. "That's great, Art. Great story!"

Old Art's sharper than he seems, thought Zoe. *I wonder if it really happened. If not, kudos to Art for good, spontaneous yarn-spinning.* "Coming off of what Coco said a few minutes ago, Mr. Glenn, you've got a good opportunity to make an act of good will in the form of acknowledging the sacred nature of the mask and making good on a pledge to return the mask to the appropriate tribe, and also to make restitution to the insurance company. You can try to convince them, maybe, that you didn't know anything about where the pots have been all this time and it was others who stashed them in the mine shaft, with the proviso that you won't name names. Maybe you can make them think it was all Gregg Neal's doing."

"What about us?" wailed Jen. "We're out ten thousand! 'Earnest money' that *we* paid *her*!" She thrust her arm out, pointing at Dahlia.

"And let's not forget my friends the Murrays," retorted Zoe. "They were the original losers in the first chapter of this criminal episode."

"They did get a decent insurance settlement," noted Ferguson. "Perhaps additional satisfaction will come when ye relate their imposters' mine shaft experience to them."

"The clients *are* going to want their money back," said Coco.

"I think Ms. Faulks and Mr. Ferguson will agree to that," said Zoe.

Ferguson sighed. Dahlia said, "We don't have a choice, do we? It was never so much about the money, anyway. There was never any criminal intent. It was about ... teaching a lesson, I suppose you could say. Poetic justice. Or maybe just a little bit of—how do you say it—what goes around comes around?—for the high and mighty Mr. Woodard Glenn."

Stan guffawed, "And bilking them—the clients—and us out of our money? That's not a crime?"

"It was more a case of 'sweet revenge,' wasn't it?" said Zoe. "Turn-about is fair play. A double-cross deserves a double-cross. You never intended to furnish the other thirteen masks. You were just going to disappear and leave Jen and Thad holding the bag and Woodard Glenn with egg all over his face and a ragged reputation. The big-bucks earnest money was a surprise, icing on the cake, the cherry on top."

"I suppose you could say that," agreed Dahlia.

"One of those securities was from you, wasn't it, Mr. Glenn? One of the securities that's now in Ms. Faulks' and Mr. Ferguson's separate bank accounts, right?" said Zoe. Woody nodded, arms folded over his chest. *He seems almost disengaged*, thought Zoe, *above it all. What machinations is he conniving to come out on top of all this?* "Then," she continued, "I suggest when Dahlia and Ferguson go to the bank and get that affidavit out of the safe deposit box and draw that money back out tomorrow, 30,000 of it should go to Jen and Thad. You're essentially buying the mask from them, Mr. Glenn. And the rest of it goes, of course, back to the clients who put down that earnest money. And you and Stan and the remaining beneficiaries to that insurance settlement will negotiate with Ferguson on just how to pay it back."

"Is that the price I pay for you *not* calling in the local equivalent of the Texas Rangers? Or having my name dragged through the mud?" asked Woody sarcastically.

"Yes, I suppose it is," responded Zoe.

Woody brought the recliner to its sit position, sat forward, clasped his hands between his legs, then drew a hand across his eyes. He shook his head. "Talk about extortion! Okay. All right."

"Whew!" expostulated Thad.

"Copacetic!" declared Jen.

"What now?" Woody looked around the room at everyone in turn. His gaze came to rest on Stan.

Stan shook his head slowly. "I'll go along with you, Woody, but only because you and I go back a long ways and we've partnered well together. But let me make it clear that's the only reason I'm going along. As a favor. Voluntarily. Nothing more than that. No erroneous conclusions to be drawn. Bread on troubled waters."

What kind of bollixed mixture of simile and metaphor is that? thought Zoe. "I think first we need to get Thad and Jen's van towed somewhere and repaired, and mostly, we need those receipts for the cash that Adrian gave you."

"They're in a metal lock box, in one of the storage bins, in our van, chained to one of the studs," said Jen. "In an envelope in there. I'll give you the keys to the padlock and the lock box." She patted her right front jeans pocket.

"I'll arrange for a tow truck, tomorrow, at first light," said Art Tatum, "and get the van towed to a repair shop. I don't know about you, but I'm plumb tuckered out with all this. I need some down time before I start dealing with all this again."

"So, Jen, you'll go out with Art to where your van is parked and retrieve that lock box? I'm assuming those receipts are made out to each ah … client? Is that right, Adrian?" said Zoe.

Adrian nodded. "That's right."

"We'll want to return the mask to the tribe," said Phil. Where is it?"

"It's in the gallery. You can get it tomorrow," said Hilary. "Right, Woody?" She looked long and hard at Woodard Glenn.

Woody sighed, nodded. "Yes." He looked at Stan. "It's real, Stan. It's not a fake. And, Hilary, you can put a sign on the gallery door to the effect that we're closed tomorrow due to … uh … unforeseen circumstances."

"I still think we oughtta call the Bernalillo County sheriff. Tell 'em all about this captivity in the mine shaft," declared Carl. "And also the Santa Fe police chief and let 'em know we've got a suspect here in a couple o' major crimes. They can work it out between them and Bernalillo County who gets arrested for what and put in the hoosegow." He nailed Stan with a withering look.

Stan shook his head. "Total fantasy. You can't make any accusations stick."

"How much of this does Nelda know?" asked Coco.

"She doesn't know anything and she doesn't need to. Leave her out of it," said Woody.

"If she did know, Mr. Glenn, she would have quite a lot of leverage in terms of letting collectors and accessorizers know about where their Mimbres pots came from and how they were made suckers in a scheme to defraud. You could declaim all you wanted, Mr. Glenn—and you, too, Mr. Joiner—but I don't think your clients and customers would want to know or will care about the intricacies of your relationship to Jane Faulks and to brokers imperson-ating legitimate antiques dealers. All they're going to be concerned about is that they couldn't, and shouldn't trust you. And Coco has the whole story; all she has to do is have a little chat with Nelda Cavaletto and there are going to be two well-connected people who know as much of the story as they need to know. They could make mincemeat out of you and Stan Joiner, and believe me," Zoe riveted Stan with a stony glare, "if anything, anything at all happens to those two ladies, the police will know just where to look. Hopefully they'll put you in irons and throw away the key, Stan Joiner. Phil and I *can* pin the insurance fraud on you and Woodard Glenn with the photos we have. All we have to do is look at public records to find who owns that particular mining claim where the pots are stored. And Mr. Ferguson may be discredited in other ways, but he can report back to Assurance Associates that he's found the remaining stolen pots and they can begin investigating and bring charges. Which they might be persuaded not to do if these two gentlemen"—she indicated Woody and Stan—"and whatever partners in the scheme are still around voluntarily agree to repay what they bilked Lloyd's out of."

"Hey, you know, I didn't bargain for any of this when I got hired as gallery manager," said Hilary. "So, you know, like, I've got a degree in art history and maybe I'd like to go into the profession on my own and, like, maybe you could help with that, Mr. Woody Glenn."

Woody Glenn leaned over, put his head in his hands, then looked up, and said quietly, "I get it. I get all the messages."

"I think this is what's going to happen tomorrow," said Zoe. "Jen and Art return here with the receipts. Hilary returns here with the sacred ceremonial item. Mr. Joiner remains the guest of Mr. Glenn tonight."

"You can't keep me here!" protested Stan. "Give me back the keys to my Jeep! You have no right to them. That's stealing!"

Zoe ignored him. "Mr. Ferguson, Ms. Faulks, and Mr. Adrian will also be Mr. Glenn's guests, sleeping arrangements to be arranged by mutual agreement. Coco, you surely have an attorney here, more or less on call? And your attorney will surely know of a notary who will agree to maintain discretion in the notarization of a couple of documents, Ms. Faulks' included."

"Oh, of course, dear."

"Tomorrow morning Jane Faulks and Brian Ferguson will be escorted to the appropriate bank in Albuquerque, where they will access the affidavit in the safe deposit box and withdraw $224,000 from their two accounts, to purchase fourteen cashier's checks, $30,000 of which go to Jen and Thad. Coco, through her attorney, will arrange for notarization of Ms. Faulks' affidavit."

"And Ms. Faulks and I will sign it in the presence of a notary," said Ferguson. Zoe noted Ferguson's accent moving away from awe-shucks Scots toward

Boston-Oxbridge officialese. "This document attests to the agreement among certain parties to waylay a van full of Mimbres pottery, seven years ago. It affirms that Ms. Faulks knows this to be the case, without any admittance of culpability or indication of how Ms. Faulks knows this. The document names the person who was to take delivery of the pots, who is here in this room. The signed and notarized document will be provided to Assurance Associates, who will in turn supply it to Lloyd's. May I point out that it will provide incentive to Mr. Glenn and Mr. Joiner to negotiate an agreement with Lloyd's to repay the insurance winnings they collected, as Ms. Dill has suggested?"

"Now see here!" exploded Stan. "Aren't you forgetting Gregg Neal and his pansy partner, perky Plumm?"

"Unfortunately," replied Zoe, "since Mr. Neal's untimely death, his estate has gone into probate. It may take quite a while and a substantial legal expense to recover that money. But I'll bet Mr. Glenn can lay his hands on a substantial amount of cash, to start making repayments?"

Woodard Glenn raised his hand in the air. "I take your meaning, Mr. Ferguson; and yes, Ms. Dill, I'll see what I can do."

"And I'll bet Mr. Joiner can scrape up some funds to begin repayment."

Stan shook his head and said slowly and carefully, "You can file all the documents and affidavits and nonsense you want with whoever you want to file them with, I'm not admitting to anything you're alleging. But if I *do* agree to this … this repayment plan, it'll only be to help out Woody here."

"There will also be a second affidavit," continued Zoe, "that Phil and I will sign—Carl and Sarah can if they choose to do so—with photos attached, about what and who we found in the strong room on what will, I have no doubt, turn out to be Stan Joiner's mining claim. It will include the arrival, hard on the heels of the perpetrators of the kidnapping, of Mr. Stan Joiner."

"You bet!" Carl nodded.

Stan guffawed. "Oh yeah? Who's gonna believe that horseshit!"

Zoe ignored him once again. "Also, tomorrow, Mr. Glenn will call the innocent parties who put up the earnest money, the down payments, the pledges, and explain that he has come upon new information that makes it inappropriate for him to continue with his offer of the ceremonial masks for sale. Now, you can do it any way you want, Woody Glenn. You can just have them come out and pick up their checks. Or you can give them to Hilary to make the rounds and distribute them."

"I think it would be better if I contact each of them individually, tell them the whole situation, and arrange for the reimbursements," said Woody.

"Oh, no. I don't think so," countered Hilary. "Maybe the best idea is for you to put on another little get-together, maybe not quite the gala you used to haul in the suck … er, clients, but rather, a little informational session—kind of a Chautauqua—where Phil, with his credentials as an anthropologist, can tell the good people about the significance and importance of ceremonial masks and the role they play in a dynamic, vital, living religion. Then you, Woody, can tell them that you've bought the mask they viewed and, as its owner, have agreed to return it to its rightful owners, right?"

Woodard Glenn seemed deflated. He was silent a moment. "Yes. All right. Have it your way." He threw up his hands. "Have it any way you want. Have it all your ways."

Zoe smiled warmly at Hilary. *She's in our camp now*, she thought. *Bye-bye, Woody.*

"So, Jen and Thad will also remain guests of Mr. Glenn while their van is repaired and the document is prepared. Oh, and that will be, of course, at Mr. Joiner's expense."

For once, Stan Joiner was silent.

"So, Carl, you and Sarah can go back home but get ready for a phone call to come back up and sign the document. And Phil, you can go with them and bring my car back to me at Coco's?"

"Will do," responded Carl.

"Happy to do it," affirmed Sarah.

"Sure," said Phil.

"But I have a suggestion," said Carl. "Somebody needs to keep a watch on these folks tonight. We don't want Ms. Dolly-Jane and Mr. Ferguson and Mr. Joiner all sneaking off in the middle of the night. Mr. Glenn, can you find room for us here tonight?"

"Oh sure!" Glenn's voice dripped sarcasm. "Everybody just move in and we can declare Los Pajaritos a kangaroo court with live-in accommodations for plaintiffs and defendants!"

"I think that's an unfair comment, Mr. Glenn," objected Art Tatum.

"Hey, you can put Ferguson and Adrian in Sansouci," said Hilary. "Carl and Sarah can stay next door in Edge of Taos Desert. Could Jen and Thad move over to Sena Court where the Motts usually stay? And why don't you give Dahlia the guest bedroom here? I'll get that sleeping bag Ms. Faulks dragged in and throw it on one of those recliners. Just in case … uh Ms. Dahlia-Jane needs anything."

Dahlia huffed.

"And Mr. Joiner," added Hilary, "you can have the go-down."

"The what?" queried Stan.

"It's perfectly comfortable. Just doesn't have indoor plumbing, but we can leave the door open here for your needs. I … uh … can find an accommodation in town for a night or two."

Zoe noted that a storm cloud passed over Woodard Glenn's face, but he remained silent.

"Oh, gawd!" complained Stan.

"And, Carl," said Zoe, "I don't see any reason why at some point you can't place our affidavit about what we witnessed at the mine site into the hands of the Bernalillo County sheriff along with the photos downloaded from Phil's phone. I think Art's right that the authorities might not be so interested in the complexities of persons, actions, times, places, and material evidence and they might simply hold onto those documents, especially if the affidavit is accompanied by a signed statement from the five victims specifically agreeing not to file complaints or press charges, regarding their brief imprisonment.

And we should include another affidavit, something to the effect that the photos we have are of pots that were stolen seven years ago and were insured, but the insurance company is satisfied that steps are being taken to rectify the mistake that they made in awarding the money in compensation for the theft, now that the pots have been found. But those affidavits will be our fail-safe in case anyone has an idea of reneging on the verbal agreement made here today, attested by all of us." Zoe nailed Stan with what she hoped was a menacing glare.

"That's quite a mouthful you just said," commented Sarah. "Are you sure you're not a lawyer?"

"Phil, can you take photos of everybody here?" Phil came over to where Zoe was sitting; she handed him her phone. He roamed the room, taking photos; as soon as he did, the subjects seemed to take this conspicuous proofing of their visibility as the unraveling of the masquerade.

Zoe now realized she was beyond tired, beyond exhausted, beyond fatigued. She felt on the verge of collapse; her adrenaline rush had drained away completely. "Whew!" She realized that Phil, Coco, Carl, and Sarah were clustered around her. "I'm beat."

"No wonder," said Carl. "That was amazing, what you did up there on the mountain. Knocking those muggers around, beating them at their own game. What was it? Something Fu?"

"Kung Fu," replied Zoe softly. "It's a martial art, intended to strengthen and discipline body, mind, spirit. It's strictly for self-reflection. It's never supposed to be used violently, as a weapon, against another person. I violated all the principles of Kung Fu when I lashed out like that."

"Huh! Good thing you did," said Sarah "Otherwise we'd all have been locked away in that mine shaft, left in freezing hell, like in Danté."

"You've had a day, dear," said Coco. "It's getting on for ten. You and I and Phil need to go home." They all made their way to the door.

Woodard Glenn seemed to regain some of his commandeering authority. "Art," he said, "Can you escort Mr. Ferguson, Mr. Adrian, Jen and Thad, and

Mr. … uh … Carl, and his companion to their quarters?" Zoe hung back, as Jen and Thad, Adrian, and Ferguson trooped out, followed by Carl and Sarah, all herded by Art Tatum.

As Ferguson was exiting, Zoe grabbed his sleeve and pulled him aside. "Ow!" he objected, "That's me bad arm!"

"One thing I'd like cleared up. Your documents that I looked at back in Croton Corners said there were ten parties involved in the Mimbres scam: six gallerists and dealers, including Stan Joiner, three ranchers and the tenth party, which was obviously the Dan Rosenstock-Dahlia/Jane combo. I noticed Glenn's face when he came into the room and spotted Dahlia/Jane. He just about had apoplexy. I thought he was going to choke. But when we marched her out of the mine shaft, Stan Joiner didn't so much as raise an eyebrow. Was he distracted by his flight attempt, or is he just that good at dissembling?"

"Ah! Maybe neither. Most likely he'd never encountered her. Woodard Glenn was the point man, so to speak, for the operation. I'll bet that bunch were organized like one of those secret cells. Glenn knew everybody and everybody knew him, but everybody dinna necessarily know everybody else, if ye take ma meaning. So that's why no mutual recognition between those two."

Zoe nodded. "Got it. So … good night, be good, sleep well, and store this in the back of your mind: you owe me one. Big time. And one of these days, I don't know when, but I'll bet there's going to be an occasion when I call it in." *I may not have gotten all of it right*, she thought. *But I think I got most of it right. Enough to make a difference.*

Ferguson nodded. "Fair enough."

Carl yelled, "Get along here, Ferguson!" Ferguson exited, hurrying to catch up with the others.

Coco, Phil, and Zoe walked to Coco's car. "Tomorrow let's start the day off with a good, rousing breakfast at Pascal's. Mounds of chili rellenos and piles of home fries!" suggested Coco.

"Sounds great!" exclaimed Zoe. "Maybe with mimosas rather than mere orange juice?"

EPILOGUE

UNDER THE SUPERVISION OF SARAH AND CARL, Dahlia and Ferguson withdrew the $224,000 that they had so recently deposited into two separate accounts, paid out in fourteen separate cashier's checks.

Learning about the important role that masks play in the religious life of the Puebloan people, that they are living spiritual entities, the potential clients agreed, upon return of their earnest money, that it was indeed just, equitable, and appropriate to forego purchase and possession of the masks.

Woody Glenn "bought" the mask from Jen and Thad for $30,000, after they had drafted a statement affirming that they had "bought" it from Dahlia, who, in the same statement, valued it at $30,000. In yet another statement, Woody Glenn then "donated" it to the tribe for a tax write-off for that amount. Phil knew from which village the mask had originated and he and Zoe would take the mask back there.

Assurance Associates agreed to exempt the now elderly rancher—who had sold his ranch to the Archaeological Preserve at considerably below market price—from the legally binding agreement negotiated with the other two living partners in the Mimbres scam, Jackson Kane and a local dealer named Mark Louwer, besides Stan and Woody. The sixth dealer, a woman named Victoria Beck could not be located; Woody claimed he had lost touch with her shortly after the pottery's disappearance. Stan and Woody, for their part, agreed to an immediate payment of $100,000 each to Assurance Associates. They and the other two agreed to annual payments ranging from $40,000 to $100,000 each, depending upon a third-party accountant's quarterly monitoring of their incomes, until they each had paid $1,000,000.

Assurance Associates' executives, mildly surprised at Ferguson's success, paid him a "recovery fee" of $30,000, with an arrangement for an annual payment of 15 percent of the amount they would garner from the agreement with the two other miscreants.

Jimmy and Horace melted back into the underworld from which they had briefly emerged.

Dahlia disappeared following her agreed-upon performance at the bank. The other thirteen masks remained sequestered, wherever and by whomever they were housed.

In the fall, a separate business opened in a newly-constructed space in the Woodard Glenn Gallery. It had a modest sign on a window, announcing it as "HiArt. Paintings, ceramics, weavings, and sculpture. Hilary Lowe, Proprietor." In one corner stood a tall, free-standing case, glassed on three sides and up-lighted, housing a complete Southern Plains woman's fancy dance regalia. The latter was labeled with two small hand-lettered index cards noting it had been collected in a Kiowa community in Oklahoma in 1923, and another noting it had been brought to Santa Fe from Cannings' Antiques, in Croton Corners, New York, courtesy of Louie Delassandro and Jen and Thad Pritchard of Suwannee Antiques, Oswego, New York. Two small paintings by John Singer Sargent and two more by George Catlin, two vintage Crystal Trading post weavings, and three contemporary ceramic pieces, two by Puebloan potters and one by Sebastian Plumm, also in up-lighted cases complemented the regalia.

Phil had done some research on the textiles that had accompanied the Shipibo pots as packing material. Stan Joiner had professed to know nothing about them. Phil discovered they were from the community of Coroma, Bolivia, and had likely been looted before falling into Joiner's hands. They were venerated as the garments of the ancestors who founded the community and, as such, were vital to its social and spiritual integrity; the spirits of those ancestors were embodied in the garments, some of which were four to five hundred years old. The garments were traditionally cared for by different families who cared for them in their homes, offering them food and prayer. Each November, on All Souls Day, the people wore the sacred garments; it was said that on this day the ancestors danced, as well. Upon learning how strikingly similar these *q'epis*, that is, bundles of sacred garments were to the Puebloan masks, Sebastian Plumm had readily agreed to work through a Bolivian anthropologist, known to Phil through Cultural Survival to repatriate them to the Coroma community. Woody Glenn, Jackson Kane in Phoenix, and the one remaining rancher agreed, over Stan Joiner's objections, that the remaining eighteen Mimbres pots stored in the mine shaft were best transferred discretely to the Mimbres Foundation.

Coco paid a visit to Sebastian Plumm just before his "fire sale." She purchased all the spears, including the broken one, concocting a story about a client who wanted to accessorize his greenhouse to evoke the Amazon rainforest. She insisted Plumm wrap them in many layers of brown paper, secured with twine. She refrained from insisting he wear gloves, but watched carefully to make sure he did not break his skin while doing the wrapping. After holding his "fire sale," from which he reaped a tidy sum, Plumm retired to San Francisco. The Neal Gallery was turned into a high-end AirBnB.

Jen and Thad Pritchard, after returning to Oswego, began making plans for shifting their enterprise, or perhaps opening a second front, at a rambling, abandoned curio shop in Corrales; they remain in contact with Carl Larsen, and, in a deliberate attempt to, as Jen put it, mend their ways, nervously and apprehensively contacted the Murrays. Cait and Robb, meanwhile, had caved to twentieth century technology and installed CCTV and a burglar-and-fire alarm. They were astonished, one day in mid-July, by the visit of a not-quite-middle-aged couple, a man and a woman, both slender, dressed in black turtlenecks and black cotton trousers, who introduced themselves as, "Jen and Thad Pritchard, the masked bandits who pulled your pants down and tied you up. And we really, really apologize," said Jen. "We are so, so sorry."

"But wait 'til you hear what *we* went through" Thad said. "We were amateurs compared to the hooligans who tied *us* up—they used fishing wire and paint cans for potties."

"We'd like to somehow make it up to you," added Jen. "Maybe we could take you out for lunch at the American Museum of Natural History?"

⁓

Art Tatum continues working as manager for Woody Glenn and the half-dozen owners of "Pueblo Estates" at Los Pajaritos. He and Nelda Cavaletto continue their affair, uncontested.

Carl Larsen and Sarah Magoffin continue to enjoy exploring old mines; they have now expanded their exploring territory to central Arizona.

Will Adrian turned up in San Francisco shortly following the arrival of Sebastian Plumm; they now live together as a couple.

Jessica Keegan enjoys a worldwide internet-facilitated network of patrons for her photographs; Mitchell Johns continues to expand his crafting of blog logos.

Nick Taylor applied for, and was granted, a one-year extensions to finish his PhD; his business takes increasingly more time and finds him increasingly far afield from Weston, Connecticut and from NYU.

Zoe stayed in Santa Fe for the summer, learning all she could about fine arts and Native arts from Coco Vanderjagt and from Nelda Victoria Cavaletto, rendezvousing every couple of weeks with Phil, either near one of his field sites in the Pueblo villages or at Coco's in Santa Fe. In August, she made her way to Washington state while Phil returned to Indiana. She and Phil vowed to keep up a "frequent flyer" relationship, while she completed her work at University of Washington and he completed his at Indiana. More than once, Zoe reflected on the ironies of her activities that summer: masquerading alternately as amateur detective and assistant to a fine art and artifacts consultant, she had unmasked impersonators; revealed a conspiracy between scammer and scam-buster; solved an insurance fraud enigma; facilitated the return of a stolen religious object; sufficiently tarnished but then salvaged the reputation of a gallery operator; brought satisfaction to traumatized victims of mistreatment who were as much mentors as employers; and pivoted successfully from an old love to a new one. Slipping behind a masque of concealment and phantasm brought excitement, renewal, and a fresh lease on life. She could understand the lure of being the person you were behind the masque of someone you weren't.

Acknowledgments

I AM TRULY GRATEFUL TO EVERYONE mentioned below for playing a part in getting the manuscript to this point. I owe a debt of gratitude first of all to my wife, Carolyn, who was always there with calm insight, consistent confidence, and enthusiastic encouragement in providing important suggestions and comments, as well as to Ray, Mell, Rudi, and Lori for their careful reading and critiques of parts of various drafts. I would also like to thank my editor, Alexandra, for her outstanding level of effort, professional expertise, insight, and sage advice, as well as Polly for her guidance and resourcefulness.

Thanks also to the following authors, whose expertise was drawn upon at various points: Aaron Elkins, (*Loot*, 1999, New York: Open Road Integrated Media); Lawrence Jeppson, (*The Fabulous Frauds*, 1970, New York: Weybright and Talley); Jonathan Lopez (*The Man Who Made Vermeers*, 2008, Orlando: Houghton Mifflin Harcourt); Ulrich Boser (*The Gardner Heist*, 2009, New York: Harper Collins); and Richard O. Clemmer (*Roads in the Sky: The Hopi Indians in a Century of Change*, 1995, Boulder: Westview). Everything that the narrator, Dahlia, Ferguson, and Zoe say about the making of art, brushstrokes, art theft, authentication, museums, auctions, marketing of illicitly obtained ritual objects, forgery, and fraud is drawn from one of the above books, or from the author's experiences. I should note, however, that any errors in that regard are my own.

Although nearly everything in this book is fictional, the sale of Native American masks, religious objects, and ritual paraphernalia in a Paris auction in 2013 is real, as is the city of Santa Fe, albeit in a bygone incarnation.